THE LOVE HATER

A SINGLE DAD BILLIONAIRE ROMANCE

BEAUFORT BILLIONAIRES
BOOK 3

ELLE NICOLL

ROSE HOPE PUBLISHING LTD.

CONTENTS

FOREWORD

Thank you so much for picking up
The Love Hater.

Although this can be read as a standalone story, **I highly recommend you start with The Matchmaker - Book 1 of Beaufort Billionaires** due to the family's backstory, which will unfold across the series.

The Love Hater is Sullivan's story, which begins near to where we left off at the end of The Matchmaker, in those months before Sterling and Halliday's wedding takes place.

Enjoy!

Time for our grumpy single daddy to tell his side...
Enjoy Sullivan.

Happy Reading

SULLIVAN
TWO YEARS EARLIER

T HE SONG'S ENDED.

Its notes drift out of the church behind us as we exit into the graveyard. It was one of his favorites, played to a montage of photographs and video clips. Seeing those familiar blue eyes was like a knife straight to my heart.

I can't believe he's gone.

I can't believe they're both gone.

All that surrounds us now is the sound of rain hammering on polished wood, accompanied by Sinclair's soft cries. A haunting symphony that will keep me awake at night. Something to keep the sounds of explosions and raging flames burning through flesh company.

My father steps toward the twin graves and drops a handful of earth on top of my brother's.

"No!" Sinclair sobs, burying her face into my shirt and clinging to me.

I wrap an arm around her, my hand skating up and down her back. Each vertebra of her spine juts out through her clothing in jagged hills and valleys. She's a walking skeleton, too consumed by grief to eat. I slant the umbrella, trying to block out the rain.

"It's nearly over, okay?" I say, pressing my lips to her blonde hair.

She shudders, letting out a whine that causes another part of me to curl up and die deep inside. I hold her tight, searching for strength in the deep pull of air I drag into my lungs.

My father takes off his ring and drops it into the grave. Uncle Mal stares at his sister's casket, before moving to my father's side and placing a hand on his back. He purses his lips, deep lines etched into his brow as the rain slides down it.

They're both soaked to the core. But they don't notice.

They're numb. We're all numb.

I meet my father's eyes as Sinclair's cries gain momentum. "I'm going to take her to wait in the car, Dad."

"All right, Son. I'll come soon."

I lead Sinclair past the black-dressed crowd of mourners, nodding at the ones that catch my eye as I pass. They're all wearing similar expressions of disbelief and loss. My mother and brother were loved. Respected. They had friends. They had us.

We were the Beauforts. New York's wealthiest family. Running our empire. One steeped in value and brilliance. Pioneers of our craft.

Beaufort Diamonds, almost as beautiful as the person wearing them.

Our company motto.

Our family's legacy.

What are we now, except broken? An empty husk of something that was once whole and magnificent.

My fiancée, Claudia, stares at me from amongst the sea of faces, concern spilling out with her tears. She wipes at her cheeks; the giant Beaufort diamond a glittering beacon on her finger. The way she'd smiled when I opened that ring box; I didn't even make it onto one knee before she was pulling it from the velvet and sliding it on with a squealed, *Yes!*

She tries to give me a reassuring smile. But it does nothing to ease my pain.

"Fuck," I mutter as Sinclair stumbles beside me, jerking on my arm.

My grip loosens on the umbrella, ready to toss it and grab her. But she's already straightening up, her eyes snagging on the face of my father's head of security, Denver, as he helps her straighten up and asks if she's okay.

"Thanks, Denver," I say.

He flicks a cursory nod my way, before his attention immediately returns to my sister.

"Are you okay?" he asks, unwilling to let her go from his grasp.

She shrugs him off, snapping that she's fine. A lie, of course. None of us are *fine*. We never will be.

"Keep walking." She sniffs, leaning into my side.

I lead us to the black town cars and help Sinclair inside. She grabs my hand, pulling me into the backseat with her.

"What are we going to do without them?" she whispers, staring at me with wide, frightened eyes.

"It'll be okay." I squeeze her hand, noting how even her fingers feel like bone.

"Dad's holding it together for us, I know he is. He was talking about the business yesterday like everything was normal. But he only found out about Mom's affair after they were gone. It's too late for him to get any answers from her. I'm scared he'll shut it all out and not deal with it."

I turn to look through the window at the dark outline of my father and uncle standing in the rain. Two matching silhouettes with shoulders weighed down by pain and loss.

Twin pillars of grief.

My temples throb as I force away the heavy threat of a migraine.

"Don't worry," I say, putting voice to the decision I made the day we lost them both and I saw the utter devastation on my father's face. "It's time I took over as CEO. Dad can take all the time he needs."

"Are you sure?" Sinclair asks; hope making her eyes twinkle.

I'm the eldest of the three of us. Now two of us. This was always the plan. I'd take over the family business. Sinclair would pursue her modeling career. And my brother would be free of the constraints that come with the duties of a first-born. He could run the global marketing like he wanted to do, while living a wild life climbing waterfalls and base-jumping off skyscrapers—two of his favorite pastimes.

I'd snorted when he'd told me I should try base-jumping with him.

Where he got his rush of adrenaline outside of work, from pushing his physical limits, I've always got mine from closing deals. From taking risks, where I already know I'll come out on top. From winning. From knowing that when it comes to business, no one has one like ours.

No one can break apart the Beaufort Empire.

Now, it's all we have left of them. I need to do everything I can to ensure its continued success.

"I'm sure," I say. "You don't need to worry, Sis. I'll take care of it."

The noise gets louder. An incessant wail that pauses briefly, then starts again with added defiance.

"What the fuck is that?" I groan, pulling the pillow over my head, but not before seeing the bedside clock reading two a.m.

The funeral, followed by half a bottle of scotch once Claudia and I got back to my apartment, and my head feels like someone's sawing it in half with a blunt object.

"I think it's a baby." Claudia frowns.

I peer out from under the pillow as she sits up in bed beside me.

"Stay. It'll shut up in a minute." I fling my forearm over her hips and pull her down onto the mattress, shoving the pillow beneath my head.

She shuffles into me, pushing her silk-clad ass into my crotch. We fit perfectly like this. My dick nestled between her tight, toned ass cheeks. Ones born from a mix of good breeding and an upbringing that included private tennis lessons, and her own pony to play polo on.

Claudia sighs as she melts inside my hold, stroking the back of my forearm tenderly.

"I'm here for you, you know that, right?" she says softly.

"I know," I reply, kissing the top of her shoulder where the strap of her camisole has slipped down. I squeeze my eyes shut and inhale the notes of her perfume that linger on her skin. "I don't know what I'd do without you."

"Ssh," she soothes, tracing light circles over my arm with a fingertip.

I kiss her shoulder again. It's the truth. She's been a constant for me when I needed one to cling to. She was the one at the end of the phone, calling me after the accident. Checking on me. The one waiting for me at the airport the day we flew their bodies home. The one who has laid beside me every night since, her gentle, sleeping breaths stopping the silence from devouring me as the memories of that day haunt me.

And she's the one I asked to marry me after a few short months of dating, because the thought of being alone with those memories was inconceivable.

"Do you think it's coming from next door?" Claudia asks as the incessant wailing increases to an impressive ear-piercing pitch.

"Fuck knows," I mutter as she throws back the covers and climbs out of bed.

She pads across the bedroom and opens the door.

The noise intensifies.

I wrench my head off my pillow, cursing at the liquor-induced fog taking up residence in my brain, and make my way out of the room after her.

I find her in the hallway, hovering by the front door.

"Sullivan." She turns to me, eyes wide as the squawking pushes its way through the door, so loud and insistent that I'm surprised the door isn't rattling in the frame.

"What the hell?" I grumble, gently maneuvering her behind me so I can open the door.

The sound pauses momentarily as I stare down at the source.

It blinks back at me.

Then it opens its mouth and wails louder than ever.

"Whose baby is that?" Claudia gasps, leaning past me to search up and down the deserted hallway.

Tiny balled up fists shake in anger as its face grows redder. It's kicked off a blanket covered in tiny teddy bears.

I reach down and slide the envelope with my name on from inside the cardboard box it's lying inside. Its body turns rigid with each outraged cry as I turn the envelope over and lift the unsealed flap, pulling the thin piece of paper out.

"What is it?" Claudia's gaze bounces between my face and the baby. The paper creases inside my grip and nausea claws its way up my windpipe. "What does it say?" she asks.

She reaches for the paper, but I shove it inside the envelope and stuff it into the pocket of my sleep shorts.

"It says her name's Molly," I croak in a voice that doesn't sound like mine.

"What?" Claudia reels back, her eyes snapping back to the baby, still crying in the box.

I clear my throat as I stare at the baby.

"She's mine."

Claudia scoffs as if I've made a joke, but the color drains from her face as she takes in my grim expression. "Sullivan... you can't be serious?"

"She's my daughter," I confirm, the paper in my pocket feeling like a live grenade. I curl my fingers around it, crushing it into a crumpled lump.

The baby pauses its wailing for a micro second. Long enough to blink at me with wide eyes the exact shade of blue as my own.

Fuck.

1

TATE

PRESENT DAY

"I'M HERE, I'M HERE!" I CALL, RACING THROUGH THE door into Caffeine Couture and maneuvering past the growing line of the morning clientele in their dark suits.

"Chill, babe, it's all good," my friend and boss, Ashley, trills, as she winks at a businessman and hands him his coffee.

He throws back a suggestive arch of a brow and tosses a generous tip into the jar.

"See you tomorrow." Ashley pouts as he turns and heads out into Manhattan's rush hour.

"Is he a regular?" I ask as I rush behind the counter to the small staff area behind it, throwing my jacket onto a peg and dumping my purse on the floor.

I tie on my candy pink apron that clashes spectacularly with my auburn hair, and return to the counter, taking my place by the coffee machine and grabbing a milk jug.

"Nope." She shrugs with an easy smile. "But he will be now. Coffee and charm." She lowers her voice, turning to me. "A little flirt keeps that tip jar of ours nice and fat. Just how we like it."

I chuckle as she turns back to the line with a bright smile

and the next guy in line reels off his order to her. She rings it up on the register and I prepare it.

"You do this one," she whispers, giving me an encouraging poke in my lower back when I don't step forward.

"Oh... um... here's your coffee, sir," I say, holding the cup out to the guy with sandy hair, who must be in his mid-forties.

As he takes it from me, I throw what I hope is a cute smile at him.

His brown eyes sparkle, dropping to my name tag. "Thanks... Tate," he says.

"Nicely done," Ashley hums after he throws a twenty and a business card into the jar.

We work in unison, the radio playing in the background as we make fast work of processing the morning rush, until the only people left are a couple of female tourists taking their time to ponder over the blends, and two businessmen adding sugar to their coffees at the end of the counter.

"So, did you get it?" Ashley asks, leaning against the counter with folded arms.

"Yeah. I'm sorry I was late. The only pharmacy that had stock was a twenty-block detour," I answer, wiping my hands on my apron and leaving cocoa powder behind on the pink fabric.

"It's fine, things like that come first," Ashley says, swatting her hand in the air.

She turns to the tourists, who make their selection, and I fix their order.

Ashley's a great boss and is becoming a good friend since I began working at Caffeine Couture. I was doing afternoon shifts for my first month. But then her morning barista, Whitney, needed some time off, so I picked up her shifts too. It's a different crowd to the day. The mornings are full of people in workout gear, stopping in after their run in Central Park, followed by the suits on their commute, taking calls as they order their espressos and double shots, setting themselves up for another cutthroat day in the city.

Then come the tourists. The ones with time to stop and soak in the magic of the city. They look up from their phones and appreciate the tiny things. Like the pictures I like to create on their coffee foam using cocoa powder.

The dreamers.

Like me.

"Here you go." I hand over the two takeaway cups, but the couple's attention is pinned to a sleek black town car that's pulled over on the street outside.

"The morning shot of tall, dark, and devastatingly anti-commitment just showed up," Ashley muses as she moves to my side and looks out of the front window.

"Huh?" I glance at her, but her attention is glued to the black car, along with the two tourists. Even the two businessmen have halted their conversation and are watching.

A suited driver, who looks like he should be auditioning for a Bond film from the way he scans the sidewalk with narrowed eyes like he's assessing for threats, exits the car. He walks around to the rear door and holds it open.

I wait for a king or queen to step out, dripping in jewels and a crown.

Instead, a guy in a suit who looks around thirty climbs out.

I swivel my head around, then glance back at him. Everyone's eyes are on him as he buttons his suit jacket with one hand, pulls a cell phone from his pocket with the other, and presses it to his ear, beneath a head of perfectly styled jet-black hair.

As he turns, a side profile of perfect angles and sharp lines cuts across the sidewalk, making a woman who passes him stop and turn back to have another look. Her expression is one of awe, like she's seen a celebrity.

"That," Ashley clips with an air of suspense, like what she's about to tell me is incredibly important. "...is Sullivan Beaufort. He has enough money to have his own coffee plantation, yet he still sends his PA to get one of ours every day, because it's *that* good." She grins with pride.

"Beaufort? Like the place next door?" I ask.

"Tate." She snorts, rolling her eyes. "Yes! Like the billion-dollar jewelry store and head offices we're lucky enough to be neighbors with."

"Oh."

The giant store next to us makes Caffeine Couture look like a speck in comparison. It's all sleek blue and gold signs, with a doorman who wears white gloves.

"I think I saw a giant fish tank through the doorway yesterday," I say.

Ashley stares at me, her mouth falling open. "You've never been inside?"

"No."

"Oh my God." She scoffs. "We have to rectify that. I go in there at least once a month to try on their most expensive designs. They're gorgeous. They have the most beautiful pieces."

"Do you own any?"

She laughs before sighing at my question. "Babe, I'd need to sell a kidney to afford even the deposit on one of the designs I like." She picks up the tip jar and fishes out the bills from inside it. "But a girl's got to have motivation, you know?" She winks as she hands me my cut.

I tuck it inside my bra.

She purses her lips as she flicks through the stack of business cards that were inside the tip jar.

"Real estate," she reads. "Hmm, means he can sell you a fantasy more than he might be willing to deliver on it." She tucks the card to the back of the pile and moves on to the next.

"Cuthbert Taylor." She wrinkles her nose. "Imagine calling that out as you come?" She tips her head to one side, studying it. "Still, he's a doctor. And I think he was the one who smelled good." She puts his card into the pocket of her apron.

"Ooh, here's one for you." She shoves a card into my hand.

"A lawyer?" I screw my nose up as I study the thick gunmetal gray card embossed with gold font.

"Yeah. Maybe he can help you with everything, you know? And you won't have to work all these extra shifts... not that I don't love you being here." She smiles at me, then sighs. "I just don't want to see you running yourself into the ground."

"I'm fine. And I'm saving faster than I thought with all the extra flirting tips," I say, forcing my tone lighter. I pat my bra as a cold prickle runs up my spine, like it does whenever I think about these past few months and how tough things have been financially.

Ashley looks at me like she doesn't buy a word of my fake bravado, but keeps her mouth shut, knowing that I won't back down. I know she's trying to be a good friend, but I'll hire a lawyer myself once I've saved enough.

"Fine." She sighs. "Keep the card, though. Call him. Go for dinner. Get some dick. You need to go out and have fun. You're twenty-seven. Not seventy."

"I'll think about it," I tell her, knowing I'll toss the card the minute I finish my shift.

She nods approvingly. "Good."

"Besides," I add. "I do go out and have fun."

"Racing around the city after some weird guy in a mask doesn't count."

"You haven't heard him play," I point out. "...Rumor has it he's appearing somewhere tonight." I raise a brow at her.

She narrows her eyes. "Fine. I'll come with you, just to make sure you don't try and chain yourself to his piano or something that'll land you in jail."

"It's not like that. No one usually gets near enough to touch him. Anyway, it's not him I go for, it's his music."

"Got to be if you can't see his face. It could be anyone under all those black outfits and ski masks."

I grab a cloth and start wiping the counter, hoping to distract Ashley from my goofy smile. He's been dubbed *The Masked Maestro*. A guy who wears all black and pops up in random places across the city with a piano, which he plays so beautifully, like he's been doing it his whole life. No one knows his identity. Although social media has conspiracy theories over who he could be. But I like not knowing. I love the mystery. And I go to hear him play rather than watch him. Sometimes I close my eyes and just feel the music running through my veins like the blood I need to live. It's my sanctuary.

"I don't care." I shrug. "I go for his music. Not knowing which song he's going to choose. How he's going to play it."

"You're such a romantic." Ashley sighs, opening up a drawer beneath the counter and tossing the remaining business cards into the pile that's already inside.

"I just think society values a person's worth based upon their beauty too often. I'd choose a guy who I felt a deep connection with over abs and biceps any day."

"Uh-huh," Ashley hums. "I want all that too. I'd just prefer it if my soulmate also comes with a big dick, muscles, and a handsome face. I want to look at him and have the urge to rip his clothes off and ride him into next week."

I laugh. "Should I call Cuthbert to give him the heads up?"

She knocks shoulders with me playfully. "Piano man better be worth it. I could have been playing doctors and nurses tonight."

"He will be." I beam. "Believe me."

2

SULLIVAN

I toss the new dildo to the woman in the black lingerie who's reclined on the bed inside the suite I have at The Lanceford Hotel. Her sleek, dark hair fans out against the silk sheets beneath her.

"Get warmed up. I don't have long tonight," I instruct as I shrug out of my jacket and tug my tie loose.

The other woman in the white lingerie who could pass as her twin pouts at me, batting her eyelashes. "Why can't we sleep over tonight?"

A muscle ticks in my jaw at her demanding tone.

"Because I have somewhere else to be," I snap, unable to keep the harshness out of my voice.

She isn't perturbed. Instead she holds my eyes suggestively and unhooks her bra, freeing her pert tits.

My eyes drop to her puckered nipples, and I take a step toward the bed.

Then my phone rings.

I reach for my jacket and pull it out of the pocket.

"Fuck's sake," I grumble at the name on the screen. I lift

my eyes to the two girls on the bed who are looking at me in anticipation. "Get started without me. I need to take this."

Their disappointed whines get cut off as I step into the bathroom and close the door behind me.

"Why are you calling?" I snap the second my phone is to my ear.

"What? No hello?"

I pinch the bridge of my nose, forcing myself to take a slow breath. Her speech is slurred. She's fucking wasted again.

"Natasha!" I snap, "I've told you. You talk to me through my lawyer."

"I just want to know how Peaches is," she drawls.

I clench my jaw so hard it hurts.

"Her name is Molly," I spit.

"Did she get any more teeth?" she continues, ignoring me.

"Like you fucking care. Cut the shit and tell me why you're really calling."

The sound of her stumbling around and knocking something over blares down the phone. With any luck, it'll be something large and heavy that lands on her skull.

"A pipe leaked in the kitchen and—"

"No."

"You don't know what I was going to say!" she protests.

"That a pipe leaked, and you need to borrow some money until you get paid? Or you lost your job and need something to tide you over until the new one starts? Or your car broke down and you need a loan?" I say with an impatient huff. "Those have all been used. Time to think up some new material."

"Sullivan..."

I lean against the marble counter, curling my free hand around its cool edge, my knuckles turning white as I grip it hard enough to rip it off the wall.

"You're not getting another cent from me," I say slowly,

even though I know she won't listen. We'll continue this fucking charade in another couple of months. Next time her latest deadbeat boyfriend has got bored of her and she needs someone to fund her habit.

"You're a goddamn billionaire, and you can't spare a few bucks for me? I'm Peaches' mom!"

"Listen to me," I spit. "Her name is Molly. And you're a fucking disgrace. You left your daughter in a box, for God's sake."

"I was thinking I could come to the city, I could—"

My blood runs cold.

"No."

"But—"

"When you get yourself clean, Natasha. That's when I'll consider discussing visitation rights with you." I screw my eyes shut, a dull throbbing at the base of my skull indicating an impending headache.

"She's mine, not yours!" she snaps, losing her soft tone, and letting the real toxic Natasha shine through.

"The DNA test says she's very much mine," I state coldly. "And if you want to fight me on that, then be my guest. I'll look forward to wiping the floor with whatever backstreet lawyer you manage to manipulate into believing you're actually capable of being a decent human being, let alone the mother that Molly deserves. The courts will never side with an addict like you."

"You bastard," she slurs.

"Don't call me again!" I spit as I hang up.

I put my phone on the counter and turn and stare at myself in the giant mirror above the twin basins. Light blue eyes hardened by two years of her shit stare back at me. The multi-billion-dollar decisions I make every day in my position as CEO of our family business I can handle. I've even found a way to exist alongside the grief that gnaws at me every day since we lost my brother and Mom.

I work.

I make obscene amounts of money.

And one or two nights a week, I fuck women—or multiple women—in a hotel suite I have permanently booked. One my sister charmingly refers to as my disgusting sex pad.

But when it comes to Molly, *my daughter*, I'm a man on the edge of losing it the second anyone does or says anything that could threaten her happiness and wellbeing.

Most of the time, that person is the woman who dares to call herself her mother—Natasha.

And the night Molly came into my life, it was my fiancée, Claudia.

"I'm not sure I can do this, Sullivan. Look after another person's daughter, I mean... I need to think about this."

I didn't need to think about it.

I packed her bags for her and called her a cab. She was gone before sunrise.

I splash some cold water on my face and walk out into the bedroom. The girls look up expectantly from where they're both naked on the bed. One is lying with her legs spread wide, teasing herself with the giant rubber dildo.

"I want you inside me first," she pants, working it inside her, showcasing exactly where she's inviting me to stick my dick.

"Not fair. In that case, I get to be the first to suck him off," the other woman mewls.

Their bickering is doing nothing to ease my oncoming headache.

I swipe up my jacket and tie.

"Get out."

They stare at me in shock. "What?"

I allow myself a cursory sweep over their naked bodies.

They're both stunning. It's a shame to waste the opportunity. But Natasha's call has put me in a foul mood.

My eyes snag on the dildo before I look away.

"Changed my mind," I clip. "You can let yourselves out."

I walk out, slamming the door behind me to the outraged cries of *asshole* and *jerk*.

3

TATE

"Hey, Dad?" I call, peering down the stairs into the basement of our building.

"We're here!" he calls back.

I head downstairs and smile when I spot Dad talking to Larry, one of the other residents. They're sitting on the old, rust-colored leather couch—cracked and sagging—left behind by a previous tenant, waiting on laundry in one of the giant, ancient washers. Honestly, a scrubbing rack and bucket would probably work better. The machines are always breaking down.

"How was work?" Dad asks as I walk over to the old piano that's been here longer than we have and take a seat. He looks paler today, the dark circles beneath his eyes more prominent. He smiles at me and my chest twinges.

"It was good," I reply, running a hand over the marked piano lid that's closed over the ivory keys, tracing the dips and grooves of tiny knicks in its dark wooden surface. Each tells its own story about the people who have played on it. All those souls connected by music.

"You going to give us a song, eh, Tate?"

I smile shyly at Larry. His old, kind eyes crinkle at the corners as he looks at me hopefully.

"Um..." I lick my lips, a flicker of nerves rustling in my stomach as I glance toward the staircase.

"It's only us here, Sweetheart," Dad says encouragingly.

He's right. We *are* the only ones here. And even though the old piano is battered and needs a good tuning, there's a charm about it that I love. I often find myself sneaking down here alone to play it.

To dream.

"I know you're good, I've heard you down here," Larry says.

He's a sweet man. He lives here alone after losing his wife a few years ago. Something my father and him bonded over. And it's a comfort knowing that when I'm at work or out with friends that Dad isn't alone.

"Okay." I give in easily because, apart from my father, this is what I love most in the world, and the pull to play is too great.

I get myself into position before taking a deep breath and lifting the lid, revealing the black and white ivory keys. I flex my fingers above them.

Then I start to play.

Once I reach the chorus, the words come on their own.

"I believed your words, but they were all pretty lies. Now I'm left empty and broken with tears in my eyes."

I close my eyes as they leave my lips, barely more than a whisper. Each syllable gets easier to sing the more times I play this song. It's as if the music is healing me note by note, the sting lessening each time.

"Is that a new one?" Dad asks, studying me as I play the final chords, letting the melody drift to an end.

"Yeah. Just something I've been working on." I shrug. "I

got inspired after watching that film. You know the one where he's killed in service?"

I can't bring myself to look my father in the eye as I wait to see if he bought my lie.

"I like it," Larry declares, giving me a bright smile.

"Me too," Dad adds.

I exhale, my tense shoulders relaxing.

Dad gestures to me, waving his hand in the air as he thinks. "Tate, play Larry that one about becoming who you are. You know which one I mean." He snaps his fingers, humming the tune to remind me. But I know exactly which song he's referring to.

I shake my head, my throat tightening. "Not right now. I'm meeting Ashley. I should get ready."

"Ah, okay." Dad nods, and the love in his eyes makes my throat ache even more.

I close the lid of the piano and stand, picking up my purse. "I'll make some dinner and leave it in the oven for you."

"Don't worry about me," he says.

"I'll leave it in the oven," I repeat firmly. I know if I leave it up to my father, he'll skip dinner altogether.

He chuckles. "Okay. Thanks, love."

"Don't wait up, it could be a late one," I tell him. "Nice to see you, Larry," I add as I head toward the stairs.

"You too, Tate," he replies.

"Have fun," Dad calls. "And bring that uniform down before you go. I'll put it in the next wash." He jerks a thumb toward one of the ancient machines. "Thing needs it; it's covered in that brown stuff again."

I look at the cocoa powder that's covered my pink shirt and black skirt. He's right. I'm covered, just like I am after every shift. The stuff gets everywhere. But I love it. I've even designed a couple of new stencils with Caffeine Couture's logo on that I can't wait to try out. Maybe it's silly, but I love the smile they bring to people's faces when they notice them.

"Will do, thanks, Dad," I call back as I head for the stairs.

"Oh my God, is it always this busy?" Ashley shouts over the crowd's cheers that erupt around us.

"There are more people each time. People fly in from overseas now if there's a rumor that he's going to do a performance," I shout back.

My eyes zone in on the man dressed all in black, including a ski mask, who's appeared seemingly from nowhere in front of a piano on wheels that's been set up in Grand Central Station, tucked away around a corner at the base of one of the staircases.

"How does he get away with it?" Ashley asks.

The sound from the crowd reaches a new high as the man takes a seat.

"I don't know. The charity donations, I guess?" I shrug as I point out the giant collection tubs that have been set up on our side of the rope fencing that surrounds the piano. They're already spilling over with bills and coins.

When I first discovered The Masked Maestro a couple of years ago, it was by accident. He had a following of two hundred people on his YouTube channel. He turned up during a 'Sing for Hope Pianos' event and blew people away with his rendition of Beethoven's *Für Elise*. Good Morning America even played a clip of him.

After that, everyone wanted to know who the guy in the mask was. And his followers jumped to over six hundred thousand overnight. Now he gets the city's permission to do random pop-up shows comprising of just four songs each time. He announces on his social media the date of when one will be. But doesn't release the location until thirty minutes before it starts. Ashley and I had a mad dash to make it here in time.

The crowd falls silent with anticipation as he rolls his shoulders, preparing to start. The broad muscles of his back rise and fall as he takes a deep breath. I wonder if he gets that bundle of nerves before he plays, like I do. I doubt it.

His first note draws a collective intake of breath from the crowd. I join them, entranced as he plays a perfect rendition of Beethoven's *Moonlight Sonata* from memory, each note delivered flawlessly.

Ashley stands beside me, dumbstruck as he flows through *Etude* by Chopin, followed by *Little Red Riding Hood* by Rachmaninoff.

"Oh wow, he's incredible," she says, her eyes glued to his dark form hunched over the keys.

"I know, right," I whisper back, unable to look away from him as he plays the final bars.

I hold my breath waiting to see which piece he'll choose for his final one. I'm hoping for an Einaudi piece. I loved hearing him play Nuvole Bianche a few months ago.

He pauses, head bowed to his chest, fists clenched above the keys. The crowd falls silent again. Waiting.

I swear I can hear the emotion thick in his lungs as he drags in a rough breath, his chest rising with it. For one long, tense second, I wonder if he's going to play at all.

Then he exhales slowly and begins.

My mouth goes dry as the first notes ring out, traveling all the way to the celestial ceiling of the station above us and scattering there like bursts of shooting stars.

"This one's different," Ashley remarks as the song builds pace.

"I know." Because for the first time, it isn't a classical piece I'm hearing, but a modern one.

"What is it? I know it, I just can't…" Ashley nods along to the tune.

"A cover of *Unstoppable* by Sia," I say, frowning as my vision blurs around the edges until all that exists in my line of sight is him, or more specifically his hands as they press down so hard on the keys it's like he wants to break them.

His head is lowered, and I bet if I could see his eyes they'd be screwed shut. He plays the song like he both hates and loves it at the same time.

The raw emotion in it brings a lump to my throat.

"I love it." Ashley grins and bumps shoulders with me.

But I don't feel it.

I can't breathe.

All I can do is stare as he finishes the song and stands abruptly from the piano.

The crowd gasps as he knocks one of the ropes to the floor and storms off toward the subway.

The sight of him striding away gets swallowed by the crowd before he disappears from view completely.

4

SULLIVAN

"Come on, lazy bones." I grab hold of the tiny ankle that's sticking out from underneath my duvet.

Molly squeals as I use it to slide her abruptly to the foot of the bed and sweep her into my arms.

"You have your own bed," I tell her.

She wraps her arms around my neck, crushing herself to me. "I sleep with Daddy."

I bury my face into her dark curls and soak her in. I thought we'd gotten over her climbing into bed with me at night. It took two whole years for her to sleep through the night. But that still isn't a given. She sneaks in with me at least twice a week, and I'm awoken by an elbow to the face, or a tiny foot to the gut as she commands ninety percent of my California King bed for herself.

I've never been one who does well without sleep. But for Molly, there are lattes with double shots.

"We need to get you ready, Sweetheart. I'm dropping you at Grandad's to spend the day with Halliday."

"Yay." Molly giggles at the same time she squishes my cheeks together until my lips pucker like a fish.

I lean closer to her like I'm trying to kiss her, and she shrieks with laughter, trying to get away.

I catch the time on the bedside clock and groan internally.

"Shall we get your clothes, and you can race Daddy to see who's dressed first?"

Molly pokes out her lower lip like she's considering my request, despite the fact we played the same game yesterday morning. And the one before that. In fact, every morning. But she humors me, carefully considering my suggestion like it's the first time she's heard it.

Every morning she wins the race.

But that's what happens when you're two and a half years old and think clothes aren't mandatory. Molly will stand in her underwear, declare she's the winner, and I'll have to wrestle her into her clothes, then dress myself after.

She gives me a serious nod, coming to her conclusion. "Okay. Race."

"I love your outfit," Halliday says as she opens the door to her and my father's apartment.

Molly beams at her and reaches for her hand, the hood of her furry panda onesie slipping off her head.

"I worked with what I had," I grumble as Halliday bites back a giggle.

It was either leave the house with a small furry panda this morning, or don't leave at all.

I hand over Molly's day bag.

"Go," Halliday says, studying the tense expression I'm sure is on my face. "She'll be fine. I've got a fun day planned. Your father already left for work, so it's just the two of us."

"Thanks." I bend to kiss Molly on the cheek. "Love you, Sweetheart. See you later."

"Bye, Daddy," she chirps.

I straighten and my eyes catch on the growing bump beneath Halliday's clothes.

"You know I can always ask Arabella to—"

"I'm good." She waves off my concern. "I'm past the sickness stage now. And if I need a nap, I'll take one with Molly later."

"Fine." I nod, knowing nothing about pregnancy to argue. I missed that part of Molly's life.

Halliday's my father's British fiancée. Twenty years his junior. A world-class dating coach who my sister hired after insisting our father needed love in his life. No one expected the two of them to fall for one another and for Halliday to get pregnant all within a matter of months. But I've discovered life likes to throw curveballs your way. Halliday's nice. Molly loves her. And my father is happy. Just like Sinclair insisted he would be if he allowed himself to move on after Mom's affair and losing her and my brother.

Sinclair was due to look after Molly today. But since she confessed she's been receiving anonymous threats, and that her car was vandalized, my father declared his head of Security, Denver, act as her personal bodyguard. Sinclair was less than thrilled. Knowing my sister, she'll give Denver hell.

"We'll have a great day. See you later," Halliday says.

My gaze drops to Molly, playing with a crystal bracelet on Halliday's wrist.

"I'll send you pictures of what we're doing," Halliday adds, before taking the bracelet off and handing it to her so she can try it on.

I clear my throat. "Please do."

"Bye, Sweetheart," I call to Molly one final time before I break away and stride down the hallway. I haven't even made it as far as the elevator before the first of many work calls rings out from my phone.

I head straight to the coffee place in the building next to Beaufort Diamonds flagship store on Fifth Avenue. The décor has a retro vibe with pops of candy pink. But it's the scent that draws me in. And the knowledge that their coffee tastes better than any of the ones the top of the range machines in my building can produce. My PA, Arabella, gets coffee from here for me each morning, but I told her she could come in late today. Something about her mother's foot and a doctor's appointment.

A bell chimes overhead as I enter. The place is busy. I join the end of the line behind a guy in a suit and answer an incoming call on my phone as I wait.

"Beaufort."

"Fairfax," I greet.

Rafael Fairfax, the owner of the company that insures Beaufort Diamonds. A ruthless British businessman whose expertise we pay through the nose for. But his company is the best one of only a handful in the world that can provide the billions of dollars' worth of cover we require.

We talk as the line moves forward. I listen to his clipped British tone telling me the new mine we've acquired in Botswana will drive up our premium. Uncle Mal handles all overseas import business, aided by a local guy, Ade, who manages the mines while Mal flies back and forth every few weeks.

"Just a second," I tell Rafael, keeping the phone held against my ear.

"Latte, double shot, for Sullivan," I reel off to the woman behind the counter.

"Coming up," she says as I hand her a twenty and walk away before getting my change.

I stand at the end of the counter, grunting the odd agreement to Rafael as he continues his spiel about rising market costs. The redhead making my coffee is humming a tune to herself. The candy pink uniform shirt she's wearing clings to her like a second skin, the gaps between the buttons gaping around a swell of generous breasts. Her skirt isn't much better. The fabric stretches over her ass like it's trying to contain it from breaking free.

"How much?" I bark, snapping my gaze away from her as Rafael tells me a number that makes me want to get on a plane and fly over to London so I can punch him in the jaw.

"Just making sure you were listening," he drawls with a soft chuckle.

I shove a lid on my takeaway cup as the redhead places it on the counter.

"Oh, I'm listening. Now it's your turn, jackass. Call me back when you're ready to talk real numbers."

I hang up, cutting off his deep, throaty laugh. This is how we operate. He gives me a number. I call him some choice names that I wouldn't use in front of Molly. We volley back and forth until we both think the other is an asshole, but that we were the one who got the better deal.

A perfect business relationship. And friendship.

I slide my phone back in my suit pocket.

"Sullivan?"

I look up into the eyes of a woman with long blonde hair wearing a patterned workout crop top and tights.

"Hello." I flash a brief smile with just enough warmth in it that it will appear like I recognize her.

Her flirty smile and glint in her eyes tell me we must have fucked once.

"Nonfat chai for Jemima!" the redhead in the ill-fitting uniform calls.

"Jemima," I say smoothly. "Nice to see you. Have a good day."

I nod politely and move to sidestep her. That call with Rafael has got me fired up and ready to unleash hell. I bet my accountant will have some choice words for him too when I inform him of the ludicrous figure the bastard gave me.

"Sullivan?" Jemima reaches out, placing her hand over my jacket sleeve. Her expression is one of unconcealed eagerness as I turn back to her. "Maybe we could have dinner soon? Catch up?"

One side of her glossed lips curl.

I narrow my eyes as images of those lips begging me to fuck her throat a couple of months ago flash back to mind. But that's all I've got.

"Sounds wonderful," I lie, injecting disappointment into my tone. "But we've just launched a new line at work. Things are busy right now."

"Oh." Her face falls before her brows pop back up. "I could come to your office and bring lunch? I'm free tomorrow."

"I'm having lunch with my daughter tomorrow," I tell her. Not a lie this time.

"That sounds great. I love kids." She beams.

Irritation prickles up my spine and my fingers tighten around my coffee.

"My daughter isn't good with new people," I say, walking away before she can respond.

As I push through the door and out onto the street, her raised voice hits the back of my navy suit jacket.

"Call me!"

5

SULLIVAN

ONE DAY OF GETTING MY OWN COFFEE BECOMES
three. Turns out Arabella's Mom's foot wasn't a small matter,
but gangrene brought on by her diabetes. I've given her leave
for a couple of weeks and hired a temp to fill in as my PA.

The new PA is fine—a young woman from an agency
who's slipped seamlessly into the role. It's not Arabella's
absence at work that's the problem. It's the extra help she gave
me with Molly. Sitting with her during meetings when I had
to bring her in. Picking her up from my father's. Taking her
home on nights when work ran late, despite my best efforts to
leave on time.

Between myself, my father, and Sinclair, we've managed
over the past two years. Molly came into all of our lives like a
thunderbolt, giving us something positive to focus on after
losing my mother and brother. I was adamant I didn't want
her going to daycare or a babysitter. I wanted family and
friends to be the ones to care for her until she can start pre-k at
age four. The idea of her being someplace unfamiliar brings
back unwelcome memories of crying boxes discarded in
hallways.

"Daddy sad."

"Daddy's not sad, Sweetheart," I tell Molly as I open the door to the coffee place and carry her inside.

She studies me as we join the line, her little face serious as she pouts.

"How can I be sad when my best friend is a lion?" I ask.

"Roar!" she shrieks, loud enough to draw amused glances from two women in line. Their eyes take in her rosy round cheeks in her fluffy lion onesie, before moving to me in my suit. They both smile as one of them not-so-subtly checks my left hand for a wedding ring.

I tighten my hold on Molly, my lips flattening. My father would chuckle if he were here. Tell me I'll have to loosen the reins as she gets older. I know he's right. He had three kids, and saw us all through scraped knees, fevers, and a broken arm when my brother tried to build a makeshift zipline in our apartment with an old rope and a coat hanger. And at age fifty, he's about to do it all again with Halliday.

But Molly's my world.

She's the one thing keeping me sane. The one thing that makes me get up in the morning after losing him. I loved my mother. And that's a loss I feel every day. But with him it was different... he was my brother. The other half of me.

The day he died it felt like a part of me went with him. I didn't know how I'd survive without him. I didn't think I could. Until the moment I opened my door to a crying baby and a handwritten note that set my life on a new course.

"Babyccino and a Latte. Double shot," I say to the woman behind the counter.

"Latte, double shot, for Sullivan," she repeats, remembering me from the previous two days, and writing my name on the cup in thick black ink. "And a babyccino..." She winks at Molly, "...for the lion."

Molly dazzles her with one of her smiles she gives out too

freely to strangers, and I ignore the bite of protectiveness that comes along with seeing it.

We move to the end of the counter to wait. My phone rings in my pocket and I keep a firm hold of Molly as I pull it out and answer.

"I'll call you back," I bark at one of the senior operations team before he can speak. I'll be in my office in ten minutes and able to talk about whatever it is he needs to in private.

I put my phone away and grab a lid for my coffee as it's placed down, taking in the plain white foam on top of it.

"Where's my—?"

"Your what?"

I glance up at the barista, but it's the same woman who took my order, not the usual redhead with the tight uniform.

She looks at me expectantly.

"Never mind," I grumble, shoving the lid on.

"I'm so sorry!"

The out of breath remark makes me look up. There she is. Red hair. Same unmistakable uniform that looks even smaller than it did yesterday, if that's possible. Her heaving breaths make her breasts appear in real danger of bursting through the buttons.

"What happened?" The other woman turns her back on me, giving the redhead her full attention as she scrabbles to tie an apron around her waist.

"Shaving cut," she mumbles in a low whisper.

"Everything okay?"

The extra layer of concern in the other woman's voice makes me frown. Since when did a shaving cut provide an acceptable reason for being late?

"Yeah," the redhead replies, seeming a little shaken. "I got the bleeding to stop, it's all good."

"All right. As long as you're okay?" The other woman squeezes her arm in a show of understanding, making my frown deepen. I'd put one of my staff on a final warning if they tried to sell that shit to me.

I look more closely at the redhead as she picks up a milk jug and sets it underneath a frother. Her too-tight skirt falls to just above her knees. Her lower legs are bare, no sign of a Band-Aid. Exactly which part of herself was she shaving?

I run my tongue over my lower lip as she pours the milk into a miniature takeaway cup and then holds a stencil over the top of it and shakes on some cocoa.

"Babyccino for Lion?" she chimes in a cheery voice.

"Me!" Molly pipes up in my arms.

The redhead looks at her, tilting her head to one side and pressing her lips together.

"Hmm. Are you sure? You look far too friendly to be a lion to me."

"Roar!" Molly cries again, louder than the first time.

The redhead's eyes pop wide. "Wow! Please accept my humble apologies. That's one impressive roar you've got there, Miss Lion. Very mighty indeed."

Molly giggles in my arms as the woman slides the small cup across the counter to me with a smile. "Here you go."

"Daddy!" Molly exclaims, pointing at the foam on her drink before I can put a lid on it. "A Bunny."

The redhead grins at her. "Do you like her? She looks like my old pet, Bumper."

"Shouldn't that have been Thumper?" I ask without thinking, studying the brown ears.

"No. She only had one eye and was always hopping into things."

I take in the redhead properly for the first time. Her light blue eyes are bright as she smiles at me, making her nose wrinkle a little and shifting the freckles around that are on her cheeks.

"She lived until she was thirteen," she adds, like the information is of great significance.

"... Right," I say.

My phone rings again. I pull it out and see the same name as earlier.

"What is it?" I snap, putting it to my ear.

"Sorry, it couldn't wait. I know you'd want to hear this straight away."

"Hear what?" I bark.

"One of the team got their hands on Fabienne's new designs."

My grip tightens on the phone. Fabienne is a jewelry brand with elevated opinions of themselves. No competition to Beaufort Diamonds, although they wish that weren't the case. The quality of their pieces is not a scratch on ours. But whenever we release a new line, they predictably push the boundaries on what they can get away with, by ripping off our designs with some gawdy low quality alternative. It takes the shine off our new launches, which are of outstanding quality. It's like getting a cab and the driver proudly showing off a Canal Street Patek Philippe timepiece on his wrist, telling you it's identical to yours, which set you back a quarter mill, but his only cost him ninety bucks.

Absolutely no comparison.

"Send them to me. And get Legal on it," I hiss, grinding my teeth as my phone chimes in my ear, indicating a new email.

"Already done. These are the boldest ones yet."

"Great," I mutter, biting back the alternative word I'd use if Molly weren't in my arms.

I end the call and walk to a small unoccupied table near the counter, depositing Molly into a chair.

"Let's have your drink here, Sweetheart. Daddy needs to look at something for work."

The tension in my neck's only going to get worse if I wait until we're back in my office to look at whatever fresh shit they're trying to pull.

Molly nods at me, swinging her legs in the chair.

I move back to the counter, grab our drinks, and return to her. She beams at the cocoa bunny as I take a seat and pull up the email.

Motherfuckers.

I suck in a sharp breath. The first design is blatantly a rip-off of our new Asscher cut diamond choker. And it only gets worse. They've even attempted a shitty copy of our new engagement ring setting. One I designed myself.

"Sweetheart, Daddy needs to make some private calls when I get into the office, okay?"

Molly's used to being in the office with me when I'm working. But whenever I need to make a call where the overuse of the word 'Fuck' and threats to shove things up the CEO of Fabienne's ass will take place, Molly stays with Arabella.

"Remember, Arabella isn't around today, so another of Daddy's work colleagues will keep you company."

"Den-Va?" Molly asks hopefully.

"No. He's with Auntie Sinclair today."

Sinclair's doing a runway show. And my father and Halliday have an ob-gyn appointment this morning. I wrack my brains. I only ever leave her with Arabella at my office. But one of the senior leadership team is recently back from maternity leave. Molly will be okay with her if they use the room opposite my office. All the walls are glass, so I'll be able to see her the entire time.

"Clare will keep you company. She's just had a baby. She'll have pictures she can show you."

"No. Me stay with Daddy." Molly scowls at me. Despite her adoration of babies and her baby dollies, the kid's smart. She knows when she's being handled.

I look back at the email and pinch the bridge of my nose, holding back a curse.

"Did you want these while you're here? We keep a few stashed under the counter."

I jerk my head up, and the redhead falters at my grimace. I force the blood boiling in my veins to cool down so I don't appear like I'm about to murder someone.

She holds a stack of coloring sheets and crayons out to me.

"For Miss Lion," she says, glancing at Molly who's poking at the foam on her drink with her finger.

"Thanks."

She places them on the table. "No problem. I like to keep things here for the kids."

Molly beams at her, clearly won over by some dust resembling an animal. "Awabella not here today," she announces.

"Oh, that's right. I hope her mom is doing okay," the redhead replies. She smiles at Molly, then glances at me before returning behind the counter.

I stare at her as she fixes a drink with a dreamy look on her face. I bet she's humming to herself again.

I go to my call list and bring up Arabella's number.

"Hi. How's your mom doing?" I force myself to ask, despite wanting to get straight to the reason I'm really calling.

"Oh, well... she's trying to keep her spirits up... and she says thank you for the flowers," Arabella tells me. "But she's not so good. It's hard to tell if the meds are working. She's scared she'll lose her foot."

"Give her all of the team's regards," I say.

"I'll be back as soon as I can."

"Don't worry about that, just be with her. Listen, I needed to ask you... You said your friend's niece works at the coffee place next door?"

"Oh, she does. Such a lovely girl."

"The kindergarten teacher?"

"That's right. She's working there while she interviews for jobs. Kids love her. She's a sweet girl. Beautiful too. Men are always giving her their number."

My eyes drop over the redhead's curves as she serves a guy at the counter. He grins at her and drops a business card into the tip jar, along with a bill.

"So I could trust her with Molly?"

"Oh God, yes. She's a gem. And HR already checked her out. She helped serve at some Beaufort events in LA before she and her boyfriend moved to the city."

Not as good as a full security check Denver could do, but it'll suffice for now. And she'll have had extra vetting if she's a teacher.

"I see. Thank you."

I sit and fire off some strongly worded emails to legal, informing them to be ready for an imminent conference call, while Molly finishes her drink and colors in a picture of a bunny eating a carrot.

"You ready, Sweetheart?" I ask after she proudly holds it up for my inspection and I take my time to study it, telling her it's the best colored-in rabbit I've ever seen.

"I want Den-va." She pouts as she takes my hand and slides off her chair.

"Denver's busy today. You'll have fun with Clare. Daddy won't be long, and then you can play in my office."

She stops walking and I ready myself for negotiations. Last time Molly dug her heels in, it cost me a day at the zoo and a custom-made princess carriage bed just to get her onboard. And she still won't sleep in it every night.

"Molly," I say as I turn.

But she's not stopped to be stubborn. She's stopped to beam at the redhead behind the counter who's fixing another drink.

Molly thrusts her picture up in the air proudly.

"That's beautiful. Did you do that yourself, or did your daddy help you?"

The redhead's light blue eyes flick from the purple scribble that's spilling over the lines of the drawing, to mine, then back to Molly as she gives her a bright smile.

"Me." Molly grins.

"Good job."

My daughter glows under her praise, and images flash into my head of all the redhead's kindergarten pupils looking at her like this. She has something about her that kids must pick up on. Some people are born naturally good with kids. The rest of us have to learn when we become parents.

"For you," Molly declares, brandishing the paper higher.

"Molly, the lady's busy," I say.

"Not too busy to admire this masterpiece," the redhead says, looking at Molly and ignoring me, as she wipes her hands on her apron, leaving brown smudges behind.

She steps closer and takes the picture from Molly, holding it between both hands as she studies it. The same guy who slipped his number in the tip jar earlier hovers at the counter even though he's already got a drink in his hand. His eyes drop to the redhead's cleavage as she leans over to talk to Molly. He sees me watching and raises his brows like we're bros sharing some harmless eye candy.

I glower at him until he looks away, clearing his throat and pulling on his collar.

"Are you sure I can keep this? It's very good."

Molly nods at her.

"Thank you. I'll hang it right up over here where people can see how pretty it is." She comes out from behind the counter and walks to a small noticeboard on the wall where there are posters about a book club, a charity of the month the coffee house is donating to, and some thank you cards that have small essays written inside. "There," she announces, pinning the picture in the center, then standing back with her hands on her hips to admire it.

The douche at the counter takes the opportunity to check out her ass.

"You waiting on something?" I snap in his direction, unable to help myself.

"Did I fix you the wrong thing? Americano with a shot of caramel syrup, wasn't it?" The redhead's eyes widen, and she looks like she's actually worried about disappointing the jerk.

"No, it tastes perfect, Tate. Yours always do." He flashes an overly toothy smile at her. "I was actually..." He glances at me, looking me up and down—a microsecond scan trying to decipher the level of competition I pose. His eyes flick to Molly and his shoulders relax like he's got nothing to worry about.

My teeth grind, and I rub my thumb over Molly's tiny hand inside mine.

"... I was thinking we could grab a coffee together when you finish your shift. There's a place I know a block from here that makes a great cup."

I snort and he flashes me a scowl before turning back to Tate.

"A great coffee?" She frowns.

The burning urge to storm back to my office and vent about Fabienne to Legal is momentarily paused as I watch the loser who thinks asking out a woman surrounded by coffee all day—with the added brilliance of telling her *he* knows a place that makes a great one, while holding the very drink *she* just made him—is too epic a fuck-up not to witness.

This is exactly the sort of shit my brother would have eaten up hearing about when he was alive.

"What time do you finish?" the guy continues, unaware he's on a sinking ship.

"She's here until lunch, but she's on a thirty-minute break starting now," the other barista pipes up from where she's just walked out from a back room. She gives Tate an encouraging smile like she's doing her a favor.

"Great," Douchebag says. "Shall we leave?"

"He wants to take me to a place he knows that makes great coffee around the corner," Tate tells her colleague.

"Great coffee?" The other woman recoils, her face screwing up as she shoots the guy a look that could freeze Hell. I glance down at Molly who's watching the whole exchange.

"I like it here, Daddy," she says, tugging on my hand and gazing at me with innocent eyes.

"I know you do, Sweetheart."

I glow with smug pride as I throw the guy a look that says, 'my almost three-year-old is smarter than you, jackass'.

"I meant bagels. The place makes great bagels." The guy backtracks furiously.

Tate looks at him the way I imagine someone looking at an injured dog would. Pity laced with a desperate need to say or do something to make them feel better before she speaks.

"Well, I—"

"She's spending her break with my daughter," I say. "They've got coloring to do."

"Yay!" Molly squeals, vibrating with excitement in her furry lion onesie next to me.

"Coloring?" This time, it's the douchebag snorting.

His smirk dies as I level him with a stare.

"That's right, I forgot. Have her back in thirty," the other barista chimes in with a giant grin.

Tate stumbles forward like she's been shoved, then shoots a warning look at her friend.

"We go now?" Molly questions.

Tate's mouth opens but nothing comes out as my daughter slips her hand inside hers and beams.

"Yes, we can go now, Sweetheart," I tell her as my gaze meets shocked, light blue eyes.

6

TATE

I FUMBLE WITH THE TIE AT THE BACK OF MY APRON as little fingers grip happily onto my other hand. I sneak a sideways glance at the little girl's father who's holding her other hand as he leads us along the sidewalk toward the building next door.

Sullivan Beaufort.

His dark hair is swept back from his penetrating cool blue eyes, and his face is set firm. I don't know whether to be afraid or not. He looks like he crushes business opponents beneath his Italian leather shoes before breakfast without even breaking a sweat. Judging by the part of his phone call I overheard and the pulsing vein in his tense neck, I'd say he has his sights on his next target.

The little girl grins at me and I smile back.

Assessing blue eyes flick over, and I swallow as they drop over my uniform and two scowl lines deepen between his brows. I yank the tie on my apron again, pulling the cocoa-marked fabric off and holding it by my side.

"Tate, isn't it?" The deep gravel of his voice saying my name sends a shiver up my spine. He sounded scary on the phone, and I bet he's terrifying in person when you're on the receiving end of his wrath.

"That's right." I fumble with my apron, not knowing what to do with it as we approach the giant glass doors of Beaufort Diamonds.

He stops on the thick blue and gold embossed sidewalk carpet and studies me like he's regretting his decision to invite me to... whatever this is.

I stuff the soiled apron underneath my armpit so I don't have to let go of his daughter's hand and thrust my other hand toward him.

"Tate Miller."

His eyes drop to my outstretched hand for a second before he lets his daughter's hand go and reaches out to curl his fingers around mine. His shake is firm and confident, like he always has to be the one in the lead. The one in control.

His hand returns to his daughter's within seconds, and maybe I imagine the way he stiffens for those brief moments their contact is broken.

"Sullivan Beaufort. And this is Molly," he clips.

His eyes soften as he looks down at the little girl with dark curls, but they regain their business-like detachment the moment they lift back to mine.

"Hello," Molly pipes up.

I can't help but break her father's eye contact and grin as she beams. "Hello," I reply, "it's nice to be formally introduced, Miss Lion." I hold my hand out to her, and she pulls hers free of mine so we can shake.

"So... coloring?" I ask lamely.

"I have an important call to make, for which my daughter cannot be present. You'll stay within my sight. And of course, I will compensate you for your time," he states, a muscle twitching in his jaw as he eyes the apron I've stuffed under my arm like he's severely regretting his choice.

"So, you're hiring me for the next thirty minutes?" I say, sounding much braver than I am. But I pull my shoulders back and lift my chin, faking confidence. He might be a billionaire who owns the ridiculously extravagant building we're about to walk inside, but I refuse to be intimidated by him, when, by the sounds of it, I'm about to help him out without being given a choice.

I pull the apron free and hold it more neatly by my side, noting the flare of his nostrils as they pass over my uniform.

"It will only take twenty," he grinds out before clearing his throat. "Is that... agreeable to you?" The words are forced like he's used to people doing what he says without question.

I don't know whether he's looking at me. I'm busy smiling at his adorable daughter who doesn't seem to have inherited any of her father's arctic abruptness.

"Color?" she asks hopefully.

"Color. I hope you have pencils? I can go back inside to get some—"

"Molly has plenty," he clips, as a suited doorman opens the giant gold-handled glass door for us with a flourish.

"Mr. Beaufort. Miss Beaufort. Ma'am."

"Good Morning, Joe," Sullivan replies, sweeping us inside.

My jaw hits the floor as we walk into the lavish interior that is Beaufort Diamonds flagship store. Ashley has some balls coming here and trying their pieces on. I feel like I should turn around and walk straight back out. I don't belong here. This place is fancy, opulent... and dripping with extravagant luxury.

"This is one of our new pieces," a sales assistant tells a couple as she presents a giant glittering ring to them on a velvet pad.

"How many carats?" the woman asks.

"Five."

"Clarity?" she purrs.

"Internally flawless. It's from one of the Beaufort mines," the sales assistant tells her proudly.

"How much is it?" the woman asks.

"One hundred and seventy."

The woman nods at her partner, an older man in a fancy suit.

"If you like it, Darling, then we'll take it," he says without giving it any thought.

My mouth goes dry. They're talking *thousands*. One hundred and seventy thousand.

"Jesus," I breathe, causing Sullivan's eyes to dart to me.

Fingers tightening around my apron, I clamp my mouth shut and keep pace with him as he walks us across the plush carpet toward a bank of elevators. The staff all greet us with bright, beautiful smiles as we pass an enormous cylindrical fish tank in the center of the space. It's filled with giant shells, over which pieces of stunning jewelry have been draped. The whole place smells expensive and high end. I wouldn't be surprised if a member of the British Royal family appeared from one of the private viewing rooms positioned at the rear of the store.

I tilt my head backward to admire an eye-catching poster taking up a floor-to-ceiling section of the wall behind one of the glass display areas.

"Auntie Sin," Molly declares.

A suited staff member greets us as he holds a white-gloved hand out, inviting us into the waiting elevator.

"My sister models for the company," Sullivan says, stepping inside.

I let go of Molly's hand as we turn to face the doors, but she slips her fingers back inside mine with ease, doing the same with her father on the opposite side. The sight of the stunning blonde wearing a sparkling diamond choker and matching earrings disappears from view as the doors slide closed.

My head's still spinning from the extravagance of the

store's ground floor level as we ride up to the highest level and step out into an immaculate marble-floored reception area.

"Cara?" Sullivan says, marching us over to a blonde sitting behind a giant, sleek, navy reception desk. She has platinum-blonde hair that shines like ice where it's cut perfectly to her jaw in a chic style.

"Good morning, Mr. Beaufort. Good Morning, Molly." She smiles at them both before her eyes land on me and she subtly reads the Caffeine Couture logo on my shirt.

"Can you issue Miss Miller a visitor's pass, please?"

"Of course." She smiles at Sullivan again, her perfectly laminated brows lifting as she ignores me and speaks directly to him. "And what is the nature of her visit?"

"Personal guest," Sullivan clips, pulling his chiming phone from his pocket and frowning at the screen.

"I see." The receptionist's lips purse as she taps something into her keyboard before reaching to a printer and taking something from it.

Sullivan's typing away on his phone as she places an ID card fastened to a clip down on the counter. She slides it toward me with one scarlet nail like touching it any further would result in her needing to scrub her hands.

"Make sure you wear it at all times so the Beaufort team knows you're *only* a visitor," she says with a fake smile.

I pick up the smooth laminated card embossed with the company's gold logo. She never told me she was taking my picture. I don't even know where the camera is. Somewhere on her ridiculously shiny desk by the looks of it, judging by the unflattering angle straight up my nose she's managed to catch.

"All done Mr. Beaufort," she trills, flashing him a megawatt smile as he looks up from his phone.

"Good," he grunts, the frown lines deepening between his brows as he eyes where I've clipped the ID to the breast pocket of my shirt. I glance at it, wondering if I should have put it somewhere else, but no one else here is wearing one for me to know if I've committed some swanky ID badge faux pas.

"Follow me."

He walks purposefully, one hand in his daughter's as he leads me past a network of glass walled offices, each filled with smart, stylish businesspeople who'd pass as runway models.

We stop outside an open door. It leads into a giant corner office with panoramic views across the city.

"Wow," I say without thinking.

"I'll be taking the call in my office," he says. "You can make yourself comfortable in here with Molly."

He opens the door to another glass walled room directly opposite his, and I walk inside. It appears to be a waiting room with sofas and bookshelves, and a coffee station set up on a large sideboard, alongside glittering jewelry brochures. But behind the corporate seating area is what can only be described as a kid's dream. There's a large crafting table covered in pens and multi-colored stacks of paper and sticker books. Giant beanbags cover the floor in one corner, next to a display stand of children's books. And in the corner is a small slide, next to a teepee tent that has rainbow bunting strung around it.

Molly trundles in happily, bypassing all the stuffy office furniture and heading straight for the wonderland behind it.

"Between my father, sister, and myself, Molly doesn't spend that much time here. But when she does, I like her to..." He presses his lips together, his eyes following Molly as she picks a teddy up from on top of a beanbag and starts talking to it.

"You like her to have her own space to play." I smile at him, a pang of sympathy tugging at my chest. He's clearly torn about having to bring her here sometimes when work gets in the way. He might be a billionaire, but I know a father's guilt when I see it.

"I used to go to work with my father a lot as a kid. I loved it," I tell him. "It helped me to appreciate how hard he worked for both of us."

"Both of you?"

I nod, my breath catching at how intense his eyes are when they're laser-focused on me.

"Yeah, just us. My mother passed away when I was a kid."

"I'm sorry," he says in a tone one degree warmer than his sub-zero business-like one.

"Thanks." I gaze around the room. "So you want me to play with Molly in here, and you'll be in there?" I gesture to the giant corner office that has a direct line of sight into this room. It's obviously been set up specifically like this so he can see inside from his office without obstruction. "It's like a fish tank. Will I find diamonds in this one like the one downstairs?"

Nerves make me laugh, but it withers as he remains silent.

"With your attention on my daughter, even if there were, I don't expect you'll have time to notice."

"No, of course not," I agree.

His eyes narrow as he stares at me like I'm a bug under a microscope. "Arabella gave you a glowing recommendation," he says slowly, like he's failing to understand his own words.

"She did?" I can't help the surprise in my voice. His PA is lovely, and I enjoy chatting with her when she comes in for their coffee. But it's always during the morning rush, so we barely exchange more than a few words before she's gone again.

"Shouldn't she have?" he rasps.

The intensity of his scrutiny steps up a level, making my stomach twist. "No, no, of course. That's really nice of her, and I love kids. Molly and I will have fun while you make your call. And I've never so much has had a parking ticket. Law abiding citizen right here." I tap the center of my rib cage and the ID rattles against my shirt.

I swallow as he stares at me.

"Molly?" he calls, his eyes trained on mine. "Daddy will be back soon, okay? Tate's going to stay with you."

"Okay," a little voice calls back.

"Give your details to Cara and she'll wire five hundred dollars to your account before you leave."

"Five hundred? For twenty minutes?" I gape at him. That's enough to get a couple of weeks' worth of the good groceries for Dad and me.

His brows flatten "Of course... this was short notice. I'll tell Cara one thousand. Now, please, excuse me."

He walks to the door before calling back to Molly. "See you in a while, Sweetheart."

Then he closes it, leaving us inside.

7

SULLIVAN

"WE'RE ALREADY ON IT. FABIENNE WON'T KNOW what hit them."

"Mm." I grunt, pacing back and forth behind my desk as Jones, the guy who heads Beaufort Diamonds legal team reels off a list of infractions he's going to hit them with over the desk phone speaker.

I stop and brace both hands on top of my desk just as Molly giggles at something Tate says to her. Tate's laughing too as she glances up and sees me watching her. Her smile falters and she looks away, her attention returning to Molly as I continue staring at her.

"Just a small glitch, don't worry," Jones continues as I lean over my desk like if I only move an inch closer I'll be able to hear whatever it is that's so funny it has my daughter gripping her sides in stitches as she laughs.

I love that laugh. I *live* for that laugh.

"This is the last time they pull this shit. I want their company ruined," I hiss, curling my hands into fists against the cool glass. "Find out what it'll take to buy them. Then once we have them, we can tear them apart and sell the pieces."

Jones chuckles, because when it comes to business, he loves nothing more than an opportunity to do what he does best. Be vicious, like a shark after blood. Be the type of moral-free lawyer that I pay him millions per year to be. I've learned money can erase most people's morals.

Tate joins Molly, laughing about whatever it is they're finding so funny, and my attention drops to the ID badge, flapping around against her shirt with each vibration from her chest. That ridiculous pink shirt that's barely keeping her ample breasts contained. The ID swung against them as we walked from reception earlier, with an irritating *pat pat* sound that's still ringing in my ears.

"Consider it done," Jones declares. "I'll call you when I have an update."

"Appreciate it," I reply.

My cell rings on the desk as I hit end call on the desk phone.

"Dad?" I answer, swiping it up.

"Hello, Son. Everything okay? How's Molly?"

One side of my mouth curls up as her dark curls bend low over the desk and she concentrates on the picture she's coloring in. She's always the first thing on my father's mind whenever we speak.

"She's good. She's coloring."

"I'm sorry I couldn't watch her today."

The regret in my father's voice brings a lump to my throat. I know how much he means that. He's always helped as much as he can with Molly. So has Sinclair. But since the arson attack at his club that put Halliday in hospital, and Sinclair's car being vandalized, and her receiving threats, they've both been pre-occupied.

We're the Beauforts. We're family. And family always comes first. But I'm Molly's father, so ultimately I'm the one who needs to care for her. I don't regret my decision to keep her out of daycare until pre-k. But with recent developments, and now losing Arabella for the foreseeable future, it does pose a new challenge. Beaufort Diamonds won't run itself, and I have a responsibility to everyone that the family's legacy is upheld. This will all belong to our next generation one day.

"It's not a problem," I tell my father as I walk to the glass wall of my office, pushing a hand into my pants pocket as I watch Molly.

"Hallie's excited to have her tomorrow," my father says.

"Molly's excited too."

"We'll pick her up early. Hallie asked if you could pack her bathing suit. She was going to take her for a swim."

"She'll love that."

Molly's looking at Tate, who's admiring her picture and saying something that makes Molly giggle. I roll my lips, pissed at myself that I kept the sound system off while I was on the call with Jones. If I hadn't, I'd be able to hear every word of what's making my little girl so carefree and happy.

"And Thursday evening, I need to move some things around a little, but—"

"It's fine," I cut in.

Molly was meant to be spending the night with Sinclair this week so that I could have my regular Thursday evening off. But I'm not comfortable with Molly being there overnight until we know more about the threats Sinclair's received.

Sighing, I stare through the glass. Part of me feared this day would come.

"I've been thinking about hiring someone," I confess. The words feel alien and wrong as they form.

"At least while Arabella is with her mom. And only for the occasions when one of us can't have Molly. And I'd base them here, where I could keep an eye on them," I add.

"I see. Do you want me to ask Killian to look into agencies?"

"That won't be necessary."

I don't want one of our family's security team going to some faceless agency and sifting through their on-paper credentials. Arabella has been working for our family business for over twenty years. I trust her judgment. And I also trust our company's vetting procedure of anyone who does any work for us. Even if that's just some waitressing at a PR event.

My eyes fall on red hair, catching the light in the opposite room. Arabella has known Tate since Tate was a child. And she's a kindergarten teacher. Molly's going to start pre-K once she turns four. It's a little over a year away. This is just... moving up the timeline a little.

"You're sure about this?" my father asks.

I curse internally. No, I'm not fucking sure. I don't want anyone who isn't family, or a close friend near my little girl, if I can help it. But what choice do I have?

"It's fine," I grit, pinching my brow.

We talk about a few business things before I end the call and march across the hallway.

I take a deep breath and open the door.

Molly's cooing about something being 'pretty'. But the sight of her is blocked by Tate's back. She's sitting back on her heels on the floor. The position makes the back zipper of her pencil skirt stretch over her ass.

Tate turns at the sound of the door opening and catches my eyes on her.

"Is it cocoa? Do I have more on me?" Her eyes widen, and she brushes her ass, twisting her head over her shoulder to try and see.

"I have a business proposition for you."

She halts her self-examination and gapes at me. "What?"

"Pardon," I correct. Jesus, I want my daughter to have manners. Perhaps I need to have a conversation with Miss

Miller about the language I deem unsuitable for use while she's in my daughter's company.

"It will be short term," I say, knowing the moment Arabella is back, I'll be happy to return to prior arrangements. "A few hours on occasion while I work, and my daughter isn't with family. And I'll pay you extra for a level of flexibility."

Her blue eyes remain wide, and I stop myself from telling her to close her mouth.

"You'll be looking after Molly," I confirm, partly because I need to spell it out from the puzzled look on her face, and partly because I'm playing dirty, knowing that if my daughter enters negotiations with me, then Tate will be less inclined to turn down my offer.

"Yay!" Molly squeals.

Tate glances at her, and the way her eyes soften upon contact with my daughter, fills me with equal parts protectiveness and tenderness.

"Um..." Tate's brow creases as Molly looks at her with pleading eyes. "Just a sec, Molly." She smiles at her.

She gets up from the floor and walks over to me, lowering her voice. "I thought you said Molly wasn't good with new people."

"When did I say that?"

She blinks, her brow scrunching up. "Earlier. To that woman in the workout gear who wanted to have lunch with you."

I place my hands on my hips and breathe in slowly through my nose to hold back a flare of temper. "My daughter has already demonstrated that she likes you."

Tate's gaze wanders back to Molly. "I like her too, but—"

"And listening to my personal conversations will not be a part of your job description."

Her gaze snaps back to mine.

"Therefore"—I arch a brow—"upon hiring you, I'd expect no questions about my dating life."

"Of c-course," she splutters.

"Good." I attempt a smile, but the way she looks more flustered makes me think it's coming out as a grimace. "Then, you're hired. You can start tomorrow evening."

Her brows shoot up, and for a couple of seconds, she just stares at me.

"I need to think about it," she says after a pause.

My boardroom face comes into play as I successfully hide my shock and irritation. I don't have time to wait for other people to *think* about things.

"Of course," I reply smoothly. I pluck a business card from my inner jacket pocket and hold it out to her. "Call me when you've decided, and assuming the position is still available, then it's yours."

"If it's still available?"

"Precisely. Now, allow Molly and I to walk you out. It's been nineteen minutes."

"Right, yes, of course." Her attention drops to the card as she takes it from me. "I need to get back to my shift," she mumbles with a frown.

"Gentlemen," my father booms as he walks ahead of me into the meeting room.

I step in behind him, followed by Uncle Mal as three voices chime back, "Boss," in unison.

Denver, and two of his team, Killian and Jenson, are sitting at the long meeting table as we enter.

"Everyone all right?" Mal asks as he pulls out a seat and

slumps into it with a low sigh, like the movement alone has taken it out of him. He pushes a hand back through his thinning hair, the bags beneath his eyes as dark as always. Losing my mother meant him losing his only sibling. And the mere mention of my brother's name brings pain to his eyes. He took losing them both hard. We all did.

There's a knock at the door and I answer it to Cara.

"Sorry to disturb you, Mr. Beaufort, but you have an urgent call."

"Miss Miller?" I enquire.

It's about time she called back to accept my obscenely generous offer. I'll overlook the fact she's taken overnight to *think* about it, because as much as I loathe to admit it; I *need* her. Molly needs her.

"The coffee girl?" Cara's face contorts before quickly smoothing out as I arch a brow at her. "No. It's the CEO of Fabienne. He says it's a matter of life or death."

"I see." My lips twitch. Life or death for him, maybe. For me it's simply another business deal that I have the upper hand in. But it's pleasing to know that he's now aware of Beaufort Diamonds' plans to buy his little company. It's just a shame for him that he's too late to do a thing about it. If you play with the sharks, you should prepare to get bitten.

"Tell him I'll call him back." I tilt my head in consideration. "... eventually."

Cara smirks. "Very well, Mr. Beaufort."

"Let's get to it, shall we?" I say as I return to the table and take a seat with the other men.

"Problem?" my father asks.

"No. Just someone calling for me. I'll call them back."

I'll fill my father in on acquiring Fabienne once the deal is finalized. Ever since Halliday arrived he's been a new man. And now that she's pregnant and they're getting married, the lightness in him is hard to miss. He deserves time to enjoy it and not be burdened with business that's already being taken care of.

I lean back in my seat and listen as a discussion about my mother's lover whom she was having an affair with behind my father's back before she died builds momentum. The guy, Neil, is back in the city for reasons unknown. The timing of it coincided with when Sinclair's car was trashed. Coincidence? Maybe. But my father won't take any chances.

"—she seems to be taking it well," my father says to Denver, talking about Sinclair and his assignment as her bodyguard.

I smirk internally at the taut expression on Denver's face. He's never gotten along with my sister. She rolls her eyes whenever she has to be in the same room as him.

"She giving you hell?" I ask.

Denver pauses like he's considering how to deliver a tactful response. His huge shoulders stiffen in his black suit jacket. "She's—"

"That's a yes," I say as he holds my eyes. "You know my sister. The harder she is on you, the closer you're getting to her."

If the guy wasn't ex special forces, I might be inclined to feel sorry for him. But if anyone can withstand my sister's defiant behavior when she's told to do something she doesn't want to, then it's Denver. Still, I reckon we'll owe the guy a vacation and a big fat bonus once Sinclair's done with him.

Jenson pipes up with something I don't catch as my phone vibrates in my pocket.

"Just look after her," I toss out, frowning at the unknown number on the screen. I hit end call and watch the screen for a few seconds, but no voicemail notification pops up.

The men are chuckling as I tune back in to my father talking about his and Halliday's wedding in Cape Town—and how the whole team's invited. Denver offers to arrange security through his contacts, and my father stands, announcing he needs to get back to Halliday and Molly.

"And I've got a call to make," I say, rising from my chair as I fire off a quick text to Jones to let him know to be ready to go on the call with me in case Fabienne's CEO tries anything.

I clap my uncle on the shoulder, and he nods at me as I pass him and follow my father out of the room.

"I'll come by as soon as I'm done here and collect Molly," I tell him.

"It's fine, Son. We'll drop her home later. We can keep her for the night if you like? You've been working hard. Maybe you need a night to yourself?"

I shake my head. "Thanks, but that's not necessary."

My father studies me, waiting to see if I'll say anything else. It's not a Thursday. Not the one night of the week that he or Sinclair have always looked after Molly for me ever since she came into our lives. The one night of the week where I leave my parental responsibilities outside the door of my suite at The Lanceford hotel, before fucking away all thoughts of lost family members, cardboard boxes found after midnight, and ex fiancées.

Thursday nights I tuck it all away and let loose. I've lost count of the women who've aided in the soul numbing process that I need to function. Lost count of the number of condoms I've come inside, then tossed out with the trash, hoping it'll help.

And it does... for a while. Because after each release, I'm granted another six nights of just about keeping my head together.

For Molly.

My father has always known where I go those nights. He gets it. My sister doesn't. She despises any mention of The Lanceford. To her, love is the one thing that can keep us going after what happened. The love of family. The love of a new partner. Hence her insistence of hiring Halliday to be my father's dating coach.

But she'll have to accept that my love for Molly is all I need. Because I hate every thought of romantic love. Romantic love tells you they can't cope with the daughter who's appeared in your life. Romantic love leaves at sunrise. Romantic love is conditional.

A father's love isn't.

I walk my father to the elevator, saying goodbye, then return to my office to call Fabienne.

"Cara?" I ask, doubling back as an after-thought and stopping at the front reception desk. She should work from Arabella's office next to mine while she's filling in. But since one of the front desk staff has been sick, she's been positioned here to assist.

"Yes, Mr. Beaufort."

She bats her lashes at me in a way that tells me she'd have no problems performing any task I ask of her while she's working here. It hasn't escaped my notice that her shirt is getting unbuttoned more each day. Slowly revealing a glimpse of perfectly smooth, tanned skin, and the hint of a pert cleavage and athletic figure. Exactly the type I go for. Elegant, slender, polished.

"Did you arrange the delivery like I asked?"

"Yes, sir." She taps something into her computer and reads the screen. "Delivery was made at six this morning."

"Six?" I echo. A burst of annoyance flares inside me, and I purse my lips. "Very well."

"Anything else I can do for you, Mr. Beaufort?" Cara asks.

"No," I bark. "Just make sure you tell me the moment Miss Miller calls, please," I say, striding away.

8

TATE

"It smells like he's got a huge dick."

I pull the apron away from my nose and scoff as Ashley gives me a suggestive smirk.

"It smells of laundry, you doofus," I cry, my shoulders shaking as I try not to laugh at her expression.

"A guy whose laundry smells like that has to have a giant dick. There's no way he doesn't."

I shake my head at her, but as I tie the freshly laundered apron around my waist, I get another waft of the scent that puffed like a cloud out of the Beaufort Diamonds box this morning when I'd opened the courier delivered package.

I left his office in such a rush yesterday to get back and continue my shift that I forgot my apron. My cocoa covered apron with a small tear in one of the ties. Only for it to be delivered back this morning in time for my shift, mended, and smelling...

Like the laundry of a billionaire with a giant dick.

I brush my hands down over the soft fabric that's been pressed to perfection. I don't think it's ever looked so good. It's better than when it was new. And Ashley's right. The

63

scent coming off it is... a subtle version of the man himself whom I spent nineteen minutes with yesterday. Well, technically no more than ten. Most was spent with his adorable daughter.

"You think he washed it with his underwear? You could be wearing something that's touched the fabric that touches his dick."

Ashley laughs as I shove her playfully.

"Cut it out."

"When do you start?"

I shrug and make myself busy, wiping down the already spotless counter as the first flurry of customers start arriving.

"You called him last night to accept, didn't you? Like we agreed?" Ashley crosses her arms, giving me the look of a teacher exhausted by a student with all the potential in the world but zero initiative. "His temp PA emailed you the offer —you have it in writing. Girl, snap it up before he changes his mind. Think what you could do with that money. Picture me as your wing-woman, perched on your shoulder. You've got talent, Tate. Dreams to chase. This offer could change everything—your song... your dad... just think about it."

"I know." I gnaw on my lower lip.

Ashley's always been better at seizing opportunities than me. She's a 'yes' person. It's how she's managed to build such a successful business by herself. She's got plans to open other coffee venues. And I know she'll achieve it, because she isn't scared of taking a chance.

Not like me.

"What did your dad say?" she asks.

"He said if I want to do it, then he thinks it's a great opportunity. And that I should be out and not home every night with him."

"He's right." Ashley gives me a pointed look. "You know he is. And we'll work it around your shifts here. The morning's the busiest when I need you, and the contract said daytimes and occasional evenings, right? Plus, it's only a few hours here and there."

"You're really trying to sell it to me, aren't you?" I laugh, wiping my clammy hands on my apron, then stopping as another subtle waft of something expensive hits me. It's weird to think that my apron was amongst Sullivan Beaufort's laundry.

"I don't get why you aren't snapping his hand off to accept."

Ashley turns to take a customer's order and I busy myself fixing it for them.

I know I have to say yes to his offer. How can I not? My father and I need the cash. And I'd give my time for free to spend it with Molly. She's a cutie. Full of smiles and giggles. But it's her father I'm concerned about. He spent the entire time pacing up and down like an angry bull when he was in his office. I caught him glaring at me more than once with those eyes of his. Piercing blue and deadly. The kind of eyes that are so mesmerizing they take you aback and you can't help but stare. They've the power to freeze you in place while he devours you alive.

Yet, I couldn't stop looking at him. Just like I couldn't stop turning his business card over and over between my fingers, feeling the smooth velvety texture as I laid in bed last night. Even that smelled incredible. The gold foiling on it is so vivid it wouldn't surprise me if it were actual gold. He's a billionaire, after all.

I snort, earning a quizzical look from Ashley.

"Fine," I whisper as I reach for the cocoa. "I'll call him after my shift."

The end of my shift comes fast because we're busy with a constant stream of customers. One has a Beaufort Diamonds bag draped over her forearm as she peruses the menu board behind the counter. The sight of it makes my stomach squirm.

"Do it now." Ashley holds Caffeine Couture's phone out to me the moment I take my apron off and fold it neatly.

"I'll use my cell as I walk to the subway."

"You'll wimp out." She presses the phone into my palm. "Do. It. Now."

I huff out a breath and pull his business card from my purse. Ashley gives a satisfied smile as I take the phone.

"Wait. This has his office number and his cell. Which should I call?"

"His cell," she says quickly.

I nod in agreement. I'm also less likely to get that snooty receptionist if I try him directly. Although a conversation with her might be a walk in the park compared to Sullivan Beaufort.

I tap it in and hold my breath.

"It's ringing," I tell Ashley as my heart rate picks up.

"Sullivan Beaufort."

My mouth goes dry the second his rich, deep voice travels down the line.

"Um, it's Tate... I mean, Miss Miller."

"Hello, Miss Miller."

Ashley twirls her fingers for me to continue as I shoot her a look of panic.

"I was calling to accept your offer to be Molly's nanny."

There's a pause and I wonder if I should ask if he's still there.

"You'll not be Molly's anything. You'll be *my* employee, as it states in the contract."

I'm pretty sure the blood has drained from my face to my feet.

Jesus, he's so rude.

"You did read the contract, correct?" he clips.

"I can read," I snap back, unable to stop myself, a newfound sass forming in response to his abruptness. His responding silence has me swallowing my surge of confidence and I curse myself. I really need the money he's offering. "So do you still require my assistance, or did you fill the position?" I ask, trying to sound more professional.

There's a pause before he clears his throat.

"The position's yours, Miss Miller. You can start once your shift ends."

"Oh..." I widen my eyes at Ashley. "Well, it's already ended for today and I—"

"In that case, wait there and my driver will come for you."

"But—"

I pull the phone away from my ear and stare at the screen.

"What did he say?" Ashley asks.

"He hung up," I tell her.

What the hell did I just agree to?

9

TATE

I GIVE THE DRIVER AN AWKWARD SMILE AS HE HOLDS
the rear door to the black town car open for me.

"Thank you."

"You're welcome, Miss Miller."

I slide into the cool leather interior and cold blue eyes drop
over my uniform. His nostrils flare as though it's personally
offended him, and he taps his fingers with impatience against
his suit pants where his legs are spread wide. Arrogance clad in
a deep blue designer suit.

"Should I put the privacy screen up, Mr. Beaufort?" his
driver asks.

His detached assessment of me ceases and he meets his
driver's eyes in the rearview mirror.

"That won't be necessary, Cliff. Miss Miller has accepted a
job offer from me."

"Ah. Congratulations, and welcome," Cliff directs to me.

"Thank you," I reply.

Sullivan's eyes return to mine and he spreads his thighs
wider. His broad chest expands as he takes in a slow breath,
sinking back into the seat a little like he's had a long day.

I wonder how many women he's had in here. How many times Cliff has put that privacy screen up at his request. Whether he fucks them on the smooth leather seats, or gets them to suck him off, kneeling between those spread thighs.

The thought hits me out of nowhere and I shove it away before it's written all over my face. I looked him up online last night after receiving his contract. It was the NDA part that made me do it. Made me wonder what he has to hide. Ashley said rich people are extra fussy about their privacy, and he probably didn't want me selling stories about all of the women I might see him with. The press is speculating over the rumor of a hotel suite he has for the sole purpose of hookups with actresses and models.

"Tonight will require an hour of your time. My lawyer is coming over with some contracts that need my attention. My father is bringing Molly home, but he can't stay. So I need you to keep her entertained while we go through them."

"Okay."

The back of the car falls silent, and I clasp my hands in my lap to stop myself from fidgeting. The quiet stretches on until my throat tickles with the need to break it.

"Thank you for laundering my apron. You didn't have to do that," I say.

Sullivan gives a brusque nod. "My housekeeper did it. It was covered in that cocoa you make smiley faces with."

I open my mouth, then close it again, holding back my own smiley face.

I thought he shoved the lid on his coffee too fast to notice. But it just goes to show, the cocoa works. Customers notice it. They like it.

"Sometimes it's two coffee beans, or our logo, or even the Empire State Building. That one's tricky to do in a rush, but the tourists appreciate it," I say. "Then of course, I do bunnies as well. Like—"

"Bumper," he clips, reaching up to loosen his tie with a frown.

"You remembered." I grin, unable to help myself.

His eyes flick to me and a muscle in his jaw flexes like he's realized he's going to have to talk to me, after all.

"Cliff will take you home later."

"It's fine, I'll take the subway."

His brow flattens. "You'll be driven home so I know that you're safe," he clips. "I won't have any of my staff at risk if I'm the one requiring them to travel home late at night."

"Oh, okay, then. Thank you, Cliff." I catch the driver's eye in the rearview mirror and his own crinkle kindly in response.

"It will be my pleasure, Miss Miller."

"Thank you," I add more quietly, glancing at Sullivan.

He gives me a curt nod before he reaches up to run a hand around the five o'clock shadow on his jaw. He exhales and pulls his buzzing phone from his jacket pocket. The frown marring his face transforms into a hint of a smile, and I sneak a look at the screen before he pockets his phone again. It's a picture of Molly in a bathing suit wearing bright yellow floaties.

The protective streak he showed with insisting that Cliff drives me home must come from being a father. It's exactly the sort of thing my dad would do.

Sullivan rolls his lips, a scowl settling on them as he trains his eyes on something out of his window.

Or maybe he just doesn't want to get sued if something happens to me. *'Employee of Billionaire mogul, Sullivan Beaufort, murdered on subway after dark,'* probably won't be good for business. Although I'm sure there was something in that six-page contract I signed about waiving my rights to sue him. Giving up all my rights, actually. There's probably even hidden small print saying I have to ask permission to pee when on his time.

"Do you ever drive yourself home?" I ask, unease making me itch to fill the silence again. Maybe I could ask Cliff to put the radio on in future if this is what it's going to be like. He seems much friendlier than the brooding hulk of a man next to me.

"Rarely. My sister is the one who likes to drive herself around. This is more effective management of my time. I work on the ride so when I get home, I can eat dinner with Molly."

Despite the brusqueness of his tone, his words bring warmth to my chest. He clearly adores his little girl, even though, I presume, a job like his requires a lot of his energy and time.

"But you're not working now. You're talking to me," I point out, my gaze dropping to a zipped-up laptop bag in the footwell he hasn't attempted to reach for.

"Hm." He grunts as those cool blue eyes meet mine again.

I regret opening my mouth as they scan over my pink shirt before flicking away. It's a couple of seconds, but I feel the depth of his scrutiny all the way to my bones.

I choose to embrace the silence for the rest of the drive.

Sullivan's low voice rumbles from the hallway, and is joined by another man's, his father, I presume, along with a happy shriek of, 'Daddy!'. He instructed me to wait in his giant living area while he went to answer the door, saying it would be Molly returning.

I can't wait to see her. Her presence will help blow some of the awkwardness away that's been making it hard to breathe since I stepped foot inside the multi-million-dollar penthouse. I'm so out of place here. Those thick, dark brows of Sullivan's had lowered, matching his terse expression as I'd hovered inside the front door, clutching my purse like it could offer support, and gazed around at the monochrome elegance, telling him what a nice living room he has.

I didn't know that was just the entryway. Who has sofas, giant artwork, and flower displays in their hallway?

The moment I walked into his actual living space, I squeaked embarrassingly at the sight of a sparkling grand piano set up in front of floor-to-ceiling windows with the city stretching into the distance behind. It's the first time I've noticed Sullivan look at me with something akin to interest in his eyes before he was summoned by a knock at the door.

Placing my purse on a side table, I wander over to the piano and gaze at it longingly. I bet it plays beautifully. More in tune than the old battered one in my building's basement. I run my finger along the sleek maple wood. It's as black as a well of thick ink. Glossy. Divine. My fingers tingle at the idea of sitting on the upholstered stool and playing it.

Sullivan clears his throat, announcing that I'm no longer alone. Molly is in his arms, and the sight of her sweet little face pressed against the front of his shirt as she clings to him makes my ovaries feel fit to bursting.

"Hello, Molly." I give her a little wave and turn my back on the piano, relieved I don't have to explain to Sullivan why I was touching it. Something tells me he might not take kindly to people interfering with his things.

"Do you remember me?" I ask, walking over slowly.

She nods, burying her cheek into Sullivan's shirt.

"She's tired. My father's fiancée took her swimming, and she woke up early from her nap," Sullivan explains, pressing a soft kiss to the top of her dark curls, the move so natural, like he does it without even thinking.

My eyes roam over him, dressed in his power suit, cradling Molly to his chest like she's the most precious thing in the world. I've witnessed first-hand the way he behaves dressed like this. When he's in his billionaire CEO persona. But here, in his own home, with his tired daughter in his arms, something else flows from him.

Love.

So much love that it tears at my heart and makes my eyes mist. Because as beautiful as it is, there's something achingly tragic too. Why I get that impression, I don't know.

Sullivan's gaze meets mine and the softness vanishes.

"Molly," he says, his voice business-like as he looks at me. "Tate's going to be spending more time with you. Helping when Daddy has to work. Like Arabella."

Molly lifts her head at the information, and gifts me with a smile, showing off two perfect rows of milk teeth between her round cheeks. I smile back as her shyness ebbs away and the Molly I met yesterday emerges.

"You see my room?" she says.

"I'd love to. If that's okay with your daddy?"

Sullivan gives a terse nod. "I'll give you a tour."

I follow him through the living and dining area to a giant kitchen filled with top of the range gadgets and sparkling marble worktops. It has a wall of floor-to-ceiling windows like the living area, making it feel like you're miles above the city below.

"You can help yourself to anything you like. If there's something you need, my housekeeper, Joan, can get it for you. That iPad," he gestures to the device on the large island, "is hers. You can leave messages for her on it. She comes every morning, so you probably won't see her because you'll be..." His eyes drop over my uniform and his nostrils flare. "...You'll be at work."

I wait until he turns and strides down a hallway lined with doors before I check my shirt for a stain, or for whatever it is that keeps stealing his attention. But there's nothing except Caffeine Couture's logo stitched onto the pink fabric.

Multiple bedrooms, a home gym, cinema room, and office —all get shown to me. I'm grateful to stop and catch my breath as we stop in a bright, fun room that's decorated like a jungle with a princess carriage bed inside it.

Sullivan puts Molly down and she runs over to a toy basket before returning with a baby doll in her arms.

"Hold baby," she instructs, thrusting the doll into my stomach.

"She has quite the collection," Sullivan says.

He's leaning against the doorframe, hands in his pant pockets. Tenderness softens the line of his mouth as his attention remains on Molly, who's picked up another baby doll and is cradling it against her, shushing it and rubbing its back.

"You sure do. A fine collection," I say to Molly as I take in the baby cot and stroller with more dollies inside. In the center of the room is the bed. The pillows are barely visible beneath the mound of stuffed animals on it.

Sullivan's phone buzzes and he pulls it out.

"My lawyer's here," he announces, falling into business mode. "I'd appreciate it if you and Molly stayed in the living area while I meet with him."

"Of course," I say, grinning at Molly as she takes my hand and tugs me from the room.

The man who Sullivan lets in appears in the living area a few moments later. He seems to be in his late thirties, and despite a designer suit that fits him almost as well as Sullivan's does, his demeanor couldn't be any more different.

"Hello." He makes a beeline for me after greeting Molly and extends his hand with a friendly smile. "I don't believe I've had the pleasure."

My cheeks heat as he closes both of his hands around mine

and pumps it enthusiastically, his eyes roaming my face like he's admiring every inch of it.

"Jones, this is Tate. Tate, this is my lawyer, Jones," Sullivan clips, moving to stand at my side, so close that the heat of his body rolls off him and seeps toward mine.

Jones grins. "Tate," he repeats. "Lovely to meet you. How long have you two been dating?"

The choked sound that comes from Sullivan's throat makes me snap my eyes to his face.

"We're not dating," he balks. "She's here to help with Molly."

"My mistake," Jones says, not looking at all shocked by Sullivan's reaction.

Meanwhile, I dampen down a surge of offense heating the blood in my veins, and picture punching him in his rude mouth. So I'm not an actress or a model. I don't look smooth and polished like Cara, and all the other people he's surrounded by in his fancy over-the-top offices. But he doesn't need to be a jerk.

"Caffeine Couture," Jones hums thoughtfully, reading the logo on my shirt. "That's the place next door to the office on Fifth Avenue, right?"

"It is." I smile back brightly for no other reason than Jones talking to me seems to be making Sullivan tenser.

"Hmm. I need a new place to grab a coffee when I'm in the area. I'll have to swing by."

"You should," I tell him. "We make the best."

"I'm sure you do." He winks.

The sharp intake of breath next to me makes my smile stretch, which Jones seems to interpret as a response to his flirting.

"So nice to meet you, Tate," he says, eyes dropping to the logo on my shirt again. "I'll be sure to come in and taste that coffee of yours."

"Contracts," Sullivan barks, stepping forward and placing himself between Jones and I. He gestures to a large dining table on the other side of the expansive room. Jones walks ahead of him, placing his briefcase on the table and snapping open the locks on it.

"I won't be long," Sullivan says, lowering his voice as he looks at Molly, happily sitting on the thick cream rug, talking to one of her baby dolls.

"It's fine. We'll be okay."

He frowns, and a fleeting look passes over his features, like he doesn't want to leave, despite the fact he isn't going into his home office, but has chosen to stay in the same room as us. Something I suspect he planned, not yet trusting me to be out of his sight with his daughter. But his protectiveness only makes me sympathize with him.

"We'll be okay. I'll look after her," I soothe, placing my hand over the forearm of his jacket without thinking.

He stiffens, his eyes dropping to my hand. I whip it away and tuck it behind me like he might rip it off if I don't.

"Sorry." I swallow, not quite understanding why I'm apologizing, but knowing I must have crossed some invisible line judging from the way his eyes are trained on mine like fierce lasers.

"I won't be long," he repeats, before spinning on his heels and striding over to Jones.

Molly and I play with her dollies while the two men discuss the pages of paperwork covering the table. But the time passes quickly and they're soon packing up.

Jones walks past with his briefcase.

"Bye, Molly. Nice to meet you, Tate," he says, glancing at my shirt logo again. "I'll come in for that coffee soon."

"You should." I smile.

I giggle internally as Sullivan sees him out. Ashley will love having a guy as flirty as Jones coming in. She'll have him overflowing our tip jar without him even realizing what's happening.

Sullivan storms back into the room, having removed his tie and jacket. The top two buttons of his shirt are undone, revealing a tense, flushed neck. He stops in front of Molly and me and stands with his hands on his hips.

"Uniform," he grumbles. "Do you want me to provide one for you, or do you have something more suitable to wear while you're working for me?"

"Um..." I hand my baby doll to Molly. "Can you please rock him to sleep for me? You've done such a good job with your baby. But he's struggling to drift off," I say softly.

"There, there, baby," she coos, taking over beautifully as I stand to face Sullivan, keeping my voice a whisper.

"What do you mean? Do you want me to wear a uniform?"

"I don't..." He purses his lips, hands still braced on his hips. "I don't *require* you to wear a uniform. But you cannot wear *that*." His eyes drag over my pink shirt and skirt again before he snaps them away, his jaw clenching.

I look down and finally understand what it is that's bothering him. My cheeks heat as I adjust the straining material, trying to close the gaps between the buttons where the material gapes.

"It shrank when my dad washed it. I know..." I swallow down the humiliation. "I know my figure doesn't exactly suit the style, but—"

"The style is fine," he barks, before his eyes flick up to the ceiling and he runs his tongue over his lips. "I just... I can't have you wearing it."

I nod, my cheeks burning. Ashley has a new one coming for me. One that will fit and not show every curve and bump.

"It's..." Sullivan's head drops down and his eyes snag on my shirt. He grimaces, like the sight angers him. "You wearing that... It's... distracting." A vein in his temple throbs and he breathes in deeply, like he's trying to maintain control.

I frown. "Distracting?"

His pupils flare, and a flash of something that looks like heat, but can't be, blazes through his eyes. It's gone in an instant.

"Um... okay, sure. I'll bring my own clothes next time."

His shoulders relax and his jaw slackens. "Make sure you do."

10

TATE

"I'll make something special tomorrow, I promise," I tell my father while I clear our plates of spaghetti from the table that I created from the meager contents of our refrigerator.

"Best damn spaghetti I ever ate." My father grins, batting away my comment.

I shake my head with a smile and finish tidying up. My first paycheck from Sullivan dropped into my account as we were sitting down to eat. I'm glad I hadn't taken a mouthful, because I'd have choked. The amount in my account was more than the contract said to expect. And it was quickly followed by a curt text message from Sullivan telling me the extra was an advance.

He's crazy, he must be. He's barely even needed me the past three days since I went to his place. Molly's been with family. Sullivan manages her care well. I doubt he'll have much need for me at all. Still, I can't complain. Not when the money couldn't have come at a better time.

"I'll see you later. Be careful while I'm gone," I say, pressing a kiss to my father's whiskery cheek.

"I'm not dead yet, Tate." He chuckles.

I grab my grocery list and purse and head toward the door. "Keep it that way," I call back with a grin.

"Do you think he'll give you a key to his place? I'd love to get a look around a billionaire's pad like that."

"I can bet my left kidney that Sullivan Beaufort will *never* give me a key to his place." I shake my head, smiling at Ashley's crestfallen expression before returning my attention to my phone.

We're taking a breather after the morning rush, and I'm checking The Masked Maestro's social media.

"Oh, oh, oh!" I squeal, thrusting the phone under Ashley's nose. "He's doing another show in a couple of weeks."

Ashley takes my phone and scrolls through the post, reading it. "Where do you think this one will be?"

"No idea. Maybe somewhere outdoors. He hasn't done a moonlight set for a while."

Ashley's brows shoot up as my phone rings.

"Is it Dad?" Worry seeps into my pores, making my stomach tighten.

"No." A sly smile spreads on Ashley's face and she turns the screen in my direction. "It's Mr. Billionaire."

"Let me answer it," I say, reaching out. Sullivan won't like being kept waiting.

"You should play hard to get," Ashley muses, holding the phone out of my reach.

I stare at her in shock. "He's hired me. This isn't some dating thing." I make a grab for my phone again but miss as Ashley curves me. She winks and answers the call.

"Tate's phone," she sings.

I widen my eyes. *What are you doing?* I mouth.

"Oh, she can't speak right now, she's helping out a customer. Oh, hold on... he's asking for her number. I think she'll be a while. Can I take a message?"

Ashley presses her lips together like she's trying not to laugh. Her eyes light up with glee. "Mm-hm, I'll tell her."

She hands the phone back to me.

"What did he want?"

"You. Tonight after your shift."

"Did he say where? Does he want me to go next door or...?" I swallow the sourness on my tongue at the thought of having to encounter the charming Cara again. I didn't know Sullivan would require me tonight. The only spare clothes I've got are some old joggers and a T-shirt I left here after helping Ashley decorate for Valentine's Day one late night. I can already feel Cara's disapproving glare if I show up at the Beaufort offices in that.

"He said he'll pick you up."

"Okay."

Ashley studies me as if she's waiting for a reaction.

"Anything else?" I ask.

She shakes her head, a small smile lifting her lips. "Is he always so terse when he speaks? Or was it because I had him picturing you being hit on when he called?"

I snort. "Don't be ridiculous. That's how he always sounds."

She shrugs. "If you say so." She turns with a bright smile to greet a customer who's walked in.

I shove my phone into my apron pocket and get back to work.

His ruthless, assessing gaze rakes over my Linkin Park T-shirt as I slide into the cool interior of his car.

"Hi, Molly." I grin, greeting her first before nodding at Sullivan.

"We need to make a stop on the way. And I have a call to make," he grumbles, frowning at my outfit.

"Sure, okay."

I give all my attention to Molly, strapped into her car seat between us as Sullivan inclines his head toward his window and barks the name 'Fairfax' into his phone.

"You had a good day, Molly?" I ask.

She gives me a toothy grin as she nods over and over. I mirror her so we look like a pair of nodding dogs, which makes her giggle.

Sullivan's eyes dart to us, and I freeze, expecting him to shush us while he's on his call. But instead, his eyes soften, and he ruffles Molly's curls.

"It's my daughter," he says into his phone. "She's in the car with me and her nanny."

I school my reaction, concealing my surprise at him referring to me as 'Molly's nanny', when less than a week ago he explicitly told me I was his 'employee' and nothing more.

A deep rumble vibrates his throat, making his Adam's apple move, and I snap my eyes away before I gawk at him after witnessing the closest thing to a laugh I've ever heard from him.

"Is this a new baby?" I ask Molly, admiring the dolly she's holding that's wearing a dinosaur onesie that matches her own.

She nods seriously, staring into the dolly's big, wide eyes. "Baby," she says.

"Baby has great style, like you," I say, bopping her on the nose, which earns me a big grin.

Sullivan's gaze darts to me as he continues his conversation, and I force myself not to squirm in my seat when he frowns at my outfit again. He ends his call, pocketing his phone.

"Didn't have you down as a fan of Linkin Park," he says, leaning his elbow on the window and running a fingertip over his lips as he looks out at the city.

I tug at the hem. "I'm not really. It was my boyfriend's."

"Was?"

"We broke up," I say, rolling my shoulders to avoid them seizing up like they do when I think about my ex.

He clears his throat. "Sorry to hear that."

"Don't be." I scoff. "He was a loser."

I clamp my lips together, but it's too late. My little outburst has caused piercing blue eyes to flick my way. I swallow under his scrutiny before he turns his attention to Cliff as the car pulls over.

"We won't be long, Cliff. Circle the block if you need to."

A moment later, my door is opened by Cliff. I climb out and watch Sullivan step out and stride toward me, fastening his suit jacket with effortless grace. He stops just inches away, towering over me. My heart skips a beat. His aftershave hits me, clean and sharp, and I can't help but breathe him in.

"Excuse me," he barks, snapping me out of my momentary step into a world of rich spicy aroma.

I step out of his way, and he leans into the backseat, unclipping Molly's car seat buckle and lifting her out.

"This can't take long. I have another call scheduled for when we get home."

I rush to keep pace with him as we walk into the grocery store.

"Joan's sick. I need to pick Molly something up for dinner," he says.

"Oh, okay," I say, reaching for a trolley with a child seat. Sullivan's lip curls in disgust and he jerks his head like he's horrified. I should have known. He's far too uptight to use a trolley. He probably thinks Molly will contract a disease.

I pick up a basket instead and Sullivan reaches to take it from me at the same time his phone rings.

"What now?" he mutters, balancing Molly in one arm as he brings the phone to his ear.

"Jesus Christ, they did what?" He sighs, sounding weary at whatever the person on the other end says.

I put the basket down by my feet and hold my hands out, gesturing to Molly. Sullivan frowns at me, his jaw tightening. But whatever the call is about, it must be important, because he hands Molly over to me, then pinches the bridge of his nose.

Molly's light as a feather in my arms, and I give her a little squeeze and maneuver her onto one hip as I bend to retrieve the basket. But Sullivan's already curling his fingers around the handle.

"Shall we look for something yummy to eat?" I ask Molly.

She nods happily, her attention snagged on my bracelet. She strokes over the giant gemstone in the center, her brow set in concentration.

I head off down the first aisle. Sullivan remains by my side, his attention glued to Molly, like he still doesn't trust me to take care of her without his supervision. I gesture to a pasta bake sauce on the shelf and he purses his lips.

"Needs to be fresh and organic," he rumbles.

"Right," I reply.

I continue wandering until we reach the fresh fruit and veg. I lift a pot of peaches and the look he gives me is like I just killed his cat, if he had one.

"Definitely no peaches," I say to Molly quietly as I stuff them back on the shelf and lift up some strawberries. He nods in approval, so I put them in the basket. "What does your daddy like to cook?" I ask Molly, hoping that maybe it'll encourage Sullivan to cut in and throw me a bone, give me something to work with.

He opens his mouth, but whatever the person on the phone says, steals his attention again, and he barks out something so harshly that it attracts glances from other shoppers.

The way the lines marring his forehead flatten the moment his eyes connect with Molly when she points to a picture of a cake on a display, has sympathy pulling at my heart for him again. He looks stressed. He always looks stressed.

"I like cooking and baking," I offer. "I could make something when we get back? It sounds like you might be needed."

The voice on the other end of the phone jabbers on, accentuating my point.

Sullivan grimaces at whatever they're saying, then places the basket down and reaches into his pocket. He pulls out a leather wallet and slides out a black Amex.

"Get whatever you need, Tate," he says, an uncharacteristic tint of gratitude warming his usually gruff voice.

I take the card from him and stare at it briefly, running my thumb over the lettering of his name. It feels like any other credit card, but the weight of it in my palm has the hairs on the back of my neck pricking up. He's a billionaire. I bet it has no limit.

I swallow as it burns into my skin.

Sullivan's lowered his voice and is hissing at the caller on the phone as I hand the card to Molly.

"Hold it tight; it's Daddy's."

She nods, her bottom lip poking out in seriousness as she steps up to her role.

"If anyone tries to take it, you could roar at them," I suggest, patting the hood of her dinosaur onesie. She grins at me like the idea is appealing.

Shopping gets a lot more fun as I wander the aisles, plucking ingredients off shelves and dropping them into the basket Sullivan's carrying. He watches me with an amused brow lift when I squeak at the sight of fresh truffles and toss them in. I wasn't entirely honest when I said I *like* cooking. I *love* it. It's one of the first things I learned growing up—me and Mom in the kitchen while Dad was at work. She taught me everything I know. And even though she's been gone for years, cooking her recipes brings her back to me. The scents alone pull me straight into those warm, messy, laughter-filled afternoons with her.

Molly and I both wear matching grins as we check out and pay before I hand Sullivan his card.

"Never seen someone so happy about buying groceries," he says as he slides it back inside his wallet.

"It was my first time shopping with a dinosaur. It was exciting," I say, making Molly giggle. I glance at Sullivan, waiting for him to take her from me, but he grunts and picks up our bags.

I walk beside him as we exit the store. An older lady taking her time to walk along the sidewalk looks at us as she passes.

"Nice family," she comments with a smile as she shuffles on.

I wait for him to correct her, but his attention is on Cliff, opening up the trunk of the car. He walks over to us, dipping his head in greeting to Molly and me, and taking the bags from Sullivan.

Something brushes my lower back. "We need to get going. Traffic could be a nightmare."

The heat of strong fingers against my lower back sends a comforting warmth over my skin. Guiding me to the car is purely out of concern for his daughter in my arms, but the move is so caring and protective that I can't help but bask in it for the few short seconds that it lasts.

11

SULLIVAN

A MOUTH-WATERING AROMA FLOWS AROUND MY living area, like a living, breathing entity, carrying the sound of music and a soft female voice singing with it. I look up from my laptop just in time to see Tate grin at Molly who is standing beside her at the cooker on a booster step. She hands Molly a spoon and helps her stir a large pot of something.

"Good job, Molly," she praises. "Do you think you can keep an eye on it while I check the cookies?"

My daughter nods, her little face glowing as she's handed responsibility.

I close the lid of my laptop and steeple my fingers as I watch.

"Ooh, they're done," Tate declares, taking a tray from the oven and placing it on a rack to cool.

My call ended a while ago, but I've remained sitting at the dining table where I have a direct line of sight to them both. Tate took Molly into the kitchen the moment we arrived home, and I've been trying to work. But every delighted laugh of Molly's has had me snapping my head up to see what she's finding so entertaining. And each time I've lowered my eyes

91

back to my screen, another sound has filled my ears, commanding my attention.

The sound of sweetly sung notes, so quiet that if I were to tap on the keys I might miss them.

Tate sings, winking at Molly as she joins her stirring the pot on the stove. I don't recognize the song she's singing, but I strain to hear every word to make sure they're suitable for Molly to hear.

"Whispers of the past, the future's calling... Unleash your potential... let the world hear your sound."

"It's ready!" Tate calls, glancing over her shoulder. "Oh." She falters when she sees me staring at her. "Um... dinner's ready."

I walk over to the places she's set at the kitchen island and help Molly up into her booster seat. Tate places down two plates of steaming pasta with mushrooms and truffle shavings on them, then steps back with a look of trepidation.

"Tell me what you think," she says.

I slide into the seat and twirl a thick ribbon of pasta around my fork, aware of her eyes on my mouth as I take it in and chew. Flavor bursts on my tongue and I lick my lips after swallowing, already loading up another forkful.

"It's good. Really good."

She exhales with a laugh like she was holding her breath. "You sound surprised."

"Sorry." I hold her eyes over the steaming pasta on my fork and she flusters.

Molly's digging in happily beside me and Tate's eyes slide to her, lighting up as she makes noises of approval. Her pasta has been cut into small pieces for her so she can get it in her mouth on her small fork. My eyes zero in on the small pieces on her plate before I look back at Tate, who's clearing up the cooking pans.

"Why aren't you eating?" It's a simple question, but it comes out as an accusatory bark.

She startles, dropping the spoon. I rise from my seat, collecting a plate from the cabinet. Tate side-eyes me as I stand beside her, depositing a serving from the pan onto it.

"You need to eat," I say.

"I can wait until I get home. It's not like I'll waste away." She laughs awkwardly, smoothing down the T-shirt that belonged to her loser ex over her curvy hips.

I flick my eyes over where the band logo covers her breasts and grind my teeth.

Tate?" I clip in a low voice.

"Yeah?" She blinks up at me innocently.

I inhale slowly to calm myself.

"My daughter will not be subjected to talk of healthy female bodies being anything other than something to be proud of."

Her eyes widen. "Oh... I..."

I lean closer, and she tilts her head back to look up at me. "So I suggest you start considering the way you talk about yourself carefully. Understand?"

She nods.

"Understand?" I repeat, holding the plate of pasta out.

She swallows, her lips parting as she holds my eyes. "I understand."

"Good girl. Now eat."

The pasta disappears quickly as the three of us eat together. Tate avoids looking at me, instead, giving her attention to Molly and telling her about animals, reeling off random facts, including how pigs are used to sniff out the truffles we just ate. My daughter hangs off her every word with big, wide eyes.

"Do you want me to get the dessert we made so you can show Daddy?" Tate asks her.

"Yay!" Molly claps. "Daddy, we made cookies."

"You did, huh? You've been busy."

She smiles at me, and Tate reaches for the plates. I stand before she can and clear them away myself. "I've got it."

"Thanks," she murmurs, stalling for a moment like she feels uneasy in my kitchen, despite the fact she seemed at home singing in it a mere twenty minutes ago.

"Side plates are in that one." I gesture to a cabinet and her shoulders soften.

"Great. I'll get them."

The cookies have Molly shouting with excitement.

"Daddy!" She points to the cat shapes.

Half are intricately designed like something from a baking magazine; the cat's faces and whiskers drawn on perfectly with icing, and pastel-colored sweaters adorn their bodies. The other half have wobbly mouths and blobs of thick icing strewn over them.

I pick up one of the inebriated-looking cats.

"This is the best cat wearing a sweater cookie I've ever seen in my life," I announce. Tate's staring at me, so I add, "Wouldn't you agree, Tate?"

Her cheeks flush and she nods. "Absolutely. The best."

Molly beams with pride.

I'm not one for cookies, but I eat the entire thing, making a show of smacking my lips against my fingertips and giving a chef's kiss when I'm done. "Well done, Sweetheart."

Molly smiles, her face covered in crumbs and icing.

Tate's eyes snap to my face as Molly grabs another cookie and takes a bite. "They're oat flour and coconut sugar. All organic," she says in a rush like she thinks I'm about to make a comment.

"Even the sweaters?" I ask, my eyes sliding in amusement to one of the neater cats wearing polka-dots.

"Yeah, even the sweaters," she says, looking at me like she was expecting me to be pissed.

She stands before I can and starts clearing up again.

"You don't need to do that."

She shakes her head, keeping her back to me, like she doesn't want to look at me. "It's okay. I made the mess; I'll clean it up before I go. Unless you want me to do Molly's bedtime routine?" She pauses and looks at me over her shoulder.

"I don't," I state, standing quickly the moment Molly finishes her cookie.

If Tate's offended by my gruff reply, she doesn't show it.

I thank her and take Molly to the bathroom to help her wash up. I'm lying on her bed, finishing up reading to her with her nightlight on when there's a soft knock on the door.

"Sorry to interrupt. I just wanted to tell you I'm leaving," Tate says, her eyes softening as she looks at a sleepy Molly with her head resting on my chest, her heavy eyelids fighting to concentrate on the cartoon image on the page in front of her.

"It's okay," I whisper. "It's time we finished for the night."

Molly mumbles sleepily and I run my fingers through her hair; the silky feel of it the only thing that calms me. Storytime with her is my favorite part of the day. No matter what shit-storm could have happened at work, this is my sanctuary. The thing that keeps me anchored and stable.

I maneuver her onto her pillow and slide from the bed, leaning down to kiss her forehead as I cover her with the duvet. "Good night, Sweetheart."

Tate's hovering in the hallway as I step out and close the door.

"That's a nice story you were reading to her," she comments, wrapping her arms around herself. "What's it called?"

"I don't recall," I say, my spine stiffening.

"It sounded like it was about an adventurer?" she says, looking at me.

"Adventurer or risk-taker, depending on how you look at it."

She laughs. "Aren't all adventures a risk?"

I press my lips together, my chest tightening.

She looks embarrassed when I don't respond. "I should go."

I swallow down the lump in my throat, regaining control. "Cliff will drive you home."

"Right, yep, thanks." She turns, and I follow her into the living area. I call down to Cliff and ask him to collect her from the door.

Tate hovers awkwardly as we wait.

"My new uniform is in," she says, stumbling over her words. "One that actually fits." She shrugs a shoulder with a forced laugh. "So I can wear that in future, if you prefer?"

"If I prefer?"

"I mean... you look at all of my clothes like you hate them. I've caught you glaring at this," she tugs on the hem of her T-shirt, "at least six times tonight."

More like six hundred.

I grind my teeth, placing my hands on my hips.

"Not all of your clothes. Just ones from loser ex boyfriends. And ones that are..." I run my tongue along the edge of my teeth, searching for the right word.

"Distracting?" Tate offers.

"Ones that incite inappropriate reactions," I say.

She laughs weakly. "I'm not worried about Jones. He's just a flirt. He acted the same with my boss, Ashley, when he came in for coffee earlier."

I pause, processing the fact that Jones has already been in for coffee, when I know he's only ever over on Fifth when he has a meeting with me. And we had nothing scheduled today.

My mind flits back to calling Tate, and Ashley telling me she was busy with a customer who wanted her number. Exactly what Arabella told me happens to Tate all the time while she's working.

"I wasn't talking about Jones."

"You weren't?" Her brow furrows. "Then, who?"

I allow myself a slow perusal of her. The clothes are a disgrace, frankly. She fidgets as my eyes rake over where the dips and curves of her body would be if they weren't covered in cheap, shapeless fabric. She's nothing like the women I like to fuck. They're put-together, styled in designer outfits that suit their slender, waif-like figures.

I know I'm scowling, trying to understand why it is that my dick's rapidly hardening as I drink her in.

There's a knock at the door, and I welcome the opportunity to stalk away from her to answer it.

"I'll call you when I need you again," I tell Tate as Cliff stands on the other side of the door, waiting to drive her home.

"Okay." She nods and pauses, waiting to see if I'll move from the doorway to give her more room to pass.

I don't. I remain solid until she slips past me, glancing at me. Her red hair is down and loose, glaring at me like a warning sign.

Cliff's arrival saved me just in time.

Stopped me from hissing out the words: *"Me. You should be fucking worried about me."*

12

TATE

"Looking good, girl." Ashley whistles as I walk in wearing my new uniform. "Although, the tip jar sure appreciated the shrunken one."

"As if." I snort, grabbing my apron and tying it around my waist.

Ashley raises a brow, watching me as I hum and get set up for opening. "Someone's perky this morning. Did Mr. Billionaire give you a big fat bonus last night or something?"

"What? No." I smile. "But guess what's now in the basement of our building?"

"A naked guy with a big dick who's chained up and exists only to perform cunnilingus?"

I laugh at her lit up face. "Why does he need a big dick if he only uses his tongue?"

She ponders my answer, tipping her head. "True. You're a clever one, Miller." She points at me. "So, what was it?"

I grin as I relay the sight my father rushed to tell me about as I walked in the door last night. "A whole row of brand new, top of the range washers and dryers."

Ashley stares at me. "Not very sexy, but that's great." A

99

grin breaks over her face. "You've been needing those forever! But I thought your landlord was an asshole? You said he ignores any requests he gets."

I shrug. "He did. But he's sold the building to a new woman, and she wants to upgrade things. Get this, that leaky tap in our bathroom? Fixed as well." I widen my eyes in excitement, still processing all the improvements that happened while I was out yesterday.

"Give me some of that good luck," Ashley says, shimmying her back up and down against mine. "I need it. The machine's playing up again, we'll have to make do with just one until the engineer comes."

"Really?" I blow out a breath as I look at the coffee machine. Ashley's been having problems with it ever since it was moved for the decorators to freshen up the paintwork on the walls a couple of months ago. Handling the morning rush with just one is going to be a pain in the ass.

"Yeah. If you didn't make such a damn good cup, I'd send you to the dumpster," she says to the machine. "Someone's coming by later this morning to take a look."

After we clear the morning rush, she turns to me with a wide smile, lifting the tip jar and giving it a shake. "Coffee and charm, what did I tell you?" She dips her hand into the stuffed jar and removes the morning's fresh business cards, sifting through them. "Come over here and rub that luck against me again. I need it, this morning's offerings are wetter than a shift at Fulton Fish Market." She tosses the cards into the drawer with a sigh.

The bell chimes and a guy in cargo pants carrying a toolkit strides in.

"Good morning," he booms, a wide grin curving inside his dark brown beard. "I'm Huck. You called about your machine?"

"Hi. I'm Tate, this is Ashley," I greet with a smile.

Ashley stares at him, her eyes dropping to his giant work boots as he wipes them on the entry mat. He walks straight to the counter, tipping his head toward the coffee machine behind it. "That the troublemaker?"

"Do you know what you're doing? It's our best machine. We can't be doing without it," Ashley says in horror as he walks around the counter and places his kit on the floor with a heavy thud.

"I picked up a thing or two over the years, Darlin'. Your baby's safe with me, don't you worry."

He pulls a tool from his kit that has Ashley's eyes widening as he taps the machine gently with it like he's issuing an old friend a greeting. "The best model we do. You been happy with it?" He turns, looking between Ashley and I, and I nod and answer when it's clear she's stuck for words. "Good," he replies, turning his attention to the machine.

"Tate," Ashley whispers out the side of her mouth. "It's your break. Go. I'll keep an eye on... *him*."

The way she stares at the engineer in alarm as he starts whistling to himself is priceless. I hope for his sake he does know how to fix it, or I have a feeling Ashley will find a new place to stuff his tool kit for him.

I head out of the store for my break, dropping in at the pharmacy, and grabbing a cute kids animal magazine I think Molly will like looking at with me. I don't know when I'll next see her, but I hope it's soon. I love spending time with her.

Sullivan... not so much.

Molly's always eager to learn and explore new things. And she's such a happy little girl, despite being a mini version of Sullivan with her dark hair and blue eyes. She must take after her mother in personality. I wonder where she is. Sullivan's never mentioned her, and there are no photographs around his place that could be her. There are barely any family photos at all. The Google search I did of him mentioned a past fiancée. But that was over two years ago.

My phone buzzes and I pull it out, hoping it's Sullivan asking me to watch Molly later. My stomach drops at the familiar name. I bite my lower lip and hover my thumb over the screen. I should decline it. But he'll just call back. Like he always does.

"What do you want, Brandon?" I huff, screwing up my face as he says my name, making the hairs on the back of my neck stand on end.

"Tate."

He uses the same drawn-out whine that I remember from the day I walked into his place and caught him balls deep in a stranger. I'd arrived at the pivotal moment, just in time to see him, eyes closed, head tipped in ecstasy, coming inside a woman who wasn't me. She saw me before he did. We stared at one another as she was thrust forward into the couch I'd sat on with Brandon that morning while he rammed into her from behind and groaned about how good she felt wrapped around his dick.

"Tate," he whines again, the same way he had after he'd chased me out into the hallway and told me it was nothing and that he loved me.

I snap out of the memory. "I told you to stop calling."

"Come on, at least hear me out. This is a great opportunity. I can get you a meeting. You know you won't get it again without my help."

I suck in a sharp breath, my fingers tightening around the pharmacy bag and magazine as I clutch them to my chest like a shield. "I don't want your help."

He blows out a disgruntled-sounding breath. "Don't be stupid. You don't mean that."

There it is. The subtle undertone I missed throughout the nine months we were dating. The one telling me I'm nothing without him. That I won't ever get a record label to give one of my songs the time of day without his help. He always dangled the carrot over me the entire time we were dating. Telling me that his position as a marketing assistant at Liberty Records would mean that I had a chance to get one of my songs heard over the thousands they receive every week.

But never once did he actually try to help me while we were dating. So why should I believe him now that we've been over for two months?

"I don't need your help. And I don't want it. Why don't you shove it down the end of your tiny cheating dick?"

I hang up on him with a triumphant swell of my chest. Ashley would be proud. She's always telling me to speak up more for myself.

I push through the door into Caffeine Couture. Ashley's still watching the engineer with an unimpressed look. But he's packed his tools away and is leaning against the counter, giant work boot clad feet crossed at the ankle, as he sips on a cup of coffee.

"You make a great cup," he comments, running his tongue over his wet lips as he eyes Ashley with amusement. "You know, I've got a conference next week."

"And?" she replies like she doesn't give a shit.

He runs a hand over his beard, but I still see his smirk.

"And I figure I'll be taking you out when I get back on Friday. Unless one of those cards you tossed in the drawer when I arrived belonged to your boyfriend?"

She ignores his question and arches a brow. "You figure, huh? Kind of arrogant to assume, don't you think?"

"Not arrogant to hope, Darlin'." He winks, then places his cup down and pulls a business card from his cargo pants. "Message me your address if you can squeeze me in."

"Dream on." Ashley purses her lips and looks at his outstretched hand.

He chuckles and drops his card into the tip jar. "I'll pick you up at seven. Looking forward to it already."

He walks out, whistling. Ashley lifts her chin, watching as he disappears out of sight, before diving for the tip jar and almost knocking it flying as she fishes out his card.

I laugh. "I thought you didn't like him?"

"I didn't before," she says.

"Before what?"

She sighs softly. "Just... before."

"But you were like the ice queen to the poor guy."

"He has to work for it, Tate. I can't have him thinking I was imagining the ways I'd mount his giant bear-like body while he was working."

"You were?" I splutter in shock.

"Hell, yeah. Did you see the way he fixed the machine? Those hands knew what they were doing. Huck," she muses, tapping his card against her chin. "Fuck me, Huck. It even rhymes."

I snort with laughter as she holds the card out to read it.

"Oh shit." She stares at the rich brown card, the color of a deep roast.

"What? Is his name really Benedict or something?"

"Nope." Her brows lift. "Huck Turner. He owns the whole damn company." She spins the card toward me so I can see the bronze lettering naming him as founder. She turns it back to her with a dreamy smile. "He said I make a good cup. Not his machine. *Me.*"

I shake my head with a grin as I put my things away and grab my apron.

"Who were you talking to earlier? I saw you through the window and you had those lines between your eyebrows I've warned you about," she asks, tucking Huck's card inside her bra.

My eyes flick to hers guiltily.

"Brandon?" she spits. "Again? I thought you blocked his number?"

"I did. But he gets new ones all the time because he loses his phone so much."

"Like he loses his pants around other women." She snorts in disgust.

"Yeah, exactly," I mumble as I join her at the counter.

"In that case, we'll get you a new one. I'll come with you after work." She looks at me pointedly, knowing I probably won't bother if she doesn't come with me and force me to do it. Brandon's an asshole, but I can ignore him.

"Fine. After work," I agree reluctantly.

"He keeps calling because he knows how good you are. He wants the bragging rights once he takes your song to his bosses and they go mad for it."

"I doubt it," I grumble.

Ashley tuts. "Believe it. I've heard your material. Although I haven't heard that finished song of yours in a while."

I concentrate on re-filling the cocoa duster. "It makes me think of Brandon," I admit.

I wrote the song Ashley's referring to—the same one my dad wanted me to play to him and Larry—on a relaxing weekend spent at Brandon's place. The weekend before I caught him cheating. I feel like an idiot when I sing it. But it invariably slips out from time to time when I'm busy doing something else.

Like cooking in Sullivan's kitchen.

I swallow past the uncomfortable dryness in my throat. I swear he was listening to me. I caught him staring with the usual glare on his face. Then he made that weird comment about my clothes. I don't get why he hired me if he dislikes me so much.

"Don't let a guy ruin what's meant for you, Tate." Ashley sighs. "You don't know how much potential you have. Not that I want to lose you. You're my star barista." She jerks her chin at my chest. "That rack had tips up thirty percent this week."

"Whatever." I laugh as she throws me a wink. "That thirty percent alone was from Sullivan's lawyer flirting with you, and you know it."

Her eyes sparkle, and she blows on her fingertips. "All in a day's work."

SULLIVAN

"Come play with us," Molly calls out.

I smirk at Denver, sitting at the kitchen island. "You've been summoned."

"Denver's coming, Sweetheart," I reply, hitting send on my email, then looking over the top of my laptop at where Molly's playing on the floor with Sinclair and her dog, Monty.

Denver rises from his stool, his thick neck contracting as he takes his gun from the holster at his hip and removes the magazine from it. He hands both parts to me and I head to my office to put them in the safe beneath my desk.

I crouch, opening the ajar door with a curse. I must have left it unlocked. Not that it matters. I have another safe with the important things in. This one's a spare. I only use it for Denver's gun when he visits, or Killian or Jenson's, if they play with Molly. That and one other thing...

I reach inside and take out the square velvet box. It's usually pushed right to the back, but it's sitting at the front like someone's been looking at it. Flicking the blue lid up, I anticipate what I'll see. But it doesn't stop me from clenching my teeth together so hard that a pain shoots up my jaw.

"Fuck," I hiss.

It's empty.

Instead of Claudia's engagement ring that she returned to me after things ended between us, there's... nothing. Just a cushion with an empty groove in it that a ninety-thousand-dollar diamond ring once occupied.

"I should have fucking known."

I slam the ring box closed and hurl it back inside the safe behind Denver's gun as I slam it closed and lock it.

My blood's boiling as I stalk back into the living area. Molly and Sinclair are munching on the cat-shaped cookies. And if they hadn't just lifted the last ones from the plate, I'd be throwing the goddamn things out of the window.

"Who's Tate?" My sister asks, looking over with a sly smile as she brandishes one of the neater cat cookies in the air. Molly must have been talking about her while I was gone.

"She's no-one," I snap, snatching up my phone from the countertop.

"Who's Tate?" Sinclair asks Molly instead.

"Daddy's friend," my daughter replies helpfully.

I inhale as I jab at my phone, punching out a message. "She's not a friend."

"Is she your new nanny?" Sinclair says something else but all I can hear is blood rushing in my ears as I click send on the message.

I glance at Denver and shake my head, reassuring his concerned expression away. He'll want to run checks on anyone coming near Molly. Damn it, I should have asked him to. It seems anyone can become a kindergarten teacher. Even curvaceous redheads without morals.

"I'm not hiring a nanny. Tate was here and I had to make a call. I was in the room the entire time. I wouldn't leave Molly with someone I barely know."

I watch as the 'read' notification comes up on the text

message. A small flare of victory ignites in my chest as I picture her face when she reads it. When she realizes I know what she did.

Jesus Christ, she cooked for us last night. What if she had put something in the food? I jerk my head up and scan Molly's little body ruthlessly. But she's the picture of health, happily petting Monty and laughing when he wags his tail furiously, hitting Denver's calf over and over with it.

"I didn't realize your friends from The Lanceford came here too," Sinclair says, her voice laced with undisguised disgust.

"They don't." I shove my phone into my pocket. "Like I said, Tate isn't a friend. Let's leave it as that, shall we, Sis?"

She huffs before returning her attention to Molly and beaming at her as she takes her time kissing her goodbye.

I wait until after they leave before I tell Molly I'm going to use the bathroom. She's busy playing with her dollies again, and I turn the TV on for her, making sure the volume is high enough that she won't hear the giant punch I drive into the bag in my home gym on my way down the hall.

"Idiot!" I berate myself with a hiss. And to think I found something about her appealing. Something about her... *sexy.*

"Stupid fucking idiot," I grit.

My knuckles are throbbing as I draw my fist back and give the bag another whack for good measure.

I sit, nursing a whiskey in one hand as I recline in the chair of my home office. I'm on my second glass, savoring the burn as it tracks down my throat.

I can't believe I let her into my home. Into Molly's home.

My phone buzzes on the desk. I lift it up, rage firing in my veins as I see her name. So she replied. It only took her four hours to think up whatever pathetic excuse or lie she's going to try and spin. I put the whiskey down beside the empty ring box that I've been staring at ever since Molly went to bed.

> Tate Miller: I don't understand. Was that message meant for me?

I scroll back to the message I sent her, snorting at her audacity. Like it would be intended for anyone else. I only work with people I can trust. Hiring her was a mistake.

> Me: Effective immediately, your assistance will no longer be required. You aren't to come anywhere near my daughter, or I'll have you arrested.

Scrolling down I fire back a reply, wishing we were face to face, so she sees how serious I am.

> Me: I will not have thieves anywhere near my daughter. I suggest you get the ring back from whatever back alley pawn shop you've taken it to and return it promptly.

> Tate Miller: I don't know what you're talking about.

I cough out an unamused laugh. "Of course you fucking don't."

Tossing my phone onto the desk I push my finger and thumb into my eyes and rub. It's been a long day. But at least the final stages of acquiring Fabienne are in motion. Some good news.

I knock back the rest of the whiskey, leaving Tate on *read*.

I don't have anything else to say to a liar.

14

TATE

"YOU SHOULD HAVE STENCILED DICKS ON HIS coffees," Ashley snarls, handing me my phone after reading the text messages from Sullivan.

"I don't even know what ring he's talking about. But he thinks I took it!"

I'm still seething about his accusation. I didn't sleep a wink last night because I was wracking my brain to think what he might be talking about. Then I was angry, so damn angry, that his first thought was to accuse me.

"He watched me like a hawk when I was there. I was only alone when he answered the door. When does he think I had time to take his precious ring?" I stuff my phone into my apron pocket with a huff.

"Relax. It's okay. The guy's obviously an entitled jerk if he thinks he can sling accusations around like that without proof."

"I knew he didn't like me. He glares at me all the time. I thought it was him being protective over Molly. I found it really sweet how much he loves her." My mouth's felt like it's been stuffed with sawdust since I received those messages.

"Now I know it's that he just didn't trust *me*. It's like he was waiting for a moment for me to slip up so he could fire me. And I just used my first paycheck from him to hire Dad a lawyer."

Ashley pulls me into a hug, and I fight back the sting of tears as I sink into it.

"And that lawyer is going to fight for your dad and get him the severance package he deserves. And you're going to start sending your songs to record labels. Then after we've all been out to celebrate your new fame, and all the cash you've made that will rival Sullivan-Asshole-Beaufort's fortune, you and I are going to take a vacation together somewhere hot with cocktails and daily massages," Ashley says, squeezing me.

"Sounds like heaven." I sniff, forcing a smile. "But what if the lawyer needs more? If the case drags on, I won't be able to pay him."

Ashley holds me by my upper arms and looks at me with confidence. "It won't. It's an open and shut case. They fired him on medical grounds, which he'd already disclosed to them. The only reason he needed time off was because he was injured *by them*, on *their* premises, because of *their negligence* to provide a safe working environment."

"I hope you're right."

"When am I not?" She winks. "Listen, Sullivan Beaufort did you a favor, taking himself out of your life. Now let's deal with the rest of the trash. Brandon won't be calling you again. Give me your phone."

I pull it from my pocket and hand it to her.

"Give me two minutes and I'll have your new number all set up for you."

"Thank you," I breathe.

Ashley came with me last night to buy a new SIM card, but I never got around to setting it up. Sullivan's message came through when Dad and I were making dinner together.

My startled gasp at his threat of arresting me caused Dad to slip and slice his hand with the chopping knife. We spent the following four hours in the ER waiting for him to get fixed up.

"All done." Ashley hands me back my phone and I immediately text my father so he has my new number.

"Thanks."

My smile is weak as I pocket my phone again, but Ashley's attention snags on something outside and she hisses, "*Motherfucker*," under her breath.

I place a hand on her arm as she steps forward like she's about to rush into battle.

"Don't," I say weakly, following her gaze to the sleek black town car that's pulled up outside.

Cliff opens the rear door, then there he is—Sullivan Beaufort, looking every inch the cold and callous billionaire that I now know him to be.

He's in a charcoal-gray three-piece suit today, and he's wearing his permanent scowl. He fastens his jacket and nods at Cliff. For a moment, he pauses. And a pathetic part of me waits to see if he'll look this way. If there'll be a flash of regret on his face or guilt. Something that indicates he knows I'm not a thief like he's making out.

But then he turns, leaning into the backseat.

Seeing him sends bile rushing up to my throat. But it's the sight of Molly that forces a quiet cross between a gasp and a sob from my lips.

She's wearing a bunny onesie. It's cream and fluffy. A tiny part of me wonders if she chose it because of me. Because when we were in the grocery store the other evening she pointed to a picture of a rabbit on a cereal box and said 'Bumper'. As if to answer my question, Molly reaches out with her tiny hand and points to the front window of Caffeine Couture. But with a single swift shake of his head, Sullivan strides away with her in his arms without even a glance my way.

My throat thickens and I drop my gaze to the counter and grab a cloth, scrubbing the gleaming surface hard enough to make my fingers bleed. I'm stupid for getting attached so quickly. Looking after Molly was a job. I was just an employee. But damn it, I'm going to miss that sweet little smile and those dark curls so much.

"He's a grade A jerk," Ashley spits.

"I can't say I disagree," I mumble as we get back to work.

We're nearing the end of the morning rush when a head of ice-blonde hair with a voice as cold to match approaches the counter.

"Latte, double-shot, and..?" I ask, waiting for her to give me the second order for her own drink.

Cara's glossy lips curl into a condescending smile. "Oh, that's such good service that you remember his order, like you actually know him. But I'm not getting Mr. Beaufort's coffee from here. He told me this place was strictly off-limits from now on." She gazes around at the candy pink walls, scrunching her nose up in distaste. "He said he can no longer *stomach it*. Seems it wasn't to his liking, after all."

I fight to maintain a professional expression, aware of the line of people behind her. "Something for yourself, then?" I ask politely, swallowing past the lump in my throat.

Can no longer stomach it? What a rude ass. The coffee here is amazing, and everyone knows it. Ashley's built up an incredible reputation. His problem isn't with the coffee. It's with me.

Cara purses her lips and flicks her eyes up to the menu board behind my head. "I guess I'll take a Cappuccino."

I ring it up for her, then Ashley steps up close behind me as Cara moves along to the waiting area.

"I'll switch. You make the witch's brew for her. And if you feel the need to spit in it, I won't say a word."

She arches a suggestive brow at me, and I smirk. As tempting as the idea is, I'd never do a thing like that. My father always says when people are jerks to you, they're the problem, not you. And that they're probably unhappy about something in their life. Using that logic, Sullivan must be downright miserable.

I make Cara's drink and use a stencil to put Caffeine Couture's logo on it. My lips quirk as I picture putting a dick on Sullivan's one, like Ashley suggested, if she'd ordered one for him.

"How cute." Cara sneers, as I slide the takeaway cup to her across the counter.

"Thanks." I smile brightly and check no one is in earshot. "I don't have any stuck-up Bitch stencils, so I went with this one."

She stares at me in shock and her glossy lips drop open. "Excuse me?"

"Enjoy your drink." I keep my smile painted on as she scoffs and looks me up and down like I'm something she stepped in.

It's petty and unlike me. But after the shit I've been dealt over the past twelve hours, I had to say something. And it feels good to wipe that smug look off her face. It's not like I'll be seeing her now that I'm no longer watching Molly. She and I both know she only came in here to gloat. She won't be coming back.

Cara huffs, spinning on her designer heels and clicking over the floor toward the door. She glances back at me, pausing for effect, then holds her hand out and opens her manicured fingers in a flourish, letting the untouched drink drop into the trash can.

15

SULLIVAN

"What's made you so pissed?"

"What makes you think I'm pissed?"

Rafe's rich brown eyes glimmer through the phone's screen, and he lets out a deep chuckle. He holds his hands out, his palms facing up as he leans back in the chair in his office. "Fair enough, if you don't want to talk about it."

Working together over the years has meant our business relationship has evolved into friendship. Even before I took over as Beaufort Diamonds CEO, I was the one who dealt with our insurance and other legal requirements. It's one of the first things Dad taught me to manage in readiness for taking the helm one day. My brother was learning to head up global marketing, because he loved to travel, and I was learning the rest. Where I was rigid and found satisfaction in following strict routines, he was fun and saw everything as an adventure.

Not a day goes by that I don't wonder why I'm the one who got to live, and he didn't.

"The nanny I hired for Molly stole Claudia's ring," I grind out.

A curse that tastes bitter on my tongue follows my confession, and I lean over my forearms on my desk. Molly went to bed hours ago, and here I am again, despite it being five days since it happened, sitting alone in my office, nursing a whiskey, and letting Tate Miller take up far too much space in my head.

I expected her to deny it, which she did. But what I didn't expect was a kids' animal magazine and a handwritten note left with Cliff to give to me when I left work. A note containing the recipe for the mushroom and truffle pasta Molly enjoyed so much. Tate didn't sign it, but it was from her. The thing even had smudges of that damn cocoa powder on it. I can just picture her writing it in that little pink shirt of hers. The one that hugs her curves like she was poured into it.

I'm a goddamn idiot for allowing myself to be momentarily blindsided by an unexpected and fleeting attraction to a woman who is clearly only out for herself.

Maybe the way she was with my daughter was all fake too.

Fuck, that thought makes me angrier than any stupid missing ring.

"Bugger. What did she say when you caught her?" Rafe asks.

"She didn't say anything. I didn't see her take it, but I found the box empty." I lift my glass and swallow a mouthful of whiskey. "Joan's been sick, not that she would ever do a thing like that. She's worked for me for years without issue. The only person who's been here, other than family, is Tate." I spit out her name like it's acid.

"Cameras?" Rafe hitches a brow in question.

"No, the security system was off," I grumble.

Another stupid mistake of mine. Lesson learned, don't run a system upgrade when there are flame-haired thieves about.

"So what are you going to do?"

"Claim it off the insurance." I smirk.

Rafe chuckles. "Your premium will go up."

"Fuck off." I let out a deep sigh, putting my glass down and pushing my hand back through my hair. "This week's been a shitshow. The only upside is that Fabienne is practically a done deal."

"It is," Rafe agrees. "Everything on our end is all set for the takeover."

"Appreciate it," I reply.

"So if it's not just the nanny thief, what else is bothering you?"

I run my tongue around the edges of my teeth as I recall my conversation with my father yesterday, and the news of who's back in the city.

"Sinclair's car was trashed, and she's been getting threats. Dad's got Denver assigned to her whenever she leaves the house," I tell Rafe.

"Shit. Sounds serious."

"Maybe. Dad's gotten it into his head that it could be something to do with Neil being back in New York."

"Neil?" Rafe runs a hand around his jaw as he contemplates my words. "That's the guy your mum was having the affair with, right?"

"It is."

I curl my hands around the arms of my chair, gripping them tight and imagining them being Neil's neck. I know Mom was just as much to blame for the seedy affair with her first love in the months before she died. But the fact remains that he's the man who's responsible for the pain in my father's eyes after he found all of the sordid evidence they left behind following her passing. I knew my parents weren't madly in love. I recognize a couple who make a conscious decision to be together because it's a good choice and they make sense, not because they can't bear to live without one another. It's exactly how I was with Claudia.

I glare at the empty ring box sitting on my desk. I've placed it here as a reminder of why I cannot afford to make another mistake like I did when I hired Tate.

"We don't know why he's here. But until we do, Dad doesn't want to take any chances. I'm not sure it's him. I have a feeling it's been going on a lot longer than Sinclair will admit. I expect she's been hiding it so we don't worry."

"Sisters." Rafe shakes his head with a mirthful smile. He's one of three brothers and one sister. If anyone gets siblings, it's him.

"Yeah."

Neil's reappearance is likely a coincidence. But I could be wrong. People can be selfish and destructive. My mind flicks to Natasha. I haven't heard from her in weeks. Hopefully it stays that way.

"Tell me something interesting. And not some shit about insurance. Something that'll distract me," I mutter.

Rafe draws in a deep breath before letting it out as a weighted sigh. "I'm *interested* in someone... and she's my sister's best friend."

"What?" I stare at him. This is Rafe. A man who never dates the same woman for more than a few weeks. And that's being generous. I've never known him to be seriously *interested* in anyone or anything, except his multi-billion-pound company.

He grimaces. "I know. What's worse is, she's thirteen years younger than me with a smart mouth and a bad attitude, and I can't stop thinking about her."

I lean back in my chair, my lips quirking, eating up the distraction like a starving man.

"You slept with her?"

"Course I bloody haven't," Rafe splutters. "Aurora's Dove's friend and... I shouldn't even like her..." He blows out a breath, before his eyes glint. "She has this fashion vlog. She films herself trying on all these outfits... dresses, skirts..."

"Let me guess? It's become your daily viewing?" I let out a throaty laugh, and it feels good.

"It's not funny, arsehole." Rafe grumbles. "It's ruining my life. I can't even enjoy sex anymore because it's not with her."

I hold back my amusement. Because as entertaining as the thought of Rafe lusting after a younger woman he can't have is, my chest still pangs with an ounce of sympathy for him. The poor bastard's a goner, I can see it in his eyes. Another reason why falling for someone just causes problems.

We talk a little longer before Rafe hangs up, and I head to Molly's room to check on her.

My heart lifts at the little dark curls splayed across her pillow, shining from the glow of her nightlight. I walk over and press a kiss to her forehead. She doesn't stir from her sleep.

"Sweet dreams, Sweetheart," I whisper.

The explorer book she loves so much is on the floor at the side of her bed. I pick it up and stare at the cartoon character on the cover.

"She'd have loved for you to read this to her," I murmur as though my brother can hear me.

But he never answers. Dead people don't.

As I place the book on the nightstand, my eye catches on a Barbie doll Molly's left there. It beams at me with a pink-lipped smile and perfect white teeth.

On its wrist is Claudia's ring.

"What the hell?"

I lift the doll, sliding the ring off its arm and holding it up at eye level. The Barbie grins mockingly and my gaze drops to the picture it was sitting on.

I swallow a sudden swell of bile. It's the picture Molly drew in my office the first time Tate watched her. There are two figures in it. Both with wide grins. A small one with dark swirls for hair. And a larger one with red hair, wearing pink.

The red-haired one has a scribble on its arm with a light blue blob in the center, like a jewel.

My gut churns as images of Tate clearing up dinner flash to mind. Her bracelet had clacked against the countertop as she'd wiped it down. A gawdy thing that looked like it came from the bargain bin at Target—one big piece of clear plastic in the middle, mounted on a silver bangle.

I look back at my peacefully sleeping daughter.

"What the fuck have I done?"

16

TATE

"Give him hell, girl," Ashley whispers as the bell chimes and Sullivan strides in like he owns the place.

It's been days since he sent me those texts. What the hell does he want?

I straighten my spine as he bypasses the line and walks straight to the counter where I'm taking payment from a customer.

"Tate. We need to talk."

His cool blue eyes fix on my face, but I don't give him any more than a brief glance before I smile at the man and take the card machine back.

"Your drink will be at the end in a few minutes."

"Thanks," the man replies, giving me a quick glance up and down before he throws a generous tip into the jar.

"Tate." Sullivan tries again, but I keep my gaze forward.

"Who's next, please?"

The couple's eyes are fixed on the menu board, still deciding.

"Tate," Sullivan says, his voice lowering. "I've been calling you. I couldn't get through. Did you block me?"

I snort. He's so full of himself if he thinks I would go to the trouble of blocking him in case he called me again.

"Why were you calling?" I keep facing forward but lower my voice, aware of the waiting line. "What are you going to accuse me of stealing this time? It's obviously not your human decency, seeing as you already lost that."

I finally look at him and his eyes are waiting to pin me in place with an intensity that scorches the back of my neck.

"I'm..." A vein pulses in his temple like he's finding it hard to get his words out. "*I'm sorry*. I know you didn't take it."

"I told you that a week ago," I reply, turning my attention back to the couple who are ready to order.

Who does he think he is? Barging in here like this. Does he expect me to accept his apology just like that? Like I haven't spent days feeling like crap and not sleeping because of what he did.

"Tate?" Sullivan leans over the counter in front of the customers and I glare at him.

"There's a line," I hiss.

His eyes narrow and his nostrils flare. "Fine," he forces out. He turns and walks to the back of the line, then stands there in his navy suit, arms folded, and legs spread in an arrogant asshole stance.

I keep serving, listening to Ashley's grumbles and derisions as she fixes the drinks. Sullivan seems unaffected by the death glares she's sending his way. His eyes remain fixed on me until only one person remains in the line ahead of him.

Taking my time serving the woman, I engage in extra chat about what her plans are for the day, drawing out my interaction with her for as long as possible. Sullivan's brow is creased so deeply when she finally moves along that I'm surprised I can't see his skull.

"Tate—"

"What will it be?" I fake a smile.

A muscle in his jaw twitches and he reaches for his wallet and pulls out his card. "The usual."

"I'm sorry, what's that?"

Ashley snorts behind me and Sullivan purses his lips like he's just sucked a lemon. To think I used to feel intimidated by him. I was so quiet in his presence. Not myself at all. I found him imposing and difficult to talk to. Rude, frankly. I felt so out of place in his company. But I no longer give a shit what he thinks of me, seeing as he's already shown me his opinion of me couldn't get any lower by calling me a thief.

The only thing I want to steal is the mistaken idea his over-inflated ego has that I'll forgive him easily.

"Latte, double shot, please," he says through gritted teeth.

I hold out the card machine and he pays.

"It'll be ready down at the end," I tell him.

Ashley clears her throat pointedly and he arches a brow before he pulls a wad of notes out of his wallet without counting them and tosses them into the tip jar.

I start making his drink.

"Tate?"

"Sorry. Can't hear you over the milk frother." I hold his eyes as I press the button, cutting him off again as he opens his mouth.

He grumbles something, his hands resting on his hips as he waits for me to make his drink.

"*Cocoa dick,*" Ashley whispers as she moves past me to take over serving the line.

"Blocking me wasn't necessary," Sullivan grumbles as I place his cup on the counter and reach for the cocoa.

"I didn't. I changed my number for another reason. The world doesn't revolve around you."

His brows perk. I bet no one's ever spoken to him like this before. It makes a thrill dance up my spine, despite the fact a small part of me still threatens to go all awkward in his presence. I can't help it. When he stares at you like he is right now, it's unnerving. He's so... intense.

"Fine," he grits. "Whatever the reason, I need your new one. I want you to come back."

I pause with the cocoa, then place it down and slide his un-dusted latte to him. "No."

"No?" He splutters like he can't possibly have heard me correctly. "I said I was sorry, because I am. *I'm sorry, Tate.* I was wrong."

He leans closer and I have to fight back the involuntary urge to shiver under his undivided attention.

"I appreciate the apology, but my answer is still no. You made me feel like a criminal. Like some low-class liar."

His jaw ticks and his attention fixes on his coffee. But when I take my hand back, his gaze follows it. It's not the coffee he's looking at. It's my bracelet. I tuck my hand into my apron pocket and wait.

"I'm sorry," he repeats slowly. "Don't let my error affect my daughter. Please."

I stare at him, my throat thickening.

"Now, can I have your new number?" He hitches one dark brow in question and my breath stalls in my lungs. His blue eyes burn into mine, heating me all the way from my toes to the top of my head.

"Hell no!" Ashley storms over before I give in. "Don't go using that cute little girl as your bargaining tool. You want Tate's new number? Well, Buddy, you can earn it." She grabs Sullivan's latte and dusts a messy digit onto it. "There!" she declares. "That's one. Buy another drink and ask nicely and you might get another."

Sullivan holds my eyes and clenches his jaw so hard it looks painful. He clears his throat, then calmly takes out his wallet, handing Ashley his card, still only looking at me.

"Put everyone's orders on this."

I glance at the line. There are people waiting and more coming in through the door.

"If you insist." Ashley gives him a sickly-sweet smile as she plucks his card from his hand.

Sullivan stands to one side, his hands stuffed into his suit pants and a scowl on his face while Ashley and I jump into action to clear the line. He lifts his chin, his attention fixed on the next drink I make as the cocoa duster hovers over it.

"Oh, would you look at that? We're out." Ashley fakes an apologetic smile as she takes the duster from me and gives it a shake, pretending it's empty.

"Use that one," Sullivan grits, jerking his sharp jaw toward another duster sitting on the counter. Ashley knocks it onto the floor with her elbow and the lid flies off, letting the powder spill out.

"Oops. Sorry. Looks like you'll have to come back another day." She hands him his card.

I don't know whether to laugh or cry. I'm internally high-fiving myself for standing up to him, but I don't have the balls that Ashley does.

He doesn't say anything, but the vein in his temple looks like it's about to rupture. He slowly places a takeaway lid on his cup, then turns his attention to the line of waiting customers.

"Enjoy your drinks," he says smoothly.

I stare at him, waiting for him to speak to me. His eyes narrow, and he lifts the cup to his lips and takes a drink, keeping his eyes on mine. The muscles in his thick neck contract, before he lowers the cup and licks a faint hint of foam from the perfect cupid's bow of his lips.

Something sparks in his eyes, but he turns and walks out without saying a word.

17

—————

SULLIVAN

"Your father called while you were in your meeting. He wanted to know if you had your usual plans this evening?"

Cara's attention snags on the trash can in the corner, and the mounting pile of takeaway coffee cups inside it as she stands in the doorway of my office.

It's Thursday. My father will be wondering if he's keeping Molly tonight for a sleepover. It's been a few weeks since I participated in my usual Thursday night activities at The Lanceford. Natasha calling, the deal with Fabienne, then hiring Tate and all the trouble that's come with that... all mean that I haven't even thought about going there.

"I'll call him back," I reply as I continue typing an email.

Cara's continued presence makes me glance up, and she mistakes our brief eye contact as an invitation to approach my desk.

"I love your office," she hums, gazing out of the floor-to-ceiling windows that showcase the city in all its glory. "You should turn your desk around so you're facing the view. It's pretty incredible from here."

129

I ignore her. She's been here long enough to know why I would never do that. The position of my desk gives me a direct line of sight into the opposite office where Molly plays when she's here.

Cara rounds the desk and stops beside me, resting her ass against the glass top. Strong musky perfume wafts around her like a cloud and she leans a little closer.

"Are you okay? You look tense?"

I stop typing and let out an irritated sigh.

"I could help. I'm good at massage. I did a course." She places a hand on my shoulder and squeezes it gently through my shirt.

"Do you have Miss Miller's new number?"

"The coffee girl?" She wrinkles her nose. "No, why do you—"

"In that case, you can get back to work. Close the door on your way out."

She yanks her hand away immediately and collects herself with a brief, embarrassed sniff. "Of course, Mr. Beaufort. Please excuse me."

The door clicks behind her, and I sink back in my seat, steepling my fingers beneath my chin. With any luck, Arabella will return to work soon. That'll solve two problems. Firstly, Cara will be gone, and I'll no longer question whether she's about to drop to her knees and offer to suck my dick in my office. A line I would never cross with an employee. I have the suite at The Lanceford for a reason. And secondly, I will no longer need to consider who can help with Molly, seeing as Miss Miller is intent on playing this silly little game of coffee bingo with me.

Five days. Five numbers. Minus the weekend because she wasn't on shift. I asked Cliff to drive by and check.

I'm down to the final two digits before I have her entire phone number. Her boss already blocked my office and mobile numbers from their landline, so I've had to resort to playing along. I should have bought their damn building. Then they'd have had to unblock my number. But the paperwork would have taken too long.

I want her back now.

I run my steepled fingers over my lips and stare at my desk phone. Those final two digits would mean what? One hundred possible combinations? And that's if the numbers I've already collected have been provided in the correct order.

Twenty minutes until my next meeting starts.

I sit forward and grab the phone, punching in the first five memorized digits.

I clear my throat as Cliff opens the rear door.

Fifty-seven minutes, uncounted wrong numbers, three guys who swore at me before hanging up, one death threat if I called back, and one lonely woman who kept me talking for eleven minutes about her pet parrot's bowel movements.

But I did it.

I'm here.

She's here.

I wanted her back. And I wasn't stopping until I had her.

The scent of her reaches me first as she lowers herself into the backseat, thanking Cliff as she does. Her blue eyes avoid mine, instead searching the backseat, like she expects to see my daughter. But she's with my father and Halliday again this evening. My father chuckled when I told him what I was doing. He doesn't know who I'm with, only that it's a woman and it's a Friday evening, not a Thursday. That seemed more than enough for him to happily volunteer to watch Molly overnight.

"Molly's with her grandfather."

"Oh."

The defiance that was in Tate's voice when I finally got her number right yesterday and she answered my call is gone. And in its place is the hesitation I'm more accustomed to from her. She asked how I knew she was innocent, and I told her I'd found the ring. That it was where I kept it all along, but my own idiocy made me miss it.

I admitted I hate being wrong and rarely apologize—but I'd keep calling until I got the chance.

"You said to wear something smart. I thought I'd be watching Molly while you attend a work dinner?" Her eyes flick to mine and something sharp pokes me in the chest then disappears.

She reaches for the door handle like she's about to climb out.

"Tate, *please.*"

The undisguised tinge of desperation in my voice surprises me, and I clear my throat as she turns back and finally looks at me properly.

I apologized again when I finally got through to her on the phone yesterday. I could sense she was waning, the anger in her voice had all but gone and been replaced by what sounded like defeat. I descended on it like a shark making its kill.

I wanted her back. And I wasn't ending that call until I had her.

"I accept that my treatment of you hasn't been how I like to conduct myself," I say. My throat feels like it's full of razor blades. "Tonight is my further apology for that. And I hope that afterward we can move forward like adults."

"You accused me of stealing from you." She scoffs, perching stiffly in her seat.

My chest relaxes as Cliff pulls out into the evening traffic. She can't get out now.

I cast my eyes down to her strappy heels, before inching them up her bare legs and over the black velvet dress that crosses over at the front, wrapping around each breast.

"A mistake I am genuinely disappointed in myself for making," I say sincerely, continuing my slow appraisal of her. "You look... *very* beautiful. That dress suits you."

Her eyes pop wide, two small patches of rouge blushing her cheeks. "You mean, it's not distracting because I'm too big for it?"

There's a hint of distrust in her voice, laced with the sparky attitude I now know she has, despite keeping it mostly hidden.

"If I recall correctly, I never once said your uniform was a distraction because you were '*too big*' for it."

"Mm," she mutters.

The urge to grasp her chin and make her look at me when I'm speaking to her wraps around my throat like a fist.

"I believe my words were, *incite inappropriate reactions*," I clip.

"What's that even mean?" She flicks her attention to me and I ignore the warning sirens in my head telling me to look away.

I drink her in again, not caring if I lack subtlety. She's a smoke show tonight. Curves for days, eyes with a new fire in them, a decadent floral scent emanating from her that's growing more alluring with each passing second.

I wet my lips. "It means ones that incite reactions that are inappropriate between a boss and an employee."

Her painted red lips part and her eyes drop to my groin before she frowns like she's chasing away an irrational thought. She drops her focus to her folded hands in her lap instead.

"Thank you for agreeing to me taking you out for a drink tonight," I say sincerely.

"A drink? So that's what we're doing? I didn't exactly have a choice. I thought Molly needed me. I wouldn't have said yes if..." She looks at me quickly, then away again just as fast. She sighs. "Is she really asking after me? Or was it a ploy to make me agree to come tonight?"

"She is asking," I admit, part of me hating that my daughter keeps pointing every time she sees a coffee cup or a bunny, and her voice lifts with hope as she says, "We see Tate?"

I don't make a habit of manipulating people's emotions to get what I want—but I was right to assume the only way to reach Tate was through Molly. Molly's taken to her. And I don't have time to hire someone new. I know full well that if it weren't for Molly, Tate wouldn't have agreed to come back at all.

When I finally got her on the phone, she didn't ask for more money—like I would have. She just demanded I treat her with respect if she returned.

I wish she'd asked for the money. That would've been easier than knowing how deeply she's come to care for my daughter—and how much Molly clearly cares for her in return.

That realization hit me like a giant neon sign.

But I'll unpack that shit later.

Right now, I need her. So she's about to find out just how respectful I can be.

The car pulls over and I climb out as Cliff does the same, opening Tate's door for her. I'm waiting at her door, hand outstretched, ready to help her climb out.

She stares at my hand for a beat like it's the jaws of an alligator, before she slides her fingers over my palm. I assist her out of the car.

"Do you like music?"

Her pupils dilate and she sucks in a quick breath. "Music?"

"Piano, specifically."

"Y-yes." Her eyes dart to the building behind me and her brow wrinkles.

"Good." I nod at Cliff, dismissing him. He'll come back later when I call.

I slide my hand to Tate's lower back and lead her toward the entrance. "This is my father's club. It's just reopened following an arson attack. You're one of the first people to see the new décor."

The doorman opens the large gold-handled door for us, and I sweep Tate inside the low-lit hallway. Another doorman opens a door at the end for us, and we enter the main bar.

"Holy cow." She gasps.

My fingers flex against her lower back and I can't stop my lips twitching at her reaction. It warrants it. The design company who headed up the re-model has done an outstanding job.

The sultry room—with a glamorous thirties era feel to it— is like stepping onto a movie set. A long bar with a smoky glass wall behind it runs along the length of one wall, and intimate tables with plush velvet seating are placed strategically around the room with enough space between them that conversations remain private.

Privacy is paramount in Seasons. Presidents drink here. Royalty drinks here. The top people in their fields all drink here. My father created a safe haven for those plagued by having their every move watched and scrutinized. Here, they're free of all constraints.

Here, they can lose themselves in the music and just *be*.

I lead Tate toward a table tucked away in a candlelit corner near the stage. Her head swivels as she admires the chandeliers hanging overhead, but it's the grand piano on stage that stops her in her tracks.

She stands, enthralled, in the center of the seating area, her eyes transfixed on Vincent as he plays a Debussy piece with skilled ease.

"He's amazing," she breathes.

"He's our resident pianist. He studied at Julliard."

We stand, watching. Tate seems to be in a trance, and it's only after Vincent plays the final notes that she allows me to lead her the remainder of the way to our table.

"It's really beautiful in here. It's like a dream," she says, looking around as I pull her seat out for her.

"It was my father's vision. I'll tell him you said so, he'll be pleased."

We order drinks, and I don't engage with Tate until the server returns with them. She's too lost in her own world, listening to Vincent play another song. Something about the way her breath hitches along with the crescendos of the music and her eyes mist like it's speaking directly to her soul has me spellbound.

I'm accustomed to seeing women's faces when they're experiencing pleasure.

But Tate is a different vision entirely.

My attention drops to the plastic bracelet on her wrist as we clink our glasses.

"I know it doesn't fit with the vibe of this place," she says, sipping her drink, then placing it down quickly so she can cover the bracelet with her hand after noticing me studying it. She strokes it gently with her thumb. "But I wear it all the time. I won it at the fair when I was with my mom. It's the last day we had out together before she died."

Jesus, I'm a bigger asshole than I thought.

I swallow my whiskey and place my glass down. "I'm sorry. What happened to her?"

Tate rubs her bracelet, smiling sadly. "Brain hemorrhage. No warning. One moment she was here. The next..." She shrugs.

"I understand what that's like."

She lifts her eyes to my face. "Of course... your mother and brother. I'm so sorry. I read about it online." She winces like she's mad at herself for reminding me that the press created a media circus reporting on their deaths, like it was a type of sick entertainment. Speculations were rife for some time afterward over whether it was an insurance coverup, or something equally underhand. It all died down after a few weeks when an investigation declared the yacht fire as an accident. Nothing more. Nothing less. Just a terrible, tragic accident.

Without conscious thought, I lean over and gently uncover her hand from her bracelet.

"My sister wears a necklace that reminds her of our brother. The diamond is made from his ashes."

Tate's eyes shine with understanding. "It's not the same as having them, but it can help to have something to hold onto in those times their loss hits you."

"Comes out of nowhere, doesn't it?"

She holds my eyes, her voice soft with understanding. "Yeah, sure does."

Vincent continues his set and I observe Tate's growing smile as she listens. I saw the way she touched the piano in my place. I was right to bring her here.

"Do you play?" I ask.

"I do. I'm not very good, though." She turns her gaze from Vincent and meets mine. "Do you?"

"Sometimes," I reply. "I've been told I'm excellent."

I hold back my smile as she breaks into a surprised laugh.

"Is excellent spelled v-a-i-n, by any chance?"

I let the smallest fragment of my smile out so that my lips

quirk. "I see you learned spelling at the same school as my sister."

Tate bites down on her bottom lip, and her laugh softens. "She gives it back to you, huh? She sounds cool."

"She is."

"I don't just play." Tate screws her face up like she's embarrassed before she takes another sip of her cocktail. "I like to write songs too."

"You do?"

"Yep. One almost got me a place in a girlband once. Until they decided my 'thunder thighs' didn't belong on an album cover."

"Thunder thighs?"

She shrugs, reluctant to meet my eyes. "Their words, not mine. They wanted thin and pretty."

"*Thin*," I echo, my eyes dropping over the neckline of her dress to the swell of her breasts. I run my tongue over my lower lip as I drag my gaze upward.

"Exactly. So that was that." She sighs. "I keep meaning to send a song I wrote to record labels. But Dad got laid off, and then the stuff with Brandon happened and I just put it on hold. But it's my dream, so I'll start again when the time's right."

"You want to give up your career?"

She laughs again like I've said something funny. Only this time I'm not joking. It takes years of studying to be a teacher, and Tate must be in her mid-twenties. She's barely begun seeing how much of an impact she can have on kids' lives.

"But you're great at it," I continue. I might not have seen her teach, but I've seen her with Molly and there's no denying the way my little girl looks at her like she hung the moon.

"O-kay." Tate looks at me like she's puzzled. "Thanks, I guess."

I pick up my whiskey and recline in my seat, studying her. "Who's Brandon?"

The way her chest deflates, and her eyes dim confirms my suspicion.

"Ah, the loser ex," I say, bringing my glass to my lips and taking a sip.

Tate's eyes fix on my mouth as I lower the glass, letting it dangle between my fingers as I rest my arm on the side of the seat.

"What did he do?"

She purses her lips, considering my question. I can see the hesitation in her eyes. She doesn't like me. And after my accusations, she probably doesn't trust me, either. But the fact she didn't insist on Cliff taking her home tonight once she realized this evening wasn't being spent with Molly was a sign that a small part of her is intrigued by me. She might think accepting my invitation tonight was a way to get to know more about the man whom she's employed by. But this evening is as much for me as it is for her. I need to know more about the woman I'm allowing around my daughter. Not the things a background check can tell me. The things she won't put on a form.

I need to know what makes Tate Miller tick. What she loves, craves. What she's scared of. I need to know everything that my daughter will be exposed to whilst in her company.

"He..." She takes a sip of her drink like she needs courage. "He was fucking another woman, and I walked in on them as he was finishing. Loudly, I might add. He was more enthusiastic than he ever was with me."

I narrow my eyes and study her. "That bothers you more than the cheating?"

"No. I don't care. I mean, why would I? That's a given with cheats, right? That they make more effort for the new person."

The fire in her eyes is muted by an undercurrent of uncertainty.

"I wasn't referring to his efforts. I meant, you're more bothered by the fact he was clearly enjoying having sex with this other woman more than he enjoyed having sex with you," I state matter of factly.

"What?" She gapes at me like I'm the rudest man she's ever laid eyes on.

"Tate," I say, taking my time to place my glass on the table and lean my forearms over my spread thighs until I'm staring straight into her eyes, ready to level with her. "How many guys left their numbers for you at work this week?"

Her nose wrinkles. "That's not import—"

"How many?"

She shakes her head, looking confused. "I don't know. Maybe twelve?"

"Twelve," I repeat slowly, the number making me clench my jaw momentarily. "And do you know how many of those twelve were imagining how you looked underneath that pink uniform you wear? How many were wondering if your nipples would be more of a pink or a brown? How many were thinking about how they'd feel against the tip of their tongue as they tasted them?" I allow my eyes to drop to the heaving swell of her cleavage as her breaths grow ragged at my words.

"Do you know how many of them were fantasizing about how loud they'd fucking *groan* like they'd visited heaven and come back to earth again if you ever gave them the opportunity to fuck you?"

"W-what?" She laughs, stopping abruptly and scanning my serious face.

I nod slowly, driving my point home.

"All of them," I say. "Every single fucking one."

18

TATE

"You didn't need to walk me to my door," I protest as I climb the stairs to my building.

"What kind of man doesn't escort a woman to her door?" Sullivan clips, sounding annoyed that I would suggest otherwise.

I glance at him over my shoulder, and he arches a dark brow at me. Cliff's waiting in the car, but he's turned the engine off like he expects to be waiting a while.

"Loser exes," I offer with a twist of a smile.

"Precisely," Sullivan grinds out and his eyes take on a menacing coldness the same way they did when I mentioned Brandon earlier this evening.

Tonight with him has been... unexpected. For the first time I found his company *tolerable*. Okay, *enjoyable*. He's actually nice and interesting, when he's not in billionaire asshole mode. We talked about music for most of the evening. He has a huge knowledge of piano songs, and listed so many of my favorites as ones he enjoys playing.

We didn't talk about Brandon again. Not after Sullivan's comments had me excusing myself to the restroom so I could splash cold water on my face. He was being complimentary. Which in itself was enough to shake me. But it was the way his eyes heated as he'd pinned me under his gaze and talked about men groaning as they fucked me.

Hearing those words in his gravelly voice had me excusing myself from the table in a rush—before he could catch the heat flooding my face. I didn't fully get it before, but now I do.

Now I get why people stop and stare when Sullivan Beaufort exits his car at the sidewalk.

Because once you put him and the idea of sex together in the same sentence, you can't unthink it.

I bet he'd fuck you into another dimension, then pull you back with those intense blue eyes, and leave you boneless.

I drank another two cocktails after returning from the restrooms before I could even look him in the eye again. Maybe he only said those things to flatter me. To cement my acceptance of coming back to work for him. But regardless, I appreciated them.

Because in that moment when I was his sole focus, I felt like a million fucking dollars.

"Oh shit!" I yelp, faltering on the steps because I'm too distracted from gazing back at him.

He reaches out and steadies me with a firm arm around my waist, but it's too late. The contents of my purse spill out over the concrete. Sullivan flexes his fingers where they've wrapped around me and flattened over my stomach. Then he takes his hand back and bends to retrieve the items scattered all over the floor.

His brow creases as he lifts a plastic bottle of pills up.

"Thank you." I swipe it from him and stuff it back inside my purse along with a packet of tampons, a lipstick, and a hairbrush.

I fumble with my keys, opening the front door, then turning back to him in relief.

"Well, that's me. Thanks for a nice evening. Your father's place really is incredible."

I turn to walk inside, but Sullivan's hand splays out on the door above my head, the same way it did against my stomach a few moments ago. He holds the door open as though he's intending to follow me inside.

"I'm fine from here," I utter unconvincingly. Because despite spending the evening with him and having the courage of numerous alcoholic cocktails flowing through my veins, the man still makes me nervous. Especially when his eyes are on me, all blue and intense, like they are now.

"To your door, Tate," he says.

"Sure, to my door." I glance at Cliff sitting in the car and throw him a small wave before walking inside.

The heat from Sullivan's broad body is like an inferno of flames licking toward my spine as he follows me up the stairs.

"Sorry, the elevator's broken again. But we have a new landlady, who's already way better than the guy before her. So I'm sure it'll be fixed next time. Not that you'll be coming here again. I mean, you're welcome too, of course. But why would you? I mean, you're my boss."

I keep my eyes fixed on the stairs ahead of me, so Sullivan doesn't see me cringe. The confidence the cocktails gave me is wearing off.

We reach my apartment and Sullivan walks beside me, before stopping at my door a split second before I do.

"How do you know this is me?"

I look up and he's already looking down at me with those eyes of his again. They're carrying the same heat they were when he talked about the men who gave me their numbers at work. I stare at him, rooted to the spot as he leans closer. My eyelids lower of their own accord as his aftershave mixes with the trace of whiskey on his breath. I incline my chin upward, wondering if his lips are about to meet mine. And whether I even want them to.

"Molly owns the building. I have a list of the tenants."

"What?" My eyes pop open.

Sullivan's frowning at the door behind me, leaning closer and studying the locks. "We'll get the security upgraded for you, and the other apartments."

He moves back, creating distance between us again. I can't believe I thought he was actually going to kiss me. Sullivan Billionaire Beaufort.

God, I'm dumb.

"What do you mean Molly owns it?"

"She has a portfolio of investments I've set up for her and will manage until she's older. You told me your dryers were broken, and Cliff knew your address, so I looked it up, knowing if your landlord wasn't maintaining the building, he'd maybe be open to selling."

"You did all that for her?"

"Of course. She's my daughter, and I want her to be financially stable outside of the family business."

"That makes sense," I say, like I have any idea what it's like to run a multi-billion-dollar empire and buy buildings around the city like I'm collecting them on my Monopoly board.

"This neighborhood is a solid investment," Sullivan adds patiently like he's explaining something to Molly. "It's just business, Tate. Don't read anything into it."

"I wasn't." I pull my eyes away from his and slide my key into the lock. This is what he sees when he looks at this place. Outdated locks. Something shabby and in need of a makeover.

I open the door and step inside, turning back to face him. He doesn't try to follow me inside, and the tightness in my stomach eases with relief... and maybe a hint of disappointment.

"Thank you for fixing the dryers. My clothes won't shrink now."

I wish I could take the words back the moment they fly out of my mouth. I'm talking too much, back to being intimidated by him again. I've gone from being nervous around him, to angry at him, to enjoying his company, to admiring him for all he does for Molly, and back to being intimidated by him, all in the space of a week.

My head hurts.

"No, they won't," he says, frowning as his eyes drop down over me in my dress. "They'll all fit perfectly." His nostrils flare before he meets my eyes. "Good night, Tate."

I stare after him as he strides off in his dark suit like he has somewhere important to be and I've taken up enough of his time.

"Good night, Sullivan," I call.

But he's already gone.

19

TATE

"Pan-da!" Molly grins as I place the plate in front of her.

"That's right. Pandas."

I've used some seaweed to make the black parts on little balls of white rice and served them to Molly with a side of cut up vegetable sticks for her lunch. I've watched her for Sullivan more than a few times over the past week. Usually after my shift ends, and at their place. It's quickly becoming a routine that I ride home with him, then make dinner while he finishes up with work calls. Joan is still sick, and Arabella is still away. The doctors say whatever Joan has is viral and will go by itself, but she didn't want to be around Molly until she was completely better.

Sullivan's face when Joan called had me offering to help out more in the evenings as soon as he hung up. He looked so stressed. His phone had rung again with something work related before he could even answer me. He'd looked at Molly with guilt in his eyes, before pinching the bridge of his nose and answering the call. "*Thank you, Tate,*" he'd whispered.

But today we aren't at his place, we're at his office. And he only needed me for an hour over lunch while he had a video meeting. Molly's grandfather is coming to collect her for the afternoon.

The two of us sit together at the table, happily munching on matching panda themed lunches while Sullivan sits at the desk in his office on the other side of the hallway with a scowl on his face as he hosts a meeting through his computer screen.

He looks up as if sensing my eyes on him and I give him a little finger wave, tipping my head toward Molly who's happily eating a cucumber stick that I arranged to look like bamboo for the panda on her plate. Sullivan told me he sometimes struggles to get her to sit still long enough to eat lunch. But if I can get her interest by making it look fun, then she'll sit and devour the whole lot.

Sullivan's lips lift into the smile he reserves especially for Molly as his eyes move to her. It's gone before he looks back at me, but there's still a touch of warmth in his eyes. One which I'm sure is gratitude. I've noticed it a few times since I came back to work for him. But he doesn't need to be grateful. Looking after Molly is a joy. I love her company and curious little questions. The way she takes delight in such small things, like a ladybug that had found its way onto a plant in their living room last week. And how she always admires my bracelet and says, *"Tate, momma, pretty,"* after I told her it helps me remember my mom.

Whatever's happening in the meeting Sullivan's taking, he doesn't look happy about it. He shakes his head with a firm bark of, *"Not good enough"*, that I hear through both glass walls, before shaking his head at whatever is said in response.

"Well done, Molly," I say, seeing her empty plate. I take the lid off the pot I packed the pandas in. "Would you like another one?"

She nods with big, eager eyes, as I put another on her plate.

"I'll have to remember that you like pandas, huh?" I say with a smile.

"Pan-das," Molly repeats.

An easy happiness fills my chest at the sight of her happy face and head of dark curls as she polishes it off, then declares, "All gone."

"Good job, Sweetheart," a deep voice praises.

I was too busy watching Molly to hear Sullivan come in.

"She ate it all, Daddy," I tell him.

Molly beams at him with pride.

"You ate all of it? You mean, Daddy doesn't get a panda?"

Sullivan walks into the room, his hands pushed into his dark blue pant pockets. No matter what suit he has on, he always manages to make me think it's my favorite. The one that suits him the most. Shows his broad shoulders the best. Highlights his blue eyes. Picks up the shine in his dark hair that he wears cut short above his collar.

It's not him I'm drawn to. I just see so many suits worn each morning on my shifts at Caffeine Couture, that I'm beginning to recognize the best fitted ones. The Tom Fords, the Brionis. And then there are the ones that are specially designed for the wearer, with specialist tailors flown in to fit them.

Like Sullivan's.

They're really quite beautiful.

"There's still one panda with your name on it, if you want it?" I hold the pot out and offer the lone rice ball to him.

"No, I'm good."

"Daddy, eat it," Molly pipes up.

I try not to laugh at Sullivan's perplexed frown as he gazes at the panda like it might get up and actually start walking.

"Not one for 'Serious Sullivan', hey?" I say as I stand and start packing up the lunch things.

"Serious Sullivan?" He arches a brow and I try not to

smirk. It's definitely gotten much easier working for him since I came back. He's kept to his promise of treating me with respect. I'd go as far to say he's even friendly on occasion.

"Yeah." I shrug, deciding to tease him. Whatever happened in his meeting has gotten him looking all tense, and I hate that. "'*Silly Sully*' would eat the panda."

He looks at me like I just suggested a 'come to work nude day' for the entire office.

"*Silly Sully*?" he repeats so slowly that my stomach twists. His eyes penetrate mine and I halt my tidying up.

I went too far.

"Eat pan-da!" Molly demands.

Sullivan's face softens and he crouches down level with her. "Daddy's not hungry, Sweetheart. But they look yummy."

"Pan-da." Molly does a great job of mimicking his scowl I often see as she stands her ground.

"Tate. A panda please, if you'd be so kind." He holds his hand out to the side, pretending to sound defeated.

Molly giggles in delight as I place the small rice animal in his palm and he stuffs it into his mouth like a monkey without table manners, then makes a big show of chewing it and making lots of 'mm' and 'yum' noises as he devours it in a few seconds.

I can't help but smile that I get to witness this side of him. The one no one else except his daughter and family see. There's something special about seeing a big, serious guy, who can go from looking like he's about to tear someone's head off in business, to ruffling his daughter's hair while he acts like a doofus to make her laugh, a moment later. Something really special.

"Grandad can't come and get you for a little while, okay?" Sullivan tells Molly. "He has to look after Halliday."

"O-kay," she answers with the easy acceptance of an almost three-year-old as she heads off to pick up a toy to play with.

"Is everything okay?" I ask, noting the way Sullivan rubs at his temples with one hand.

"Halliday's bleeding. Not much, but enough that they want to get checked out and make sure the baby is okay. He said he'll call when he knows more."

"Gosh, I hope everything's all right." I follow his gaze to where Molly's happily playing, sensing the tension rolling off him in waves. "I can stay longer if you need me to? While you work?"

"It's fine, Tate," he replies, his attention staying on Molly. "You do enough. You have your shift to get back to."

"Not today. Ashley gave me the afternoon off. I was going to enjoy the sun and read in the park. I could... take Molly with me?"

Sullivan stiffens the moment the words leave my mouth.

"... Or we can stay here. There's plenty to play with. She might like to color." I backtrack furiously, ignoring the pang of disappointment that he still doesn't trust me. But I'm being stupid. This isn't about me. This is about Molly. Sullivan's a very protective father. And I shouldn't take it personally.

"No." He sighs. "She's spent the morning here with me while I answered emails. She needs to get out."

"We go park?" Molly pipes up hopefully.

Sullivan smirks. "For a kid who looks like they aren't listening, you sure don't miss anything, do you?"

Molly looks at him, the picture of innocence until he blows out a breath. "Okay, park, Sweetheart. But Daddy might have to make some calls while we all go, okay?"

"Is that okay with you?" He turns his piercing blue eyes on me, and I stare into them.

"That you come along and work, and I'll watch her? Sure."

"Great." His shoulders soften like he's relieved. "I'll get my laptop."

A few minutes later we're heading into reception to catch the elevator. Molly's holding my hand and humming a cute little tune as we walk.

"Cara?" Sullivan pauses, one hand holding Molly's, the other carrying his laptop bag. "I'm heading out for a while."

Her ice-blonde head snaps up from behind the desk, eyes narrowing into daggers as they flick over my Caffeine Couture uniform and the sight of Molly's hand in mine.

"Are you escorting Miss Miller back next door?" she asks.

"No. I'm escorting them both to the park," Sullivan replies.

"What should I do if I need you?" she questions, batting her lashes at him.

"Call my cell," he says, a hint of agitation creeping into his tone.

"How long will you be?" she calls as we stop in front of the elevators and Sullivan punches the call button.

"As long as the girls want me to be," he barks back, clearly annoyed now.

The girls. Not my daughter. *The girls.* Like I'm part of the gang.

I don't know why that makes my stomach flutter like it's full of bubbles, but it does. I smile at Molly, and she beams, then looks over at Sullivan and beams at him too.

We step into the elevator and Cara's pinched face is the last thing I see as the doors slide closed.

20

SULLIVAN

MOLLY'S SMALL "OOH" AS TATE SITS ON THE GRASS and slides a daisy chain over her curls like a headband has my heart seizing painfully like it's in a vise.

She has this with Sinclair. But not often enough. Tate coming into her life has filled my little girl's eyes with something I haven't been able to give her.

The happiness of time spent with other women.

I can do the dressing up, the games, the nail painting. But I can't give her this.

Once or twice, I've questioned whether keeping Natasha away from Molly was the right decision. But I only have to hear her slurred, drunken pleading for more money, to reassure myself that it was. I wouldn't be surprised if it isn't just alcohol she's addicted to. I can't have Molly exposed to that. Natasha's been given the choice. Get clean and have the opportunity to see Molly. Or carry on the way she is, and possibly lose her life to substance abuse before Molly even starts school.

She's chosen the latter.

Tate looks up and her smile falters as she sees me staring.

"Is it time to go? Do you need to get back?" She checks her watch.

I close my laptop and place it on the grass beside me, leaning back on my hands and stretching out my shoulders. These pants alone cost twenty thousand dollars. But Molly's happy giggle floating over to me makes all concerns about grass stains and dirt evaporate.

"No," I say, pulling out my phone and snapping a picture of Molly with the flowers in her hair.

"Okay then." Tate smiles and plucks another daisy from the ground, winking at Molly. "I think Daddy would look good with a necklace. What do you think?"

Molly's stroking the daisies around my neck with one small fingertip, tracing over each flower with care as I carry her back along Fifth Avenue. She claimed her legs were too tired from chasing the pigeons outside The Songbird hotel that faces onto Central Park to walk the rest of the way back.

"The park was a good call," I tell Tate as we stop on the sidewalk between Caffeine Couture and Beaufort Diamonds. "Someone's tired and should sleep well tonight." I kiss the top of Molly's head.

"It was all this one's idea," Tate replies, tickling Molly under one arm and making her squirm and giggle in my arms. "I'll see you soon, okay?" she says to Molly.

My daughter reaches for Tate and Tate glances at me with an unsure expression.

"You want a cuddle, Sweetheart?" I ask Molly.

She nods enthusiastically and reaches for Tate.

I pass Molly into Tate's arms and hold back the bite of

protectiveness that fills my chest as Molly sinks happily into her embrace and Tate closes her eyes and presses her face into Molly's curls.

My father's right. I need to loosen the reins a little. What kind of man would I be to deny my daughter the affection Tate obviously has for her, because I find it difficult to let go?

Molly deserves love and attention. She deserves the damn world, and I'm going to do whatever it takes for her to get it.

"What a lovely big squeeze," Tate says as Molly kisses her on the cheek with a 'mwah' sound.

Our eyes connect over Molly's shoulder and Tate smiles at me before she kisses Molly back. "Next time I see you, we'll have bear pancakes, okay?"

"Yay!" Molly grins as Tate hands her back to me.

I hold her in one arm as my phone rings in my pocket. I place my laptop down so I can pull it out and answer.

"Dad? Everything okay?"

I hold Tate's questioning gaze and give her a small nod when my father tells me that Halliday and the baby are both fine, but that he's going to stay at home with her, and I can drop Molly over for the rest of the afternoon.

Tate exhales and her face softens like she's relieved.

"Yeah, I can do that now," I tell my father after he asks me to go to Seasons for him. "We'll head over there, and I'll bring Molly to you after."

I hang up and text Cliff before pocketing my phone.

"My father needs me to check on something at Seasons. I'm going to head over there now."

"You're close, aren't you? Always helping one another. It's really nice."

I look at Tate's innocent expression. "We're Beauforts, Tate," I say by way of explanation. "It's what we do. Family always comes first. Cliff can drop you home after."

"What? No, it's fine. I'll get the subway."

"Cliff always takes you home," I clip.

"Yeah, because it's usually evening. It's the middle of the afternoon."

Tate blows out a breath as I remain silent, refusing to negotiate.

"Fine, okay. Thanks," she says.

"Good." I nod. "He's bringing the car around now."

"Sullivan?"

The voice makes me stiffen, and I turn slowly toward the woman approaching us, wondering if I'm imagining it.

"Hi..." Her eyes rake over me, stalling on Molly in my arms. "I was hoping I'd find you."

Her blonde hair is longer than when I last saw her, flowing over the shoulders of the fitted white dress she's wearing. And her makeup is immaculate, highlighting her natural beauty. She was always stunning and perfectly presented.

Except that night when her eyes were red from crying as she walked out.

"Claudia?" I reply.

"It's good to see you." She leans forward and kisses me on the cheek, one hand resting on my upper arm.

Her perfume wafts over me. It's the same one she's always worn. One I bought for her.

Molly snuggles closer to me. "Who that lady, Daddy?"

Claudia's brows shoot up at hearing Molly's voice.

"I'm an old friend of your daddy's," she says, her attention glued to Molly like she's an exhibit in a museum. "Gosh, she looks just like you, doesn't she?"

My grip on Molly tightens.

Claudia's trance is broken as Molly looks toward Tate as if for reassurance.

"Oh, sorry. Were you about to get a coffee?" Claudia asks, spotting Tate in her uniform. "I could... I could join you. I thought we could talk?"

"I'm actually about to leave," I say as Cliff parks the car along the sidewalk behind her.

Claudia glances at Cliff climbing out of the car. "Hi, Cliff." She smiles.

"Miss Hayward." Cliff nods in greeting, recognizing her immediately.

He drove us home the night I proposed. He also drove her to the airport the night she left. He's never asked what happened. Instead, he helped me install Molly's first baby car seat the morning after, his only words about what a special baby she was. He was smitten the first time he laid eyes on Molly. Just like we all were.

Except Claudia.

Claudia looks back at me and pulls a card from her purse. "I'm staying at The Songbird for a few days for work before I go back to Boston. I'd love to have dinner and catch up. I've got a table booked at seven tomorrow night. Join me?"

I take the embossed card and read it. *Claudia Hayward Designs.*

"You started your interior design company?"

She nods. "You always told me I could do it. You were always so supportive." Her eyes slide to Molly, and she smiles sadly before looking back at me. "Please come, Sullivan. I'll be waiting for you."

She reaches out and squeezes my hand, then leaves.

My grip on my glass of water tightens and my attention wanders from Seasons bar manager chatting to me about how New York's mayor had been in the previous night as laughter rings out from the stage.

Tate's smiling and chatting with Vincent as he plays cartoon theme tunes on the piano. Molly claps enthusiastically beside her as he comes to the end of another one.

"Give me a minute," I tell Phillipe.

I move further along the bar, closer to the stage, and lean back, sipping my water, pulling out my phone so it appears like I've moved to make a call.

"Sullivan and I aren't a... thing," Tate tells Vincent in a low voice, glancing at Molly as she happily holds her baby doll and mimics it pressing the keys on the piano. "I'm helping out with Molly. He's my boss."

"Sorry, my mistake. I thought he mentioned a dinner date," Vincent says, sounding far too friendly for my liking. I've heard that tone before when he's flirted with women who gush over his piano playing.

"Oh, that's with a woman we just bumped into. Claudia, I think her name was," Tate replies.

"Blonde? Tall? Beautiful?" Vincent asks.

"Yes to all the above." Tate smiles.

"Uh-huh." He runs a hand around his jaw. "That's his ex-fiancée."

"Really? Wow. Well, yeah, he's going on a date with her," Tate replies.

Damn it. The only reason I told Vincent I might be dining at The Songbird soon is because I know he's desperate to know what set the pianist they have plays. She's excellent apparently. And Vincent's intrigued.

Like he's too fucking intrigued about Tate's personal life right now.

"No boyfriend, then?" he asks.

Tate's smile widens. "No boyfriend."

"Do you want one?" He winks.

She laughs. "That sounds like an offer?"

"How about I take you on a date, and you can decide if I'm in with a shot?"

"Um…" Tate's laughter strains like she's shy, and she tucks a strand of hair behind her ear.

I lean closer, straining to hear her response.

"Sure, why not."

I slam my glass down so hard on the bar it echoes through the room.

"Time to go!" I bark.

Tate looks over in surprise. "You're done?"

"I'm done," I reply through gritted teeth.

I questioned whether having Tate back working for me was a wise decision or a monumental mistake. The way my hands are curling into fists like I want to punch something tells me… it's the latter.

21

TATE

Unleash your potential... let the world hear your sound."

I play the notes that accompany the gentle words, and the melody fills the room.

Molly sits beside me on the piano stool, her eyes wide as she watches my fingers glide over the keys.

"Did you write that?" a deep voice rumbles.

"Oh!" I cease playing immediately, heat blooming in my cheeks at the sight of Sullivan leaning against the doorframe. "I'm sorry, I should have asked before I..." My gaze drops to the piano.

"It's fine. I told you to help yourself to what you needed while you're here. That includes our piano."

He walks over and stops beside the sleek black wood, resting his hand on it.

"You told me you weren't very good."

"I... I guess I'm okay." I give him a shy smile.

"You're very talented, Tate," he says.

My breath catches at his rare compliment. "Thank you."

He holds my eyes for a brief moment, then holds his hand out toward Molly.

"Time for bed, Sweetheart."

She slides off the stool and walks to him. He pulls her into his arms and his eyes crinkle as she places her palms on his cheeks and squishes his face.

My heart swells at the sight of them.

He's always so patient with her, but the dullness around his eyes tells me he's tired tonight. I see him taking call after call, meeting after meeting, when I'm here in the evenings with Molly. He always makes sure to stop and eat dinner with her. And he always reads to her at bedtime, never asking me to do it. But I swear after I leave he goes straight back to work again. He told me she gets in his bed some nights too, and usually wakes at 6 a.m..

No wonder he's exhausted.

I stand from the piano and tuck the stool under. "I'll let myself out. Sweet dreams, Molly." I bop her on the nose, making her giggle.

"Enjoy your date," Sullivan rasps.

His eyes flick over my outfit, nostrils flaring. I changed after cleaning up from dinner, slipping into a navy, figure-hugging dress—far sexier than anything I'd normally wear. Ashley insisted I borrow it, though I'm convinced she bought it specifically for my date with Vincent tonight. It's in my size, even though she's at least one dress size smaller.

"I intend to. We're going to a new jazz bar in Midtown." I brush my hands over my dress, checking for loose threads or lint. "Vincent said they have some great singers there."

"Did he now?"

Sullivan's skeptical tone has me snapping my eyes up to meet his. "Is there... Are you unhappy that I'm going out with him? I know he's a friend of yours, but it won't get weird if it doesn't work out. I'm not going to start bad-mouthing him to you."

Blue eyes pierce mine before Sullivan exhales.

"Of course not. You can date whoever you like. Cliff will drop you off. Call him when you're ready to go home. I don't want you getting a cab late at night."

I clear my throat softly, considering my words.

"Problem?" Sullivan arches one of his perfect dark brows at me.

I glance at Molly before giving him a 'you know' look, which he completely fails to interpret.

"I..." I lick my lips, wondering how to word it. "That's really nice, but Vincent will give me a ride. We might... decide to go on to somewhere else after drinks."

I might decide enough is enough and it's time I got laid.

Ashley made me promise I had to consider it. Vincent's a nice guy and we have music in common. I agree with her. I need this. Finding Brandon with that other woman drained my confidence. And Vincent seems quite happy to help me find it again, so...

Sullivan stares, and the silence between us turns awkward. His rapidly deepening grimace has me growing hot and trying not to fidget. Does he really think I'm that hideous? I know I'm not his type, but he doesn't have to look so horrified by the idea of me being with someone.

"Fine," he grits.

"Good."

The two of us stare at each other for another tense few seconds before he gives a tight nod.

"I'm taking Molly to bed."

He turns and strides off, then stops as he reaches the hallway leading to her bedroom.

"Tate?" he calls, looking back at me with something dark burning in his gaze. "Can you wait until I've read to Molly?

I..." He purses his lips. "I think we need to discuss some things before you leave."

Something dangerous about his tone has every sense heightening in my body.

"Sure," I reply, trying to keep my voice breezy.

If he's going to fire me or accuse me of stealing something again, I swear I'll lose it.

He nods again, the movement stiff, before he walks away.

I head to the bathroom and take my time touching up my makeup and spritzing some perfume on. I'm waiting in the living area when Sullivan returns. His shirt is unfastened at the neck, and his hair is ruffled from where he's laid on Molly's bed with her.

"Am I fired again?" I blurt out, unable to stop myself as he walks over to me.

"What? No. Why would you think that?" He frowns like it's the last thing he was expecting me to say.

"I..." I shrug, the fire in my stomach simmering down. I've been sitting here thinking of all the smart come backs I could use if he were to pull that crap with me again. He looked so tense, I assumed he wasn't happy with something I've done.

"Do you want me to fire you?"

"What? No! Why would you think that?"

He arches a brow as I repeat his words.

I exhale a ragged breath. "Sorry... I just never know where I stand with you. You're kind of intimidating."

"I intimidate you?" He moves a little closer, and I tilt my head back to look him in the eye. Even with heels on, he's still inches taller than me.

The heat from his body pours off him and reaches out to me like coaxing fingers.

"Come on." I scoff. "You're..." I gesture a hand up and down his broad, muscular body. "You look... like *that*. And you're really successful. Plus, kind of scary. I saw a grown man leave your office looking like he was about to have a heart attack."

"He did. He died in the elevator."

Sullivan's eyes glint. The only sign that he's joking. *I think.*

"So what do you want to talk about?" I ask.

His expression hardens and he swallows thickly, his eyes dropping over my dress. "I—"

The bell from the building's concierge rings out, indicating he has a visitor. He grumbles something and walks over to the panel on the wall, pressing a button to answer it.

"Mr. Beaufort? There's a Miss Hayward here to see you. Shall I send her up?"

"I should get going," I whisper as Sullivan looks at me.

His jaw tightens and he rests one hand against the wall and talks into the panel. "That's fine, thank you."

His hand curls into a fist against the wall and he mutters out a hushed curse before turning to me.

"Enjoy your date, Tate," he says, a cool detachment taking over his eyes as he pushes away from the wall to escort me to the front door.

I hover before he opens it and glance up at him. "Is everything okay?"

I'm overstepping. We're not friends. But I don't like seeing him all tense like he is. Maybe it's nerves, knowing his ex-fiancée is here. Perhaps he wants to get rid of me so they can have some privacy. Ashley was salivating over the gossip when she saw us all outside yesterday, wondering why his ex was back in the city. She said it was a huge thing when they broke up, with the New York press reporting that the engagement was off, and speculating over whose decision it was.

"Everything's fine," he bites out.

A vein pulses in his temple and his brow is so deeply creased he must have a headache.

"Okay then," I answer.

He opens the door for me, and I almost walk face-first into Claudia.

"Oh, hi." She smiles without a hint of recognition, like my uniform yesterday made me invisible.

"Hi," I reply.

"I didn't know you had company?" Her eyes meet Sullivan's and I look at the way he's staring at her, like he can't look away.

"I'm not company. I work here," I say, returning Claudia's smile. "And I'm late for my date, so..."

"Of course." Her voice softens like she's relieved as she steps aside so I can slide past her.

"Nice to meet you," I say to be polite.

"You met yesterday," Sullivan snaps, his eyes still on Claudia.

She looks at him and her eyes widen before she blinks and looks at me. "Of course, I remember."

I'd bet the contents of this week's tip jar she doesn't.

"We weren't introduced, though." I smile wider, trying to ease the weird tension that's building between us all. "I'm—"

"Tate," Sullivan clips. "This is Tate. She's Molly's nanny." His eyes are still on Claudia. "Tate, this is Claudia."

"Nice to meet you." I step past her and make my way down the hallway toward the elevators.

"Tate?" Sullivan calls after me.

I turn back just as Claudia is slipping past Sullivan and shrugging her coat from her shoulders, revealing a red lacy dress beneath it.

"Yes?"

He glowers like he's pissed, his eyes dropping to my feet and back up to my face.

"Have a nice time."

"Thanks. I wi—"

My words are cut off as he disappears inside and slams the door.

22

SULLIVAN

"You still have the couch we bought together?"

Claudia runs her hand along the back of the white fabric, and I stuff my hands into my pant pockets, watching her walk around the living area like she never left.

"Did we? I don't recall."

She gives me a look that says she knows I'm lying before wandering around more, inspecting what's changed since she was last here.

My phone chimes and I pull it out, reading the text Cliff sent to confirm Tate just got into the car. I pocket it again. He'll let me know once she reaches her destination safely.

On her date.

With Vincent.

I drag in a slow breath as Claudia strokes a fingertip over the piano like she's admiring it.

She hated it.

She would tell me it was too loud when I played.

My jaw clenches as she presses down on a key making a lone note ring out.

"Where's Molly?"

"She's two years old. She's in bed," I answer harshly, but she doesn't flinch, continuing to hover by the piano.

"Oh, of course," she murmurs.

"Why are you here, Claudia?"

She tilts her head to one side, exposing her slender neck before she turns and faces me.

"I'm here to quote a newly married couple on their apartment re-design. They want a whole re-style." Her eyes slide over to a white vase on a side table, and she smiles. "That was an engagement present, remember?"

"I meant here. In mine and Molly's home?" I grind out each word, noting the way her eyes pinch a fraction when I use Molly's name.

She leans back against the piano, arching her spine in a stretch, and pushing her breasts forward in her dress. Her expression softens. "You're looking really well, Sull. Being a daddy suits you.... How are you finding it?"

"What kind of a question is that?" I spit.

Her face falls and for a brief moment I feel guilty. She was never a bad person. She just couldn't love my daughter the way she deserves. Because Molly isn't hers and she couldn't see past that.

Claudia's attention moves to a photograph on top of the piano. It's of Molly on her first birthday. She's sitting on my lap while she blows out the candle on her cake. Her curls were shorter then. She had one that would stick up on top of her head no matter how much I tried to brush it down.

"I was wrong, Sull," Claudia says gently. She picks up the frame and I walk closer to her, fighting the urge to snatch it from her hands and place it back where it belongs.

"Yeah, you were. She's the best thing to ever happen to me."

Claudia puts the frame back and nods. "I can see how

much you love her." She sweeps her long blonde hair over her shoulder and a hint of her perfume washes over me. "We loved one another once too, remember?"

She's still looking at the picture of Molly, which means she doesn't see the way I stiffen. We were going to get married. I was the one who proposed. But I never actually told her those words.

I never said it.

"Nothing's been that good since. I've tried, I really have. I met someone great and then…" She turns and looks at me with glassy eyes. "I've never been able to forget about you, Sull. You were my one. You've always been my one."

"Two," I utter.

"What?" Her eyes narrow, trying to catch my words.

"Two," I repeat. "I'm not a one anymore. I'm a two. Me and Molly. You know that. You had that choice."

"And I'd make a different one if I could go back, I swear." She reaches for me and winds her arms around my neck.

A small groan vibrates my throat at her touch, and I lean into it, my eyelids hooding. It's been weeks since I've made it to The Lanceford. What the hell have I been thinking? I need sex to help me de-stress. No wonder I've felt so tightly coiled recently. I barely even get the opportunity to jerk off with Molly climbing into bed with me some nights. And then she wakes up so early and wants to play in the shower with her toys as I wash, so even that's off-limits.

"We could try again. I can move back to New York. We could be us again."

Soft lips press kiss after kiss to my throat.

"Sull," Claudia breathes, pushing her body against mine so her breasts sink into my shirt. "I want you." She drops a hand to my belt and starts unfastening it. "Remember what it was like? All those nights we wouldn't sleep."

"I remember," I groan, closing my eyes.

"When it was just you and me?" she purrs.

"Just you and me," I repeat.

My hands drop to her waist on instinct just as she pulls my lips down to meet hers.

23

TATE

My heart's racing as we reach the door.

"Did he say what was so urgent?" I ask in a rush, my mind racing with possibilities of something happening to Molly, or him, or both of them.

"He didn't," Cliff replies. "Only that I should bring you back as soon as possible."

"Okay, thank you," I say as Cliff opens the door to Sullivan and Molly's penthouse.

I rush inside and Cliff closes it behind me, remaining outside. My heels click on the floor until the sound of the piano overtakes them.

Rushing into the main living area I spot Sullivan, head hung over the piano, eyes screwed shut, the haunting melody of *Lacrimosa* by Mozart spreading like a cloud of darkness around him.

"Sullivan?"

He stops abruptly.

One lone lamp is on, casting the room into shadows.

"Where's Molly?" I look around for signs of her, my feet slowing from Sullivan's lack of urgency. "Is she okay?"

"She's fine. Fast asleep," he says, his voice a rough whisper.

He's sitting with his head hung. His broad shoulders lift, then slowly drop as he breathes deeply.

"Then... what's happened?" I drop my purse on the floor and reach down to pull my shoes off. My heart continues to hammer as I study him.

Something isn't right.

I walk toward the piano.

"Stop!"

His sudden outburst has me freezing on the spot and staring at him in shock. He lifts his head and despite the darkness, his eyes shine like bright blue daggers as he looks at me, before his attention drops to my feet.

On the floor in front of me are pieces of a broken vase.

"You could cut yourself," he warns.

His body goes taut as he watches me navigate the shards carefully on my way toward him. Once I pass them, he exhales, turning his attention back to the piano. He starts playing again.

"Sullivan?" I frown. "What's going on?"

"Claudia kissed me," he rasps.

"What?" I scoff out a surprised snort, swallowing it back down as his pressure on the keys ramps up and he plays with more determination. "You asked Cliff to come in and tear me away from my date and bring me here, so you could tell me your ex kissed you?"

"He had to *tear* you away, did he?"

The snarl in his tone has the tips of my fingers tingling by my sides.

"What's going on? I don't understand."

"You wouldn't because I've given you no reason to understand." He snorts as he continues to play the piece so beautifully, like he doesn't even need to think. His fingers glide over the keys effortlessly.

"I—"

"She *kissed* me. And she tried to undo my pants, telling me she was going to suck me off."

I recoil. "Are you drunk? Why are you telling me this?"

"I'm not *drunk*," he snaps, sneering like the suggestion disgusts him.

"Then, what—"

"I couldn't stop thinking about you. On your date with Vincent. How was it? Are you going to marry him and have his babies?" he snipes cruelly.

"What?"

What the hell has gotten into him?

"If you must know, it was great. We talked about music. He made me laugh and feel relaxed. And I even saw an apartment block for sale on the ride there and took a photo of it to show you for Molly's portfolio."

I cross my arms, irritation slithering up my spine as he continues playing, not even having the manners to look at me after he ended my evening prematurely because for some unknown reason it suited him. He's so used to people bending to his whim. But I can't figure out what his angle is right now, and why he's being like this.

"Not interested in whatever building you saw, Tate," he says without an ounce of enthusiasm.

"But it was—"

"Not. Interested," he repeats.

He's an asshole. An uptight, arrogant prick. So what? He thinks because I saw it that it can't possibly be a good investment? That the area can't be right? That I wouldn't know what I'm talking about?

"I live here, too. I know the good neighborhoods," I argue. "I—"

"I only bought your building to get you new dryers," he

hisses, moving seamlessly into another song on the piano, his playing unaffected despite his harsh tone.

"What? Why?"

"Because!" he thunders, his lips twisting into a grimace as he plays.

"Because what?" I step closer.

"That *uniform*," he spits, like it's a curse word.

The music flows effortlessly around him. It's as if the angrier he gets, the better he plays.

"Oh my God! Because you hated it that much? Because it offended you that much when it shrunk? That's...wow..." I blow out a breath, all of my nerves from being around him evaporating as they're replaced with white-hot rage.

How dare he?

I'm never going to let him make me feel intimidated or awkward again.

"Nice way to tear a woman down, hey? Tell her you hate clothing that shows the shape of her body. So I have hips and breasts. And my thighs touch in the middle. So fucking what?"

Sullivan stops playing and flies to his feet, knocking the stool to the floor.

The sudden stillness in the room heightens the sound of my angry breaths as my chest heaves.

He steps toe to toe with me, blue eyes burning.

"You think I hated it because I didn't like the way it clung to you? The way your shirt looked like your breasts were going to spill out of it any minute? The way your skirt showed these..." He sucks his bottom lip between his teeth, his eyes dropping down my body. "These curves near your hips... like fucking handles made to grip on to?"

"What?" I choke.

He rakes his gaze over my body, his tongue sliding out to wet his lower lip.

"So your date?" he whispers darkly. "How was it?"

He continues his perusal of me without apology, drinking me in with heated eyes.

"Over now... thanks to you."

His lips curl a little on one side. But it isn't a smile.

"Before it ended? Do you like Vincent? Would you have gone home with him? *Fucked him?*"

"Fucked him?" I echo in a disbelieving gasp.

I take him in, dressed in his suit pants, his white shirt undone to the top of his chest, showing a hint of dark hair disappearing beneath the fabric. His brows are pulled together in his signature scowl.

"No," I say, not sure why I'm sharing this with him. It's none of his goddamn business. "I wouldn't have. There's no spark. It was a fun evening with a new friend. But it was *comfortable.*"

I regret the shred of information I let slip free instantly. Sullivan homes in on it like a shark after a drop of blood.

"Comfortable? You don't want comfortable?"

"No."

His eyes pass over my folded arms, before settling on my cleavage in the plunging neckline.

"What *do* you want?"

I open my mouth, but nothing comes out.

He finally looks up at me, hitching one brow in question. He isn't going to let this go until I answer him.

I swallow. "I want *more*... I want my heart to race when I see him... I want my spine to tingle, knowing he's close... I want a rush when I lock eyes with him and see the way he looks at me... I want... I want something that's almost frightening because of how intense it is."

I'm pinned in place by show-stopping bright blue irises.

I don't move. I don't breathe.

"Ask me what *I* want, Tate," he says, his voice a rich husky gravel.

I pause, my pulse galloping in my ears. I should keep quiet. This is... this is too much... He can't honestly think that he and I...

"What do you want?" I whisper, unable to stop myself, the urge to have him finally share his private thoughts with me too great of an opportunity to pass up.

He reaches up and brushes the back of his fingers over my hair, stopping before he reaches the ends that fan over the swell of my breasts.

"I want you."

"But... you don't like me," I splutter.

"I'm good at hiding things I don't want other people to know about. Believe me, Tate, I want nothing more than you out of this dress right now."

I choke out a laugh. I misheard him. I must have.

He leans closer, his heady, expensive aftershave lingering in the air. The aroma is decadent and dark, mixed with warm skin. Creating a scent that's so uniquely... him.

"I want you, Tate," he says simply, like he needs to spell it out. "I want to kiss you, taste you... sink my head between your thighs and fucking drown in you. I want your curves filling my hands, and your moans filling my ears."

"You what?" I squeak, my breath ragged.

Heat flares deep in my core as he looks at me with hungry eyes.

"I want you," he rasps.

He leans down, lowering his mouth to mine.

"But I won't touch you." His breath fans over my parted lips. "I won't..." He licks his lips. "Not unless you want me to."

"Unless I want you to?"

"Precisely. The choice is yours." He exhales, and I breathe in his air, my nipples pebbling beneath my dress.

"And if I say no?" The piano presses into my back. I don't know when we moved, and I became trapped.

"Then we'll forget this ever happened," Sullivan murmurs, his attention dropping to my mouth.

"And you'll what?" My lips tingle as I search for the right words.

Go back to looking like you hate my clothes? Go back to being curt with me, bordering on rude? Go back to scowling at me when you think I'm not looking?

"You'll go back to—"

"I'll go back to dreaming about if you'd said yes. That's what I'll do."

24

SULLIVAN

I stay rooted to the spot, waiting to see what her next move will be. Waiting to see if she wants me like I want her.

My name breathed so softly from her lips has my eyes hooding with lust as I stare down at her. She rises on her toes and lightly dusts her lips over mine with trepidation like she's testing out how it feels.

"Say the word, Tate," I whisper. "Let me kiss you."

She sinks her teeth into her pouty lower lip, looking at me from beneath her lashes, still toeing that line between what her body wants and what her head is telling her to do.

I cradle her face in a way that leaves no room for hesitation, stroking her cheeks with my thumbs. "I want to kiss you so badly. Let me. Please."

She nods. It's so slight that if I weren't enraptured by her every move, I'd miss it.

"Is that a yes?"

"Yes," she whispers.

"Thank you."

I crush my lips to hers, the move making us stumble back

181

into the piano. I drop my hand to her hip, squeezing it as I steady her.

"Tate," I groan.

She's had me wanting her for weeks. She's in my dreams, in my head. She's every-fucking-where.

I'm ready to devour her, but she's frozen in place like she can't move.

"Kiss me back. Really fucking kiss me, Tate. I need you in this with me," I plead, sliding a hand to her neck, pinning her gently in place as I drag my tongue over the seam of her mouth. "Let me in, Baby."

She sucks in a breath as if she's remembering where she is.

Then she surges forward, answering my prayers, meeting me in the middle with a wild hunger that rivals my own.

Our mouths crash together. It's a crushing kiss. One that ignites the blood in my veins and draws a deep groan from my chest. It's a kiss that has me delving deeper and deeper, seeking to tether her to me. To make sure she's right here alongside me. Feeling this undeniable pull between us.

I snag her lower lip between my teeth and bite down gently on it until she whimpers.

"You're so damn sexy, you know that?"

I lean over her, swallowing her small gasps as I take, and take, and take. Using my tongue to taste her, to steal her whimpers and store them away to replay in my head when I'm alone.

I fucking obliterate her final hesitations about what we're doing. Kissing her the way I want to. The way I *need* to.

Deep, urgent, raw.

A man possessed.

"Sullivan," she gasps.

I break apart so she can breathe, resting my forehead against hers. "Don't ask me to stop," I beg, even though it sounds more like a command. "Please don't ask me to stop."

She shakes her head, before grabbing my hair and dragging my mouth down to hers with renewed urgency. Her tongue seeks mine, matching me stroke for stroke, as eager for my taste as I am for hers.

"Oh my God," she pants as I drop my hands to those fucking curves of her hips and yank her body against mine.

She gasps as my cock presses into her.

"This is what you do to me," I growl, flexing the thick length against her so she can appreciate just how painfully hard I am.

I need to be inside her, burying myself to the hilt. It's more than an obsession now; it's goddamn essential to my survival.

"Tate," I moan. "Jesus fucking Christ."

I dig my fingers into her flesh, my mouth dropping to suck the point where her pulse is pounding in her neck. I could bite right through her flesh. Drink her down. I'm that fucking starved to get a taste of her. There's no time for subtle. She needs to understand how crazed I am for her. She's consumed my mind for weeks.

Her curves. Her defiance when she stands up to me. Her damn obliviousness to the way I stalk her with my eyes like a predator when she's in my apartment. When she's in my kitchen teaching my daughter how to cook. When she's playing my piano and filling my home with laughter and lightness and... *her*.

Whatever she's doing, I see it. I watch. I notice every single thing. And it's fueled the obsession to have her more each day, until it's become too powerful for me to resist.

"Sullivan," she whines, clawing at my shirt as she drops her head back, exposing more of her neck.

I suck it roughly, knowing I'll leave a mark. But I don't care. I want her marked by me. I want her to look in the mirror and remember this. Remember how damn good it is with me.

"That feels amazing," she mewls, sliding her hand between us to the front of my pants.

Her touch is soft and slow.

I grab her wrist and hold it still.

"That's it, get a good hold on it, Baby." My breath stutters in fevered groans as she wraps her fingers around my dick and I drag her hand up and down, jerking myself roughly. "Treat it like you own it."

"You like it like this?" she breathes.

"God, yes. Don't stop," I grit, shoving her dress up around her waist. I yank her panties to the side and curse as I swipe through silky wetness.

"Sullivan," she moans.

"Soaked for me," I growl in appreciation.

She gasps as I sink two fingers inside her. I should take it slow. But fuck...

"Knew you'd feel good. I fucking knew it." I look down at my palm meeting her skin with each forward thrust.

I'm rough, taking my cues from the way she's crooning my name and clawing at my hair as she pulls me in for another kiss.

"When was the last time a man made you come?" I ask, pulling back to look at her heaving cleavage.

I drag down one side of her dress, freeing her breast.

Pink nipples. Goddamn perfect.

"I don't... Oh lord!" She whimpers as I close my lips around her nipple and suck.

"Don't what? Don't remember?" I alternate between kisses and bites over the heavy flesh surrounding it, before sucking on her tightly puckered nipple again.

"I can't..." she pants as I fuck her with my fingers and circle her nipple. "God, Sullivan, don't stop."

"Wild fucking horses couldn't stop me right now, Tate."

I take the weight of her breast in my palm and knead it, teasing that delicious pink nipple with my teeth.

"Jesus, you're so sexy."

She rubs me faster through my pants, and I match her pace, burying my fingers inside her.

"Oh God... Oh my God... I..."

Her lower stomach tenses and a fresh wave of wetness flows into my palm as she clenches around my fingers.

"That's it, Baby. Let it go. Come all over my hand like a good girl."

"God, yes," she cries.

"That's it." I rise so I can see her expression.

"Sullivan," she whispers, her pupils dilating.

I drag in a breath, almost choking on it as her eyelashes flutter uncontrollably and her cheeks flush brightly.

"Tate?"

She nods, answering my unspoken question.

"Good girl." I exhale roughly. "Good. Fucking. Girl."

A whimper escapes her and her back bows.

She's silent for a beat.

Then she sucks in a breath and lets it shatter out in a cry as she comes. "Sullivan! I can't... fuck... I'm coming, I'm... oh fuckfuckfuck..."

I look into her trusting blue eyes as she comes apart for me, riding each clench and wave out with me, sharing every part of her pleasure with me as she keeps her eyes locked on mine.

Like a fucking goddess.

"Sullivan," she whines my name in awe as her orgasm fades, like she was in ecstasy, and I'm the one who put her there.

"Come with me."

I lift her into my arms, and she wraps her trembling legs around my waist.

"Where are you taking me?"

"Where I've dreamed of seeing you."

I carry her into my bedroom and drop her onto the bed, standing back to look at her. Her red hair fans out against the white sheets like a scorching flame.

I unbutton my shirt as I drink her in.

"Take your dress off."

She complies slowly, watching me undress as she reaches around and slides down her zipper. Her eyes roam over my chest before dipping lower and snagging on the tented fabric of my pants.

"Don't get distracted," I scold as I unfasten my belt.

Her eyes glitter, and she slips the dress from her shoulders rolling it down her body, uncovering inch after inch of soft, smooth, feminine flesh.

"Now your bra and panties."

I drag my zipper down, my cock twitching as I shove my pants down and step out of them.

Tate's eyes darken as they fix on my erection straining inside my boxers. I study her as I push them down and free my cock. Her eyes widen and her mouth pops open in a silent gasp.

My lips twitch and I make a show of wrapping my hand around my dick and giving it a slow stroke.

"Now show me what I'm getting," I rasp, gesturing to her deep blue silk lingerie that's still covering too much of her body.

She unclasps her bra at the front and her magnificent tits spill free, both nipples puckered into delicious pink peaks.

I squeeze my cock and the end of it drips.

"Keep going." My voice comes out strained.

She wriggles, hooking her thumbs underneath the sides of her panties and lifting her hips from the bed in order to slide them off.

It's the little arch of her hips that does it.

Like an invitation.

I lose all fucking patience.

"Fuck!"

I grab her legs and lift them onto my shoulders. I don't give her time to react. I sink my face between her thighs and press my mouth against her soaking flesh, my body going taut as her taste hits my tongue.

"Fuck, yes, oh sweet Jesus..." I groan.

I suck and lick and grunt and swallow, eating up her quivering little pussy like my life depends on it.

"Sullivan." She arches on the bed, her hands twisting my hair at the roots. "Oh my God, You'll make me come again."

"Exactly what I was aiming for," I murmur against her skin, holding her eyes as I scissor my fingers, parting her and exposing her clit to me.

I tongue the sweet swollen flesh, watching the way her back bows.

"Please," she whimpers. "It's... oh my God... so good..."

I press my lips to her, humming a soft tune before I continue to work her with my tongue.

"What... what is that?" she moans.

"Don't you recognize it?"

She stares at me as I hum the song against her again.

"It feels..." Her eyes roll and her grip on my hair tightens.

"Feels beautiful," I say, humming and licking her again.

"Sullivan... Oh fuck."

She comes on my tongue, sending a rush of wetness that I swallow down with a rough curse, hungry for more.

I keep kissing and sucking, pinning her down by her hips when she tries to pull back and get away from me.

"It's so sensitive. Stop," she squeals.

I close my eyes, kissing between her legs with a tortured groan.

"I could do that all night," I tell her as I move up onto my knees. I keep her legs held to my shoulders so she's lying beneath me as I kneel over her.

"I want to be inside you so damn much, Tate," I say, gripping my cock with one hand and running it up and down through her wetness, watching the swollen lips of her pussy part for me in invitation. "But you'll have to take me bare if you want me."

"You don't use condoms?" She frowns at me, her cheeks glowing from her orgasm.

"I always use them. But I don't have any in the house."

I rub my cock over her clit, inhaling sharply as it touches my slit and my precum drips onto it. I don't want to use one with her, even if I did have some. I want to feel every damn inch as I slide inside her. I want to watch her eyes widen at that first stretch as I take her.

"You'll be safe if you say yes. Are you on birth control?"

"The pill," she answers, studying me like she's confused.

"What is it?" I turn my head and kiss her leg propped up on my shoulder.

She shakes her head. "Nothing."

I run my hand up and down her leg, pressing kisses to it as I gaze down at her.

"Can we do this, Tate?"

I tap the glistening crown of my cock against her clit, loving the way her lower lip trembles in response.

"Yes," she breathes.

Thank fuck.

I hold my cock in position, pinning my eyes on hers as I feed the fat head inside her.

"Oh..." Her pupils blow wide, and her body resists me.

"You're so wet. It'll feel good in a minute. Just relax."

She gasps beneath me as I push forward, sinking inside her tight wet heat with a grunt. "So fucking good."

"That's so—"

"You feel full?" I run my tongue over my teeth and look down at her stretched around me. My cock is hard as steel and shining with her arousal at the point she's taken me up to.

"Yeah, you're big."

"I know I am. But we're almost there," I soothe.

"What?" Tate lifts her head from the pillow and looks down her body. Her eyes widen when she sees how much more of my cock she still has to take.

"You like watching?" I bite my lower lip with an appreciative moan. "Me too."

I grab a spare pillow and slide it under her ass, so it's lifted higher.

On a goddamn platter just for me.

"Fuck, you look good like this." I kiss her leg again and reach forward with both hands, grabbing her tits and squeezing them. They're round, full and fuckable. The image of sliding my cock between them makes me twitch inside her.

Tate whimpers at the movement and I take my opportunity to push the rest of the way inside her until my balls meet her skin.

"Fuck, yes." I tilt my head back to the ceiling and exhale slowly, closing my eyes to savor it.

Damn, I needed this.

I slide out and drive back inside her, keeping my head back and my eyes closed, relishing the feeling of her sucking me back in. The coiled muscles of my torso pop beneath my skin as I bottom out inside her again.

Dropping my head back down, I peel my eyes open and look at her through hooded lids. "So fucking good, Baby."

I pull back and thrust in harder making her tits bounce.

She gazes up at me as I build up a rhythm, my eyes glued to those fucking magnificent tits as they move.

But it's not enough. I want to be so deep inside her that she doesn't know where I end, and she begins.

I curl one hand around her hip and plant the other next to her head, folding her beneath me until her knees are almost touching her ears.

"This is how I've dreamed of you. Beneath me with my cock buried inside you." I pump my hips, and I steal her gasp, kissing it from her lips and swallowing it down.

I want all her whimpers, all her cries.

All her goddamn noises.

Mine.

I thrust again. The angle is deep, but I can't move fast enough. I can't do it hard enough. I need to fuck her the way my body is screaming at me to.

"Tate," I groan, kissing her again and sliding my tongue against hers. "You're fucking delicious. Now hold on."

I move back, widening my knees and pushing them into the mattress for leverage. My forearm strains as I keep a hand planted by her head, and her hip grasped inside an iron grip with the other.

Then I let her have it.

I slam into her again over and over. She can't move beneath me, except to push her tits up as her spine curls from pleasure.

"Fuck, like that," I urge. "Like fucking that, Baby. Do you know how good you feel?" I grind out, driving harder, deeper.

I thrust in and out, my cock getting covered in her slick arousal.

I grunt. "That's it, Baby. Cream my cock up for me. Why don't you come again and milk it for me, because I'm so damn close."

"Sullivan... that's..." Tate mewls as I drive my hips with force, slamming into her.

She shudders and lets out a whine.

"That's what I'm talking about," I praise as her pussy

strangles my cock like she's barely managing to take all of me stuffed so deep inside her.

I keep fucking her. Hard and deep. I hold onto her hip, sinking my fingers into her flesh so hard I know she'll have bruises.

"So, so, good," she pants.

"I knew we'd be good together," I hiss. "A body like yours was made to drive me wild. Look at it."

My gaze drops to her magnificent juicy tits, bouncing up and down her chest.

"Perfection, Baby. Just what I fucking needed."

I thrust hard again and sink my teeth into my lower lip.

"Sullivan!" Tate cries, rippling around my cock like she's trying to wring it out.

"That's it, squeeze me." I turn and nip her leg, as my balls draw tight to my body. "Come all over that cock, Baby. Give it to me."

She holds my eyes, her brows pinched together and her mouth wide open as she lets go and comes with a cry.

No... *a scream.*

It's been weeks since I've heard that kind of noise from a woman. But none have ever sounded as good as Tate's.

Euphoria floods my brain and my vision blurs as the end of my cock throbs, ready to explode.

"I'm going to come. Fuck, I'm going to come, Tate."

My ears fill with the deep relief of my groan as I release and come deep inside her.

We hold each other's gazes, pupils dilating, locked in a moment where nothing else exists. Both witnessing the other unravel and tip over into bliss, letting it take us because it's no longer under our control.

We aren't in control.

I'm not in control.

My chest tenses, and my head grows light.

Spurt after spurt spills from me inside her as I pin her in place beneath me. My vision blurs as I fight to stay focused on her eyes. She's looking up at me with so much desire. So much... *feeling*.

She wriggles in my grasp, but I tighten my hold on her hip and keep her still, the need to finish outweighing everything else.

Shadowed memories of drowning in grief flood back to me, ripping the air from my lungs.

This is what I do.

I fuck.

Needing the sweet relief it brings.

Needing to just fucking come to function.

The instinct to take what I need is suddenly overwhelming, pounding in my ears, tearing at my chest.

"Take it," I grunt.

I give her hip a firm squeeze and force out as much from my body as possible, tensing my abs and doing all I can to make sure I'm getting rid of it all.

"Fuck, Baby, that's it."

The final drops leave my body, and I shudder with a rough exhale, screwing my eyes closed.

"Sullivan..." Tate's sweet voice murmurs my name and soft, delicate hands reach up, brushing my hair back from my forehead.

I can sense the happy, trusting smile on her face without needing to see it.

Fuck.

25

TATE

MY EARS ARE RINGING FROM THE BREATH-STEALING orgasms as I wilt against the cool sheets.

Sullivan leans into my touch and I caress his hair. His eyes are closed, and I smile and admire how beautiful he is. All dark hair, and a strong jaw, like it was cut from glass. And those brilliant blue eyes that are like staring into the ocean under a midday sun.

He turns his face into my palm, kissing it with a deep sigh. But our moment is over before it has a chance to bloom. He opens his eyes, meeting mine for the briefest flash, and the pure relief on his face from moments ago is already replaced by terse lines between his pinched brows.

I wait for a kiss. A word. A rare smile from him.

Nothing.

"Daddy?" a small voice calls out.

Sullivan's eyes pop wide. "Shit!" He pulls out of me and scrabbles off the bed at breakneck speed.

"Daddy's coming, Sweetheart," he calls, yanking his pants on.

His expression is one of pure panic as he races from the room.

A moment later, his soft, loving voice carries from the hallway. "Hey, what are you doing up? Let's get you back to bed, okay?"

His voice moves further away, joined by a sweet, tired murmur from Molly.

I look around the room wondering what to do. I climb out of the bed and am gathering up my clothes when Sullivan walks back in.

"Is she okay?" I ask.

"She's fine." He scrubs a hand through his disheveled hair.

I hold my clothes in front of me, covering myself, even though he still hasn't looked directly at me.

"I didn't know what I should do—"

"You should go."

"Oh."

His shoulders are stiff, his forearms rippling with corded muscles as he keeps his gaze fixed to the floor by my feet.

"Tate," he says, his voice devoid of emotion.

My stomach rolls as the temperature in the room plummets, the atmosphere changing in an instant.

"You need to go." He sucks in a breath. "And you need to forget about what just happened."

"Are you serious?" I splutter.

I grip my clothes tighter against me and try to breathe. Try to process what he's doing right now. I'm naked in his bedroom. My body is still warm from where he was inside it moments ago.

He glances to the side, toward his bedroom door, his face cast in shadows. But I see the rigid planes of his grimace. The tightening of his jaw.

"Molly will get confused if she wakes up again and you're still here this late."

He's just concerned about Molly. Of course he is. It would be weird for her to see me in here like this.

"It's okay. I understand. I'll get dressed."

I feel his eyes on me as I pull my panties and bra back on.

"I'm sorry. Tonight was... it was a mistake," he tries to say it softly, but the edge is still there. Sharp jagged edges that slice into me like razor blades.

Regret.

"Wow..." I breathe. "It's like that... I get it."

"Tate."

"It's fine. I get it. This was a fuck. Nothing more. Shame you didn't make that clearer before we did it." I seethe.

I rush to pull my dress on and zip it up. My face burns with humiliation. If I'd known that's what this was to him, I'd have never...

Tears threaten my eyes, and I blink as fast as I can praying I can hold them back long enough to get away from him.

"Don't make this more awkward than it needs to be," he warns.

"Awkward?" I scoff. "God, you're so full of yourself."

I push past him and tear out of the door.

He spins to stride after me.

"Watch the vase!" he snaps, panic mixing with something else in his tone as I enter the living area.

But he needn't worry about his precious floors getting scratched by me stepping the broken shards into them. I'm not like him. I don't damage things for the sake of it. For my own perverse pleasure.

I sidestep the mess and reach down, swiping up my purse and shoes from where I left them.

"Tate?"

I turn. He's stopped at the end of the hallway on the other side of the living area, not even bothering to try and catch up to me.

I pull my shoes on. The two of us stare at each other across the room, broken white china strewn like shrapnel between our feet.

The aftermath of destruction.

Irreparable.

"What?" I snap.

I fight to keep my voice steady, so it doesn't betray my emotions. Doesn't show the way that humiliation and shame are coursing through me, telling me what an idiot I am.

I *will not* cry in front of him.

He stares at me like he wants to say something but won't allow himself to.

Instead, his eyes glaze over with the cool professionalism I see him use all the time when he's working. He stands there in just his suit pants with his broad chest, lightly touched by silky dark hair, on show. The chest that was heaving with exertion as he fucked me minutes ago. The chest that was grinding out husky praises and delivering groaned rasps of my name as he told me how good I felt, how much he desired me.

All lies to get what he wanted.

Warm wetness trickles down my inner thigh and I gulp down a sob.

He clears his throat.

"Cliff will take you home."

"Monumental fucking prick!" Ashley hisses.

"Can we talk about something else please?"

I wipe the counter, preparing for the early morning rush. I arrived ten minutes ago. Ashley took one look at my face and asked me what was wrong, and it all came pouring out.

How Sullivan made me feel so sexy. How he hummed my song as he made me come, like he'd been listening... *noticing*.

How he spouted off lie after lie to make me believe he actually felt something, before callously throwing me out. I would never have done it if I'd known he just wanted a one-night stand.

I'm not stupid, I didn't expect a proposal or anything. But I didn't expect to be leaving before I could even use the bathroom to clean away the mess he'd left behind.

I swallow around the thick lump in my throat. No one's ever come inside me before. And I gave that first to Sullivan Beaufort, like a pathetic idiot. All because I was caught up in the moment and he was looking at me like I was... *like it meant something*.

Everything felt so real.

I'm so stupid.

"He's early today. Let's pray it's his conscience keeping him up all night. Bastard," Ashley snarls as the familiar black town car pulls up outside.

My stomach's in my feet as Cliff exits and holds the rear door open. Sullivan appears, all black suit, crisp white shirt, and dark hair shining in the morning light. He's a devil in disguise. All those harsh edges clothed in the finest fabrics, looking like a wet dream. But I've seen beneath the flashy exterior now. And nothing about it is pretty.

Sullivan's cool blue eyes pierce through the glass window and across the room like he's only inches away. I stare back, unable to breathe as he locks eyes with me.

"If the jerk comes in here, he better be prepared," Ashley says.

He strides toward the door like he's on a mission, his eyes penetrating mine and rendering me unable to move. I suck in a deep breath, preparing to give him hell. Fighting the memory of those eyes holding mine as he towered over me and made me come harder than I ever have. Those same eyes that flared with molten desire as he came inside me, filling me so deeply that I still have part of him inside me now.

I hate him.

Stepping forward, I curl my hands into fists against the countertop. But Sullivan's gaze breaks away and he pulls his phone from his jacket pocket and looks at the screen.

Then he pivots, storming toward next door without looking back.

"Oh no, he didn't! He doesn't get to ignore you." Ashley tugs the cloth from my hand that I've got in a death grip. "Go tell that asshole you aren't going to be treated like this."

"I will," I agree, my resolve strengthening.

I've thought about nothing else since Cliff took me home last night. I can't work for Sullivan anymore. Not after what happened. And as angry as I am at him for how he's made me feel, I'm angriest for Molly. For how he's let his own selfish actions affect her. She's the one who will suffer most in all of this. She isn't going to understand why I suddenly stopped coming over.

The thought hurts me more than anything Sullivan can possibly do to me.

I rip my apron off and toss it on the counter.

"I won't be long."

"Give him hell, girl," Ashley says.

I storm next door, painting a polite smile on my face as the security officer inside the store lets me inside with a smile. The staff recognize me now. Sullivan even gave me a staff ID, one with a better picture on it than Cara took.

Riding the staff elevator up to his level, I take slow, deep breaths to calm my racing heart. I need to say what I've come to, then I'm walking out of here with my head held high.

Cara's handbag is on her empty desk as I stomp past. But there's no sign of her or any other staff.

Sullivan's office door is closed, and the blinds are shut. I don't knock. The bastard's lucky I don't boot the door down as way of an entrance.

He's sitting, leaning over his desk, one hand over his mouth, the other holding his cell phone to his ear. His eyes are red-rimmed and glassy.

I stall on the threshold as his throat contracts with a strained swallow and he ends his call without saying a word to the person on the other end.

"What's wrong?" My voice comes out far too soft. Far too caring. But the ashen color of his face suggests whatever the call was, it was bad news.

"Nothing." He blinks, his expression morphing back into his usual terse one with practiced ease.

I stare at him for a beat. He's lying. I shouldn't be surprised. It seems that's all he does.

"You're here to discuss last night, I presume?" he says smoothly, slipping into business mode like I'm nothing more than a client he needs to manage.

"I'm here to hand in my resignation."

That gets his attention.

"No."

So simple. So confident. Like he has control.

"Yes."

"No," he snarls.

"Yes!" I step inside his office. "Do you seriously expect me to work for you after you used me like that? You don't respect me—"

"I do."

I snort. "You don't. You don't care about my feelings—"

"I do." His voice is so deep, so sure of himself.

So fucking arrogant.

"Stop talking!" I snap. "You're a liar! You wouldn't throw me out like trash if any of that were true. At least admit it.

You're nothing but a selfish jerk with charm. And I fell for it."

He stares at me, his nostrils flaring as he flattens his hands on top of his desk like he's fighting to remain calm. "I'm sorry, Tate."

I walk over to his desk, wanting to make him see what a terrible bullshitter he is, show him I can see right through him.

It all happens so fast. I'm not paying attention, too intent on glaring at him. I slam my hands down on his desk and bring one straight down on top of a letter opener, catching it at an awkward angle.

"Shit!" I yelp as white-hot fire races up my arm.

My finger throbs, bright red blood dripping from it and dropping onto the desk.

"Jesus!" Sullivan barks.

He flies out of his chair. His eyes widen as more blood runs down my finger and onto my hand.

He jabs the desk phone. "Cara! Call an ambulance!" he barks before rounding the desk. "It's okay. I've got you, Baby."

With one giant sweep of his arm, he sends everything on his desk crashing to the floor, then lifts me up to sit on top of it.

"Tate," he hisses, taking my hand between his and surveying the bleeding cut. "Fuck."

He lifts my finger to his mouth and slides it past his lips, sucking it gently. His warm tongue swirls over it, cleaning off the blood, before holding it inside his mouth.

"What are you doing? It's just a cut."

He pulls my finger out, grunting something, before sliding it back in and against his tongue again. He yanks his tie free, then slides my finger out again so he can wrap the silver silk around it.

"What's happened?" Cara appears in the open doorway,

her eyes bouncing off the mess on the floor before locking onto us.

Sullivan doesn't look her way. His attention is fixed on wrapping my finger with his tie.

"Miss Miller cut herself. She's a hemophiliac. Where's the damn ambulance?"

"I'll go and call it."

"You haven't fucking called it?" Sullivan roars, snapping his face toward her.

She withers under his death glare. "I didn't know. I came to see what was happ—"

"You're fired!" he snaps. "Get your stuff and get the hell out."

"Sullivan," I say.

He sucks in a deep breath through his nose, his jaw so tense that his teeth are probably being ground away to nothing.

"It's okay," I say, placing my uninjured hand to his cheek and turning his face to mine.

Wild, panicked blue eyes meet mine.

"I'm not a hemophiliac. And it's just a cut. See?"

I unwrap the silver silk from my finger and show him my finger. It's bloodied, but the flow is already easing, showing just a small cut on the tip.

He puffs out a ragged breath, studying my finger with a frown. His lower lip has a smudge of blood on it.

"I saw your medication when it fell out of your bag."

"It was my father's."

Sullivan flicks his attention toward a sniveling Cara.

"You can go, Cara. We'll discuss this later."

She flees, and as awful as she's been to me, I feel sorry for her. Being on the receiving end of Sullivan's wrath is not a place I'd wish upon anyone.

"Your father?" he asks, holding his tie back against my finger to stem the remaining bleeding.

"Yes. It's why he lost his job at the engineering firm. He got injured and almost died. They fired him saying he was unfit to perform his job. I hired him a lawyer. He's fighting it."

"You paid for a lawyer yourself?"

"Yes."

He blows out a breath. "Jesus, Tate. You should have told me. I'd have helped you."

"What?"

"I'd have helped you," he repeats. "Got him the best lawyer. Torn his old company to shreds, if that's what you wanted."

I stare at him.

I came in here because of the way he treated me last night. That hasn't suddenly been made all better because he got concerned over a cut and is talking like this.

"It's not your problem."

"It's affecting you, so it is my problem," he all but growls.

"What the hell's that supposed to mean?"

He's going to give me whiplash, acting like he did last night, then going wild with concern this morning, and saying things like this.

"Keep it there," he instructs, ignoring me and placing my hand over his tie on my finger.

He walks over to a cabinet and opens a drawer, coming back with a first aid kit. He places it on the desk and opens it.

"Let me see," he instructs softly.

I remove his tie and hold my finger up. His brow furrows and he curses quietly like the sight of the small cut upsets him as he inspects it.

"It won't need stitches. It's not that deep," he says.

"I know."

He arches a brow at me, his eyes meeting mine momentarily, before he gets an antiseptic wipe and takes his time cleaning the cut. Once he's done he unwraps a band-aid and secures it on my skin.

"Teddy bears?"

His eyes flick to mine, the grim line of his mouth softening as he packs the kit away.

"They're Molly's. And they're explorer bears."

I scan his profile, before looking back at the band-aid. The tiny bears are wearing clothes and carrying compasses.

"Uh-huh," I murmur.

Sullivan's jaw clenches and he clears his throat. "I'm sorry about last night. I've never... no one's ever been at the house with me like that since Molly came along."

Something about his tone and difficulty in getting the words out makes me believe he's being honest.

"And I'd have understood if that's what you told me. But you didn't. You threw me out afterward, saying it meant nothing."

I turn away, pretending to look around his office, instead of at him. I came here to give him a piece of my mind. Yet here I am again, weakening the moment he's nice to me. So desperate to cling onto something that isn't there. To believe the glimpses of the man I thought he is, are real.

They aren't.

I slide off his desk. Coming here was pointless. It's time to walk out and not look back.

"I made a mistake. It meant everything," he says to my back.

I freeze halfway across the room at his choked confession.

"Tate," he urges. "Look at me."

If I do as he asks, that could be it. I'll be sucked into his gaze, never to return.

He exhales slowly when I don't turn around.

"Molly's mother is an addict who left her on my doorstep in a peaches delivery box. A fucking box, Tate."

I move slowly, braving a glance at him over my shoulder first. He's standing in front of his desk, the room around him chaos where he threw everything off his desk to help me.

His eyes have an emotional sheen to them I've never seen before.

"She was three months old. And it's been just me and her ever since."

"I thought Claudia—"

"She's not Molly's mother. We were engaged. And that ended the night Molly came into my life."

"She didn't want to stick around?" I turn to face him, my heart clenching at the way his entire body seems to have lost its fight.

"She wasn't sure."

"But now she is? Is that why she came back?"

His face hardens. "It doesn't matter. I don't give second chances where my daughter is concerned."

I stare at him, unsure where this sudden barrage of openness has come from.

"Molly isn't baggage, Tate. I won't have her being seen as a catch to being with me. She's everything to me. She's the reason I'm still here. After my brother, I—"

"You wondered how you'd keep going," I say.

He nods. "You understand."

"After my mother died I knew my father needed someone to make sure he was careful. Make sure he took his medication. His need for me stopped my grief from taking everything from me." I give Sullivan a weak smile.

He walks over to me slowly, like he's concerned I might still run out.

"I should never have treated you like I did last night. I panicked when Molly woke up."

I look into his open gaze. "I don't know whether to believe you or not."

His eyes pinch and he presses his lips together as his eyes roam over my face. "I've given you no reason to trust me. But I'm telling you the truth. I wanted last night to happen. I wanted you. And even though forgetting it would be easier; I know I can't do that. I don't *want* to do that. Not if it means you walking out of here and never coming back. There's something between us. You can't deny it. Not after how we were together last night. You can't fake that kind of connection."

He takes my hands, lifting them to his lips.

Warm breath skates over my fingertips as he gently kisses the teddy bear Band-Aid.

"I can't let you walk out of here hating me."

My throat's too dry to speak easily, so it comes out as an uneven whisper.

"I don't hate you."

"Thank you—"

"I did twenty minutes ago."

Sullivan's mouth softens. "I hated myself twenty minutes ago too."

"And now?"

He brings my finger to his lips again.

"That depends on whether you'll let me make it up to you."

His eyes warm as he runs the tip of his nose down my fingers and presses a soft kiss into my palm.

"Keep talking."

26

SULLIVAN

"Two dozen," I clip. "Thank you."

Cara hovers in the doorway and I wave her in as I end the call.

"I'm sorry about earlier," she starts. "I came to check what the emergency was and—"

"It's fine. But regardless, I've called the agency and they're reassigning you."

Her face falls. "I thought my work was good."

"There's nothing wrong with your work. It's your attitude about certain things I have an issue with."

"The waitress?" She scoffs.

I stretch my fingers against my suit pants as I lean back in my chair, composing myself.

"Miss Miller, *Tate*," I roll her name off my tongue, "is important to me. So I suggest you watch your tone if you'd prefer I don't inform the agency of my concerns regarding your work ethic."

"You just said there's nothing wrong with my work," she argues.

I sigh.

"Do you suggest embarking on physical relationships with all of the CEOs you're assigned to?"

Her face pales. "What?"

I wave a hand in the air. "It doesn't matter. If they want to take you up on your offer, that's up to them. But that was never going to happen with me. Now, please pack up your things. Your replacement is on their way."

The air is heavy and thick.

"You're a jerk," she hisses.

My attention is already on my emails as I scroll through the new ones.

"Maybe if I'd offered on a Thursday, you'd have taken me to The Lanceford, and we'd be having a different conversation entirely."

There's a cold smile on her face as I flick my eyes up to her.

"I don't think so, Cara. And seeing as you know so much about my personal life, perhaps you'd like to update your notes. I haven't set foot in The Lanceford since meeting Miss Miller. Because she—" I pause for effect. "Is the epitome of a woman whom I would do whatever it took to get a moment of her time, *any* day of the week."

Natasha: Peaches is my daughter. You can't stop me from seeing her.

I rub at my temples with one hand, pocketing my phone with the other. Natasha's demands are becoming more frequent.

She's a problem that I don't have the energy to fucking deal with right now.

"Everything okay, Son?"

I drop my hand to my thigh, holding back a curse.

"Fine."

My father's eyes narrow and he studies me. He knows me better than anyone. But any concerns he might have are shoved aside as Uncle Mal slams his hand on the table.

"What the hell does he think he's doing?" he rages. "Leaving notes on Elaina's grave... ambushing Sinclair like that?"

My sister's head swivels in our direction at his outburst from across the room where she's sitting coloring with Molly and Halliday. It's early and Seasons isn't open yet. My father called us all here for a meeting to discuss the latest updates with Neil, my mother's ex-lover, being in New York.

The man is either brave or stupid if he thinks coming here and approaching Sinclair was a good idea. Denver had his gun trained on him, prepared to blow his brains out if it had come to that.

But it didn't.

Neil says he has questions. He claims he saw a man walking away from the yacht before the fire took over and caused the explosion that killed them both.

He followed my mother that day to ask her to leave my father. I don't believe a word out of the asshole's mouth knowing that. This could all be a cruel lie to mess with our family.

They're both dead. Nothing will bring them back.

"We don't trust a word he says without evidence," my father says, lowering his voice.

"We'll get on it, Boss," Denver says. "And we'll pay Neil a visit tonight. See if there's anything else we can *squeeze* out of him."

Killian and Jenson nod in agreement beside him.

"I'm coming," I add, meeting Denver's eyes.

He holds mine, understanding passing between us. If this

fucker is messing with my family. It means he's going to have to answer to all of us.

"Me too." Uncle Mal seethes. "I want to know what the asshole thinks he's doing. Visiting my sister's grave."

He drops his head into his hands, pushing his fingers through his thinning dyed blond hair. We've all had to live with the aftermath of that day. But Uncle Mal is the one who wears his grief more obviously in the weathered lines on his face, and the deep hollow shadows around his eyes.

It fucking ruined us all.

"Denver," my father says, leaning back in his chair with a weighted sigh. "Stay with Sinclair tonight. She's shaken. Let the boys handle this. If Neil gives us anything useful, then you can pay him a visit yourself, okay?"

Denver's shoulders bunch as he rests his forearms on his thighs and cracks his knuckles. "Yes, Boss."

His eyes flick to my sister across the room and I almost feel sorry for the poor guy. She's made no secret of the fact she doesn't like him. And they've been stuck together for weeks while he acts as her bodyguard.

"You sure everything's okay? Fabienne still trying to give you grief?" my father asks as the other men stand and disperse.

"When are they not?" I snort. "But now that we own them, they can't do a lot about it. I've got a team dismantling their operations as we speak. Any employees who might be valuable to Beaufort Diamonds will be given the opportunity to prove themselves. The rest will be getting their severance checks in the mail."

"Another opponent gone," my father muses with a chuckle. "You're more ruthless as CEO than I was, Son. I'm proud of you." He squeezes my knee.

"Culling the competition is therapeutic," I reply, looking over at Molly as my mind flicks to Natasha. If she were a company, I'd have dealt with her by now. She'd be a distant memory. But money doesn't solve issues with her, it just creates more.

"Speaking of things that are good for us." My father follows my gaze, only his settles on Halliday. His eyes soften, the love he has for her rolling off him in waves. "The girls were talking about arranging Hallie's bachelorette. They want it in London so her friend over there can join them."

"Sounds good," I reply, my chest tightening with realization from the way he can't take his eyes off Halliday.

I'm envious of my own father.

He's found love after loss. He's opened himself up to possibilities.

"How are things working out with finding Molly a nanny?"

"There's... a suitable candidate. But it's early days. Molly's still getting to know her."

"You mean you're still analyzing her every move before you let Molly out of your sight with her?" He's looking straight at me, a knowing glint in his eyes. "I get it, Son. This is Molly we're talking about. But kids need space to grow, and we have to let them."

"I hate that you're right."

He chuckles. "Call it experience. You don't get to my age and not learn a lesson or two. Including when to just be damn well grateful for what's right in front of you."

Halliday beams back when she sees him looking at her again.

He's right. I need to learn how to relax when it comes to Molly's care. The thought of my overprotectiveness hindering her in any way makes me want to tear the world in two.

I just don't know how to start.

27

TATE

"THEY'RE PAPER?" I EXCLAIM, TAKING THE GIANT bouquet from Sullivan.

He stands beside his car, hands pushed casually into his pant pockets as he regards me carefully, gauging my reaction to the roses.

"And they're made from music sheets." I touch a petal, gently peeling it back so I can read it. "This is the song you were playing the night we—"

"The night we?" He arches a brow, and I shake my head, heat pinching at my cheeks.

"The other night," I finish, checking another flower. "Are these... can you play all of them?"

"By memory."

"Wow."

I sneak a look at him and he's watching me intently.

"Do you like them?"

"Are you kidding? I love them! No one's ever given me something like this before."

If I didn't know better, I'd say his shoulders loosen in relief. But this is Sullivan Beaufort. Nothing flusters him.

"They're one way of showing you I meant it when I said I wish to make it up to you."

He gestures inside the backseat of the car, holding the door open for me. Cliff is sitting in the driver's seat, and I smile at the fact Sullivan must have insisted on greeting me after work and opening the door for me himself.

I hand the paper roses to Sullivan so that I can climb inside.

"Hi Cliff," I greet. "Oh, and hello, little rabbit."

Molly grins from her car seat before I hold my arms out and take the flowers that Sullivan passes back to me.

He's climbing in through the opposite door and into the backseat as I bop the ears on Molly's onesie.

"I like this one. I think it's my favorite," I tell her.

Her little face turns serious, and she nods. "It a nice one."

The way she takes her time over the word 'nice', making sure to pronounce it properly makes my heart melt. I've missed her this past couple of days.

Sullivan's blue eyes capture mine over the top of the cream furry ears, and they crease at the corners as he listens to Molly.

I've missed *him* too.

Ashley wasn't sure when I told her I was giving working for him another go. She said I should make him grovel until his knees bleed. But I don't need fancy displays of him pouring his heart out to me.

I just want his honesty.

And the wild look in his eyes as he threw the contents of his desk off so he could help me when I hurt myself told me a lot more than extravagant gifts could.

He cares.

He even sucked my wound without a thought, getting my blood in his mouth. But seeing the edge of despair that was entwined with his actions pained me a billion times more than any cut could.

He was scared.

The way he yelled for the ambulance... I hate that something about that situation stirred up memories for him. Memories of people getting hurt. Memories of not having control.

I drop my attention back to the bouquet, smiling as I search through the petals, discovering note after note of beautiful, classical tunes.

This is Sullivan's way of sharing a part of himself with me without actually needing to speak.

Maybe he finds words hard.

But these roses are something I am more than willing to listen to.

"You got a new sofa?" I say to Molly as I hold her hand and walk inside their home the following evening.

Last night I played with her while Sullivan worked. After, he made dinner for the three of us. That in itself was a surprise. But then I saw he made lasagna, one of my favorite dishes, which I'm sure I told Molly about once while he was busy working across the room.

Joan is back at work now. But Sullivan asked if I minded if he gave her the afternoons off when I'm helping with Molly. He said he likes that Molly gets to learn how to cook with me. Although last night it was him showing her how to layer the pasta sheets and spreading the sauce in-between.

I just got to sit and enjoy watching them.

My eyes slide over the new giant gray sectional sofa. Something else new. Yesterday it was a sculpture of a musical cleft, occupying the space on the table where the broken vase used to be. Today it's a new sofa, even though their last one looked like new.

Molly runs over to the new sofa and climbs onto it.

"Did you feel like a change?" I ask Sullivan as he walks in behind us both, loosening his tie and undoing the top button of his shirt.

He swallows, making the five o'clock shadow dusting his throat move against his collar.

"The old one was itchy."

I frown. His old sofa was beautiful. And comfy.

"But it was velvet."

He shrugs. "I didn't like it."

Pulling something from his pocket, he walks over to me.

"Memorize this number, then throw this away." He hands me a piece of paper with eight digits on it.

"What is it?"

"The alarm code. Now, come over here."

He's walked over to the security panel and is tapping something into it.

"Tate?" He looks back at me, hitching a brow.

I move to join him. "I don't understand."

"Thumb?"

He takes my hand when I don't move. His brows flatten and he pauses, studying my fingertip that's healing well enough. A quiet grumble leaves his throat, like the sight of the damaged skin bothers him. Then he gently places my thumb against the screen on the panel.

"What are you doing?"

"Scanning your thumbprint." He's focused on the lit-up panel as he keeps my hand held in place.

"Why?"

"Because that's how you'll gain access through the front door and to our level in the elevator."

"But I'm always with you and Molly. Why would I need to be added?"

"There might be an occasion where I need you and Molly to come home ahead of me. Or I might require you to come and collect something for Molly without me. There are any number of reasons I might want you here, Tate," Sullivan says, his face the picture of intent concentration as he completes my security set-up on the panel.

"Sure, that makes sense."

My stomach does a tiny victory leap. This must be huge for him. He watches me like a hawk when I'm with Molly. He doesn't even leave the room. Even if he never asks me to use the scanner, the act of him adding me speaks volumes alone.

Ashley is going to flip out when I tell her.

"Do you have much work to do?" I ask once he's finished.

"I always have work to do." He exhales, meeting my eyes. "But no, it can wait."

"Oh... okay. Should I get started on dinner, then?"

I look at him, growing hot under his intense gaze. He hasn't mentioned our night together once in the past two days. I thought perhaps he's changed his mind and decided me coming back to work for him would be where he drew the line. That we should only have a professional relationship.

That would be the sensible thing to do. The wise decision.

He was nothing but a gentleman last night. Working when we came in, while I played with Molly, until he declared he wished to make dinner for us all. I expected him to need to work tonight too. Otherwise, why am I here?

"I thought..." His eyes drop to my lips, and he runs his tongue along his own, the move so sexy that I can't not stare. "Perhaps you'd like to bathe Molly with me first?"

"Really?" I snap out of my trance. "You want me to help?"

His eyes glitter. "I do. But be warned, she likes to splash."

The smile remains glued to my face while I run the bath in

Molly's bathroom. He's never asked me to help with bathtime before.

Sullivan helps Molly undress by pretending to be a tummy-loving monster whose sole purpose is to deliver noisy, wet raspberries to unguarded tummies. Her high-pitched squeals of delight as he presses one after another to her little round belly make my heart feel like it's about to fly out of my chest. It's hard to believe the same ruthless, suited billionaire is the same doting father who is now kneeling on the bathroom floor in designer suit pants, and a shirt rolled up to his elbows.

He drops his hand past all of the bubbles and tests the water temperature, before depositing a still giggling Molly in.

"Toys, Daddy!"

"How could I forget?" He winks at her and reaches for a plastic tub on the floor.

"This one?" he asks, tossing a little yellow duck in so it disappears underneath the bubbles.

Molly giggles and pushes her hands through the foam to search for it, sending water sloshing up the sides of the bath.

"Or did you mean this one?" He sends a small plastic monkey somersaulting through the air and into the water.

Molly laughs with all the unbridled joy of an almost three-year-old as toy after toy are sent sailing into the water in a succession of splashes and plops.

"Daddy!" she shrieks, like she's telling him off.

"Sorry, Sweetheart," he says. "Too many? Hold on, I'll take some out."

Sullivan bends over the side of the tub and sticks his head in the bubbles and swivels his head side to side like he's searching out the submerged toys.

Molly's laugh erupts into more belly shaking as he lifts his face and it's completely covered in bubbles.

He blows out through his mouth, sending a shot of white foam up into the air.

Molly swipes at his face with a tiny hand, displacing enough bubbles that he can see out of one eye. "Daddy!"

"A towel, if you'd be so kind please, Tate?" he says, holding out a hand behind him.

I laugh and grab one, pressing it into his palm. He moves it to his face like he's about to wipe himself, then stops.

"Just one kiss first," he declares.

Molly pushes at his face with a toothy grin, obviously having played this game before. I lean one elbow on the side of the tub as I watch her tip her head back with a gurgling laugh as he presses kiss after kiss to her neck and face, covering her in bubbles too.

A sweet and fuzzy feeling soaks through my body like a warm tide as I'm allowed to witness the moment between them, and the special bond they have.

Sullivan wipes Molly's face for her before he does his own. Then he sets about expertly washing her dark curls for her as she sits happily.

I reach beneath the water and feel around.

"It's like a treasure trove down here," I exclaim, widening my eyes at Molly, which makes her grin.

I pull up the first thing—a small mermaid.

"Pretty," Molly comments, fishing around, then brandishing her own discovery of a small frog playing a guitar.

"Ooh, and a talented musician," I say, looking at the green toy.

"Pretty and talented," Sullivan muses, his voice a deep husk that has me lifting my eyes to him.

He's watching me, his dark hair curled a little around the front where it's wet. A small patch of bubbles is still clinging to the top of his dark chest hair beneath his unbuttoned shirt.

"Very pretty and talented," he repeats.

28

TATE

A FUN AND SPLASHY BATHTIME IS FOLLOWED BY Sullivan insisting on making dinner for us all again. Molly's not even finished her dessert before the first of many yawns begin.

"She's had a busy couple of days. Swimming with Halliday, chasing Monty around," he says, reaching over to stroke her head. "Haven't you, Sweetheart?"

Molly stays quiet, confirmation in itself that she's ready to pass out.

"I'm going to take her to bed," Sullivan says, rising from his seat at the island, before lifting her out of hers. "Stay until I'm back?"

"Sure. Good night, Molly." I blow her a kiss, earning myself a sleepy smile over Sullivan's shoulder as he carries her from the room.

Sullivan didn't need to ask, it's become our routine that I always stay, at least until Molly's asleep, just in case he gets a work call and needs me to take over. Not that he ever has. Storytime with Molly is something he's reluctant to hand over to me. It's his special time with her and he wants to protect that. Something about that makes me like him even more.

Everything he does with Molly seems to make me like him more.

"Oh God. This could be a really bad idea," I murmur as I tidy up alone, waiting for him to return.

I load the dishwasher, then wander over to the piano, running my hand along it and admiring the photo of him and Molly on top of it.

"Sinclair put it there."

I look up as he re-enters the room. He wasn't gone long; Molly must have gone straight to sleep.

"You don't have many photos," I say, more a question than an observation.

"I know." He walks over and looks at the photograph. "After they died I took a lot down. Seeing them every day made it harder. But maybe it's time I put some up again."

"Maybe," I agree.

I don't think I'd ever be able to take the photograph of my mother down from my bedside cabinet. I love seeing her smile every day, as a reminder that I had her once. But we all deal with grief in different ways, and I can't judge Sullivan for what he's needed to do in order to cope with his.

He clears his throat. "You know my mother was having an affair before she died? With her childhood love."

I don't say anything to confirm I already knew. He doesn't need reminding that one Google search of his name, and all of his family's tragic past comes up for the world to read about.

"The guy came back to New York recently. I paid him a visit with my uncle and a couple of our security team."

"You did?"

His profile is rigid as he keeps his attention fixed on the photograph and my gut twists at what that could mean.

"I didn't hurt him, Tate. But I damn well wanted to."

I breathe in and let it out slowly, the knots in my gut loosening in relief that he hasn't put himself in danger of legal repercussions because of this man.

"That must have been tough. Seeing him."

"It was. I hate him for what he did to my father. He didn't find out about their affair until after she was gone. He's lived with questions ever since. One's he can never get answers to. And then this guy walks back into our lives more than two years later and churns everything up again with some flimsy story he's concocted about their deaths. All just lies with no proof. That much was obvious when we paid him a visit. I think he just wanted to cause us all pain again out of bitterness that she was never going to leave my father for him."

"I'm sorry."

Sullivan's eyes pinch at the corners, and he inhales slowly before tipping his head back and blowing out a deep sigh toward the ceiling. "Thanks, Tate."

"Is there anything I can do?"

The question is pointless, I know it is. I can't possibly have anything to offer, other than listening if Sullivan wishes to talk to me.

He lowers his head, his gaze capturing mine, and runs his tongue over his teeth like he's contemplating whatever it is he's thinking about saying.

"Go on," I encourage.

His attention drops over my uniform, roaming over my hips and breasts.

"You could let me kiss you again."

"You want to kiss me?"

"More than anything."

I twist my head to one side and study him with a smile. "You ask so nicely, yet in business I know you're a man who takes what he wants."

He steps closer. "That's business."

"So what's this?" I slowly wave my finger between our chests.

His gaze heats as he looks down at me. "This is me spending time with the woman I can't stop thinking about... You know I can't stop, right?" He hitches one of those sinful brows.

I search his eyes, wanting to dive into them and swim alongside every sexy husked word that leaves his lips. But a niggling part of me is still reluctant.

"Why? I'm—"

"Magnificent," he breathes, reaching up and taking hold of my chin gently, tilting it so I have to maintain eye contact with him and can't shy away.

I wet my lips. "That's a very specific word."

His eyes narrow with intensity. "I feel a very specific way around you."

He mirrors my movements, wetting his own lips slowly as he runs the pad of his thumb along my lower one.

"You don't care who I am. You stand up to me when I'm an asshole. And you're gentle and sweet when I'm not." He dips his thumb inside my parted lips, just a fraction, so it grazes the tip of my tongue. "You treat my daughter like she's precious."

"She is," I breathe.

"I know." He smiles softly and I'm blindsided by how rare and beautiful he looks when he lets his guard down.

"It's the first thing I noticed about you. Not your hair." He tucks a strand behind my ear. "Not your eyes. Not your..." His gaze rolls down my body, drinking in my cleavage. "... not your... that's a lie. I noticed your curves in that tight little uniform, how could I not?"

His lips curl into a hint of a smirk as a small laugh dances past my lips.

"But I only *noticed*. The way you spoke to Molly when

you dusted that rabbit onto her drink, that's when I *looked*. *Really damn looked.*"

A tingle runs up my spine.

"You're so natural with her. So genuine. I didn't want to look, Tate. But I couldn't tear my eyes away, even if that meant..."

"Meant?" I inhale slowly as he cups my face.

"Meant letting you get close to Molly... close to *me*."

"It's natural for a father to be protective, Sullivan."

His eyes pinch. "She saved me. She's my reason for everything."

"I understand."

"And that's another reason I can't stop looking at you..." He dips his head and his breath fans over my lips. "Now, *please*, let me fucking kiss you."

My core clenches at the deep groan of relief that leaves Sullivan's throat when I nod my agreement. But before he can slant his lips over mine, I rise up and press mine to his, loving the way he sucks in a surprised breath as we connect.

Our kiss starts off slow and sensual, full of unspoken promises and teases of what's to come.

I reach up and wrap my arms around his neck, inhaling the scent of his aftershave on warm skin. It's a scent I know I'll recognize anywhere for the rest of my life. One that's so uniquely him—a confident sexy man who knows how to turn me inside out with pleasure.

"Tate," he murmurs into my mouth, making my core clench with need. "*Baby*..."

That single word is husky and rough, weighted with desire and pure carnal need. And I know from now on I'll melt whenever he calls me it.

He sinks into me, angling my face in his hands so he can kiss me deeply, taking his time to slide his tongue against mine until I'm practically panting into his mouth. His erection digs into my stomach, and I grind against it.

"Fuck, yeah," he hisses, teasing my lower lip between his teeth.

He kisses me again, then pulls away with a groan, creating a gap between our bodies. His lids hood as he looks down at me.

"Sit on the stool."

I glance at the piano stool. "That one?"

"There's only one stool here, Tate," he rasps, hitching a brow. "Sit. On. It."

I perch on the cool buttoned leather cushion and look at him as he tilts my chin up and leans down to press a lingering kiss to my mouth.

"I've been dreaming of having you sit here while I make you come," he says darkly.

He drops to the floor and slides my skirt up my thighs.

"Lift," he instructs.

I glance toward the hallway where Molly's bedroom is. "Sull—"

"I turned the monitor on. I'll know if she gets out of bed."

He hooks his thumbs underneath the edges of my panties.

I lift my hips for him, allowing him to slide the black lace all the way down my legs. He holds the fabric up to his face, and my wetness gleams on it.

My breath hitches as Sullivan extends his tongue and licks the fabric. "Fuck, Tate. Do you have any idea..." He shakes his head, balling the fabric in his hand, and turning his attention back to me.

"Any idea what?" I breathe as he pushes my skirt higher, exposing my pussy.

He presses a kiss directly to it and pauses to inhale before pressing another, longer one against me.

I whimper and part my thighs wider, needing to feel him closer.

"Any idea what you do to me?" he rasps, shoving my skirt so high that it bunches around my waist.

He slips his hands around my knees and yanks me forward on the stool.

"Wider," he growls. "Wide enough that I can taste your cunt the way I need to."

His words send a shot of molten heat hurtling through my veins, and I part my legs as far as I can, leaning against the piano for support.

"Fuck," Sullivan groans as he pushes his head between my legs and licks me from my asshole to my clit.

I cry out and grab his hair. My back hits the piano keys and a deep crash of notes blare out.

"Open those eyes, Tate. You're going to watch this."

I peel open my heavy lids and look at him on his knees at my feet. His blue eyes spark as he holds my eyes and eats me out with rich groans, sliding his tongue over me, kissing me, and lapping up each new wave of wetness that my body creates.

He's making me so insanely wet that my cheeks heat with embarrassment.

He grips my thighs and holds them wide, massaging the sensitive skin with his thumbs.

"Don't you dare hold back," he groans. "I want you to drown me in it."

He sucks on my clit and slides two fingers inside me, curling them toward my G-spot.

I cry out, corkscrewing his hair and making him grunt.

Wet sounds echo between us as my body greedily sucks him in, his arm flexing with each thrust as he finger-fucks me until I'm gasping.

"That's it, Baby." He tongues my clit and squeezes the flesh on my thigh with one hand.

He groans against my soaked flesh, pushing his whole face into me and twisting it side to side as he eats me out savagely, pushing me right to my limit.

Any concerns I had over them once being referred to as 'thunder thighs' vanish as Sullivan looks at me like he's a man on the edge, barely holding back from throwing me to the ground and fucking me into next year.

As if reading my thoughts, he holds my eyes and growls, "I always loved a good storm, Baby."

I come in a sudden rush, my cry a breathy squeal as my body spasms around his fingers and a new surge of wetness spills over them.

"Fuck, so pretty when you come."

I can't control my expression. My forehead is bunched up tight, my mouth working out gasp after gasp, and my eyes... they're held in place by a devilish blue gaze full of filthy intent.

"Sullivan," I gasp, my lungs clawing in deep breaths in order to cope with the blinding pleasure that's taken me out like a bat to the knees. "Oh my God, Sullivan."

Notes wring out from the piano as I grip onto his hair and keep coming around his fingers. I can't stop. It's like one orgasm has been pushed into another, then another.

"Look at you," Sullivan groans. "Fucking look at you."

I jerk and fall into another ripple of needy clenches around his fingers before my orgasms begin to subside.

Sullivan keeps kissing me leisurely, over and over, murmuring about how good I taste as I catch my breath.

"That was..." I pant.

"Can you take a bit more?" His eyes swim with lust as he tongues my clit again, making a soft whimper fall from my lips.

"Y-yes."

He slides his fingers from inside me, holding my eyes as he sucks them clean. My legs tremble, and he holds out a hand, helping me to my feet. He kisses me without warning, scrunching up a handful of my hair as he pulls me close and groans softly, filling my mouth with my own taste.

"So delicious," he rasps, letting his lips linger over mine for a beat.

I curl my fingers around his as he leads me to the new sofa and turns to face me, pulling me into another heady kiss.

The sound of his belt buckle and zipper being undone has my thighs clenching in anticipation.

"So damn sexy," he growls, kissing me again before dropping to the sofa and pulling me down to straddle him.

"I love your curves." He runs his hands up my thighs and grips my hips, circling me over the straining dick that's fighting to get out of his pants.

I bite my lower lip at how big and hard he is.

He tips his head back against the cushion, his dark gaze intent on me as I reach between us and push his pants down out of the way, freeing his cock. I rub myself up and down it, smearing it in my wetness.

"Ride me," he whispers.

"You want me to ride you?" I whisper back, leaning in to kiss him lightly on his flushed lips, loving the way his voice has taken on a rough, pleading edge.

"Fuck, yeah. Slide down onto it, Baby."

I hold his eyes as I position the slick head of him against me. Sullivan's pupils dilate, and his teeth sink into his lower lip in a long hiss as I take every inch of him slowly, until I'm full and fluttering around him.

"Damn," he rasps.

His fingers flex on my hips, and he eases me up, then pulls me back onto him with a groan. I rest my forearms on his shoulders as we work together, rocking and grinding.

"So fucking good." He grunts, lifting his hips each time so his balls meet my skin.

"So, so good," I agree, circling down onto him, loving the way he feels filling me.

He tears open my shirt, unhooking the front fastening of my bra.

"Damn, Baby," he growls, watching my breasts spill free.

He pulls me to him, pinning himself between me and the sofa as he drags his tongue over each breast and kisses the swells of skin.

"Keep going," he groans, leaving me to take over our pace.

He cups my breasts, kneading and stroking them as his mouth slides all over them, kissing, sucking, and biting.

My nipple throbs as he sucks it, and arousal runs from me and over his cock that's buried inside me.

"Tate," he groans. "Fuck."

I grip his shoulders tighter, using them as an anchor so I can ride him harder. Each time I slide down, the coiling pressure in my core winds tighter.

"Sullivan, I'm going to come," I whimper.

"Yeah, you are. I can feel your cunt getting wetter. Let me have it, Baby."

His filthy words only make me clench harder around him.

"Good girl," he hisses as I squeeze him.

His hands drop to my ass and his lips slide up my windpipe in rough kisses as I arch up, chasing my release.

"Fuck. Let it go. Let me feel it."

I dig my nails into his shoulders as I come. It's just as hard as when I came on his mouth, but this time I have more to grip onto. My body clenches around his thick length as it slides in and out of me with growing urgency.

"I can feel you coming on me, Tate. Fuck, you make me lose my goddamn mind," Sullivan grits, his grasp moving to hold my hips with bruising force as he thrusts faster.

His entire torso stiffens and his cock swells inside me.

"Tate," he growls, coming hard.

He drags me up and down his cock, slick heat slipping all over where we join as we both succumb to our orgasms with rough need and wring out every tiny bit of pleasure we can from them.

"Jesus." Sullivan drops his head back against the sofa cushion, his grip softening on me.

I pant, trying to catch my breath as the corners of his lips curl. His dark lashes fan out over his hooded lids as he gazes at me.

"You're so beautiful," he murmurs, seeming intent to just sit and look at me.

I reach up and trace one of his dark brows with the tip of one finger.

"I could say the same about you."

"Stay," he breathes.

"What?"

He licks his lips, eyes intent on mine. And even though his gaze is soft and filled with bliss, there's a deadly seriousness beneath the surface.

"I want you in my bed all night."

"What about Molly? What if she wakes up?"

"Let me worry about that," he says.

He leans forward, capturing my lips in a soft kiss.

"Stay."

SULLIVAN

"Tate, Baby?" I press a kiss to her bare shoulder as I climb onto the bed, fully suited after my shower.

She stirs, nuzzling her head into the pillow. I lean on one elbow, admiring how damn good she looks in my bed. We only fell asleep a couple of hours ago. We spent the night wrapped up in each other, kissing, touching, tasting... coming.

I couldn't quell the raw need to be inside her. It controlled me, making sleep impossible until I'd felt her body bend and quiver to my touch, again and again.

We fucked until we lost count. Her sweet cries are still echoing in my ears.

Sliding the cover lower, I kiss a trail down her spine, pausing to run a hand over the beautiful curve of her ass. I give it a squeeze and my dick flexes in my pants against her thigh.

"You're a fiend." She peels her eyes open. "Does your designer dick not need a rest?"

"Designer dick?"

She gives me a sexy smile. "Yeah. It felt pretty good quality last night."

I sink my teeth into her ass cheek, playfully nipping it. She giggles and the sound makes my fucking chest tight with emotion. I haven't woken up with a woman in my own bed since Claudia. But that never felt like this.

I like how good this feels.

I like how *Tate* makes me feel.

"What time is it?" she murmurs sleepily, eyeing up my suit.

"Almost five thirty."

"Molly?" Her eyes widen and the fact she's concerned makes me slide up the bed and pull her mouth to mine for a slow kiss.

"She could get up any minute. That's why I woke you. I'm going to keep an eye out for her. You stay here. Take as long as you need and text me when you're ready. I'll take her to check the mail downstairs, and when we come back we can tell her you let yourself in so you could have breakfast with us."

"Okay." Tate bites her lower lip, her eyes sparkling. "Are you sure you want me to be here for breakfast, though? I'll understand if you'd rather I leave so she doesn't find anything odd."

I hold her chin and lift her mouth to mine again, giving her another slow, deep kiss.

"Text me when you're ready," I repeat, not dignifying her absurd question with an answer.

I give her one last look, drinking in her smooth feminine curves before I leave the room, closing the door behind me.

"How's your father's case progressing?" I ask Tate two days later, while she sits beside Molly, eating bagels she somehow managed to bake in the shape of curled-up dachshunds.

She's spent the last two nights at our house. I can't call it sleeping over because we hardly sleep. But despite clocking the least hours I have since Molly was a baby and woke for night feeds, I've got enough energy to run a marathon.

I reach over, taking Tate's glass and re-filling it with orange juice. Our fingers touch and she blushes. I narrow my eyes at her in amusement. How can she blush when only a few hours ago she was watching me fuck her from behind in the mirror, so hard that her tits were bouncing?

"Really good." She smiles. "They made him a settlement offer, and he was going to accept, but his lawyer said he could get him more. Dad can't believe it."

"Hmm, good." I nod, pleased that my suggestions to the engineering company her father worked for were taken onboard. Knowing the right people in this city can get you anything you want. Or at least, knowing things they don't want you to know. Like engineering firm CFO's committing tax fraud.

Tate doesn't need to know that small detail. As long as her father is happy with the outcome, then my hand in it is a mere insignificant detail.

"It's a relief that it didn't take longer. I'd have been working triple shifts if we'd had to pay the lawyer more."

She lifts her bagel and takes a bite, her gaze warming as she watches Molly stroke her own dog shaped one.

"A teacher's salary will be more though, once you get a position," I say, packing Molly some snacks into her bag, ready for a day with my father and Halliday.

"What do you mean?"

"Arabella said you're interviewing, and the barista role is just temporary."

I screw the lid on Molly's snack pot, smirking at the cartoon fruit sticker on it that Sinclair gave her. *"I'm searching for berried treasure."*

"Oh. No, that's Whitney. She does the afternoon shifts now."

"Whitney?" My grip on the pot tightens and I shove it into Molly's bag with unnecessary force as warning tingles prick up over my skin.

"Yeah. She's a kindergarten teacher. Blonde? Tall?"

Tate looks at me like I should know who she's talking about, and I vaguely recall another blonde who works there. But Arabella told me her friend's cousin is beautiful. She could have only been talking about Tate. There's no one else who's even remotely as attractive…

"Whitney's a teacher?"

"Yeah. She's lovely. The kids adore her."

I place my hands flat on the counter and suck in a deep breath, forcing myself to count to ten.

"You okay?" Tate asks, studying me. She places her bagel down as realization dawns over her. "You told me I was great at my job. You knew I was a barista, right?"

I roll my lips, choosing my words carefully. "I meant how great you are with Molly. I thought—"

"You thought I was Whitney?" She glances at Molly who's busy talking to her bagel rather than eating it. "I understand if you don't want me to watch her anymore. I'm not qualified. I'm not—"

"I don't care about some piece of paper," I bark a little too harshly. Then I look at Molly. "Sweetheart? Can you go and get Baby from your room, ready to take to Grandad's, please?"

"Okay," she replies happily.

I plant a kiss to the top of her head as I help her down from her seat.

As she leaves the room, I sit beside Tate and lower my voice, the words coming so easily I surprise myself. My father will be proud.

"I care about the smile on my daughter's face when she

sees you. I care about the way she sleeps better after spending time with you. I care about the way she comes to you if she's worried or hurts herself." I reach for her hand and entwine our fingers. "I care about the way you can give her something I can't."

I inhale deeply at Tate's puzzled expression.

"She has Sinclair and Halliday. And she loves them. I watch her blossom from their attention... just like she does with you. Only with you, it's more. Because you aren't family. Molly's chosen you all by herself."

Tate's eyes shine as she looks between me and Molly, who's walking back into the room, hugging her baby doll, preventing me from saying something else that I can't take back. Something about the way I feel. About what I care about.

Because this isn't about me.

Emotion makes my throat thicken as I step back into reality from wherever I just went that made me confess those things.

They're true. Every word.

But their weighted meaning hanging in the air and making Tate look at me like she's seeing something for the first time makes my chest tighten and my heartbeat crash loudly in my ears like storm waves over rocks.

It's always been Molly and me.

And that day I saw her left in a box, I promised myself it always would be. I read that note Natasha left, and I knew beyond doubt that everything I did from that moment on wouldn't be about me.

It would *always* be about Molly.

She comes first. Not me.

30

TATE

"YES!" I GASP.

The cool wood of the desk in Sullivan's home office is a refreshing shot to my flushed cheek as he holds me in place with a hand on the back of my neck, bent over for him as he thrusts into me from behind.

"Fuck, Baby. You just came again, didn't you?"

I whimper.

"Good girl," he groans.

The telling swell of his cock draws a happy murmur from me as his movements speed up.

"Fuck, Tate," he growls, coming hard, his fingers tightening on the back of my neck.

He thrusts a few more times, emptying all he has, before dropping his heaving body over mine and replacing his hand with tender kisses against the top of my spine.

"I can't keep my hands off you," he breathes.

"That's good, because I don't want you to."

He kisses me again, a rumble of amusement vibrating through his lips and over my skin.

This is how it's been for the past couple of weeks. I've slept here every night apart from weekends, wanting to make sure I spend time with my father. But he'd just chuckled and told me to enjoy myself with my new mystery man. He and Larry have taken to eating together and watching some new detective series together each night. So I believe him when he says he's fine with me being around less.

Only Ashley knows it's Sullivan I'm seeing. And I don't think his family knows about me, either. He's never mentioned telling them or talked about me meeting them. Perhaps I'm getting ahead of myself. It's only been a couple of weeks. But him opening up about Molly choosing me made me think maybe he saw whatever this is between us as something serious. Something with a future.

But he hasn't mentioned anything like that again since. And as wonderful as things are when we're together at his place, it stops when I step outside into the real world.

Sullivan behind closed doors is attentive and passionate.

Sullivan Beaufort in public is the ruthless billionaire whose scowl is as sharp as his specially tailored suits.

He pulls out of me, smoothing my panties into place and zipping up his pants. Molly went to bed a little while ago and Sullivan needed to finish some work in his office. I'd only come in to see if he wanted a drink.

Somehow that quickly turned into getting fucked over his desk.

I stand and slide my skirt down. Sullivan pulls me to him by a gentle hold on my hips.

"I'll be done soon." He kisses me softly. "Why don't you go and play for a bit?"

"Okay," I agree, kissing him back.

I head out into the living area and take a seat at the piano. I lose track of time as I play, working on a new song. It's only the sight of Sullivan's bare feet coming to a standstill beside the piano that alerts me to no longer being alone.

"What are those?" I grin.

"Sweatpants. I do casual." He shoves his hands into the pockets of the black pants and arches a challenging brow at me.

I run my gaze all the way up his torso, over every dip and groove of taut, muscular skin, and over the dark smattering of silky hair on his broad chest.

"You know I don't mean the sweatpants."

"No?" His gaze heats before I look back at his feet.

"Pink glitter suits you," I say, admiring his bright toenails that Barbie would envy.

"Thank you," he rumbles.

"When did she do them?"

"This afternoon, while I was on a call with the CEO of our insurance company."

I snort out a giggle. "I'm sorry I couldn't help out earlier. But Whitney got sick, and I had to cover."

"It's fine, Tate. I know you have your own life."

My own life.

Silence stretches between us. Those few words tell me more than any others could about how Sullivan sees this situation between us. That morning in his kitchen must have been a blip. Something he regrets saying out loud. He can't take it back, but he *can* act like it never happened.

I turn my eyes to the sheet of music I've been working on so I don't have to look at him.

"Tate?"

"Yeah?"

"Stand up."

I glance at him before doing as he asks. He slides onto the stool behind me and pulls me onto his lap.

"Tell me what to play," he says softly, resting his chin on my shoulder and pressing a kiss beneath my ear.

Goosebumps run up my spine at his touch and I sink into his hold, unable to stop the way my body reacts to him.

"What do you want to play?" I ask.

"Surprise me."

I bite my lower lip and picture the twelve paper roses he gave me that now live in my bedroom. He says he knows each classical piece by heart. But there are some especially difficult versions in the bouquet. Ones that even the most accomplished pianist would struggle with.

"How about..." The hairs on my arms prick to attention as his warm breath coasts over my neck with more kisses. "How about Chopin's *Etude*?"

"Hmm. Good choice." He kisses me again, sliding his long fingers onto the ivory keys.

His face stays buried in my neck, and he presses kiss after kiss to my skin, barely concentrating on what his hands are doing. Yet he hits each note with precision, playing the piece more beautifully than I've ever heard it. My heart is in my throat as I sit, entranced. When he plays the final notes, I blink away the mist threatening to take over my eyes.

"*Moonlight Sonata*," I say, naming another song from the bouquet.

He plays the second song with the same skilled ease as the first, his lips sliding up and down my neck like he can't bear to let them leave my skin.

The final notes of the song that sounded so beautiful when I heard The Masked Maestro play it in Grand Central Station ring out, just as beautiful. Like a twin echo of that night.

I slide my hands forward, over the backs of his until our fingers sandwich together.

"Will you play one more?" I ask.

I feel his smile against my neck. "For you, I'll play anything."

"Play *Unstoppable*," I whisper.

His hands tense beneath mine and he pauses.

"I don't know that one, Baby," he says, resuming his kisses.

I swallow, something pulling at my gut. He's lying. I know he is.

"You know when I went on that date with Vincent?" I ask.

Sullivan grunts. "I recall."

"Part of me went because I was curious after hearing him play the piano so beautifully at your father's club."

"You aren't the first woman to be seduced by his musical abilities, Tate," Sullivan says with a hint of amusement in his tone.

"I thought he was The Masked Maestro."

Sullivan lifts his chin from my shoulder and lets out a deep, rich chuckle that I feel in my spine. "Did you tell him that? It would make his day. I've heard of that guy. He plays excellently."

"I didn't tell him, no." I turn to look into his eyes. "I remember you telling me that *you* played excellently once."

"What are you asking me, Tate?" His blue eyes penetrate mine with the intensity that only he can create. One that makes every moment with him feel like it's significant. Like it's meaningful.

Like he sees deep inside you.

The way I'd felt listening to The Masked Maestro with Ashley that night stole my breath. I've listened to him numerous times. But something about that night was different. It was... *more*.

"Are you The Masked Maestro?" I whisper, reaching up to run the backs of my fingers down his cheekbone.

He leans into my touch, inclining his face and pressing the softest of kisses to my fingertips.

"Are you?" I breathe, my heart climbing up to my throat as I wait for him to answer.

Maybe he walked into the coffee shop that day for a reason. Maybe I chose to stencil a bunny on Molly's cup, and not a bear, or a cat, for a reason. So that I'd mention Bumper when I took her the pictures to color. So that Sullivan would look at me and question the name. So that he'd then ask me to watch Molly for him.

Maybe it was *all* meant to happen.

Because that moment in Grand Central Station when he played a song that wasn't classical for the first time, I felt something.

I felt *him*, through the music.

I was supposed to hear him play that song. I know it.

Sullivan shakes his head, holding my eyes with a heartbreaking clarity in his.

"No, Tate. I swear to you. I'm not him."

Ashley slams an espresso on the counter. "It's not vodka, but we need something strong for this. Drink."

"What?" I laugh.

"Drink." She points at the cup.

I lift it and she clinks hers against mine and then knocks it back like she's doing a shot on a night out.

"You're in love with him."

I spray the espresso out and Ashley calmly hands me a napkin.

"Let it sink in," she soothes.

She waits for me to dry my mouth, before I stare at her in shock.

"I…" I shake my head. "No… I…"

She looks at me with a patient smile, and my throat turns scratchy.

"Sullivan?" I squeak. "I do… I am… I mean…" My shoulders fall. "I'm… *in love* with him?"

"There it is." She pulls me into a hug, and I stare over her shoulder at the noticeboard. Molly's purple rabbit coloring is still pinned in the center, in pride of place.

"I can't be. He's… I don't think he feels the same. He's not said anything about going public, or anything. I only ever see him at his place. We don't go out like a regular couple. We don't do anything."

She pulls back to look at me. "Apart from banging each other's brains out, I get it. Why do you think Huck was grinning like an idiot when he picked me up the other day? It's not just his swanky coffee machines that are receiving full services."

Despite the gnawing in my gut, I laugh. "He's lucky to have you."

"He is. But I've got a latte love for him too, you know?" She winks at me.

"Oh God." I sink my head into my hands, leaning over the counter.

"It was probably the painted toenails that did it. Single dad porn, right there. He does cute stuff for his adorable kid. Of course you're going to be falling in love in the wet panties that he's given you. And despite, you know, the asshole tendencies, he's smoking hot and rich. Every woman in the city would hit that. The men too."

My stomach somersaults as I think of his pink glittery painted toes. Ashley's right. That totally made my heart melt, knowing that he's going to work, talking about billion-dollar deals with a detached coldness that makes him brilliant at what he does, all whilst his love for his daughter is literally painted on him beneath his suit.

You'd have to have no heart not to be affected by that.

"I didn't exactly plan this," I groan, looking up at the exact time Cliff pulls up in the black town car on the street outside. I frown. Sullivan told me he had a meeting across town this morning. Right after I'd moaned out my orgasm into his mouth as he'd pinned me to the mattress beneath him.

"Breathe," Ashley instructs. "It's too late now, it's done."

"Thanks for the reassurance." I scoff.

She flicks a hand in the air. "Life's short, Tate. If he makes you happy, then don't overthink it. Guys are sometimes slow about the whole labeling relationships thing. It'll all work out how it's supposed to."

"I believe you," I murmur, closing my eyes and rubbing my temples.

I can't stop picturing his eyes when he told me he wasn't The Masked Maestro. It's like he felt bad that he couldn't tell me something I longed to hear. I've studied every YouTube video I could find in the last couple of days. Analyzing the curve of his shoulders, the width of his back. Even the angle of his head as he gives over to the music and loses himself as he plays.

And I still don't know.

Every cell in my body tells me that was Sullivan playing that night. That his music was the one that reached into my soul and danced with it.

I want it to be him.

I *need* it to be him.

Ashley's right.

I'm in love with Sullivan Beaufort.

The bell over the door goes.

"Or you could just ask him yourself how he'd label your relationship status?" Ashley whispers, nudging me.

I look up to find Sullivan striding in, wearing the same navy-blue tie with gold flecks I twirled around my hand while kissing him this morning.

His expression is his usual business-like mask of indifference.

"I thought you had a meeting across town?" I say.

"I do. I just needed this." He rounds the counter and pulls me into his arms, gifting me with a passionate kiss that's over far too quickly. I choke out a tiny, surprised gasp and his lips curl against mine as he plants another softer kiss to them.

"I'll pick you up later and we can stop by your place to get some clothes. There's somewhere I want to take you tonight."

"Oh, okay."

The customers stare after him as he strides out and climbs into his car without looking back.

Ashley gives me a knowing smirk. "You're no longer just his private obsession, girl. Billionaire Boy's taking you on a date."

31

SULLIVAN

"Nice to meet you, Mr. Miller." I extend a hand, and Tate's father pulls it between two calloused palms and pumps enthusiastically.

"Ah. You're the man I have to blame for taking my daughter away from me most evenings?"

I clear my throat. "Sir, I—"

"Dad!" Tate laughs.

"I'm messing with you." He breaks into a chuckle as we move further into their apartment, and I get my first look at the inside of Tate's home.

I take it in subtly. The peeling paintwork. What looks like damp on the walls. The way the sounds of the city pass through the old windows like there's no glass in the battered frames.

The maintenance company I employ to look after the buildings in Molly's portfolio will have a new priority on their list first thing tomorrow morning.

"Going somewhere special tonight, are you?" he asks, taking in my suit.

"Somewhere I believe your daughter will enjoy, yes," I reply.

He nods, his warm eyes, so much like Tate's, twinkling. "Well, enjoy yourselves. Nice to meet you, Sully." He claps me on the shoulder, then says to Tate, "Larry's cooking tonight. Wish me luck."

Giggling, she kisses his cheek. "You'll be fine, Dad. I gave him some pointers."

She turns to me as he leaves. "I'm sorry. I called you Sully *once*, and he's latched on to it."

"I can't say anyone else calls me that, but he's your father, Tate. The man can call me whatever he wants, seeing as he's letting me date his daughter."

Her lips twist into a smile. "Is that what we're doing? Dating?"

"That's what we're about to do. If you'll go and get changed." I look at her pointedly. "Because as much as you know I love you in your uniform, I think you'll want to wear something else for this."

"Sounds mysterious. Can you at least tell me if I should do smart, or—?"

I clear my throat. "I actually had Cliff deliver something here for you this afternoon that I thought you might like."

Her brows hitch, and I hold my breath. She might think I've overstepped. Or interpret this as further evidence that I hate all of her clothes, which I've already told her, I do not. I just hate how I can't think straight seeing how sexy she is in the ones that hug her curves. And then there are the ones that cover her body like it's something to hide. Those ones, I really do hate.

"You bought me an outfit?"

"And shoes, jewelry, and... lingerie."

She holds my eyes, and I stare back.

Put them on, Baby. You'll look breathtaking.

"Thank you," she whispers.

She grabs my hand and pulls me down the hall and into her bedroom. The smile that bursts over her face at the sight of the silk-ribbon tied boxes on her bed makes my chest tighten. She's never been treated in this way, that much is obvious. But she deserves to be lavished with gifts and beautiful things.

She deserves me to spoil her like I intend to.

"Oh my God," she gasps, tentatively lifting the lid off the largest box and gazing at the gold silk dress inside. "Did you choose this?"

"I did."

Listening to Sinclair talk about designers of gowns who she models for came in useful. A few calls to the right people, and Tate now has a dress that isn't even available to the public yet.

"It's incredible." She runs her hand over the glistening fabric. "And shoes?" she gasps, pulling the red-soled stilettos from their box. "I'm not sure how I'll be able to walk in these."

"I'll carry you."

She looks up at me like I'm joking.

Her cheeks blush with the same beautiful color that stains them when I make her come as she opens another box to reveal a lace bodysuit, cut high at the hips and low at the cleavage.

She'll look fucking incredible in it.

"It's so beautiful. Thank you."

"There's one more." I tip my chin toward a blue velvet box and push my hands into my pants pockets, happy to hang back and just watch her understand that this is all for her.

She picks the Beaufort Diamonds box up and traces the gold logo on the top.

"Open it," I encourage, eager to see her reaction.

She eases the lid up and goes silent.

"Don't you like it?" I step forward, scowling at the box like it's to blame for her frozen expression.

She twists her face up to mine. "I can't wear this," she whispers. "I know what your pieces cost."

"They're the best diamonds in the world, Tate, so yes, they attract a price to reflect that."

I take the diamond choker from our new collection from the box and arch a brow at her. She lifts her hair up, her breath hitching as I fasten it around her neck and let the back of my fingers dust the top of her spine before I move them away.

I resist the urge to call her a good girl for allowing me to place it on her.

Her hand flies to the gleaming chain of our finest diamonds decorating her neck, and something about her wearing one of my own designs has my dick rock hard.

"But until someone actually wears them, their true potential is unmet." I run my hands up her arms and press a kiss beneath her ear. "It's all about the owner, Tate," I whisper. "They're almost as beautiful as the person wearing them."

Her pulse flutters beneath my lips as I recite the company slogan softly, pressing another kiss to her neck.

"Maybe I should take this off before we leave. It won't go with everything else," Tate says in a low voice as she reaches for her bracelet.

I grab her wrist and smooth my thumb over the gawdy gemstone tenderly.

"Don't you dare take it off. It's a part of you and I love it."

"Really?"

"Really."

I kiss her neck again and she arches into me, making my hard cock press against her ass.

"Sullivan?" she breathes.

"Tate," I rasp.

"How long until we need to leave?"

"We've got time, Baby."

She turns to face me, blinking at me through thick lashes. Her hand drops to my pants, and she palms my cock through the fabric.

"Time for this?"

"Time for anything you want," I answer, grasping her face and crashing my lips to hers.

Her hand tightens on my dick, and I groan into our kiss, claiming her mouth with my tongue. She unzips my pants and pulls my cock free, moaning against my lips as my pre-cum leaks all over her wrist.

"Sullivan," she moans, tightening her grip on me as she jerks me up and down.

"That looks so damn good, Baby," I say, dropping my gaze between our bodies to where her delicate hand is working my dick.

The large plastic jewel on her bracelet taps against my inner thigh with each stroke, and I pull in a tortured groan, wanting to prolong the feeling, because right now I could blow all over her fingers.

I reach for her shirt, unbuttoning it and pulling it free of her skirt's waistband, before unhooking her bra.

"You're wearing too many clothes," I grumble as I rid her of everything from the waist up.

She arches up, pushing her breasts into my waiting hands.

"Fuck, these tits will ruin me, Baby." I bend and snag one rosy nipple, sucking on it with a rich groan of appreciation. "So perfect."

I reach around and unzip her skirt, grabbing handfuls of her ass as I slide it over her curves and let it drop to the floor.

My lips slant over hers again as I rid her of her panties until she's wearing nothing but my diamonds around her neck and a blush on her cheeks.

Something about the way I'm still fully suited, and she's

naked and vulnerable makes the blood in my veins ready to ignite.

"So beautiful," I rasp as I push a hand between her thighs and find her wet for me. "So needy, too." I sink two fingers inside her and smile against her mouth as I swallow down her gasp with a kiss.

"Baby?" I purr.

"Y-yeah," she pants as I move my hand, finding her little sweet spot and fucking her the way she likes, with my thumb slipping over her clit.

"When I said we had time, I wasn't completely truthful. We don't have the time for me to fuck you all the ways I want to. But we have time for me to make you come all over my fingers."

Her grip on me tightens and I hiss as my cock drips from the tip, landing on her stomach.

"Are you going to be a good girl and come for me? Or are you going to need my cock?"

"God!"

Her body ripples around my fingers, squeezing them hard. I groan and suck on her neck as she comes. Just like I knew she would if I sprinkled a little filth her way. My baby is so sweet at times. But I know a few of the right words, coupled with the way she likes to be handled, and she'll come for me the same way she is now—wet, whimpering, and wrung out.

"Sullivan," she whimpers.

I smile against her skin, kissing her again, but she pushes my hand away while I'm still enjoying the lingering pulses from her cunt.

"Tate," I grit, annoyed that she's denying me all of the tremors from her body that I love to bask in.

But my flare of displeasure ceases as she drops to her knees and gazes up at me with trusting eyes.

"Look at you, Baby. You want to suck it, don't you?"

She nods and parts her lips, teasing the head of my dick with her tongue before she licks the wetness from my slit in one slow drag.

I groan as my balls pull tight to my body.

Tate keeps her eyes on mine as she takes me in her mouth and sucks.

"Good girl," I rasp, gathering up her hair in one hand and holding it gently at the back of her head.

She blinks up at me, mouth full of my cock as she sucks.

The half a million-dollar set of diamonds glitters around her neck as she pulls back, leaving a thin string of salvia between her lips and the swollen head of my cock.

"Fuck, yeah."

I push her back onto my dick, my eyes roaming between her lips wrapped around me, her eyes shining up at me, and my diamonds around her neck.

She couldn't look more like mine if I tattooed my name across those magnificent tits of hers and put them on a billboard in Times Square.

"That's it, Baby," I growl, jutting my hips, fucking her mouth in time with her eager sucks.

I reach down and pull my pants out of the way, freeing my balls to hit her chin as she gags.

"Such a good little cock sucker," I croon, stroking her cheek as her eyes water. "You know mine's the only one you'll ever taste again?" I thrust faster, my balls tightening with the need to release.

"I'm never letting you go, Tate," I growl, holding her gaze. "That's what you want, isn't it? You want to be mine?"

She chokes on my cock, looking up at me with pleading eyes as she nods.

"Good girl." I thrust deeper. "Good fucking girl."

The first spurt spills over her tongue and I draw back,

pulling free of her mouth while I still have the self-control to do so.

"Chin up, Baby," I groan as cum shoots out of the head of my dick, plastering thick, shining ropes over her tits.

She gasps as I point my cock higher, shooting across the diamond choker with a satisfied grunt.

The stones glitter and shine as my cum drips over them, running over her collarbone.

"You're not going to wash it off your tits, Baby. You're going to wear me beneath your dress tonight so you remember whose girl you are."

"Yes," she whimpers, gazing up at me as I squeeze the final drops out onto the crown of my dick.

"Open."

She complies and I wipe the head of my cock over her tongue.

"Now swallow."

Her eyes spark with arousal and her throat contracts, drinking me down.

I don't need to tattoo my name on her. She's wearing me all over her. From the cum on her skin, to the spark in her eyes when she looks at me.

I run my thumb over her lower lip. "You're mine, Tate. Say it."

"I'm yours," she breathes.

My eyes burn into hers.

"I'm keeping you, Baby," I say, allowing the careless promise to slip past my lips.

Even though I fear the day is rapidly approaching where I must break it.

32

TATE

THE WIND WHIPS AROUND US AS WE CUT ACROSS THE water of the Hudson like a hot knife on butter. Sullivan commands the sleek speedboat like he was born to do it.

"I can't believe you never mentioned you have a boat. Do you have any others? Slower ones?"

Sullivan glances at me, his lips quirking as I grip onto my seat with white knuckles. He pulls on a lever and reduces the speed. The city skyline begins to form back into shapes instead of just a blur.

"My father prefers the slower ones... yachts," he replies, his eyes pinching a fraction. "I don't have time to float and take in the scenery."

"I've noticed. The only time you sit still is when you're playing the piano."

I curl my hand around his bicep when he doesn't say anything and lean my head against his arm.

"This is lovely. I've had a great evening. Thank you."

"It's not over yet," he says, kissing my hair.

"A new outfit that I feel incredible in, and dinner in a

private dining room at a restaurant I know has a six-month long waiting list. What else do I need?"

"You'll see," he replies, steering the boat over the moonlit water.

I run my hand over the diamond choker. The weight of it has pressed against my skin all evening. But it's not been unpleasant. In fact, the choker has served as a wonderful reminder of how Sullivan must trust me in order to allow me to borrow such an exquisite piece.

He flicks his eyes in my direction. "I've insured it for you. I'll get a safe installed at your place. But until then you can keep it in one of mine when you aren't wearing it."

"What? I thought you'd borrowed it from the store?"

A small curl of his lips is the only sign that he heard what I said.

His profile is dark and determined as he keeps his eyes fixed ahead on wherever he's taking us. His suit is as black as his hair today. The cut as sharp as his jaw.

He's devastatingly handsome. And only growing more so the longer I look at him. The more I get to know him, and who he really is beneath his CEO persona.

"Sullivan?" I press. "I can't keep it. I—"

"Why not?"

"Because it's... it's expensive. They're *diamonds*," I splutter.

"Would you have preferred rubies?" His head snaps in my direction, a serious, questioning expression on it.

I scoff. "Oh my God, you actually want me to keep it, don't you?"

His eyes drop to my neck and his gaze heats like the sight of the diamonds sitting there pleases him.

"I *insist* on you keeping it."

"I don't own anything like this." I stroke the jewels, the cool, smooth surface of the piece moving against my fingers as

I swallow. "When will I ever wear it? When I'm making coffees?"

"If you want to."

I snort at the ridiculousness of the idea. "Sullivan…"

"Tate," he counters, dropping the boat into neutral so we slow down to a gentle bob. "You can wear it whenever you like. But if it makes you uncomfortable, then save it for when I take you out on dates."

"Dates?" I bite my lower lip. "You mean I get more of this?"

"You get more of this." He sucks his bottom lip, his gaze sliding down my body. "As long as I get all of you."

"Do I get all of you too? All the secret parts no one else does?" I ask playfully.

His brows pinch and he focuses on the choker, reaching out to run his thumb over my skin above it.

"You could just wear it naked if you like. I could fuck you in every piece Beaufort Diamonds has ever made," he murmurs.

His eyes flare with desire and I shake off the feeling that he deflected my question on purpose as he pulls me into a passionate kiss that has my stomach filling with butterflies.

"I could kiss you forever," he whispers against my lips, tracing my cheek with the back of his hand. "But then you'd miss what I brought you here to see."

He sits back, spreading his arm around me over the back of the seat cushion. He delicately circles my bare shoulder with gentle, skilled fingers.

"Watch. And listen."

I look over the water at a floating platform we've drifted closer to. A lone piano is set up on it.

A man dressed all in black wearing a balaclava sits at it.

"That's not…?"

Sullivan smiles at me as my throat goes dry. He pulls me into his side and kisses my temple.

"It is," he whispers.

The first notes of *Nuvole Bianche* by Einaudi ring out over the water like a haunted introduction.

My stomach drops as the crowd lining the harbor comes into focus. Hundreds of cell phone lights illuminate the gathering like fireflies as they film him.

The Masked Maestro.

Here in the flesh. Playing as well as he always has. Exactly how he's always sounded when I've raced to one of his concerts to lose myself inside his music.

Sullivan strokes my skin, but I no longer feel it. I'm numb.

"I thought it was you," I say, my voice a strained whisper.

"I told you it wasn't," Sullivan says calmly, like the realization isn't crushing something inside me.

"I heard him play a song that wasn't like the others. It was..."

I grow tenser in his hold. I sound ridiculous. A woman with stupid dreams about feeling a man's soul through his music. Feeling his passion. His pain.

Feeling *him*.

"It was what?" Sullivan asks, relaxing into the seat, enjoying the music.

"It doesn't matter," I breathe, forcing down the illogical swell of disappointment in my gut.

I thought it was him.

I wanted it to be him.

I swore it was him because the way I feel around him has become so intense so...

I love him.

But as stupid as I know it is, a tiny part of me fell in love that day at Grand Central Station.

And the rest of me fell for Sullivan.

I wanted it to be him.

Forty-eight hours of replaying our date in my head and I've finally come to terms with it.

I spent so many months wondering who The Masked Maestro could be. It was part of the magic, that element of mystery. But now I know for certain that it isn't Sullivan, I no longer care who The Masked Maestro really is.

His music is still beautiful. But the magic is gone.

He isn't the man I've fallen in love with. The song that touched my soul in Grand Central Station was just a fleeting moment where I imagined feeling something. Maybe I'm a fool, for wishing it was Sullivan. The way he plays, the emotion that flows through his fingertips onto the keys; I thought it had to be him. Because the only time I've felt such a spark of light inside me except when he plays, is that one time in the station.

I was sure he was lying when he said he didn't know how to play Unstoppable. But he wasn't, because it isn't him. Time to move on and appreciate what's right in front of me.

"Everything okay?"

I turn at Sullivan's deep, concerned tone and am met with a brilliant blue gaze that blazes with an intensity that thrums through my body like an electric charge.

"Fine." I smile at him, resting against the cool leather car seat and looking at Molly beside me. She's stroking her baby doll's eyelashes. She's so much like Sullivan. She even pulls her brows together in the same look of concentration. *So adorable.*

Sullivan had to stay in the office for a meeting with Jones and a few others, so I watched Molly. She was telling me about her auntie's dog who she sneaks into her bed with her when they look after him.

Sullivan's meeting ran over and we all got takeout and ate together in the conference room. It was strange seeing him relax at work, chatting with everyone as we ate.

Everything felt so natural.

Me, him, Molly.

I glance at him, and his eyes lift from his phone like he senses me. The way they sparkle has my stomach erupting into butterflies. It's a look that says he suspects what I'm thinking. But he can't. Because that would mean he's aware of how hopelessly in love with him I am.

And if he knows but isn't saying anything back, then...

"Tate?" he murmurs.

"I'm fine," I repeat, like saying it out loud makes it true.

His eyes narrow like he's about to ask me something, but the song playing from the car's radio grabs my attention.

"Cliff? Can you please turn it up?"

I shoot forward, hanging off the edge of my seat, straining to hear.

It's the same words, the same melody, but it's completely... *wrong*.

Bile rushes up my windpipe.

Sullivan straightens in his seat. "That's your—"

"My song," I choke, turning to him in horror.

Ice slithers up my spine as the unknown female artist continues to sing my words like they're hers. Like they're her hopes and dreams. Her work.

Not mine.

"You didn't know about this?" Sullivan states, studying me as I blink rapidly, the back of my neck on fire.

"I think I'm going to..." I swallow.

"Cliff, pull over," Sullivan commands calmly.

The moment the car rolls to a gentle stop, Sullivan flings

his door open and strides around to my side. He opens my door just in time as I fold at the waist and throw up violently in the gutter.

"It's all right," he says, gathering my hair from my face as my heaves turn dry.

"Tate?" Molly pipes up.

"I'm okay. Just got a little sick," I say, giving her a weak smile, not wanting to worry her.

"I'm good now," I tell Sullivan.

He passes me a bottle of water that Cliff's got from the trunk. I take a sip and hand it back to him. He watches me like a hawk, a dark determination in his gaze. My head's still spinning as he passes the water to me again.

I wave it away. "I'm fine. We need to get back. It's almost Molly's bedtime."

"Drink," he instructs, his voice a steady calm, a direct contrast to the thudding in my temples.

I take the bottle and glug some more down until the concerned look on his face eases a fraction.

"Who else has heard you play that song?"

The deep frown lines between his brows are matched with a dangerous undercurrent in his tone.

I shake my head. "No one, I…" I swallow down the threat of more vomit. "My ex, Brandon. He works at a record label. He's not high up or anything, but he keeps telling me he can get my song in front of the producers."

"He keeps telling you?" Sullivan questions, more than a hint of suspicion in his tone.

I wince at how stupid I've been. How I didn't see this coming.

"It's why I changed my number. He kept calling after we broke up."

Sullivan's nostrils flare.

"Last name?"

A muscle in his cheek clenches when I don't immediately answer, and his eyes bore into mine.

I swallow. "Rutter... Brandon Rutter. He works at Liberty Records."

He nods once.

I know the look on his face. Laser-focused eyes. Jaw set like stone. It's how he looks when he's about to go into battle in the boardroom.

"Sullivan—"

"Are you okay for us to keep driving?" he asks.

I nod weakly.

"Good." He reaches into his breast pocket and hands me a monogrammed handkerchief before closing my door softly.

He climbs back into the car and as we pull out into the city traffic, Molly's lower lip trembles.

"Hey, I'm okay," I reassure her.

She rubs her eyes, a mix of tiredness and confusion swimming in them.

"I am. All good now, see?" I smile at her.

But I'm not convincing enough.

As the final notes of what used to be my song play out, her little face screws up and she tilts her head back against her car seat.

And cries.

33

SULLIVAN

"Did she go down okay?" Tate questions, looking up with glassy eyes from the piano stool.

She's been sitting there ever since I took Molly to bed. Usually the faint notes of whatever she's playing drift through to the bedroom.

Tonight there's silence.

"She was asleep before her head hit the pillow, didn't even have a story."

"I'm so sorry. It's my fault. Seeing me sick upset her."

"She's just tired, Tate. It's been a long day."

She nods, her gaze returning to the untouched keys in front of her.

"I can't believe Brandon would do this," she whispers.

The hopelessness in her voice is like a knife to my heart.

"It can be fixed."

"It can't. It's out there now. It can't be unheard. That song will never be mine again. It's gone."

Her shoulders heave and the first sob breaks free. I knew she'd been holding it together in front of Molly.

But now it's just me.

Me and her.

"Come here."

I lift her gently, sliding onto the stool beneath her and cradling her sideways across my lap.

"I'm sorry," she chokes.

"Shh. Never apologize for sharing your feelings with me. I'm here for you. I'll do whatever you need, okay?"

I thumb away her tears but more fall.

"He stole my future. I was going to send that song to record labels. Ashley helped me write the query letters. I might not have gotten anywhere, but I would have done it myself, on my terms."

"And you still will. I promise you."

She squeezes her eyes shut. "It's too late."

Plans are already forming in my mind as she opens her eyes and blinks in an attempt to clear the tears.

"Do you want to hear something silly?"

I raise my brows at her. "Am I not 'Silly Sully'?"

She snorts, wiping at her eyes as the first hint of emotion that isn't despair passes over her face.

"I swore you were The Masked Maestro. I even had a bet going with Ashley."

"Really?"

"Yeah... Stupid, huh?" She glances at the piano, shaking her head softly. "When I saw him in Grand Central Station, he played a song I've never heard him perform before. It wasn't as technical as all the classical pieces he's known for. But there was something about the way he played it. It was *heartbreaking*."

"That's the song you asked me to play? *Unstoppable*?"

She looks back at me, reaching up to brush my hair from my face.

"But you said you didn't know it. I thought maybe you just didn't want to tell me who you really are."

I look into her eyes, my mouth going dry. If she knew the truth... the consequences are far too damaging to even consider.

"Then you took me in your boat to see him play and I knew it couldn't be you. It's stupid but I felt a connection to him after hearing him play that song. And you know I suspected Vincent, too. He's a great pianist, but..."

"But?"

"But when I had dinner with him, it was obvious he wasn't the same man I'd felt that connection to that night. I can't explain it, I just knew. And I started spending time with you and Molly and..."

She looks at the ceiling, like she can't believe what she's about to say but that whatever it is, it means something to her, and she believes it, deep in her soul.

"I thought for sure it had to be you. The way I felt when I first heard you play, the way you are with Molly, so different to what the outside world sees. You're a beautiful man, Sullivan."

She gazes at me, so open and trusting. So perfect.

My throat seizes up.

"I was disappointed. That split second when I saw him on the water and realized it wasn't you. But this..." She places her hand over my thundering heart. "This is so much more than one beautiful song. This is real. This is—"

"Living," I breathe.

Her gaze softens. "Exactly."

She sniffs and glances at the keys again. "It didn't even sound like my song. They ruined it. The key was off."

"I know. It should have been like this."

I place my hands on the keys either side of her.

And play.

The opening chords surround us, sounding exactly the way they should have before the record label and her worthless piece of shit ex massacred them.

"How do you know that?" She clasps a hand over her mouth, her eyes filling with more tears.

"You've been singing it to Molly for weeks. I told you; I *look*. And I pay attention."

I hold her eyes and add in the words, singing them softly. They've taken over my mind since I first heard them drift from her lips and I know every single one. I sing them the way they deserve... with depth. With feeling. With raw emotion.

"Whispers of the past, the future's calling... Unleash your potential... let the world hear your sound."

She bursts into fresh sobs, and I stop and cup her face.

"*Baby*," I breathe.

Beautiful, dazzling irises gaze back at me. Tears cling to her lashes, but the sadness in her eyes clears, making way for something else. Something that has the power to bring me to my knees.

I swallow around the lump in my throat and bring my forehead to hers.

"You are more perfect than any song that's ever been written or is yet to be written. I need you to understand that, Tate."

The front of my shirt crumples as she fists it.

"Sullivan?" Her breath fans softly over my lips and I slide my hands from her cheeks to cradle her neck gently. Her beating pulse grounds me in a way nothing has ever been able to. I breathe in and out slowly, concentrating on its steady rhythm.

"Tell me what you need."

"I need you," she whispers. "I need you to kiss me all night and never stop. I need you to never let me go."

"I don't want to let you go," I confess.

Her breath hitches and our eyes connect again for a fraction of a second. But it's long enough for me to see everything. To see exactly where we're heading together.

"Tate—"

Her mouth crashes to mine, pleading and urgent. Begging me for what she needs.

I wrap her in my arms and give it to her.

I give her everything I can.

"Bedroom," I rasp into our kiss, before breaking it long enough to stand from the stool with her in my arms and carry her away.

The journey there takes far longer than necessary because I keep pausing to lower my mouth to hers and kiss her.

Her chest rises and falls with gentle puffs as I place her onto my bed, climbing up over her. She reaches for my shirt buttons, and as her delicate fingers undo them, I sink my face into her neck, peppering kisses over her silky skin.

The small whimper that slips from her has me moving back to kiss her, stealing it for myself.

It's mine. She's mine.

The trace of salt from her tears hits the tip of my tongue and I screw my face up, holding her in place by her neck and deepening our kiss until she's writhing beneath me, desperately pushing my shirt from my shoulders.

"No more tears, Baby," I say into another searing kiss.

"No more tears," she pants.

"Good girl," I breathe. "It can all be fixed. Now, all you have to think about tonight is lying back and letting me do everything, okay?"

"You want to do everything?"

I squeeze her breast, groaning as her hard nipple pokes through her shirt against the pad of my thumb.

"Everything," I rasp. "I don't want you to worry about a thing."

I unbutton her shirt, sliding my hand up over the warm, soft skin above her ribs as I kiss her. Her perfect breast spills into my waiting palm as I pull her bra down.

"I'm taking control, Tate. Just relax and let me make you feel good."

My gaze zeroes in on her puckered pink nipple before I swoop on it, sucking it past my lips.

"Oh God." She arches up, pushing against my tongue. I pull the other side of her bra down and nip the sweet flesh where her breast is its fullest, before sucking that one past my lips too.

"So, so, good," she whines, stroking the back of my neck as I look up at her, watching her every movement. The softening of her brows, the slackening of her jaw. The flutter of her lashes as my teeth graze her.

"I'm going to undress you," I tell her, swirling my tongue around her nipple. "And then I'm going to bury my head between your legs until you've soaked my face."

Her eyes widen as I bare my teeth, nipping her breast gently. The resulting intake of breath she makes has my dick leaking in my pants.

"Then I'm going to take my clothes off and spend the night inside you, until the only thing you feel is pleasure, okay?"

She nods.

My voice drops to a low husk. "I'm going to take care of you, Baby."

She needs this. She needs to be worshipped, and to know that despite today's blow, it isn't all gone. She still has a future. She can still follow her dreams.

I'll make sure she does.

I pull her up to a sitting position. She watches me,

entranced as I take my time removing her shirt, kissing each shoulder as it's bared to me.

"So beautiful," I whisper.

I kiss every damn inch of skin that's revealed as I slowly rid her of everything, until she's naked with only a blush staining her cheeks as she looks at me in anticipation.

"Now lie back."

I wait for her to get comfortable, then sink to the mattress between her thighs, leisurely sliding my arms beneath them until they rest over my biceps.

"Give me your hands."

Tate holds my eyes, sliding her hands into my waiting ones. I wrap her fingers between each of mine and rest them against her lower stomach.

"Now, pay attention," I rasp, before dipping to press a lingering kiss between her thighs.

She jolts, her breath catching.

"You and me," I declare, pressing another kiss to her and looking up into her eyes. "Tell me."

"Me and you," she whispers, her words turning into a moan as I lick her in one long, languid stroke.

"That's right. I'm right here. I'm not going anywhere."

"Sullivan," she whimpers.

I sink into her, groaning as I take my time eating her out until her flesh quivers against my tongue. I told her I was going to take care of her. But as her first orgasm spills into my mouth and she shudders against me, there's no doubt in my mind that I need this just as much as she does.

"Fuck," I groan, sliding two fingers inside her and making her come again before I ease up.

She's breathless and flushed as I stand and remove my clothes.

"Sullivan," she whispers, reaching for me as I climb onto the bed, settling my hips between her thighs.

"What is it, Baby?" I murmur, kissing her pouty lower lip.

My dick slides against her, getting coated in a mix of her arousal and my saliva. I hook one of her legs behind the knee and lift it, wrapping it over my hip.

Her lids hood, her eyes glazed over in a post-orgasmic haze. She's exactly how I want her to be. Relaxed. Sated. Not thinking about anything else except how good it feels to let me take care of her.

I push forward, sliding into her slowly.

She whimpers against my mouth and stretches around me, gripping me in a way that makes my eyes roll back in ecstasy.

"You don't have to talk. You don't have to do anything. I've got you," I tell her, kissing her softly.

I pull back a little, then push forward again, sinking deep inside her.

She trembles around me, each tiny flutter like a goddamn signal to my cock to take it easy, or I'll be done in a matter of seconds.

"Sullivan," she moans, sinking her hands into my hair.

We pause, foreheads pressed together, eyes held in weighted meaning, lips hovering over one another, the sound of our soft breaths passing between us.

She doesn't need to say anything. Neither of us do.

This time, our silence speaks volumes, louder than any words, any notes played on a piano, any words sang.

"I know, Baby," I whisper, my voice coming out hoarse as I slide a thumb over her jaw. "I feel it too."

Her breath catches and my heart jackknifes as I realize the magnitude of my confession. The impact it could have for Molly and me.

I screw my face up and kiss her again before she can say anything. Keeping us in this moment. A moment where I can allude to the way I feel without having to consider the ramifications.

A moment where it's just me and her. And my daughter sleeping soundly in another room.

A moment that's perfect, even if it is fleeting.

I kiss Tate deeply, savoring her taste as I move inside her.

In this moment, my body is free to dream alongside hers.

Tonight, I'm sleeping without nightmares.

34

SULLIVAN

THE ROOM IS DIMLY LIT WHEN I WAKE. BUT IT'S light enough for me to realize that I didn't set my alarm and overslept.

"Shit," I whisper-curse, my thoughts immediately flying to Molly.

I scoot out from beneath the covers and swipe my underwear from the floor, pulling it on in a frenzy. I'm out of the door, pulling it closed behind me, and heading to Molly's bedroom within a matter of seconds.

It's fine. She must have slept later, too. Yesterday was a long and emotional day. But despite my self-reassurance, my heart is thundering as I approach her room and find her door open, despite closing it when I put her to bed last night.

"Molly?" I say, stepping into the room.

Her bed's empty.

"Molly?"

I check her bathroom, but that's deserted too. She'll be playing with her dolls in the living area.

I stride down the hallway.

The living area is silent.

A cold slither inches up my spine and pins me by the throat.

"Molly?"

I race over to the kitchen, checking all of the places she could be where she'd be hidden from view.

Nothing.

My head grows light, my pulse an erratic pounding in my skull. I run from room to room, my home office, gym, guest rooms, bathrooms.

Every room, every closet. Even beneath the couch.

She's gone.

"Jesus!" I choke, fear gripping and making me gasp for air.

I've only ever felt like this once in my life.

The day that death showed my family no mercy.

I stumble over my own feet, sprinting to the bedroom to wake Tate. I need to call the cops, call Dad. Call the fucking president.

Molly's gone.

"Tate!" I wheeze, opening my bedroom door and practically collapsing through it. Every nerve in my body is sparking with adrenaline. It's the only thing keeping me standing as terror slices through my veins like a lethal injection.

I round her side of the bed and slam to a halt.

She's lying on her side, sleeping. Her lips are parted, and each soft exhale spills out over her pillow... gently ruffling the delicate dark curls lying beside her.

I fall to my knees beside the bed, a silent, relieved sob caught in my throat.

They both look so peaceful. Molly must have climbed in during the night, the way she used to before I linked the monitor to her door, so I'd know if she left her room.

I didn't set it last night. The silence from Tate's lack of playing as I took Molly to bed distracted me. I wanted to get back to her. To make sure she was okay. I hated seeing her so obviously torn up from hearing her song on the radio. I needed to take care of her, for my own sanity.

I *needed* Tate to be okay.

For a brief moment, my subconscious was focused on my needs. Not those of my daughter.

Guilt weaves its way up my windpipe, replacing the fear. But it still chokes me up, lashing at me without restraint.

Molly comes first. Always.

As my daughter's eyelashes flutter sleepily over her chubby little cheeks, dancing in time to a dream, a glimmer of hope unearths from a dark place inside me that I thought was long buried, if not snuffed out altogether.

But hope can be destructive.

I hoped my brother and mother could survive an explosion that blew out one side of my father's yacht in the marina that day.

I hoped that if they did, then they'd also survive the fire that spread in front of my eyes as we all raced down the jetty toward them.

I hoped that my father would find them alive when he ran onboard through the flames to try and reach them.

All of that hope was for nothing.

I swallow around the lump in my throat and stand on weak legs.

Leaning down, I press a kiss to first Molly's, then Tate's forehead.

"Look after her for me," I whisper.

"You'd like her, Brother. She adores Molly."

The gray headstone stares back at me, silent and still. A complete contrast to what he was like when he was alive.

We called him the 'Risk Taker'. It was a joke, of course. He assured us that the skydives and the base jumps, and all the other crazy shit he called fun were completely safe. And I guess they were.

It was an accident that killed him.

A pointless, tragic accident.

"And she plays piano," I say to the matching headstone on the left. "Not just plays, composes her own songs."

Elaina Marigold Beaufort.

The deep chiseled letters of my mother's name remain lifeless and empty. A shell devoid of emotion, when I know had she been here to hear those words, they'd have made her eyes light up with joy, and she'd have asked me a barrage of questions about Tate's music.

That was Mom's love. Music. It's why I was given lessons from a young age. My brother wouldn't sit still long enough to practice, and Sinclair lacked the coordination, her body too intent on growing at an alarming rate in order to give her career-making supermodel height.

We would sit beside one another at the piano, learning new songs together. Perfecting them.

She couldn't love my father enough not to cheat on him, but her heart loved music so much that she could play a piece by Mozart in her sleep.

"You'd both love Tate," I murmur, sighing deeply as I bend to straighten a wilting flower that's been planted. But it's not wilting, it's broken. The stem has severed and comes away between my fingers.

"Sinclair said you never come here."

I turn at the familiar voice, meeting Uncle Mal's saddened gaze as it lifts from the broken stem in my hand.

"As far as she's aware, I don't." I look back at the delicate white rose, running my nail up one of its thorns. One prick and I'd bleed. Just like Tate did that day in my office.

The day I freaked out thinking she was in physical danger.

But physical pain isn't the only one a person can endure. And sometimes it's the wounds we don't see that are the ones that never heal.

And it's exactly the type of wounds I fear I'm exposing Tate to more with each passing day.

"I'd prefer if Sinclair continues to think that way," I say, standing and turning to my uncle. "I promised her when they died that I'd hold things together for us... And now we know about..." I swallow. Something another model said to Sinclair caused her to want her necklace tested. The necklace I made for her. The one that I thought had my brother inside it. The one that turned out to have ashes in it that didn't belong to him.

"Now we know her necklace isn't... I don't want her having any more reasons to think about that day." I grimace.

He nods in understanding, walking to my side and stooping to place a single flower on each of their graves, before gathering up two almost identical ones that can't be more than a few days old.

"Grief isn't a weakness, Sullivan," he says with a deep sigh as he stands and looks at both headstones in turn. "It's a sign of how much they were loved."

I press my lips together, every inch of my windpipe burning, all the way from my stomach to my throat as we stand in silence for a few minutes, both prisoners to our own thoughts.

"I've met someone," I say, the words piercing my lips like daggers as I allow them out into the world.

Uncle Mal doesn't look surprised. He looks sad. Remorseful. *Pitying.*

"I see." He inhales slowly, before letting it out.

"Tate..." I wince as I say her name, here of all places, in

front of their graves. "She doesn't know what happened. She can't ever know."

The look of grief that pulls at his face, drawing it down and deepening every crease and shadow, matches how I feel inside.

"I'm lying to her."

He doesn't say anything. Just jerks his chin in acknowledgment.

What is there to say?

Tate doesn't know the truth about my family.

We're The Beauforts.

No one knows the real us.

"I'm sorry, Sull," Uncle Mal says, patting me on the shoulder.

I press my lips together, not trusting myself to speak.

"I'll see you before I leave, okay?"

Mal's stayed in New York longer than usual, knowing Neil was here. But after some careful surveillance, Neil's no longer deemed a threat. Denver and the team have uncovered his plans to move to Chicago to be near his brother. He'll be gone in a matter of days, where they'll still have eyes on him. But they doubt he'll be back. And Mal's needed in Botswana again.

I clear my throat and nod. "Okay."

Uncle Mal walks away and I stay for a while, staring at the headstones with only my thoughts for company.

Cliff's sitting in the car, reading the paper as I finally turn and head back in its direction. It's a Friday, the day of the week he arrives early in case I need to drive here in silence when the sun has barely risen.

No one knew I came here. Until Uncle Mal saw me just now.

Cliff's brought me here so many times over the last two or so years that the car could probably drive itself.

My old Thursday night routine served a double purpose. Molly was still on one of her sleepovers with Dad or Sinclair Friday mornings. I'd usually have spent the evening at The Lanceford before my visit, not awoken to find my daughter asleep in my bed with the woman who's slotted into our life so perfectly, like she belongs with us, like I did today.

A woman who only sees the version of myself that I portray to her. A version lacking so much that I can never share with her.

I pull out my phone and bring up my home surveillance system that Denver had installed for me after Molly arrived. My chest tightens as Tate walks into the living area with Molly in her arms. Molly's rubbing her eyes like she's still waking up, and Tate's wearing one of my T-shirts, with her hair tied up in a messy knot on top of her head.

Tate swivels her head side to side and her mouth opens. Even though the sound is off, I know she's calling for me. She walks over to her purse on the table and pulls her phone out.

Mine rings in my hand.

"Sullivan? Is everything okay?" Her tone is breathy, an edge of concern in it.

I watch the way she balances Molly on one hip, and my daughter rests her head against her, so naturally at ease in her arms.

"Everything's fine. I just had to go out for something. I'm on my way back now."

"Okay." She still sounds unsure, but she smiles at Molly. "Daddy's coming home now."

"We make him breakfast?" Molly asks, completely unfazed by the fact that she has never been alone in our home with anyone who isn't family before.

"That's a good idea," Tate tells her.

"I won't be long," I say, hanging up.

Tate puts her phone down and wraps Molly inside both of

her arms. Molly's face splits in half with a beaming grin. My heart staccatos in my chest as I stab the sound on, turning it up.

A soft, sweet melody I haven't heard Tate sing before drifts from my phone. But I only catch the words *'blue eyes'* before the rest of the words are muffled into Molly's hair as Tate sinks her face into it and carries her toward the kitchen.

"Jesus Christ," I choke.

I shove my phone back in my pocket, reaching out to steady myself on the trunk of a large tree. The back of my neck heats, sweat pricking up along my hairline.

I'm lying to her.

I'm lying to the woman I've just watched care for my daughter like she's her own.

The woman I've pictured multiple times in my head doing exactly what she is doing right now.

Cuddling my daughter and singing to her.

Only in the image in my head, she's wearing my ring on her finger and growing my baby in her belly as well.

I pinch the bridge of my nose and suck in a deep breath, willing myself to get a fucking grip. This isn't just about protecting Molly now. It's about protecting Tate too. Doing what's best for her. No matter what I want. Being a parent means being selfless, putting another before yourself. Molly's prepared me for this.

I pull my phone out again and fire off a text to Jones. He replies immediately, no doubt surprised by my instructions, but not perturbed. He lives for this kind of shit.

No limit. Just make it happen.

I text in answer to his question concerning the budget he has to work with. He replies with a thumbs up. They should make a shark emoji with a shit-eating grin especially for him.

Scrolling through my recent calls I find Denver and hit call.

"Sullivan?" he grunts, sounding out of breath like I've just interrupted his workout.

"Denver? Can you talk?"

There's a muffle that sounds like a female's voice, and despite myself, I smirk. The poor guy's been assigned to Sinclair for months. But since the culprit who was sending Sinclair anonymous threats was caught and dealt with by the cops, and Neil was also ruled out as a threat, my father has removed Denver from being her bodyguard.

The guy's probably making the most of having some of his freedom back.

"Yes," he clips.

"Okay..." I exhale, tilting my head side to side, making it crack.

"What is it?"

"Tate," I reply, her name rolling off my tongue with familiar ease. "Listen, can I count on your discretion?"

"You wouldn't believe how good I am at keeping secrets," Denver rasps.

I look over at Cliff, who's folded up his paper, and is waiting patiently. "Good. Because what I need you to help me with isn't exactly legal."

"Don't tell me any more until I get there. I'll come to you now."

"Thanks," I clip, ending our call. I'll be home before Denver gets there. And Cliff can take Tate to work. This isn't a conversation I want to have in front of her.

I walk to the car and climb inside, nodding at Cliff. He pulls away without uttering a word. He knows I rarely want to talk after I've been here.

Bringing up another number, I hit call again, before realizing it's the middle of the night in London.

"Beaufort," he answers, sounding far too alert for me to have woken him up.

"Fairfax," I greet back. "Am I interrupting something?"

He lets out a rich chuckle. "Nothing more than a guy struggling to sleep. Give me something new to focus on instead of trying to count sheep. You know that shit doesn't work, right?"

"Try having an almost three-year-old that never stops moving, you'll learn to fall asleep in five seconds flat if you ever get the chance."

He chuckles again.

"Can you insure a record label?" I ask, cutting straight to it.

"What have you done now? This about that woman? Molly's nanny?" Rafe drawls in amusement.

"Have you told Aurora how much you *enjoy* watching her vlog?" I counter, wishing I'd never mentioned Tate to Rafe. The guy doesn't miss a thing.

"Fuck off." Rafe snorts.

"In that case, don't ask. Just tell me, can you do it? Or do I need to find someone else?"

"Course I can bloody well do it," he replies with the sharpness in his tone that he only gets when he's pissed.

My lips lift into a ghost of a smile. He'll do it twice as fast now, just to prove his point. I know he will, because it's exactly what I'd do in retaliation to a comment like that.

He knows I've played him. I'd never go anywhere else.

But I also know he won't care.

Because Rafe and I are the same.

When it comes to getting what we want. It's only the winning that matters.

35

TATE

"I haven't heard from Brandon in a while."

Ashley snorts. "Perhaps, he's fallen in a ravine and been eaten by rabid rats."

I study the counter as I wipe up a drip of coffee, then buff the surface until it shines, the ache in my arm helping to take the edge off the nausea I've felt since hearing my song on the radio.

"You can prove you wrote that song. You kept all of Brandon's text messages begging you to let him pitch it. You have the power to ruin that asshole."

"I know," I say, finding a new blemish on the counter to scrub. "And I'm going to go to the record label after my shift today."

Ashley grins. "Want a wing woman?"

"Please." I've spent the past two days going over what I want to say, and how I intend to get past the front desk and into the CEO's office. I've got my evidence all printed out in a folder, ready to slam at them.

Ashley's right. I have a good case to put forward. And I'm determined not to leave that office until I get what I deserve.

My song back.

"I know that look on your face. What else is eating you?" Ashley muses.

"It's Sullivan, he's been... I don't know, acting weird since I woke up and Molly was in bed with me."

"You think he's worried about her finding you there?"

"No, that's just it. Molly wasn't bothered at all. I told her I was feeling sick, and that Sullivan had looked after me, and I'd had to sleep over. She saw me get sick in the car the night before, so it made sense."

"So what is it, then?" Ashley leans back against the counter.

"I don't know. He's been distant. I keep catching him on the phone, but he hangs up when he sees me. Then last night he told me it was a wrong number. But I swear before I walked into the room, he said something."

"Like what?"

I shake my head. "I don't know. It sounded like, 'I'm sorry' and 'I miss you'."

Ashley's brows shoot up. "I'll grind his balls in the coffee machine if he's cheating on you."

I give her a grateful smile. Knowing Brandon cheated has made her extra protective.

"I don't think he'd have the time, even if I did think he was capable, which I don't. He's always working. And in the evenings we're together." Except the past two nights. He told me he thought it was a good idea if I didn't stay over for a while, just until he was sure Molly wasn't going to have any questions about finding me in his bed.

Goosebumps prick up over my arms, and I desperately want to ignore the warning bells making my gut churn. Despite me not staying over, I've still spent the evenings with them both. And he's still wanted me to stay after Molly's asleep.

Sex has become more intense.

Sullivan's been intent on fucking me all over his penthouse, like he's trying to impregnate the memory of us together throughout it. Just last night he lifted me into his arms as I was about to leave and fucked me desperately against the front door.

He tore my skirt in his haste to shove it to my waist and sink inside me, despite us only just having finished fucking in his bed minutes earlier.

"Well, I'd do it without question. Just so you know." Ashley winks at me and pats the coffee machine.

"I know you would." I smile. "And that's why I love you so much."

"I hate you," I tell Ashley.

"No, you don't," she whispers back as she marches toward the sleek reception desk inside the lobby of Liberty Records with her hand on my lower back, herding me along. "I know you're nervous, but you'll thank me later for not letting you wimp out."

I take a deep breath and let it out slowly. She's right. I was ready to turn back around once we made it here. If it weren't for Ashley's insistence and strong grip on me, I'd be back home now, instead of fearing I'm about to hyperventilate.

"Did Sullivan give you pointers on what to say? He's used to dealing with huge businesses and getting what he wants from them, right?"

"He did. He wanted to come with me, but I need to do this myself."

"And you will. You'll blow them out of the water." Ashley

smiles, enjoying every minute of this. She's been role-playing my argument with me on the cab ride over, preparing me.

I straighten my shoulders and approach the young man at the desk.

"Hello. My name's Tate Miller, and this is my colleague, Ashley. We're here to talk about my song that Liberty Records has produced without my permission." I drop my folder of evidence on the desk and tap a finger on it. "All of my evidence is in here and I will be going to the press if this isn't resolved."

My voice is loud enough that we attract curious glances from people moving around the large marble lobby.

The man at the desk looks taken aback and clears his throat. "Just a moment, please."

He picks up his desk phone, his attention bouncing from me to Ashley and back again as he waits for it to connect.

"Mr. Drayton. Apologies, Sir, I know you didn't want to be disturbed. But there's a Miss Tate Miller here." He nods. "Yes, Sir."

He places the phone down and beckons another staff member over, saying something quietly to her that we can't hear.

"Hilary will take you to Mr. Drayton's office."

The woman smiles brightly at us. "Right this way."

We follow her into the elevator. This is going smoother than I expected. I was prepared for more push back before I made it anywhere near the head producer, Kyle Drayton. Brandon always told me getting a meeting with him was harder than playing "La Campanella" by Liszt with your eyes closed. Although, I bet Sullivan could do it.

We step out into a huge office, filled with people working, making calls, and walking around with steaming cups of coffee. On the walls are giant posters of musicians and album covers the label is famous for. We walk past one of a female artist who picked up no fewer than nine Grammys at the last awards ceremony.

"You're lucky," the lady says, as she stops in front of a closed door and knocks. "Mr. Drayton was about to leave for a meeting."

I take another deep breath for courage as the door is opened by a suited man in his forties. His skin lacks brightness, the area beneath each eye dark like he's had too many late nights. But he forces a welcoming smile onto his face and extends a hand.

"Miss Miller. Nice to meet you."

I shake his hand and stop myself from glancing at Ashley as he greets her with the same professional, albeit unexpected warmth. Not what I was expecting when I came in here slinging around accusations like confetti.

"Please, come in."

He shows us into the large office, decorated with multiple music awards and framed gold albums on the walls. We take a seat on one side of a large glass desk, and he falls into the seat behind it.

"I believe I know why you're here."

"You do?" I stare at him, and his chest deflates like a sad old balloon.

My death grip on my folder loosens a fraction. Adrenaline pumps through my veins, ready for battle. But he looks defeated, and we haven't even begun.

"Brandon Rutter." He sighs the name like it's one he's heard far too many times. "He came to us yesterday and confessed to stealing a song you wrote. We opened an investigation immediately and discovered..." He rolls his lips, leaning over his desk and clasping his hands together. "This might not be the only time he's done something like this. Thankfully, yours is the only song that's actually been released."

Nausea coils its way up from my stomach. Brandon's done

this to other people. Other songs. Other dreams. Taken without remorse. How did I date a guy like that and not see it?

Kyle scrubs a hand around his jaw, continuing, "He no longer works for the company. And Mya's song... *your* song," he corrects himself, "has been removed from all stations. It won't ever be played again."

Won't ever be played again? His words crash over me, stinging everything they touch. I wanted my song to be heard. Just not like this. I wanted it done my way, and—

"I'm sorry... Mya?" I ask, the name sparking something.

"The artist. She signed with us six months ago. We've been looking for the right song for her," Kyle confirms, looking at me as I shift in my seat, memories making my skin prickle.

Mya.

The name Brandon was groaning when I caught him balls deep in another woman.

"He gave my song to his mistress," I tell Ashley while I maintain eye contact with Kyle, who doesn't react, suggesting he also found out this little nugget of information during his investigation.

"Personal relationships within the company are expressly prohibited. Another reason Mr. Rutter will not be receiving a recommendation from us for his future employment," Kyle says, confirming my suspicions.

Brandon fucked her. And then he fucked me over.

Ashley snorts, making Kyle's attention slide to her.

"I can assure you both, Liberty Records is taking this matter very seriously. Frankly, we're appalled that this happened."

"It's a little late for apologies, what are you going to do about it?" Ashley probes.

I'm grateful for her cutting in and focusing her wrath toward Kyle, because all of the phone calls and text messages from Brandon are shuffling their way to the front of my head, making it pound. I never suspected a thing. And now, not only did Brandon cheat on me and steal my song, but he's the reason it will never be played again.

"Do you have any more?"

"I'm sorry, what?" I snap my focus back to Kyle.

He rubs his hands together, leaning further over his desk. The remorse on his face has vanished and been replaced with a weird mix of eagerness and desperation.

"More songs," he says, eyes pinned on me.

"You want to know if I've written any other songs?" I ask, needing to clarify what I think I heard for a third time, because it makes no sense.

"Yes. And then I have a proposition for you."

Ashley and I ride the elevator back to the lobby twenty minutes later. Her fingernails dig into my forearm and she bounces on her toes.

"They want you!" she squeals.

"I know," I murmur.

"They want all your songs!" she squeaks.

"I know."

"And they want you to perform them on stage!"

My tongue thickens and sourness creeps over it.

"Why do you look like you're about to hurl? This is amazing!"

I force a smile. "It is," I agree. "Amazing."

I gnaw on my bottom lip. It's my dream... kind of. Having my songs played on the radio, seeing them made into an album, feeling the excitement in a crowd as they wait to watch them performed live.

I wanted to believe that this day would come. And now that it has, all I feel is... confused.

Kyle wants me to record an album with Liberty Records after going straight out on tour as a support act for a band they represent. He said it'll be an explosive way to introduce my songs to the world and drum up fan excitement.

It means spending months away from New York.

Away from Dad and Ashley.

Away from Sullivan and Molly.

The elevator doors slide open, revealing the same marble lobby I walked into. Only now, I'm seeing it with fresh eyes. As a potential artist who could be signed here. I told Kyle I needed to think about it and have his contract looked over. But at a glance it all looks legitimate.

It's a dream.

It doesn't seem real.

A familiar jean and rock band T-shirt clad form stands at the reception desk with his back to us, arguing with the guy there.

"Come on, man. I had personal stuff on my laptop. Can I just get it off? Then I'll leave?"

"Sorry. It's company property. Mr. Drayton said everything that belongs to you is in there." He tips his head to a cardboard box sitting on top of the desk.

The guy curses and whacks the box, causing it to topple off and land on the floor.

"Fuck's sake!" he spits, bending to throw pens and notebooks back inside. He clutches his side with a hiss like it hurts.

"Brandon?" I breathe, stalling and staring down at him.

Ashley stops beside me, folding her arms. He turns around, and I let out a gasp at the state of him. His face is bruised, and he has a fresh black eye.

The eye that isn't swollen shut slides up and down me

slowly, making my skin crawl by the suggestive way he licks his lips before he speaks.

"Tate. What are you doing here?"

"I came to get my song back." I study the bruises on his face with a flicker of empathy. "What happened to your face?"

His expression shuts down and his top lip curls into a sneer. "I fell into a fucking door shaped like some asshole's fist, what do you think?"

He takes a step toward me.

"Good luck, yeah? I'm sure the fans will love you." He throws another leery eye crawl over my body.

"What's that supposed to mean?"

I shouldn't have asked. The glint in his eye as he sniggers makes my stomach drop to my feet.

"You can sing your little heart out and ask yourself whether it's your voice or your tits the guys come for."

"Excuse me?"

"You heard." He sneers.

I slap him across the face before I realize what I'm doing.

"And while you beg for someone to give you another job, which will never be in music, by the way, you can ask yourself whether all of this was worth it. Whether being an asshole was the only thing you'll ever be good at in your measly existence."

"Ouch. Slay," Ashley sings beside me as Brandon throws me a parting glare and storms away.

He gets as far as the sidewalk outside before his box collapses, sending all of his stuff scattering across the concrete. His yelled 'Fuck!' reverberates through the glass doors as he bends to retrieve everything. But then he turns to the side and looks at something.

The next moment he takes off at a sprint.

"What do you think made him shit his pants?" Ashley asks as we step outside, weaving through the objects on the floor.

I look up and my eyes connect with brilliant blue, like two

stormy seas, as Sullivan climbs out of his town car a little way up the street.

"I think it just arrived."

Ashley follows my gaze to where Sullivan is striding toward us purposefully. "Do you think he did that to Brandon? If he did, then I like him even more now. You have my permission to marry him and pop out his cute dark-haired babies."

I narrow my eyes at him, and he stares back with a blistering intensity.

"I don't know, but I intend to find out."

36

SULLIVAN

"Did you beat Brandon up?"

Tate and I have been driving for fifteen minutes since dropping Ashley off and she's finally spoken to me.

"Yes."

"What?"

"You look surprised, but I think you knew the answer before asking the question."

I meet Cliff's eyes in the rearview mirror and dip my chin. The soundproofed privacy screen slides up into position.

"You don't want Cliff to hear that you beat a guy up and gave him a black eye? Probably some broken ribs?" Tate scoffs.

"Pretty sure Cliff knows seeing as he's the one who helped toss your ex into the trunk of this very car two days ago."

Tate blinks, her pouty lower lip falling open. "What?"

"He deserved it, Tate. He stole from you."

"I know, but—"

"But nothing."

I adjust my cufflinks, tension oozing up my spine at the hint of concern in her voice for the jackass.

I inhale slowly and recall his sniveling pleas as he'd

hammered on the inside of the trunk as Denver and I sat in the backseat together and chatted about the Yankees' latest game while we drove out to his cabin in the woods. They replay in my head like a sweet melody, easing my tension.

It was the perfect place to scare a pathetic asshole shitless while letting him believe I was going to murder and bury him where no one will find him. Denver even had an axe. A little steak blood on it in preparation of our arrival and Brandon Rutter pissed himself thinking that's the last place his head was going to be attached to his body.

I don't recall the last time I hit actual flesh and blood, and not the punching bag in my home gym.

It was rather therapeutic.

I turn and pin Tate under a pointed gaze.

"If you're waiting for an apology, then you'll be disappointed. My only regret is the guy's still able to walk. Now tell me how your meeting went."

Tate shakes her head, breaking my gaze and looking out of her window. I fight the urge to take her chin and turn her back to me so I can see her eyes. So I can gauge what she's thinking.

"They want to sign me," she says.

She flicks a look in my direction when I remain silent.

"Did you hear me? They want to sign me?"

"I heard you." I hold back my smile at the spark of defiance in her eyes. It's only when she's pissed at me that I see it. But I love the times she lets her fire out.

"I suppose I should thank you. If Brandon hadn't come forward, it might have been harder to prove what he did." She turns away again.

"No. You had all the evidence. Him getting his ass kicked was for my benefit, not yours."

She whirls in her seat to face me, her cheeks blazing.

"Are you serious? You beat him up for nothing?"

"You're not getting my point," I clip in irritation.

"Maybe because your point sucks!"

"Why are you suddenly concerned about an ex who treated you like shit? An ex who enjoyed fucking another woman more than he enjoyed fucking you?"

My words land straight on target. But they hurt me as much as her as a shimmer of self-consciousness passes through her eyes and she moves back, faltering in her attack on me.

I've gone too far. Put her back in a place she should never have been. Reminded her of a way she should never have been made to feel.

"Come here."

"No," she spits, jerking her face toward the window and crossing her arms.

"Tate," I instruct, my voice soft, but firm. "Come. Here."

"Make me."

I unfasten my belt, and in one swift move, I unfasten hers and pull her into my lap to straddle me.

"I'm not going to apologize for my actions."

"Well, what a surprise. Sullivan Beaufort doing exactly what he wants."

Her eyes are like two flames trying to destroy me, but her words lack conviction. Especially because her panties are soaking as I rub the tips of my fingers over them.

"Don't think that's me forgiving you, just because my body reacts to you." She pouts.

"No one will ever treat you like he did and not have to deal with the consequences. And you can fight with me as much as you want. It won't change a thing."

I unzip my pants and pull my dripping dick out.

"Does anyone ever say no to you? Refuse to let you have your own way?" she snaps, even as she shivers in my arms, letting out a soft moan.

I yank her panties to one side roughly, my heart rate skyrocketing as she does nothing to stop me.

"If they do, then they soon say yes. I can be very persuasive."

Holding her glare, I grip her hips and lift her, bringing her down slowly onto my aching cock.

She feels like fucking ecstasy.

I tip my head back, keeping my eyes on hers as I groan, sinking my teeth into my lower lip.

"You're mine, Baby. And I protect what's mine." The words spill out before I can stop them. I shouldn't be saying them, no matter how much I want to.

"I'm mad at you," she breathes, unable to hide the way her voice pitches.

"So fuck out your anger right now so that I can kiss you and tell you how damn proud of you I am."

Her pupils dilate and she stares at me. "Proud of me?"

I stroke her cheek, sliding my hand down to curl around her jaw possessively, but oh so gently.

"So fucking proud," I whisper.

"Asshole," she breathes.

Then she launches herself at me, hands sinking into my hair, thighs clamping tight over my hips.

And my girl fucks me.

She fucks me like a star in the backseat of my car.

"Wipe that smug smirk off your face," she pants. "The moment I come, we're done, whether you've finished or not."

But her threat is wasted on me. Seeing her like this is enough to make me blow on the spot.

I wait until the telling rush of wetness swirls around the head of my dick, and she clenches, indicating she's about to come.

Then I bring her to me by her neck, pulling her lips to mine, and release deep inside her with a groan.

"Fuck, Baby. That's my girl."

37

TATE

"Shall we go and tell Daddy you're ready for bed?"

Molly nods, her dark curls bobbing as I take her empty milk cup from her and place it on the counter. I walk with her toward Sullivan's home office. He said he had a call to make to Jones, but he's been gone the entire time Molly took to drink her milk, and I haven't heard the low rumbling of his voice carrying down the hallway in a while.

Molly opens the door and barges straight inside, running over to him, sitting at his desk.

"Hey, Sweetheart." His eyes snap up from his phone and he tosses it onto the desk and pulls Molly up into his arms.

"Sorry, it took longer than I thought," he says to me, his eyes falling closed as he sinks his face into Molly's shoulder and breathes her in.

I glance at his phone. The screen is still lit up, showing his call list. Jones is the second one down. But the most recent is a number with no name.

The same number repeats over and over down the list.

Whoever it is, he must call them multiple times a day yet chooses not to save their name.

"It's okay." I glance up to find Sullivan watching me over Molly's shoulder, his gaze sharp. Heat creeps into my cheeks like I've been caught snooping.

"Let's get you to bed," he says to Molly.

He reaches out and presses the button on the side of his phone, turning the screen off, then stands with her in his arms.

"I'll wait in here for you," I say as we walk into the living room. "Good night, Molly." I ruffle her curls, and she gives me a sleepy smile.

I watch Sullivan's retreating back as he leaves the room, then drop onto the sofa to wait. I can't bring myself to play the piano tonight. My mind's too busy, even though playing might help to distract me.

The last few days have been a whirlwind.

I didn't dream about Liberty Records, despite wondering if my mind had made it all up. Their contract is fair, and I'm actually getting a great deal for a first-time artist. Sullivan insisted that Jones look over it for me, and he made a few adjustments that were in my favor.

Ashley has already covered my shifts with someone Huck knows, and my father can't stop telling Larry how excited he is that he gets to join me for the whole four months of the tour.

It's all booked and paid for. Our plane tickets are sitting in my email, and my suitcase is half-packed in my room at home.

But aside from practical things that Sullivan's asked about to reassure himself that I'm prepared, we haven't spoken about me leaving.

He's either avoiding it, or he doesn't care.

I pray it's avoiding, because the alternative makes every cell in my body ache. He can't not care. Not with the way we are together. Not after all these months.

We have something, I know we do.

"Tate?" Sullivan calls, pulling me out of my head.

"Yeah?" I stand and head toward Molly's bedroom. The two of them are lying on her bed together, Molly beneath the covers, and Sullivan on top.

"Come and read?"

I must have misheard.

"You want me to read with you?"

"We want you to read *to* us," Sullivan says softly.

"Yay!" Molly grins.

"Okay, sure." Somehow my voice sounds natural, hiding the way my heart is thumping in my chest. This is Sullivan and Molly's special time. He never asks me to join them.

I walk to the bed and Sullivan shuffles Molly over so there's space for me to lie on the opposite side of her. I climb on and stretch out beside her.

She smiles up at me as Sullivan passes me a book.

"Ooh, your favorite," I exclaim to Molly, taking the illustrated jungle cover with the dark-haired explorer on it from him.

I settle down and read. The character is on a search for lost treasure and has to figure out a clever way to descend a waterfall without being swept away. He uses a rope from his backpack and manages to craft a zipline that he whizzes down using his shirt as a hand strap.

"He's quite the adventurer," I remark, coming to the end of another page.

"More like a risk taker," Sullivan mumbles.

I look up and his gaze is cast down on Molly, who's fast asleep between us.

"Risk taker?" I echo.

Sullivan's brow creases and he strokes a curl back from Molly's forehead.

"It's what I called my brother as a joke. He did some crazy stunts."

I close the book and study the character on the front. Dark hair, blue eyes, a giant I-can-do-anything grin on his cartoon face.

"Do you read this because it reminds you of him?"

"Molly likes it." He frowns.

"What was he like?"

Sullivan rarely talks about his mother and brother, but I'd love to know more about them. The press stories all center around their deaths, not who they were when they lived.

"He was the fun brother. And he'd also argue that he was the better looking one."

I rest the book against my chest and turn toward him, studying the groove between his dark brows. In the photos, his brother wore his hair longer, his smile wider. There was a freedom in him—a lightness Sullivan never seemed to carry, even in the pictures taken before the loss.

"I happen to find scary CEOs the best looking. Maybe even irresistible."

He arches a brow. "Really?"

"Really," I whisper. "Do you want to talk about him? And your mom?"

A shutter slides down behind his blue eyes, like a cloud passing in front of the sun. "I can't, Tate," he breathes.

I nod, ignoring the sudden lump in my throat that he doesn't want to let me in. Maybe he's just not ready. "I found it hard to talk about losing Mom those first few years. I thought if I pretended she was away on a trip, and that she was coming back one day, then it would be easier. I guess, I denied it, hoping I could escape the grief."

"And did you?" Sullivan asks, holding my eyes.

"No. You can't escape it. It's always waiting for you."

He clears his throat, his gaze sliding to Molly.

"Sweet dreams." He kisses her on her forehead and rises from the bed.

I kiss her in the exact spot Sullivan did and get up too. He takes the book from me and looks at it for a few seconds before putting it on the nightstand.

"Come on."

He holds his hand out and I slide mine into his and follow him from the room. We walk into the living area, but a part of me is still in Molly's room, watching her sleep, listening to her innocent little breaths as she dreams of whatever almost three-year-olds dream of.

Daisy chains and explorers, maybe.

Sullivan lets go of my hand and walks to the kitchen, taking out a bottle of whiskey. He lifts the bottle in question, and I shake my head. I've never seen him drink after putting Molly to bed before.

He pours himself a glass and knocks back a large mouthful.

I sit on the couch, waiting for him to join me. "I leave in a couple of days if I go on this tour—"

"You're going." His deep voice travels across the space between us, reaching me before he does. He sinks into the couch beside me and leans back, widening his knees and sighing.

"Sull—"

"You're going, Tate. There's no *if* about it. It's an incredible opportunity."

"I'll be gone for four months."

"And three days," he adds, tipping his head back and drinking more of the whiskey.

"And three days," I echo. "Will you... What will that mean?"

"It will mean you're following the path you're supposed to."

"I mean for us?"

"Tate..."

He looks at me, his eyes red-rimmed from tiredness. They soften as he exhales. The sigh leaving his lips is gentle, but it might as well be a nuclear bomb for what it means.

We're over.

It's written all over his face.

I turn away, blinking rapidly. I fight not to shiver from the iciness that's rushed through me. He cannot be serious.

I take deep breaths, unable to face him, afraid of what I'll see if I look into his eyes.

The piano sits across the room, illuminated by New York's twinkling lights behind it. Its surface is the same glossy black that I once thought looked like ink. Now it resembles tar. The kind that will suck you inside it. Devour you. Drown you silently.

"It's four months. I'll be back before you know it. You and Molly can come and watch me perform. It'll be fun for her," I force out brightly, like if I ignore the ominous tension that's surrounded us suddenly, it will disappear, and everything will be fine again.

I keep staring at the piano.

"Tate." He sighs again.

"I don't understand. Do you want me to choose?" I spin to face him, ready to throw the tour out of his skyscraper window and watch it shatter on the street below if that's what it takes. "Because there is no choice. It's you and Molly for me. It always has been. I'll stay here with you both. I don't need to sing."

His eyes are glassy and he looks at me with a sad finality. "It's more complicated than that."

"Why is it? Who says it has to be?"

"I won't hold you back, Tate. It's not fair. You deserve more. Go and sing. You have to."

"I don't want to unless you tell me you'll wait for me." I sniff, not caring that I sound like I'm begging.

Because I am.

I'll beg until my voice deserts me if that's what it takes. I love him. And I love Molly.

He puts his glass on the table and takes my hand, lifting it to his lips. He screws his eyes closed and kisses my fingertips one by one before dropping his forehead to them.

"My life changed the day they both died. I will always be in New York. For my family. Your career could take you all over the world, but I will *never* leave here. And you'll never have more than this with me."

"It's enough. It's more than enough," I urge, a bubble threatening to burst in my throat and bring a barrage of ugly tears with it.

"It shouldn't be." He shakes his head. "You shouldn't have to give up your dreams for us."

"The night I heard my song on the radio, you said you were right here, that you weren't going anywhere," I say, searching his face for a hint of surrender, but he's as cool and collected as he is at work, CEO poker face well and truly in place.

"And that's true. I am right here. And I was there for you that night. But I will always be *here*, Tate. With Molly. You don't see it, but we have to stay as we are. Me and Molly."

"What about you, me, and Molly? I lov…"

I bite back the word before it slips out, hating how pathetic I sound.

He pins me with one of his intense stares. The ones that usually make me weak at the knees.

This time he brings me to them.

"I'll never marry you, Tate. I'll never want kids with you. You will never be more than a girlfriend who I hide my daughter from seeing first thing in the morning."

The bubble detonates spectacularly, and I choke out a sob.

His voice is so soft, so caring.

But his words are brutal, shredding my heart to pieces.

"I'm sorry. That is all I can ever offer you. Nothing more."

"You're not in love with me," I breathe, my bottom lip trembling. "Why don't you just say that?"

The first hint of emotion flashes in his eyes and they pinch at the corners.

"I *can't* love you. Not the way I want to."

"What does that even mean?" I yank my hands from his and swipe at my eyes, hating the look of pity that's growing in his.

"It means tonight is our last night together. Cliff will drive you home now if that's what you want."

Silence stretches between us. I give him time to take back his cruel confession. Time to retract the last five minutes and start over.

To make it all good again.

He just watches me with those damn eyes that I can never seem to look away from.

"What other option do I have?" I snap.

"You can stay," he says. "You can give us one more night. *Please.*"

38

SULLIVAN

"I DON'T KNOW."

"Please, Tate," I beg. "Just one more night."

"What will you tell Molly?"

Her voice tears my soul from my body. She's holding it together, but the tremor is there, beneath the surface.

She blinks at me, tears pooling along her lower lashes. I hate myself for being the reason they're there. I should have kept away from her. I could have prevented all of this from happening. I could have spared her the inevitable outcome that was always going to come if she got involved with me.

"I'll tell her you went on an adventure."

She sucks in a sharp breath.

"Tate," I murmur, reaching for her hands.

She yanks them away.

"No. Don't say my name like that. Don't you dare make out you're doing this for me."

"I'm sorry," I rasp, meaning it down to the very core of who I am. I lean closer, reaching for her again, taking her hands and running my thumbs over the back of them. "I really am."

"This can't be real. Tell me you don't feel this between us." She searches my eyes, but I can't answer her.

Of course I fucking feel it. I feel it so much my heart wants to burst out of my chest when I think about what I have with her.

"Tell me you don't feel this," she repeats with more determination, climbing into my lap and straddling me.

She crushes her lips to mine desperately.

"If you were sorry, you wouldn't be doing this."

I deepen our kiss until I'm groaning into her mouth and gripping her hips like my life depends on it. I don't want it to be this way anymore than she does.

But I don't want to keep lying to her.

And I *can't* tell her the truth.

She pulls away and rests her forehead against mine. "I know you feel this." She places her hand over my thundering heart.

"It doesn't matter what I feel. This is the way it's got to be." I run the backs of my fingers down her cheek. "I am so sorry, Baby," I whisper, my voice hoarse.

She pushes away, hands flattened against my chest.

"Don't call me that!"

She shoves at my chest over and over as I wrap my arms around her and pin her to me. My head pounds at the thought she'll walk out the door like this. Hating me.

"Get off!" she snaps, wriggling in my hold and shoving at me harder.

But there's no real strength behind her attack. She isn't trying to hurt me.

She's trying not to fall apart in front of me.

I did this to her.

"Tate," I plead. "I'll let you go. Just breathe."

She freezes, meeting my eyes with a glare hot enough to brand me. Her shoulders rise and fall with rage-fueled pants, and I welcome them. I welcome anything that takes away from the sadness in her eyes. I'd rather she lets her hurt out like this. Seeing her cry is too much. Absorbing her anger is easier, even if the thought of her walking out and hating me is more than I can handle.

"Just breathe," I repeat.

We stare at one another, and I try to commit the exact pattern in her irises to memory, tracing over each swirl of blue in them that fan out from her pupils like notes suspended on the lines of a musical staff.

A song I don't deserve to ever hear, let alone play.

"I don't love you." Her words fly from her lips as she spits them out. She's lying. But the venom in her tone still cuts deeply. "I don't love you, Sullivan Beaufort."

I scan her face, swallowing down a burning in my throat as I do what I have to for both of our sakes.

I pretend I believe her.

"Good. I don't deserve your love."

"You don't," she agrees, holding my eyes. "But Molly does. And I *do* love her. You don't get to tell me I can't. You can tell me we're over. You can stop me from seeing her again. But you can't stop me from loving your daughter. No one can."

My heart seizes.

Molly.

Tate shoves at my chest one final time and my arms fall from around her, letting her go without hesitation. My eyes sting and I work my throat to hold back the prickling sensation behind them that's threatening to erupt.

She loves Molly.

I didn't cry at my mother and brother's funeral. And I'm not going to cry now.

This is what has to happen, even though letting her go just became a billion times harder.

I wait for her to climb from my lap. To walk out of my home. Out of my life.

"I'm sorry," I utter.

Tate searches my eyes, and the fire burning in them flares as she leans closer.

Then her lips are on mine again.

She rips at my shirt and tugs at my belt with determination.

"What are you doing?" I say into her fierce kiss.

"Shut up."

She yanks my shirt out of my pants, a high-pitched tear piercing the air as the fabric rips.

Her kiss grows more frantic, her teeth sliding over my lower lip.

"I'm sorry," I rasp into her mouth.

My words only feed her anger, and she bites me, sending a shot of metallic warmth coating our tongues as they wrap together.

"Shut up and touch me," she grits. "You don't get to be the one who controls this. If this is over, then I'm ending things my way."

She bites my lip again and my hands fly to her breasts. I knead them roughly through her shirt, pinching her nipples and making her hiss.

"I'm sorry," I say again, earning myself another bite.

I groan into our kiss as her nails scrape down my chest, snagging on the flesh.

"Stop talking," Tate cries, yanking down my zipper.

She shoves at my pants and pushes her hand into them, pulling my weeping dick out and squeezing it hard.

"Fuck." Blood rushes painfully to my groin, making me even harder.

She jerks me, and I curse, my cock leaking in a nonstop stream all over her hand.

"Damn it, Tate. I'm sorry," I groan as she discards my cock against my lower abs and pulls harshly on my balls, digging her nails in.

"Don't talk to me," she snaps, shoving her tongue inside my mouth again.

It's not goodbye sex.

It's 'I hate you for what you've done' sex.

But she needs this.

And I need her to have whatever she needs.

If that means scratching me and hurting me, I'll take it all. I'll take whatever she gives me if it makes this any easier for her.

"I'm sorry, *Baby*," I breathe, knowing it'll push her over the edge.

She screams into our kiss, and I seize my opportunity, lifting her in my arms and tossing her on the floor beneath me.

Hips bucking against me, she wraps her legs around my waist and digs her heels into my ass, drawing me closer to her.

I hold her eyes, rip her panties to the side, and spear her with two fingers.

"This what you need?" I grunt, watching her eyelashes flutter in undisguised pleasure.

"Fuck you!"

"I want you to, Baby. You're so damn good at it."

I swirl my fingers deeper, hitting the spot that makes her tremble. But it's not enough to push her over the edge. I sit back on my heels and look at her, giving her one last opportunity to leave.

She stays as she is. Legs parted, pussy glistening, and eyes narrowed into hateful slits.

"Get on with it, Sullivan," she snarls.

"You sure this is what you want?"

"Yes, Just fucking do it already." She forces her lips together, holding back a sob.

My cock leaks as I lift her leg onto my shoulder and kiss her ankle, sliding my tongue up her calf to her knee as I take her other leg and place it on my other shoulder.

I fold her in half and let out a guttural groan as I thrust inside her.

"How fitting. Just like the first time," she snipes as my face hovers over hers. "You told me to forget it had ever happened after that. Well, guess what?" She stares into my eyes. "This time, that's exactly what I'm going to do."

I suck in a rough breath. "You want to forget me?" I flex my cock inside her, making her whimper.

She gives me a cold smile. "I've already started."

"Fuck!"

I pull out and drive back inside her, fucking her as hard as I physically can. My knees burn against the rug like the skin is being torn off.

She stares at me the whole time, anger blowing her pupils wide as her tits bounce in the gap between us. I know she's holding my eyes on purpose. It's not about intimacy this time. It's about showing me what I'm throwing away. What she will never give me again after tonight.

It's about giving me one last great big 'fuck you' before she leaves.

She tips her head back and moans, coming around my cock in rippling waves.

"Tate," I growl, the feel of her setting off my own release. I come so hard inside her that my head spins. "Fuck, I'm sorry. I'm so fucking sorry."

I keep thrusting as she comes again and tears her nails down my back.

If this is the last time I'll ever have her like this, then God knows I'm going to make it count.

It's 5.30 a.m. when she slides out of my bed. Our bodies parted for the final time less than an hour ago, and we've been lying beside one another in silence since.

The last proper words I said to her were the rough, *"I'm so fucking sorry"*, as I came inside her in the living room.

I've come inside her more times since then. And on her breasts, over her ass, down her throat. All in groans and grunts. Sometimes, I've not even pulled out in between. We've just stared at each other in silence.

No words. Just the warmth of each other's bodies, the taste of each other's kisses, the scent of each other's skin.

And the sight of each other's eyes as we held on to them like anchors.

Neither of us wanted to break it. Because once that final time was over, that would be it.

We'd be here.

In the moment where it's come for her to leave.

Muffled crying comes from inside my bathroom, and I stare at the strip of light spilling from underneath the door. The sound of her pain reaches my body like a beckoning finger, urging me to climb out of bed and go to her. To find a way to fix this.

But there isn't one.

I screw my eyes closed and turn my back to the bathroom door.

It opens and she walks into the room, but she doesn't falter.

She pads softly across the carpet and opens the door.

Then she's gone.

39

TATE

TWO WEEKS LATER

"Go and sing." My dad beams, nodding enthusiastically at me where we're standing backstage.

I wiggle my fingers by my sides, trying to shake the tingling nerves from them. I'm about to play the piano and sing a new song in front of thousands of people. We're in LA. I've already done it multiple times. I should be used to it by now.

"I'm going to be sick again," I blurt, before one of the stage crew calmly hands me a bucket.

I deposit the contents of my twisting stomach into it and take the cold washcloth Dad hands to me. It's all part of my pre-show routine now. Everyone knows what to do.

"Thank you." I wipe my mouth and try to ignore the prickling sensation crawling over my skin as the crowd roars in response to the stage lighting changing, illuminating the piano with a spotlight.

I'm up.

"Go and sing," my father repeats, gently patting my upper arm. "You'll be fine once you get out there."

I nod weakly, not wanting to break the look of pride and love in his eyes.

I am not fine.

I hate every second of it.

And even though he doesn't know it, his choice of words makes me feel like I might throw up again.

"Go and sing."

It's exactly what Sullivan told me to do.

Right before he broke my heart.

I thought staying for that final night might have changed his mind. But it didn't. The last time I walked out of his place, I saw what he'd left on the table by the front door, placed so conspicuously for me to see.

A key for a private suite at The Lanceford Hotel.

The press didn't concoct the story because it sounds scandalous. That part of Sullivan's life is real, and he wanted me to know it. It was his way of telling me that he intended to move on the moment I left. He's probably there now, fucking some beautiful woman with toned thighs that looks like Cara.

But it's not the sight of that key that cut the deepest. It was the realization I came to after I left his place and replayed that night in my head.

He'd asked me to read to Molly as a way of saying goodbye to her without knowing that's what I was doing. I hate him for it. But equally, I understand why he did it. Molly might have got upset if I'd said goodbye, because I would have probably cried. I wouldn't have been able to hold back the pain I feel at knowing I'll never hold her in my arms again or sink my nose into her soft little curls and feel her giggling in my embrace.

I loved her as much as I loved him. Only, I can force myself to get over Sullivan. I'll never stop loving Molly. And that's something I'll have to learn to live with.

"I'm good now," I assure my dad, brushing down my dress and taking a deep breath.

"Show them what you've got, love."

I pull my shoulders back and walk onstage, into the heat of

the spotlight. Cellphone lights cover the sea of people staring at me, and I'm grateful I can't make out their faces. The only way I get through each show is if I close my eyes and pretend no one else is here. Kind of like The Masked Maestro did that day in Grand Central Station on his final song. Maybe that song was the hardest one he's ever played too.

That day feels like a lifetime ago now.

I sit at the piano and stare at the ivory and black keys, my heart sinking.

"This song's called *Blue Eyes*," I say into the microphone as I slide my fingers over the cool keys.

The crowd roars.

I squeeze my eyes shut and sing.

40

SULLIVAN

"I'M RAISING OUR FEE BY TWO HUNDRED PERCENT. That's fine, right? Actually, you're listening so hard, you're thinking three hundred sounds better, aren't you?"

"Mm." I grunt, staring across my desk and into the office opposite. Molly's in there with Arabella.

She's coloring, her face set in a scowl of concentration. My happy little girl has changed. Arabella thought it could be the 'terrible twos' coming late, seeing as Molly is turning three soon.

But it isn't just the increase in tantrums. It's the way she's stopped sleeping through the night and has been climbing into bed with me again. And the way she's gone back to refusing to eat all of her meals.

"I tried to make bear pancakes last week and she threw them on the floor, then cried."

"What? Oh, I see," Rafe says in understanding through the phone speaker. "She'll be okay. She's adjusting, that's all."

"It's been almost three weeks. I thought kids were supposed to adjust fast." I lean over my desk and scrub a hand around my jaw. "She won't wear anything else except this bunny onesie. I have to sneak the thing out of her room at night to get it into the laundry."

"You could call Tate? Maybe Molly would be happier if she speaks to her."

"I think it'll just confuse her," I say.

I don't know that for certain. But I do know I'm too fucking scared to find out. This is the way things have to be.

"How was LA?" Rafe asks, sensing my need to change the subject.

"Fine. The store is thriving. The new manager has it handled."

"Had to go check in person, though, right?"

"Yeah," I mutter.

"Like you checked San Diego last week."

"Exactly," I clip back.

"And San Francisco," Rafe adds, letting his unspoken knowledge of where I've really been hang in the air.

"You told your sister that you're jerking off to videos of her best friend yet?"

"Arsehole." Rafe chuckles. "Fine. Point taken. I won't mention your sudden increase in airmiles again."

"Good," I grumble.

"Speaking of women we aren't supposed to be speaking about..." Rafe murmurs. "My sister and Aurora just walked in. I've got to go."

"Stay sitting at your desk. That way they won't see your boner."

"Fuck off," he rumbles, hanging up.

I look up as my father, Sinclair, and her dog, Monty, arrive and go in to greet Molly and Arabella. I stand and make my way to the office opposite, thanking Arabella as she passes me on her way back out to her office.

"Ready for a sleepover with Grandad?" my father asks as he swoops down and pulls Molly into his arms.

She grins at him, obviously saving her recent tantrums for my personal enjoyment only.

"See baby?" she asks hopefully.

"I think we can arrange that." He chuckles.

My father bought a home scan machine when Halliday fell pregnant. He says it's for peace of mind. But we all know it's because he's excited and wants to see the baby every day.

He was never like this with our mother. Halliday's been good for him.

"Hallie said if you're lucky, you might even feel the baby move," he adds.

Molly's eyes widen in wonder, and she looks at Sinclair, who reaches out to grab her little hand and kiss her fingers.

"I'm going to come with you and Grandad. I've got some wedding things to talk about with Halliday. That okay?"

"It okay," Molly replies seriously, like she's given it great thought.

"Good."

My sister's gaze slides to me.

"I guess you're busy tonight, huh? Since it's Thursday." The repulsion in her voice is palpable.

I bristle, straightening my shoulders. "I have plans, if that's what you're asking, Sis?"

"I can't believe you still have that place."

"I have good reason to, not that I have to explain myself."

"Whatever." Sinclair snorts. "I'm going to go to the bathroom before we leave."

She spins and storms off, Monty trailing obediently behind her.

"She'll be fine," my father assures.

"Denver's a saint for being her bodyguard for as long as he was," I mutter. "How's finding his replacement going?"

"Damn impossible," my father says, lowering his voice as

he places Molly down and tells her to collect her baby from where she's left it strapped in a toy stroller across the room.

Not long after the girls came home from Halliday's bachelorette, Denver handed in his notice. He's worked as my father's Head of Security for years. He's like one of the family. I never thought he'd leave.

Then one day he was gone.

Just like that. Handed his notice in and left the city the same day.

"You'll find someone. I can help you interview if you like?"

He nods and claps me between the shoulder blades. "Thanks, Son. Mal said he will too now that he's back from Botswana for a couple of weeks. We'll get something set up."

"I'm sorry if she disturbs you tonight," I say, keeping my voice low and gesturing to Molly.

"She still getting out of bed?"

"Yeah." I blow out a breath. "Every night since Tate left."

My father nods. I told him about Tate nannying for Molly. And he understands why she is now on the other side of the country.

I had to do it.

"Have you heard from Natasha recently?" he asks.

Just hearing her name has me grinding my teeth until my jaw throbs.

"She texted again. Same old story. Says she wants to see Molly, but all she really wants is money. She didn't even mention Molly's birthday. I'm not sure she even remembers it's coming up."

"Hmm," my father grumbles as I crouch and hold my arms out for Molly.

"Come and give Daddy a hug before you go, Sweetheart. And I'll see you first thing in the morning, okay?"

She runs over to me, and I wrap my arms around her, stroking her back beneath the furry bunny onesie.

"I love you so much," I tell her.

It's the truth. But what's also true is how badly I need tonight. I haven't been to The Lanceford since meeting Tate.

It's time to move on.

"Did my father send you? Or was it Sinclair?" I ask as I open the door to a tired-looking Uncle Mal on the other side.

"Neither. But they are concerned about you."

"I could have had company." I grunt.

He looks past me into the hotel room and raises a brow.

"I got a headache and decided to be alone," I lie, following his gaze to the untouched bed and single glass of whiskey sitting next to a half-empty bottle on the table.

"If I were wallowing in guilt over losing someone, I'd go to the place where I can remind myself of who I once was too," Mal murmurs, stepping past me and into the room.

He walks over to the whiskey bottle and lifts it.

"Go ahead," I invite, pointing at a clean glass. "It'll stop me from drinking the whole damn thing."

"Thanks." He sighs, pouring a generous amount into the glass.

"Dad told you Tate left, then?"

He slides one hand into his pant pockets and takes a slow drink with the other.

"He did. She's the woman you were talking about at the cemetery? When you said you'd met someone?"

"Yeah." I refill my glass then walk over to join him where

he's standing in front of the floor-to-ceiling windows looking out at the city.

"I see." He doesn't need to say anything else. He knows why Tate had to leave. The whole family knows.

Beauforts stick together.

"I'm sorry, Sull," he says after a few minutes.

"Yeah," I mutter. "Me too."

"So, are you?"

"Am I what?"

"Expecting company?"

He tips his head toward the room behind us—the one with the giant bed. The cabinet beside it is stocked with condoms, lube, and everything else I need for my stays at The Lanceford. It's why I had none that first time with Tate. I don't share the home Molly and I live in with anyone. Sex happens here. And here only.

Until Tate, of course. And I didn't want to wear condoms with her. I wanted every damn inch of her as close to me as I could get it.

It was reckless. So fucking risky. She could have gotten pregnant; then where would we be?

I look at the room through new eyes. No wonder Sinclair hates hearing about this place. I bring women here to fuck, nothing more.

Because I don't do feelings. I don't do love.

I mean, I didn't.

I shake my head, turning back to the window. "I don't want to be that version of myself anymore. Molly deserves better than a father who has women approach him in front of her and he has to wrack his brains to recall if he's had sex with them or not. She's going to grow up into an incredible, smart, and funny young woman. I can't jeopardize her belief in how she should be treated as a woman by being the prime example of the type of man she should avoid at all costs because he treats her as nothing more than an object for his own sexual gratification."

"Very eloquent words after half a bottle of whiskey," Uncle Mal remarks.

I snort, taking another drink. "Yeah. Sin would be fucking proud of me if she weren't already disgusted."

"She's your sister. She'll always be savage when she doesn't agree with you. It's because she loves you that she cares so much."

I exhale slowly as Uncle Mal squeezes my shoulder.

"You're right."

"I am." He chuckles softly. "I know sisters."

I turn to him and the deeply etched lines of grief pulling at his eyes make it hard to swallow. When I lost my mother, he lost his sister. The only sibling he had.

"You can't deny your past, Sull. You can only do your best from this moment on. That's all any of us can do."

"What if my best isn't good enough?"

"It will be. You'll figure it out. And if you need help, you've got it right here." He tips his head back and drains his glass. "We've been through hell as a family. But we stick together."

He gives me a weighted look like he wants to say something else. But instead, he pulls me into a one-armed hug, slapping me on the back.

"You'll be fine, boy. Just fine."

He gives me a parting nod and deposits his empty glass on the table as he leaves.

I collapse into a seat and take my time finishing my glass of whiskey. I could drink the whole damn bottle and pass out on the bed. But with each passing second the walls of the room seem to close in on me, making it hard to breathe.

Pulling out my phone, I scroll to a number and lift it to my ear.

My empty glass falls from my hand and lands softly on the carpet. I pinch my nose and drag in a shuddery breath as I listen.

I end the call without saying anything and haul myself to my feet. Grabbing the trash can, I rip the nightstand drawer out and turn it upside down, shaking the contents into the trash. Then I walk into the bathroom and throw in my toothbrush and floss. I storm around, stripping the place of every last shred of me.

I drop the trash can on the floor and catch sight of myself in the mirror. Bloodshot eyes stare back at me.

"Sort yourself the fuck out," I mutter.

I walk out of the room and let the door slam shut behind me.

The young woman on reception looks up with a bright smile as I exit the elevator and walk over.

"Mr. Beaufort. It's good to see you again. Is everything okay with your suite?"

I press the keycard down on the counter, sliding it over to her.

"Cancel my contract, please."

Her eyes pop wide. "You've been a valued guest for almost three years. We'll be very sad to see you go."

"Nothing lasts forever," I grunt, the whiskey making my head too foggy for small talk.

She takes the keycard and taps into her computer. "You're paid up until the end of next month, so it will remain yours until then, should you change your mind."

"I won't," I clip, already turning away. "But thank you."

41

TATE

ONE MONTH LATER

I DROP MY TOOTHBRUSH BACK INTO THE GLASS beside the sink.

Another city. Another show.

Another round of pre-show stage fright hurling.

"You okay in there, love?" Dad calls through the door.

I splash cold water on my face and plaster on a smile. "Fine," I reply, walking out of the bathroom and into the small dressing room.

My father looks up from the chair he's sitting in, worried creases lining his brow. "You sure it's only—?"

"I'm not pregnant, Dad."

His shoulders fall, but he doesn't look relieved. If he's hoping to be a grandad any time soon, then he'll have a long wait ahead. I've had two periods since leaving New York. And I'm still taking my pill, despite the idea of letting a man near me again making me break out in hives.

"I'll never marry you, Tate. I'll never want to have children with you."

It's been weeks, yet Sullivan's words still circle around my

327

head like a cruel merry-go-round. He had to put it out there so callously. Make sure I understood.

I meant *nothing* to him.

"It's just pre-performance jitters. Completely normal," I tell my father.

"It's getting worse, love. You only used to be sick once before a show. Now you're in the bathroom for an hour each time."

"It's the traveling. All the different food's messing with my stomach," I lie.

My father nods, looking unconvinced.

I walk over to the vase of flowers and inhale their creamy scent to remove the smell of vomit from my nostrils—white roses, like the paper ones Sullivan gave me that are still at home in my bedroom.

A wave of nausea threatens to rise again, and I step back, grabbing a bottle of water to sip instead.

"This is the one!" a voice yells in the hallway.

The door bursts open and Ashley flies in, red and flustered.

"Jesus, where's the air conditioning?"

She tosses her purse onto the floor and makes a beeline for me, pulling me into her arms.

"Tate? Oh my God. Girl, I've missed you!"

"Ash!" I squeal, wrapping my arms around her and laughing at how tight she's squeezing me. "What are you doing here? You didn't tell me you were coming."

"We wanted to surprise you."

I look up, and Huck is hovering inside the doorway wearing jeans and a lumberjack shirt.

"Hey, Tate." He lifts a hand in greeting first to me, then my father. The other is curled around a steaming travel mug.

"I can't believe you're here," I say, holding her tight. "You've no idea how much I needed this."

"About as much as I did too, I expect," Ashley replies, letting me go and turning to smile at Huck. "Give it to her, then."

She pulls my father into a hug almost as enthusiastically as she did me.

Huck steps forward and brandishes the travel mug to me like it's filled with liquid gold.

"You brought me one from Caffeine Couture because you knew I missed home? No way. You're amazing!" I grin, taking the mug and inhaling the rich, decadent scent, waiting for the blast of familiarity to envelop me like a warm hug on a cold night.

"Oh? Is it a new blend?" I ask, taking a sip. It's smooth and creamy, and something about it makes my throat thicken with emotion, even though it isn't one of our house blends I've spent hours drinking with Ashley.

"My first thought was to bring you one of ours in a flask. But then Huck made this," Ashley says, her eyes moving to him proudly.

He runs a hand around the back of his head sheepishly. "It came out of a new portable machine I've designed a prototype for, so people traveling don't have to miss their favorite cup of coffee in the morning."

"It's phenomenal," I say, taking another sip. "Thank you."

"He's a genius." Ashley beams, patting him on his giant, bear-like chest and pressing a kiss to his cheek.

I bite back my smile. All those times she would complain about never meeting a good guy as she sorted through the business cards from suited businessmen we'd get left. And now here she is, looking completely besotted with the guy who owns the best coffee company in the country and turns up to work in ripped jeans and steel toe-capped boots.

I'm so happy it's working out for one of us.

"He's also really good at packing, aren't you, Babe? Let's

start with the closet." Ashley points at the open closet, and my father nods at her in agreement. "Good idea."

"What are you doing?" I gape as the three of them spring into action like a well-choreographed military unit.

"We're calling time on this shit for you. Because you're too nice to do it and will worry that you're letting people down. But you're not," Ashley says.

"What?"

She walks over to where my phone is charging and unplugs it, before tucking it into my purse.

"I called them, love," Dad says, hesitation creeping into his tone. "You don't play like you did in the basement. You're getting more sick, not less. I began to suspect you were pretending. For me. And... for yourself, perhaps. But you don't have to do that. I'm proud of you no matter what. Dusty old piano or sold-out arena. As long as you play because you love to, and not because you think you have to, that's all I care about."

"Dad..."

I look around the dressing room. We've only been here for a day. I've not even unpacked. Ashley and Huck barely have anything to do. But Dad hasn't called them because we needed help packing.

He's called them because he could see I needed support from those I love.

"It's okay to say enough is enough. You don't owe anyone anything, Tate," he says, stopping in front of me. "Tell me you honestly love this, and that you're in your element out on that stage, and we'll all pretend this never happened. Ashley and Huck will go back to New York. And you and I will continue with the tour."

I stare at them, while they wait for my answer.

Going back to New York means throwing away an opportunity that so many musicians would kill for.

Going back to New York means admitting this isn't the life I want.

Going back to New York means being back in the same city as Sullivan and Molly.

I push the final thought to the back of my mind because it's the one with the most power to stop me from doing what I know in my heart is the right thing for me.

"I hate it," I admit in a rush. "When I'm not throwing up, I'm thinking about throwing up. And when I'm on stage, I wish I was throwing up, because it's the more enjoyable option to me."

The entire room audibly exhales in relief at my words. Maybe they thought they'd have to fight me into seeing what's so obvious. I don't know how I've lasted as long as I have on this tour.

"I want to write songs, not perform them," I say with newfound determination.

"All right, then," my father says with a relieved smile.

"Thank God!" Ashley sighs as Huck smiles at me from beside her.

"I need to talk to the tour manager. And we need to look into flights back," I say, my mind running a million miles per minute.

"It's all taken care of, Girl," Ashley says, pulling me into another hug. "All taken care of."

Two hours later, we're sitting onboard a private jet, having just taken off from Las Vegas.

"How did you arrange all this?" I whisper to Ashley as Huck shows my father around the interior.

The whole thing is plush carpets and soft, buttery leather in shades of silvery, pale gray. It looks like something out of a movie.

"Huck's friend is some bigshot and loaned it to us. He met them at some entrepreneur convention or something. I don't know. But it just shows that coffee brings people together." She bumps shoulders with me and winks.

"Sure does." I rest my head on her shoulder, and she puts hers on top of mine, letting out a happy sigh.

"I'm so happy you're coming home."

"Me too," I agree.

"Were you really sick before every show?"

"And after," I confess quietly. My father doesn't know about the after as well.

"Damn," Ashley mumbles.

"Did you…" I lift my head and check my father and Huck are out of earshot. "Did you ask Huck about Liberty Records?"

"I did." Ashley pulls her lower lip into her mouth, and I can tell from the way her shoulders drop that I'm not going to like what she has to tell me. Huck knows a lot of people in business, so I hoped he'd know someone who could answer some questions for me.

"Was it Brandon? Did he somehow—?"

"No, he had nothing to do with it."

She reaches into her purse and pulls out a folded piece of paper, handing it to me.

I stare at it, heat flaring across the back of my neck.

Everything about that meeting with Kyle Drayton at Liberty Records felt off. It was too easy to get time with him. He was too quick to admit their mistake. And far too eager to offer me a deal on the spot in order to make it all right.

An offer that was way out of line with what an unknown artist could ever hope to receive as their first offer.

I may be naïve at times, but I'm not completely stupid. Something didn't add up. I ignored it at first. But the feeling has only grown.

"A company bought it. The sale finalized the day before we went to the head office together. It was rushed through. They paid well above what it was worth in order to obtain it."

"A company bought it?" I echo, nausea climbing up my windpipe.

"Yeah." Ashley nods. "Huck said his friend was able to pull some strings and get hold of a copy of that." She gestures to the document in my hands.

I unfold the piece of paper and hold my breath as I scan it. It's the first page of a contract.

One between Liberty Records and their new owner—a company called Slade Investments.

My eyes snag on the name listed alongside the company name.

Miss Molly Beaufort.

42

TATE

I come to the closing bars of the song and shake my head at my father with a soft smile.

"That's what you said about the last one I played."

"True." His eyes crinkle at the corners and he chuckles. "I'm just happy to see you playing again without getting sick."

"Yeah, me too," I murmur, letting my fingers linger on the old piano keys.

Coming home's not been as strange as I thought it would be. It's been a couple of days, and I feel like I never left. Larry was waiting for us when we got back, eager to show us the brand-new working elevator that's been installed, and the new locks that have been fitted to all of the apartment doors. He supervised the work crew doing ours, which I'm grateful for. I know it isn't Sullivan doing the work himself, but he's still the reason it's getting done in the first place.

The fewer reminders of him, the better.

"Could have given it a polish while they were here, though," Dad grumbles, his attention sliding over the dusty, battered woodwork of the piano.

"I'm glad they didn't. It's the one part of this place I hope no one ever touches," I muse, lowering the cover over the keys and stroking it tenderly.

It doesn't matter that it needs a good tune and some TLC. Money can't improve the memories I have of writing my songs on it.

"Have you heard anything yet?" my father asks, pulling the clean laundry from the state-of-the-art dryer that looks like it belongs in a mansion, not in our communal basement.

"Yeah. Mr. Drayton called just before you came down here."

"And?" My father lifts a questioning brow.

"And he said I can take my time thinking about what I want to do. They aren't going to enforce my contract and make me finish the tour. Or hold me to recording in the studio with them if I don't want to."

"That's good news."

"It is," I agree, my smile growing tight.

I suspect Kyle Drayton knew I had doubts. He had a replacement support act filling my spot before our flight even touched down back in New York.

I was replaceable in an instant.

The feeling is all too familiar.

I made the error of looking on a local news site before I came downstairs to play. There was Sullivan, top story of the gossip column, leaving The Lanceford late one evening. The press delighted in that juicy story; after stating he hadn't been seen there in months.

But it looks like he moved on after I left a lot faster than I'll be able to.

I was still soaking in the feeling of betrayal when Kyle Drayton called and delivered his very 'no-pressure' speech. I can't believe I was so stupid and didn't see it. Sullivan bought Liberty Records so he could engineer a recording contract and a tour for me. He made certain I wasn't going to be in the vicinity of him or Molly.

He wanted me gone that badly.

"What are your plans this afternoon?" my father asks, breaking me out of my self-pity.

"I'm visiting Ashley."

"Have you decided if you're going to go back to work for her?"

"I don't know."

Ashley's offer was appreciated. In fact, it was less of an offer, and more of an assumption. But she realized her error the second I grimaced. Returning to work at Caffeine Couture means working next door to Beaufort Diamonds again. A move I'm not sure I'm ready for, even though I know I shouldn't allow Sullivan to influence my decisions.

"I thought going there this afternoon to hang out with her might help me decide."

"Hm, good idea. Test out how you feel being back there." My father nods thoughtfully. He knows the words I'm not saying. He met Sullivan that night he took me to see The Masked Maestro play. He heard me talk about him and Molly.

And he wouldn't have missed the fact that I hadn't mentioned either of them in the days prior to accepting Kyle's offer.

He knows his daughter had her heart broken. He's just waiting until I'm ready to invite him to help with fixing it.

"Exactly. Test out how I feel," I murmur, stroking the bumps and grooves in the worn wooden piano lid.

Sullivan might have brought our song to an abrupt end. But it's time for me to write a new one now.

"He wants at least three kids. I'll tear in half pushing them out if they take after him. You've seen the size of him."

I snort at Ashley's shudder before she throws me a cautious smile. But she doesn't need to worry. I'm not that newly single friend who everyone has to be careful not to upset by talking about how happy they are. I *want* to hear about her and Huck. I've been asking her questions about him for the past fifteen minutes, greedy to revel in every detail of my friend's happiness.

It also helps distract me from scanning the sidewalk outside every few minutes searching for a sign of a black town car.

"First this place became a smash hit. And now you've found Huck. You've got everything we bitched about taking so long to happen." I grin as she bites her lip shyly, completely out of character.

"What is it?" I coax. She never gets coy for no reason.

"He asked me to make him a coffee using his new machine at his place this morning."

I narrow my eyes at her blushing cheeks. Ashley has regaled me with all the sordid details of her one night stands over the course of our friendship. Yet now she's blushing over making a guy a coffee.

"And...?"

"And he..." She shrugs, taking her hand out of her apron pocket. "He left me a surprise inside the bean compartment. And when I turned around, the big bear was down on one knee."

I grab her left hand and pull it toward me.

"Holy... Wow, it's massive!"

"I know," she squeals with undisguised joy. "It's an oval cut, but it looks like a coffee bean to me. I know that's why he chose it."

I turn her hand side to side, admiring the giant engagement ring as it glitters.

"Congratulations," I cry, happiness bubbling in my stomach. "You're getting married. Oh my God!"

I pull her into a giant, crushing hug and am wiping at the tears in my eyes as the bell chimes over the door.

"Hold that hug. I'm coming back for seconds." Ashley sniffs through her laugh as she pulls away to serve the customer.

"Oh." Her laugh dies abruptly.

I look over and my heart stalls.

A pair of brilliant blue eyes stare back at me, hostile and cold enough to freeze hell over. But even his hard expression can't detract from how breathtakingly handsome he is.

I hate him.

I love him.

No, I don't. Not anymore. I can't allow myself to. I hate that even after all these weeks the mere sight of him still causes heat to flood my core.

"You're back," Sullivan states, his lips flattening into a grim line as he approaches the counter.

I step out from behind it and my spine stiffens at hearing his voice again after all these weeks. "Well done on your impeccable observation skills," I remark, wrapping my arms around myself.

He's alone, which I'm grateful for. I couldn't have handled seeing Molly walk in here today. Not when her father is looking at me like he's about to pop a vein.

"You're supposed to be on tour, Tate. Singing."

The gut punch I expect when he says my name doesn't come. It's the word 'singing' that does it.

"I hate performing in front of a big audience," I snap. "You know that."

He jerks back, his brow furrowing like he's shocked. He's such a good actor he deserves an Oscar.

To think I used to get flustered in his presence seems like a joke to me now. He's nothing but a man who uses money to get what he wants.

"I didn't," he says.

"I told you!"

"When?"

"When you... When I... It was that time when..." I suck in a breath and clamp my lips together as my heart pounds.

I told him. Didn't I?

"I never told you I wanted to perform," I hiss.

"You never told me you didn't," he replies calmly. He's already composed himself from the surprise of seeing me again. Yet my insides have turned to jelly.

I hate that he has the upper hand. That he's talking to me in his business voice. The voice he uses when it doesn't matter how much the other person protests, he knows by the end of their conversation he will come away as the victor.

"You were verging on being inconsolable when you found out that your song was stolen," he says.

His phone rings in his pocket, but he ignores it.

"I wasn't inconsolable!" I scoff as my cheeks flare with heat. "I was fine. You calmed me down and then spent the night—"

I grimace, clawing back the words before it's too late. He spent the night taking care of me, telling me I didn't need to do a thing. It was the first time in my life I felt treasured by anyone who wasn't my mother, father, or Ashley.

The first time I've felt truly loved by someone else.

"I hated seeing you hurting," Sullivan says, tenderness creeping into his tone and bringing with it a flash of the man I thought I knew.

He clears his throat, his features hardening again. "What

did Liberty Records do? I'll call Jones. Whatever it is, he'll help you get your contract amended. You can do different shows. Smaller ones. Whatever you're comfortable with."

Throw money at the problem, of course that's his answer.

I rub my temples and screw my eyes shut. "Please stop talking."

My head pounds, made worse by the fact the scent of his cologne, mixed with his warm skin, is reaching over to me and making memories flash to the front of my mind.

Memories of intense gazes and whispered words as he kissed me and covered my body with his.

"But it's your dream," he says slowly, like he's explaining it to me.

"No. Me being gone was *your* dream. You didn't care about what *I* wanted. You made that clear when you ended things between us."

"I thought performing your songs was what you wanted." He scowls at me like it's my fault that I'm back here.

Anger builds inside me until my veins are practically vibrating with it. Sullivan stands perfectly calm in a new designer suit I don't recognize. He looks incredible in it. He always does. *Asshole.*

"No! I hated it. God, do you not see anything?"

His eyes narrow. "I see clearly, Tate. Believe me. I make hard decisions because I can see the consequences of what can happen if we are too weak to make them. If we allow ourselves the indulgence of wanting something we cannot have."

"What the hell's that supposed to mean?"

He told me he had to end things because he couldn't give me more than what we had. That him and Molly had to stay as they were, and that he can't love me the way he wants to.

It was all just a fancy bullshit way of saying he didn't want to try.

That what we had wasn't special enough.

He purses his lips, his eyes blazing into mine.

"Nothing," he clips.

Ashley's carried on serving the slow stream of customers, throwing me glances every few minutes, checking if I need back up.

But Sullivan is all mine. I've had weeks to think about what I'd like to say to him, given the chance. Time to pore over the words he used when he ended things. I've tried to make sense of them. But no matter how many ways I look at it, they don't.

They never will.

I lower my voice, grateful that it's quiet and no one's bothering to pay attention to the two of us. "You bought Liberty Records and got them to make me an offer no sane person could refuse."

"And yet here you are, back in New York, giving up," he says, arching a brow.

I step closer to him, my head threatening to explode with how much he's hurt me.

"Giving up?" I snort. "You're one to talk."

He blanches momentarily before his mask of indifference slides back into place over his face.

"You made me think they believed in me. That they thought my songs were good and I had talent. When you paid for it all with your billions of morally bankrupt dollars."

His nostrils flare and he stares down his nose at me. *Morally bankrupt?*

"Money can buy a lot of things. But it sure as hell can't buy basic human decency. I thought Liberty Records were interested in *me*, not your money."

His lips twist into a grimace. "They already produced your song, didn't they? When they thought your shithead ex wrote it? Why would they do that if they thought it was trash?"

"Because—"

He lifts two fingers in the air, signaling me to let him finish. *Arrogant ass.*

"Why would they sink hundreds of thousands of dollars into getting every radio station to play it?"

"They did what?"

"Why would they fight like hell with me when I told them that if they wanted their record label to continue to exist, then they'd make sure every single copy of that girl your ex fucked behind your back, singing your song, was destroyed?"

"What?" I gasp.

"Why would they do all of that for something mediocre written by someone with no talent?"

My eyes burn, tears building in them.

He leans closer, his eyes roaming over my face intently, like he's finally allowing himself to accept that I'm back and standing right in front of him.

"They wouldn't, Tate," he breathes. "They fucking wouldn't. And if me telling you that isn't enough, then what about all those screaming fans at the concerts? The ones who sang along, reciting every word of your music as you performed? The ones holding up homemade banners with blue eyes on? What about them? Were they all fake, too? Were they all lying too?"

"How do you know about the banners?" I choke out in a strained whisper.

Sullivan moves back, creating more distance between us.

"How do you know?" I press.

He remains silent, refusing to give me anything. Something I should be used to from him by now.

"Why can't you just admit it, Sullivan?" I sigh, my fight seeping away and leaving me deflated and empty. "You wanted me gone because being with me was too complicated. It meant opening yourself up. You wanted me to leave so you could go back to The Lanceford and fuck on schedule. In fact, it's

Thursday." I shrug. "If you leave now, you can have an extra-long evening with whichever woman you select for the night."

I give him a sad smile.

"You got scared about how close I was getting to you and Molly. So you got rid of me in the easiest way you knew how. You used something dear to me to manipulate me. Well, congratulations, you won. We're over, and you don't have to pretend anymore. You don't have to worry about what could happen. Because we are done."

"Tate," he murmurs.

I ignore the pang in my heart at the emotion that's crept into his tone.

It's all an act. But I don't see why he's insisting on dragging it out. He can walk out of here and forget about me. Just like he planned to do all along. He has no reason to stay. No reason to be staring at me from where he's towering in front of me like a dark-suited inferno, brimming with tension that makes it appear like he's barely holding himself together.

If he's going to stay here, prolonging it, then he can listen to my next words. Maybe he needs to hear them as much as I need to say them.

I whisper softly, sadness overtaking the hurt in my voice. "You're a coward, Sullivan Beaufort. A beautiful coward who doesn't know how to let someone love him and his daughter."

A muscle twitches in his cheek, his eyes penetrating deep into my soul.

But I've locked him out of it now.

I won't let him hurt me again.

He speaks slowly through gritted teeth. "You're right, Tate. I am a coward."

I inhale sharply as he reaches up and brushes the backs of his fingers down my cheek with aching tenderness.

"I am a coward," he repeats. "Because I was fucking *terri-*

fied of you. Terrified of what you staying could have done to me."

I freeze as he leans closer, his breath fanning over my face. He pauses with his lips inches from mine.

"Happy now, Baby?" he asks in a strained whisper.

My mouth falls open, and I struggle to take a breath, let alone answer him.

His eyes burn into mine, and he licks his lips, making me shiver like an idiot.

Then he storms off, throwing open the door with a punch as he leaves.

43

SULLIVAN

How fucking dare she?

She thinks she doesn't have talent? That the label only wanted her because I bought them? She blamed it all on me, using me as her scapegoat for giving up. She could have had it all. Everything that being with me could never give her.

"I hated it."

"Me being gone was your dream."

"Jesus Christ." I slam my head into my hands, scrunching up the roots of my hair and slumping forward.

Cliff wisely put the privacy screen up the moment I threw myself into the backseat of the car after work, sensing I needed space on the drive to Seasons where I'm going to meet my father and collect Molly.

Tate has no idea why I can't be with her the way I wish I could. I would kill for the chance to be able to live my life how I wanted to. But it's more complicated than that. Just like I told her it was.

I thought the tour would make her happy. Make her forget about us. I hoped it would ease my guilt at having lied to her for so long.

347

I'm a deluded asshole, because it's achieved nothing except making her hate me.

I yank my tie loose as the memory of her calling me a coward assaults me, making my chest tighten. I screw my eyes shut, rubbing them. But it's no use. The disappointment and hurt in her eyes are seared into the backs of my eyelids.

Something new to add to the nightmares.

My phone rings and I pull it out, my jaw clenching at the name on the screen.

"Natasha?" I snap. "What is it?"

"You didn't answer my call earlier. Are you avoiding me?"

Praying for you to disappear would be more accurate.

"I don't have time to concern myself over missing one of your many pointless calls. I have a business to run, and a daughter to care for. What the hell do you want?"

I've had enough. I'm stressed to the max today after fighting with Tate, and Natasha always calls with the same bullshit. I should ignore her calls altogether. It's always money she's after.

"Charming way to talk to Peaches' mom," she drawls.

It's barely six p.m., but I wouldn't put it past her to be on her way to being drunk already. I doubt she recalls what it feels like not to be either drunk or hungover anymore.

I ignore her jibe. Rising to it will only prolong our conversation.

"I'm not giving you any money. I told you. Get clean, then we'll talk."

"I'm in New York. I went by your office, but they said I missed you."

"What?" I snap, my eyes threatening to bug out of my head.

"I want to see her, Sullivan," she demands, suddenly sounding far more lucid.

Cold sweat pricks along my hairline.

"No."

"I'm not leaving until I do."

"She doesn't know you," I spit. "You'll be a stranger to her."

"You managed it when I left her for you to look after. She didn't know you then, either."

"She was a baby!"

My grip on the phone tightens so much that it could shatter it at any second.

"I want my daughter back," Natasha continues.

"You gave up the right to call her yours when you left her in a fucking box on my doorstep!"

She sighs like she's bored of hearing it. But she needs to. She's the shittiest excuse for a mother that's ever existed. And I'll do whatever it takes to protect Molly from her.

"I have every right. She's mine."

I suck in a blistering breath. Her argument is the same old one. But this time it's different. This time she's actually come to New York. Away from Florida where Molly was conceived on a stupid bachelor weekend years ago. Natasha was a drunk then too. But it wasn't obvious. Not when everyone was having fun and partying.

I hate that Molly was the result of a one-night stand that meant absolutely nothing.

"She's mine, Natasha," I grit dangerously. "You don't want to play this game with me."

"You're a fucking entitled asshole; you know that?"

She hangs up on me, but instead of feeling relieved, anger courses through my blood like liquid fire.

She's in New York. Far too close for comfort.

The car rolls to a stop outside Seasons, and I leap out, tipping my head at Cliff before I storm inside.

Molly's playing on the floor with Sinclair and Halliday. She looks so happy fussing Monty, and Sinclair's new puppy,

Mabel. I give her a brief kiss and cuddle, not wanting her to pick up on my tense mood and ruin the innocent smile on her face.

Instead, I make my way over to the piano and sit down while I wait for my father to appear from his office.

The keys are cool and comforting beneath my fingers as I hang my head and play. Music doesn't ask questions. It doesn't threaten to take your daughter from you. It doesn't demand anything.

It gives me a release like nothing else.

I continue playing, the stiffness in my neck easing a fraction with each song I finish. But the second I allow Natasha's threats back in, it all comes crashing back with full gut-wrenching force.

"Damn it!" I curse, slamming my hands down on the keys, making a foreboding crash of notes echo around the room.

I fly to my feet and stride over to where my father has appeared with Uncle Mal and taken a seat with the recently returned Denver, Killian, and Jenson at one of the low tables on the far side of the room, away from where Molly is still playing with Sinclair, Halliday, and the dogs.

Tossing myself into an empty chair, I don't wait for any of them to greet me.

I simply spit out, "She's fucking back."

"Who?" My sister demands, stalking over to our table.

I don't miss the way Denver's eyes track to her. I feared he'd left for good after he told my father he could no longer work for our family. We all did. But as it turns out, we felt his absence as much as he felt ours. Sinclair's eyes meet his and she's drawn into his gaze for a beat. I never thought I'd see the day my sister looked at Denver in anything other than detached disinterest. But now it's out in the open that the two fell hopelessly in love while he was her bodyguard, I can't imagine ever seeing her any other way.

Happiness suits her.

"Natasha," I hiss, my anger spiking from saying her name.

Sinclair's eyes go round. "Molly's mom?"

"Do you know any others?" I grit.

"Don't speak to me like that." She whacks me gently on the back of the head, the only person who would ever dare talk to, or treat me in such a way, and not face repercussions for it. "What does she want?" she asks.

All eyes around the table pin on me as I grind the words out with a menacing quietness so they don't carry across the room. "Molly. She says she wants to take Molly."

"What?" Sinclair shrieks. "She can't! Tell her she can't."

"I did fucking tell her that. But she's her biological mother and—"

"And she's also an addict who can't look after herself, let alone a little girl. She *left* her on your doorstep in a *fucking box*, Sullivan. For God's sake, what kind of mother does that?"

"I know."

I scrub a hand down my face. But I'm worried. I'm fucking worried. Natasha has never taken it this far before. She went to my office, for Christ's sake. Molly could have been there. And she's her mother. As much as I know I can fight her, the fact remains that she's Molly's flesh and blood. What if by some miracle she gets a good lawyer? Or a judge who feels sorry for her and thinks a mother and a child shouldn't be kept apart, even if that mother is a fucking liability?

What the hell happens then?

"She gave up all rights to be her mother when she did that," Sinclair continues. "We'll fight her, won't we, Dad?"

My father nods. "You bet your ass we will, Sweetheart. Molly isn't going anywhere."

A burst of hope ignites in my chest as I look around the table at my family, and the security team. Any person sitting at this table would die for Molly. I know that for a fact.

Natasha doesn't know what she's up against.

"Just slam some DNA tests at the courts along with her failed rehab stints. Then she can crawl back to where she came from."

"DNA results?" I echo Sinclair's words.

"It'll show you're her biological father, won't it?" Sinclair quips.

It's been my main threat against Natasha whenever she's tried to pull shit in the past. But this time it's not been enough to keep her away.

I grit my teeth. "You know it will, but it's not that simple—"

"You're her father," Uncle Mal says.

"You are," my father confirms.

"I know." I lean my head back against the chair, exhaling. "It's just the last thing I need right now." My head's still reeling from seeing Tate back in the city again. And now Natasha goes and pulls a stunt like this?

"Okay," my father says, his deep, commanding voice bringing a calm order to the table. "We all know what's going on. And we've got each other's backs. We're family. And family looks out for one another. We'll get this all sorted."

"Yeah." I scrub at my eyes, not wanting him to see how deeply Natasha has gotten to me this time. "Thanks, Dad."

"You're okay, Son. It'll all be okay." He squeezes my knee.

"Mabel licked me." Molly giggles happily as I carry her into the lobby of our building.

"Auntie Sin's new puppy loves you and thinks you taste yummy," I reply, hiding the weariness in my voice.

Today has drained me. All I want now is to go upstairs with Molly and eat whatever Joan has left us for dinner, then lie in bed with my little girl and read to her.

I head straight for the elevators, passing the empty concierge desk on the way.

Movement to my left catches my eye and I turn to see a woman walking toward us, her steps slow and uncoordinated.

"Natasha?!"

I pull Molly into my chest and cradle her head, nestling it into my shoulder. My heart hammers against my ribs.

"What the hell are you doing?" I spit.

"Daddy?" Molly pipes up.

"It's okay, Sweetheart," I say, stroking the back of her head in her bunny onesie, keeping her firmly planted against my shoulder so she can't turn around.

Natasha's glazed eyes scan over Molly and she has the audacity to look interested as she admires her outfit.

"You like rabbits, Peaches?" she slurs.

"You're drunk," I spit, stepping back quickly as she reaches out, attempting to stroke Molly's back.

"Peaches?" Molly echoes innocently, making my heart crack in two. If only she knew why I hated that fucking nickname so damn much.

"Get. Out," I snarl.

"I want to see my daughter, Sullivan," she says.

I step back again. She fucking stinks of liquor.

She changes her approach, realizing she isn't going to get any closer to Molly.

"Aren't you going to tell me how good I look? I've not seen you since that weekend in Miami. That was a wild one, huh?" She winks and lets out a laugh that scrapes at my bones.

"You need to leave."

I turn my face toward Molly who's shuffling in my arms.

"It's okay, Sweetheart," I whisper. "We're going home in a minute. The lady's leaving."

Natasha snorts, shaking her head with a lopsided sneer. "What a loving daddy. So sweet."

"Get out," I clip.

"Make me." She shrugs, pushing her long dark hair over her shoulder.

She's wearing heels and a tight dress, suitable for a night out in a club. Disgust oozes from my pores. The outfit isn't for my benefit. It's for whoever she's going to flirt with all evening in order to have her night funded.

Small bruises are fading in the crook of her elbow, and I stiffen, tightening my grip on Molly. God knows what she's moved on to in addition to the alcohol.

Natasha twists her lips in amusement at the look on my face, then breaks into a cold laugh that makes her look unhinged.

My mouth goes dry.

I will not have her anywhere near Molly like this.

Without thinking I reach for my phone, pulling it from my pocket with one hand.

"This is a one-time fucking offer. So name your goddamn price," I grind out, each word laced with threatening promise.

But Natasha ignores my tone, lighting up like a fucking Fourth of July fireworks show as I open up my banking app.

"I dunno. You're asking a lot here." She licks her lips, drawing it out. "You want me not to come back again? But now I know you live in such a beautiful place." She opens her arms, gesturing around the grand reception area before turning to smile at Molly's head of dark curls.

Bile gathers in my throat.

"And you want me to give up the chance to see my only daughter," she whines theatrically, reaching for Molly again.

I step back, glaring at her in warning.

She tilts her head, narrowing her eyes. "One million."

I tap the number into my phone without hesitation.

"Make that two million," Natasha adds, watching me closely. "After all, you can afford it."

I give her a tight grimace. Whatever her price is, I can afford it. There isn't a number in existence I wouldn't pay to get her away from Molly.

I hit send and turn the screen toward her.

"It's all yours. Now get the fuck out," I breathe.

Her eyes widen and she pulls out her own phone, a smile splitting her face in two as she checks her bank account.

"I need somewhere to stay. My flight back isn't until tomorrow," she adds.

My head spins. She was going to keep coming back until she saw Molly. She was damn determined this time.

Through gritted teeth, I snarl, "I have a suite at The Lanceford Hotel. Go to the front desk. I'll call and tell them to expect you. But, Natasha...?"

She lifts her glazed eyes to mine, blinking at me through heavy smudged eye makeup.

"Yeah?"

"This is the last time we ever see you. Understand? You don't ever turn up like this again. And you never call. It all stops now."

She wobbles in her heels and gives me a sarcastic salute.

"With pleasure, *Daddy*," she slurs.

I watch her as she weaves over to the main doors and spills out onto the street.

"Who that, Daddy?" Molly asks.

I press a kiss to her head, keeping her from seeing the tears that are seconds away from racing down my cheeks.

She didn't even look at her.

Molly's own fucking mother didn't even look at her once after that money dropped into her account.

She walked away without a glance back.

"No one, Sweetheart," I choke, squeezing my eyes shut and sinking my nose into her hair to breathe her in.

"It was no one."

The night creeps by, painstakingly slowly knowing that Natasha is nearby. She checked in at The Lanceford. That much I know after asking them to inform me once she had. After a call to my father, he placed Jenson on surveillance. Natasha went out, as I expected her to, getting more drunk and leeching off some random guy she met. But she returned to The Lanceford alone, and I told Jenson to stand down until midday. Natasha will be too wasted to surface before that, and even if she does, the hotel will inform me when she checks out.

I'll be able to breathe again once I know she's caught her flight and left for good.

I close Molly's bedroom door quietly after checking on her. She's slept later this morning. I'll have to wake her soon to get ready. Sinclair's expecting her at her place after breakfast. And Denver will be with them. I can trust Molly will be safe with them. Natasha won't be back now she got what she came for.

I gave her two million reasons to walk away. Something she did far too easily for a mother who claims to care about her daughter.

Fucking disgusting.

Flicking the coffee machine on I brace my arms on the countertop and roll my neck side to side in an attempt to ease the knotted muscles. I'm used to running on little to no sleep.

Today will be no different. And tonight I can go to bed knowing that Natasha will be out of our lives.

Maybe I'll even sleep well.

The buzzer goes and I walk to the security panel.

"Mr. Beaufort?" the concierge greets. "There are some members of the NYPD here who want to speak with you."

"Detective Field," a gravelly voice that sounds like its owner hasn't slept either cuts in. "And Officer Jones. It's an urgent matter, Mr. Beaufort. Your cooperation here, and not at the precinct, would be appreciated."

The hairs on the back of my neck prickle.

"Of course," I reply. "Come on up."

I let go of the speaker button.

Fuck.

What the hell do they want at this time of the morning? I grab my phone from the kitchen counter and check it. There's a text from Sinclair telling me she can't wait to see Molly, and an email from my father with some business news article Uncle Mal sent to him that he thinks I should read.

My family is fine, so why are they here?

Tate...

My blood turns cold, and I storm to the door, yanking it open as a suited detective and uniformed officer step off the elevator. They head toward me with matching stony expressions.

"Mr. Beaufort," the detective greets, extending a hand. "I'm Detective Field, this is Officer Jones."

"What's happened? Is she okay?" I clench his hand a little too hard as my heart races.

His eyes pinch at the corners, his mouth flattening into a grim line. "Can we come in?"

Not an answer. *What the hell's going on?*

I step back, granting them both entry. I lead them into the living area before spinning to face them.

"What's happened?"

I've seen enough law enforcement faces to recognize when they're about to deliver life-changing news. I know it's their job. But fuck, in the moment all you want to do is hit something. Hard.

"We have some news that might be upsetting," the detective says with a morbid finality. "A woman has been found deceased in one of your residences."

"Tate," I choke under my breath, unable to think of anything other than her face before I walked away from her yesterday.

At the way she looked at me.... So *disappointed*.

"Jesus." I drag a hand over my jaw, my throat unbearably tight like it's got a chain being pulled tight around it. "I don't... Wait. You said residence?"

"A suite registered to you at The Lanceford Hotel," he confirms. "The staff advised that you gave them permission to allow a guest to stay there last night?"

"Yes, I did."

The air that's expelled from my lungs makes my head light and I almost laugh.

Natasha.

But the relief that it's not Tate they're talking about is destroyed in an instant as the rest of his words sink in.

"Natasha's dead?"

"We'd like you to formally identify her. Her driver's license lists her as a resident of Miami," the detective says. "A family member will be required to complete the identification if you're unable—"

"I'll do it."

I blow out a breath, standing with my hands on my hips. My father was the one who was going to identify my mother and brother. But they were too badly burned. As horrific as it was hearing that, it was a small mercy to me that my father didn't have to see them like that. It was done using dental records instead. I'd never wish to put a family member through seeing their loved one in that way.

"The only family Natasha's ever mentioned is an uncle. I don't think he's in good health. I'll do it."

"Very well." The detective nods. "We'll get that arranged, Mr. Beaufort."

"How did she...? What happened?"

"It appears to be an accidental overdose. The autopsy will confirm it. But there were narcotics and methods to administer them found by the body."

I step back, slumping onto one of the kitchen stools.

"Drugs?" I whisper, pushing my finger and thumb into my stinging eye sockets.

Fucking drugs.

I knew she was probably using, and it wasn't just the alcohol. But I did nothing. I gave her two million dollars to go out and score whatever she wanted.

I handed her the means to acquire whatever she wanted on a golden fucking platter.

I might as well have killed her myself.

Small footsteps pad toward me, making my eyes snap open.

"Molly?" I breathe, standing from my chair and reaching down to pull her into my arms as she rushes over to me in her pajamas, eyeing the cops with an unsure expression.

"It's okay, Sweetheart. The police came to talk to Daddy about something."

Molly's eyes drop to the gun in the officer's holster and my jaw tightens at the parting of her lips as she stares at it in wonder. She's never seen Denver's in all of the times he's been here. He's either kept it discreetly hidden, or it's been placed inside my safe.

My daughter hasn't turned three yet, and I'm already

failing at protecting her innocence. Failing to keep the ugly side of the world away from her. The side that results in uniformed officers showing up at your home before breakfast.

The detective seems to sense my discomfort and tips his head at his colleague. "Jones, go and see if you can get us an update on when we can take Mr. Beaufort with us to assist."

He doesn't say assist in identifying Natasha's dead body, for which I will be eternally grateful. Molly might not understand yet who Natasha was to her. But I don't want her to have any more reasons than necessary to remember this moment.

The officer heads down the hallway toward the front door, the sound of his radio faint as he talks with someone over it.

"Good morning, Miss Beaufort." The detective smiles kindly at Molly, but my grip remains firm on her.

"Hello," Molly answers shyly.

The officer returns, but hangs back near the hallway, making a signal to the detective, before he turns his attention back to me.

"Is there someone you can call?" he gestures to Molly.

I nod. They want me to go with them now. Wherever they've taken Natasha, they're waiting for me to confirm it's her before they do anything else.

Clearing my throat, I reach for my phone, pulling up my father's number first.

"I'll call my family," I tell the detective. "They'll all want to be here."

44

TATE

My hands shake, creasing the envelope that's clutched so tightly in my palm that I swear my skin will have nail marks in it by the time I let go.

The elevator doors slide open, and I step out, heading to Sullivan and Molly's door. A route that's so familiar, yet feels so alien to me today. This is the last time I'll come here. Once my signed letter cutting all ties with Liberty Records is received, then that'll be it.

I will no longer have any reason to talk to Sullivan Beaufort.

And every reason to still love him and his daughter so much that my body physically aches at their loss from my life.

I could have taken the letter to Kyle Drayton. That would have been the sensible thing to do. Sullivan might own the label now, but I don't know how involved he is with the actual running of it. Besides constructing contracts and tours to get ex-girlfriends out of the city and away from him, that is.

But something told me I had to do this. Delivering this last confirmation that we are over is what I need. A sort of closure, even though I know it's going to hurt like hell.

I want Sullivan to look me in the eye one final time as I leave his life for good. I need him to understand that even though he did this, that I'm okay without him. That I. Will. Be. Okay.

Taking a deep breath, I reach to knock on the door, but the sound of notes drifting from inside halt me.

He's playing Chopin's *Funeral March*. The foreboding notes ring out like deep bells, signifying the end of something.

His despair seeps through the door like a living breathing entity until my legs go weak and I have to reach out to steady myself.

I clutch the envelope to my chest as I listen. Each note rings out sharply like he's striking the keys so hard they're in danger of splintering from his touch. The piece isn't complete before the notes merge into one another un-ceremonially like they've been slammed all at once.

I sink back against the door as silence engulfs the air in a thick cloud.

The only sound is my shallow breaths and pulse in my ears...

...and crying.

Swallowing hard, I turn my ear to the door and strain to hear the faint muffles.

Sullivan's crying.

It's barely audible, but it's real.

My heart flies to my throat and I force back a sob. This isn't anything to do with me. Whatever he has going on the other side of this door is his private business. He closed me off from being a part of it months ago. If I was ever really a part of it to begin with.

I bend and push the envelope underneath the door, my breath coming in tightly drawn tenses of my lungs. *This is nothing to do with me.*

I stalk back to the elevator, hitting the button harshly. I

wrap my arms around myself, rubbing at the goosebumps that have skittered up over my skin.

The doors slide open, but my feet don't move.

I whip my head to his door. Maybe it's Molly. Maybe something happened.

My heart's in my throat as I race over and scan my thumb to let myself in. Relief sags my chest as it unlocks with a click. He hasn't shut me out completely. Not yet.

The envelope crumples beneath my feet as I step on it in my haste to get inside. I ignore it, leaving it sitting on the floor like a ruined scrap of something worthless.

"Sullivan?"

I head into the living area, but it's deserted. The piano sits in silence like a dark, oppressive mass, its stool upended on the floor.

The sounds of choked whispers spills from somewhere close by and I follow it on autopilot until I come to a stop outside Sullivan's closed office door.

"I'm so fucking sorry. She's lost her mom now... I can't do this without you."

There's no other voice, only his.

I breathe in slowly and open the door.

Blue eyes meet mine, stealing my breath. As long as I live, I know I will never be able to forget the way he looks in this moment. He's sitting on the floor, propped up with his back against his desk like he's collapsed there and doesn't have it in himself to get up again. He's wearing his usual shirt and suit pants but lacking the suave sophistication that usually fills out the designer fabric.

It's like seeing a shell of the man he is.

"Sullivan?"

Tears course down his cheeks and he shakes his head.

"T-Tate? I don't... I c-can't..."

I fall to my knees, pulling him to me without an ounce of hesitation. "It's okay. It's okay."

His phone drops from his hand, thudding on the plush carpet as he puts his arms around me and grips me hard, sinking his face into the crook of my neck.

"What's wrong?" I ask, fighting to keep my own emotions from bubbling up at seeing him like this.

Wracking sobs shake his torso, and he falls apart in my arms.

"Molly's mother is dead. She died of an overdose. I gave her the fucking money. I wanted her gone. And now she is. I took Molly's mother from her."

"What do you mean, you gave her the money?"

"She came here looking for Molly. She was drunk and I wanted her as far away as possible. I gave her two million dollars to never come back. And now she never will." His voice cracks. "I k-killed her."

"No," I say with force. "No, you didn't."

Sullivan's told me about Molly's mother's addictions. And as awful as this is, he needs to understand this wasn't his fault.

"Sullivan? Look at me," I urge.

He pulls back and the broken man I see makes my heart bleed for him.

"I didn't know that's what she'd do. But I should have. I should have seen it coming. I should have protected Molly from this happening."

"You did protect her," I say, begging him to believe me. "You could never have known what would happen. You were doing what was best for Molly at the time."

His face crumples. "Her mother's gone, Tate."

"And I am so, so sorry about that," I say, meaning every word. I know Sullivan never forgave Molly's mom after the way she abandoned her. But she's still her mother. This must be a horrible shock for him.

He crushes himself against me even tighter, and I stroke his heaving back as he struggles to catch his breath.

"I'm supposed to protect her," he utters.

"You do," I soothe, reaching up to stroke the hair at the nape of his neck. "No one loves and protects her like you do. You're an amazing father."

My words cause him to suck in a sharp breath, and he pulls away from me.

"I'm not."

Any remaining light in his eyes extinguishes as he looks at me. My heart breaks for him. No matter what's happened between the two of us, I can't stand by and not feel like my soul is falling apart seeing him like this.

"Sullivan," I plead softly. "Don't do this to yourself. You told me Natasha had her struggles. This isn't your fault. She chose to go down that path a long time ago."

"Don't make excuses for me, Tate." He blinks away lingering tears, his eyes taking on a cold detachment. "This is on me. I failed."

"You didn't fail." I search his eyes, begging him to see what I do, what everyone does. A loving father who will always put his daughter first.

He breaks my gaze and reaches for his phone. I sink onto my heels in front of him, not wanting to move any further away, because despite him regaining his composure momentarily I can see he's dancing on a knife's edge of losing it again.

I know him better than he thinks, and I can see when it's taking everything in him to hold it together.

His brow furrows as he unlocks his phone and hands it to me. As I close my fingers around it, our skin touches and a bolt of energy bites me low in my stomach.

"Call it."

"What?"

"Call it," Sullivan repeats.

"Call what?" I look down at the phone, but only the screensaver image of Molly in her bunny onesie with a big grin looks back at me.

"You know what."

Something about Sullivan's voice makes my stomach sink. I open up his call history. The number with no name is listed line after line, filling the screen.

"I know you've seen me call it. But you've never pushed to know who it is. If you had, I'd have lied to you about it, anyway."

His eyes are on his phone as I look up at him in shock.

"You'd have lied?"

He grimaces. "I wouldn't have had any other choice."

My throat thickens and I hover my thumb over the number.

"Call it, Tate," he urges in a hoarse whisper. "I don't have to lie to you anymore."

A stupid, small part of me wondered if this was a number for another woman. It was a fleeting thought, probably brought on by Brandon cheating on me. But I never thought that was something Sullivan would do. Not with the way things were between us.

But then he left that key out for The Lanceford for me to see.

Maybe we were always more to me than we ever were to him.

"I don't understand," I whisper.

"You will." He reaches over and presses the number for me, lifting my hand to my ear as the phone connects the call.

"Hey, you've reached Slade. I'm probably jumping out of a plane right now and freaking out my brother. But if you leave a message, I'll call you back."

Sullivan holds my gaze as the message ends. Emotion swirls in them as I end the call.

"He sounds just like you, only…" I swallow down the word *happy* before it leaves my lips.

"Younger?" Sullivan quirks a brow, and that small, simple hint of himself shining through his grief is a lifeline I want to cling onto for dear life.

"Three minutes and fourteen seconds younger. Although Slade would talk about it like I was ancient compared to him some days. Especially because I didn't share in his thrill around taking unnecessary risks."

A rare, bittersweet smile forms on his lips before he frowns at the phone.

"I've paid my dead twin brother's phone bill for almost three years, just so I can hear his voice and leave him messages he'll never return."

"Sullivan," I breathe.

He stares back at me with shining eyes, his neck contracting like he's trying to hold back the onslaught of thickness that comes to your throat before you cry.

"I don't want to not hear his voice anymore," he confesses quietly.

I reach for his hand and intertwine my fingers with his. The warmth of them brings back a rush of memories that I push down straight away. This isn't about us right now.

"It's okay if you need to call it. No one's saying you shouldn't. There is no right way to grieve. And you can trust me. I would *never* tell anyone about this. You don't need to worry about that."

"Tate," he murmurs with a sad smile. "That's not why I didn't tell you who I was calling."

"It isn't?"

"No."

He strokes my hand with his thumb. Back and forth. Slow and gentle. Calm and in control. *Barely.*

I study his face. Study the deep frown lines that are back

on his brow. Study the way his cheek clenches and his eyes pinch like it physically pains him to consider the words he's about to say.

"Natasha left Molly on my doorstep with a note," he says in a thick, measured voice. "And even though she walked away from her own daughter, I've spent every day terrified of the thought that she could come back and take her away again."

I hold back my argument of him being her father and Natasha not being able to just walk back into Molly's life and do that. Sullivan knows as well as I do that he has the means to protect Molly legally. But knowing it, and keeping the faith in it, are two different things.

Instead, I squeeze his hand in reassurance, and after a beat he squeezes mine back.

"I was terrified. It would keep me up at night, thinking of all the ways it could happen. As long as my family supported me, and I stayed strong, the chances were kept to a minimum. But then..."

"But then?"

He looks straight into my eyes. "Then I met you."

"Me?"

"I haven't been in a relationship since the day Molly came into my life and Claudia left it."

"I don't understand what that's got to do with me."

"It has everything to do with you." He shakes his head. "For the first time Molly was at risk because I met someone who I didn't want to lie to. I met someone who I allowed myself the indulgence of picturing a future with. I let myself imagine how you'd look the day we got married. I let myself dream about you taking my hand and putting it on your stomach so I could feel *our* baby moving inside you. I let myself hope, Tate. I knew better, yet I still did it anyway. Everything I put you through as a result is my fault, because I was selfish."

"Are you saying you were lying to me? Sullivan…?" I press when he says nothing.

He blinks, fresh tears escaping from his lower lids.

"She's not mine," he whispers. "Molly isn't mine."

His grip tightens on his phone, drawing my attention to it again. Suddenly the magnitude of his grief takes on a new, deeper significance.

"She's—?"

"Slade's," he confirms in a husky breath. "She's my brother's. He died, never even knowing she existed."

He taps something into his phone, then turns the screen toward me. I've seen photos of his brother before when I searched Sullivan up online. But they were press shots, and ones taken at business events. The one Sullivan's showing me is of the two of them sitting together with drinks in their hands and the sunset behind them, painting the sky a vivid orange. Slade's hair is longer and his physique more muscular, but he still looks so much like Sullivan and vice versa.

Twins.

"The last photo of us. He died the following day."

"I'm so sorry," I whisper, knowing nothing I can say will help.

Sullivan winces as he studies the image. "They say losing a child is one of the hardest things to endure. And I'd have argued that losing a twin was on the same level. He was my *brother*. I was created from the same cells as him," he chokes. "But then Molly came along, and I became a father. And despite missing him so much that I didn't want to wake up some days, I understood. Losing a child really is the worst thing someone could endure. And every time I saw Natasha's name flash up on my phone, I wondered if that was the day I'd finally lose everything."

"I had no idea," I say, unable to stop my own tears from falling.

"Molly gave me a reason to keep going. It's like Slade brought her to me the exact moment I needed her. I was so close to giving up. And I swore the second I read Natasha's note telling me she was his, but that now she heard he was dead that Molly was my *problem*, that I'd protect her with my own life. She's family. She's his. And that means she's mine too. I wouldn't have survived without her.

"I've never been able to understand how a parent can abandon their child like Natasha did. She left Molly with me. With a stranger."

"You're not a stranger," I say, cradling his face so he'll look at me. "You're her daddy."

"I'm..." He blinks at me before screwing his face up and sobbing.

I pull him to me again, wrapping my arms around him. Although this time it isn't only Sullivan who's crying, it's me too.

"She's lucky to have you. I've never met such a loved little girl. Such an *amazing* little girl. You've done an incredible job."

"Thank you," he whispers.

I pull back and look into his eyes. My heart's beating so deeply that I feel it through every fiber of my body.

"You're an amazing father," I breathe.

I run the pads of my thumbs over his damp cheekbones. He's always been a beautiful man. But now, with fragments of his soul laid bare in the remaining tears coating his dark, thick lashes, he's breathtaking.

I lean closer and press my lips to his in a gentle kiss. His breath stutters, and he kisses me back softly. Tenderly. *So heartbreakingly gentle.*

"I couldn't give you what you deserved, Tate." His soft words mix with our slow, light kisses. The kind of kisses that you know can't go any further, but yet you aren't strong enough to hold back from giving, because they spill from you like whispered promises and shared secrets.

Carrying the weight of everything with them.

Sullivan rests his hands on my hips as I position myself in his lap and continue to stroke his face and press delicate kisses to his mouth.

"DNA tests will show that I'm Molly's biological father because we were twins. Natasha knew the results coupled with her behavior meant she would never get near Molly without getting herself clean first. But for me to have a future with someone it would have meant telling them the truth. It's why I kept away from relationships. Only my family know the truth. I lied to Claudia and told her Molly was mine because of the way she reacted when we found her. And I decided I would never fall in love, because it would mean I'd have to tell someone the truth. I'd have to trust them. And if something happened one day. If they changed their mind and decided bringing up another woman's daughter was too much for them, like Claudia did, then it would be Molly who paid the price. My word against Natasha's was one thing. But the possibility of someone else knowing and telling someone? Having people look into it and ask questions? It could have meant me losing Molly forever if the truth had come out."

"And yet, somehow you still think you're not an amazing father," I say through tears. "Everything you do is for Molly. I understand that. And I admire it. I grew up with just my dad looking out for me for most of my childhood, remember?" I take a deep breath and look him straight in the eye. "All those decisions you've made for Molly... It's okay to have made them. Every single one."

The breath leaves his chest in a sob.

"It's okay," I repeat gently.

He pulls me to him, and our lips crush together in a single, bruising kiss before he rests his forehead against mine.

"I had to ID Natasha. I had to—"

"Shh." I kiss him again.

"I'm sorry it had to be this way."

"It's okay," I whisper.

"I wanted to trust you so much, Tate. More than anything, I wanted it to be different with you. I used to keep everyone from getting close to me." He winces. "I had a hotel suite and... the only time I've been there since we met was to be alone. And I hated myself more than ever when I went. I never want to set foot in it again. I... wanted to trust you..."

I press a finger to his lips. "You could have trusted me. But we'll never know how things might have been now, because you didn't."

He pulls my hand away, his pupils flaring. "I was too scared to try. It could have blown up in our faces. I've woken up thinking it's just another day, and then witnessed my life get torn apart in front of me and been unable to do a fucking thing to stop it. I've seen destruction. I've lived in nightmares."

"And I'm so sorry that you have. I really, truly am. I'm not saying it to be hurtful. It is what it is. And I understand why you didn't tell me."

"I had to protect Molly at all costs. And I was scared of what it would do to me if you left. Even if you never told anyone. Just the thought of you leaving us, I..."

I kiss him again, silencing the wounded noise that rumbles from deep inside his chest.

It's heartbreaking seeing him like this. But it finally makes sense. Why he pushed me away like he did. Why he told me he couldn't love me the way he wanted.

Why he encouraged me to walk out of their lives and live my own.

It all makes sense. But answers don't make it any less tragic.

I pull back and look into his bloodshot eyes. "When did you last sleep properly?"

"The last time you were here," he confesses in a voice so quiet I swear my heart disintegrates.

I stroke back the dark hair from his eyes.

"We should do something about that."

It's growing light outside, spilling a thin crack of sunshine through the drapes in Sullivan's bedroom. I press a kiss to his forehead, making him stir. His exhaustion won over the moment we climbed onto his bed. He's still wearing his shirt and suit pants.

Nothing happened.

He spent the night sleeping with his head resting on my chest.

I spent the night awake, watching him frown and mutter as his dreams tormented him like demons in the dark.

"Tate?" he murmurs sleepily, his arm tightening around my waist.

I check my watch. It's almost six a.m.

"It's okay," I soothe, extracting myself from his grip and climbing gently from the bed.

He looks at me. I smile softly and he smiles back. But neither of us speak.

There's nothing to say. Not right now.

Sullivan told me the truth, because Natasha died, and he was freed of the fear of her taking Molly. I meant every word I said about understanding why he chose to do things the way in which he has.

But it doesn't make it any easier.

He's told me the truth because now he can.

And as freeing as that might be. It's also made something else glaringly obvious.

Sullivan Beaufort needs to grieve. For his brother, his mother.

And for Natasha.

It's hit him hard that Molly's mother is gone. She might have been a terrible one, but while she was alive there was a possibility that she could turn things around. That she could sort her life out and be a healthy and valuable part of Molly's life.

As much as Sullivan won't admit it, even to himself, I believe a small part of him hoped that one day Molly might have had a relationship of sorts with her mother.

Because he's a good man. And an amazing father.

And right now while wounds are fresh I could be a distraction that keeps them open and bleeding.

He needs his family right now. And that's not me.

"Can we..." He clears his throat. "Can Molly and I see you again soon?"

I look back at him from the doorway.

"I don't know," I answer honestly. "Can you? Are you ready for that after everything?"

His silence as he looks back at me still steals the air from my lungs even though I expected nothing else.

"It's okay," I reassure him. "I'm not sure I'm ready either."

I open the door.

"Tate?" he calls.

I swallow, not turning around.

"I'm sorry."

I swallow past the thick lump in my throat, my eyes burning.

"I know. Me too," I whisper.

45

TATE

ONE MONTH LATER

THE NECKLACE IS HEAVY IN MY HAND AS I PLACE IT back into its case and snap it shut to the echo of his words in my head.

"You're mine. I'm keeping you, Baby."

"You should wear it," Ashley says, looking over from my wardrobe where she's helping me choose an outfit to wear for the grand opening tomorrow of her new branch of Caffeine Couture that's going to be inside the iconic Songbird Hotel that faces Central Park.

"It's stupidly expensive. What if I lose it?"

She gives me a pointed look. "Jewelry is made to be worn and enjoyed. Besides, if you did lose it, you could wear another. You've got enough options." She shrugs with a sympathetic smile.

"Isn't that the truth," I murmur.

I place the box back on top of the growing stack inside my lingerie drawer and slide the drawer shut, sealing off the sight of all those blue velvet boxes.

They started arriving within a couple of days of me leaving Sullivan and Molly's place for that final time. The pieces are different. Sometimes he sends me earrings, sometimes bracelets, once it was a keychain. But they all carry the same heavy feeling in my gut when I open them and see the same words on the accompanying card.

"I'm sorry. We miss you."

It's all he can say. He's not ready to say anything else. Not ready to make suggestions of a future, or whether there's even a chance of one where we all exist in it together anymore. And that's okay. Like I told him so many times the night I held him while he cried.

It's okay.

It has to be okay. Because if I falter for even a moment and allow a flicker of how *I am not okay* without them both surface from my subconscious, then I might fall and never get up.

"You've got that look again," Ashley pipes up, carrying a dress over to me on its hanger. "You need a good night out, drinking ridiculously overpriced champagne courtesy of The Songbird Hotel."

I smile at her. "I'm sorry I'm that horribly dull friend who's no fun anymore."

"Girl, you don't know dull until you listen to Huck talk about components of his machines. I love the giant bear, and I love his coffee, but honestly, sometimes I just jump his bones to get him to shut up. He can't talk about shit like that when I sit on his face."

I snort out a laugh as Ashley pulls me into a one-armed hug. She's been the person who's gotten me through the last month. As much as I love my father, I haven't told him too much about what happened with Sullivan since we came back to New York. I thought maybe he'd think severing my contract with Liberty Records is what's gotten me into a slump, even though it was my idea. But he's not stupid, he knows I spent the night at Sullivan and Molly's place, and that I haven't been back, or laughed much, since.

Ashley knows as much as I felt able to share with her. She knows Molly's mother died and that Sullivan needs some time to process it all.

She doesn't know Molly isn't Sullivan's.

To me, Molly will always be his. There's no more loved little girl than her. He's a perfect father to her.

And I miss them both so much that if I let myself think about it too much I struggle to breathe.

My father appears in the doorway of my bedroom, knocking lightly on the door to get our attention.

"Tate?"

I swallow hard when I see what's in his hand.

"Another one?" Ashley asks.

"Another one," he confirms, holding the box out to me. The silk ribbon sits in a perfect bow on top of it; beauty papering over the heartache lying in wait inside.

They always arrive like this, by private courier without excessive packaging. It's a small mercy at least. The process of opening them and seeing yet another apology note isn't drawn out. Because no matter how many notes I get, reading those words still brings a lump to my throat every time.

I sigh and hold my hand out.

My father walks over and places the buttery velvet box into my hand. This one's shallow and square. I lift the lid, bracing myself for another beautiful, expensive piece that I won't be able to bring myself to look at much, let alone wear.

But this one is... *different.*

My hand flies to my mouth. "Oh my God," I breathe.

"Why'd he send that?" Ashley asks, peering into the box.

I lift out the small square card from the center of the velvet cushion, careful not to damage any of the pressed daisies that run around it in a circle.

A daisy chain. So perfectly intact, like it's been treasured and preserved. Treated like it's more valuable than any of the precious jewels the boxes usually contain.

"Molly and I made it for him," I say.

Any further explanation I have freezes on the tip of my tongue as I read the card. Then read it again. And again. It's as though my brain is unable to register that this one doesn't say: *"I'm sorry. We miss you."*

It doesn't say anything like that.

"Molly's turning three?" Ashley comments, her eyes widening at the tiny invitation decorated in gold line-drawn bears carrying compasses.

Explorer bears.

"In three days," I whisper. "And he wants me to be there."

46

SULLIVAN

"You want me to take door duty for a while?" Jenson asks, gesturing to the hallway that leads out from the main bar area of Seasons, where we are, and toward the side-walk entrance.

"You want to be on the street dressed in that?" Killian smirks.

Jenson scratches at the giant fluffy tummy on his bear outfit with a shrug. "The single moms will dig it, man. This suit's going to do wonders for my game."

"If the game involves Molly's future pre-k friends' moms, then you aren't playing," I grumble.

"She doesn't even start for another year," Jenson complains.

"And I've had her on the waiting list since she was three months' old. It's the best pre-K in the city, and your dick won't be doing anything that might affect my daughter's future education. The last thing I need is one of her future friends having an aggrieved mother because you screwed up."

"Hey, I resent that. I'm a great boyfriend. You could be keeping me from my future wife," Jenson pipes up.

"Uh-huh... In that case, you can date whichever mother you want."

"Really?" He raises both brows at me.

"When Molly turns eighteen," I clip.

Killian and Denver burst into chuckles.

"But yeah, take the door and greet the guests as they arrive. Thanks for offering." I clap him on the shoulder and give him a wink.

"Dunno why I like you, man," he mutters before ambling away in slow, wide steps, the round tail of his costume bobbing behind him.

"He drew the short straw, huh?"

"We made sure all Jenson's straws were short," Denver rumbles with a smirk.

"He wanted to win really. He was born to play that part. He'll be loving getting all sweaty in all those pounds of synthetic fur. We did him a solid." Killian chuckles, holding out his fist for Denver to bump it.

Jenson makes it almost all the way to the doorway before losing his footing in the giant paws of his costume and stacking it spectacularly.

We watch as he rolls over onto his back, but the awkwardness of his costume prevents him from getting back on his feet.

"Someone should help him," Denver says.

"Someone should," Killian agrees.

They both snort with laughter as Jenson waves his arms in the air trying to get momentum to swing back onto his feet. Molly runs over to him and throws herself on his belly.

"Bear!" she shrieks in delight, bouncing up and down on him until he's coughing and laughing at the same time.

"All right, Mol. This bear needs to go and greet your friends. Make sure they know where the best party of the year is at."

Molly slides off his belly and tugs at his sleeve as he rolls onto his knees and manages to climb to his feet by gripping onto the doorframe.

"I'm expecting a giant bonus for this," he quips, shooting us all a look.

"Maybe the Boss will put a nice little pot of honey in your next paycheck," Killian says.

"Whatever, man. Just you wait. This bear's going to be getting a whole different kind of honey." He ruffles Molly's hair and plods out.

"You really think women are going to fall for the costume?" Killian asks.

"Jenson will make sure that they do," Denver replies.

"Yeah. Lucky fucker. He never has any issues. Must be the baby face. You two will be having your own parties like this before me."

Denver's eyes slide guiltily to mine at Killian's comment, but I keep my mouth firmly clamped shut. Denver's been one of the family for years. He's my father's most trusted hire and has become a friend.

But I still don't need the image of him and Sinclair in my head.

The guy's built like a wrestler, and three times the width of my sister. But she's never smiled as much as she has since he came back to work again and declared that he loved her, and was going to be with her, whether we liked it or not.

Bold move. Lucky for him, it worked.

Molly races past me, back over to the door as a large bunny-shaped balloon is brought through it. But it's not the balloon that's got her running.

"Tate!" she squeals, flinging her arms up in the air.

She's whisked up into the air, her face half-covered by auburn hair as she's hugged fiercely.

My lungs cease to work, leaving me bereft of the oxygen I so badly need.

Adrenaline courses through my veins, my heart pumping erratically.

"Jesus," I choke under my breath as I watch two of the most important women in my life greet one another after months apart.

"Daddy! Look!" Molly calls, the excitement in her voice making my mouth dry.

I've kept them apart. Me. I did this. I'm responsible for the watery blue eyes and tremble in Tate's voice that she tries to hide as she wishes my daughter a happy birthday and embraces her like she's the most precious thing in her world.

Like she loves her.

Because she does.

She told me as much. And then I went and screwed everything up and we all suffered.

"You okay?" Denver asks quietly.

"Yeah."

I continue staring at the two of them, soaking in their happiness that's radiating around them as bright as the damn sun.

Tate looks up over Molly's shoulder, and the second our eyes connect it's like all the air in the world has rushed back into my lungs at once.

I can breathe again.

"Tate?" I stride over with purpose, needing to close the gap between us, but the pinch at the corners of her eyes makes me halt.

She lowers Molly to the ground and hands her a ribbon-handled gift bag.

"I brought you a little something," she says, lowering her eyes to Molly like she can't bring herself to look at me.

"Thank you," Molly says, turning all serious as she reaches inside the bag and pulls out a stuffed rabbit.

"She's the same color as Bumper," Tate tells Molly as my

daughter strokes the creamy fur. "And she has a surprise in her tummy."

Molly turns the bunny over and pulls open a pouch on its stomach. Three small bunnies in varying colors spill out.

"Baby bunnies!" Molly grins, scooping them up and rushing off, calling out for Halliday and my father who are on the far side of the room chatting with Uncle Mal and Aunt Trudy.

Tate hovers like she's unsure what to do. I want to pull her into my arms and greet her properly. Sink my nose into her hair and fill it with the scent of her, instead of having to make do with just the memory of it. Kiss her soft lips. The lips that held me together the last time I saw her.

I want to tell her how I *feel* about her.

"I wouldn't have recognized it in here. It looks amazing," Tate exclaims, her gaze roaming around the animal jungle themed décor that I hired one of the city's top event management companies to create. "It's like being inside Molly's favorite book."

She bites her lip, like she's regretting her words, but also doesn't know what else to say. What's safe to bring up, and what isn't.

"It is," I agree, trying to convey with my tone that she doesn't need to worry. Nothing is off-limits anymore. There are no more secrets.

"And one day she'll understand why it's her favorite," I add.

Tate's eyes widen. "You're going to tell her?"

"Eventually."

It's something I've thought about a great deal over the past month. This secret was only ever something myself and all of my family have kept because it was protecting Molly.

"I always intended to tell her when she was an adult. But

now Natasha is no longer with us, maybe that day will come sooner, if I think she's ready," I tell Tate.

"You're her father. You'll know when the time's right."

Tate's words and faith in me come so easily, making me look at her with a mix of intense adoration and tenderness, that I'm sure conveys exactly what I want to tell her. At least, I must be looking at her like that because she rubs the back of her neck and looks away like she feels awkward.

"How have you been?" she asks, flicking her eyes to mine, then away again.

"I've—"

Before I can tell her the truth—that I've missed her every damn day, but that as much of a mess as I am without her, everything else is slowly coming together, and that I've started seeing a grief counsellor—Sinclair arrives, brimming with excitement.

"Oh wow! You're Tate the cookie baker."

She pulls Tate into a hug and lets out a little squeal.

"I've only heard about you recently because my brother is a huge doofus and kept you all to himself." She tosses a mock dirty look my way, before turning to Tate with a grin. "But I can't wait to hang out. And you need to meet Halliday. You're going to love her. She's into crystals and matching energies and stuff. It's so interesting. Magical."

Tate's lips part, but she clamps them shut again, throwing me a genuine smile as Sinclair leads her away.

And just like that, Tate meets my family.

She's all smiles and laughs, her shoulders softening more by the second as Sinclair introduces her to everyone.

She becomes one of us seamlessly, slotting into the place I never knew was sitting empty, just waiting for her.

The room fills as some of Molly's future classmates and their parents I've connected with to ease her transition into pre-K arrive. And Arabella comes in, armed with more gifts from the team at work.

The party roars to life.

I stand, like a human island in the middle of it all.

The excited squeals muffle into white noise.

The decorations and balloons all blur and merge like a kaleidoscope.

All I see, hear, and feel is her. Back in the same room as me.

Back in my life where she belongs.

"You okay, Son?"

My father's strong palm on my shoulder brings with it a sense of calm, and I inhale slowly.

I look up from behind the bar where I'm making a coffee and take in the party. Everyone's having a great time. The entertainer I hired is busy making balloon animals. And all of the children now resemble different creatures, courtesy of the face paint artist who's here.

"Have you spoken to her?" he asks.

"Not since she arrived." I sigh, dropping my gaze away from where Tate's talking animatedly to Molly and admiring the rabbit whiskers on her cheeks.

"She's been popular." My father chuckles.

"Everyone who meets her loves her," I mumble, reaching for the sugar.

"Everyone loves her, huh?" my father muses, arching a knowing brow at me.

I shake my head with a frown. "Halliday's turned you into a romantic."

"I always was one. It just took Hallie to bring it out."

I nod in understanding. I know my father never loved my mother the way he loves Halliday. But he tried. For years he was the best husband and father he could be. And my mother gambled with it all by having an affair with Neil. We'll never know what would have happened if she hadn't died that day. But I can be certain that my father's eyes wouldn't sparkle the way they do whenever he says Halliday's name.

"Don't let opportunities pass you, Son. I know something worth fighting for when I see it." His eyes track to where Sinclair's wrapped around Denver's side, whispering something into his ear.

My chest tightens, the way it has every time Tate's looked up and caught me staring at her. But she's never come over. It's like she doesn't want to talk to me.

"I don't know what she's thinking," I confess, hating that I'm showing weakness. I always get my own way in business. I'm the one that's in control. The one with the upper hand. The one who always knows the outcome will be in my favor. Because I won't allow it not to be.

"She's here isn't she? She came," my father says. "And if that doesn't tell you enough, then just ask her."

"That easy?" I snort, knowing full well this is one outcome I'm not in control of.

He claps me on the shoulder again. "It's as hard as you want to make it, Son."

"I wouldn't know where to start."

"Find a way that speaks to her."

He moves away and I look up, seeing the reason for his smooth departure.

"The kids are having a great time." Tate smiles shyly from the other side of the bar, curling her hands around the edge of it and gripping on like she's glad of its presence. It's like a barrier shielding her from any more hurt I can cause her.

"They are," I agree.

"Are you?"

Her question catches me off guard, and I look into her eyes. She isn't looking away anymore. She's looking right at me like my answer means something.

"I have a photo of Slade out on display in our apartment."

Her brows pop up. "You do?"

"A few, actually."

She smiles softly. "I'm glad."

"You should come over? See what's different and…"

I run my tongue over my teeth, unable to finish due to the way her lips part like she's moments away from thinking up an excuse. But then my father's words ring in my ears and I take a deep breath, remembering who I am.

"I want you to come back around," I say, holding her gaze without apology. "I want you to come and cook with us again. Bathe Molly with me. Read to her with me. I want you back in both of our lives. And this time I won't ever try and make you walk out of it again."

"Sull—"

"I'll do whatever it takes to show you how much I mean that."

I continue what I'm doing, aware of her gaze on my face as I fix the coffee, then slide the mug toward her.

"Forgive me," I say.

"I already have," she whispers, her eyes shining. "It's not about that, it's…"

Her gaze drops to the cup and a smile that squeezes at my heart tilts her lips as she looks at the smiley cocoa face in the foam.

"My cup's been half empty without you. My *life's* felt half empty without you. You are more beautiful to me than any song ever written," I add in a rough whisper, repeating the words I said to her the night she needed me after hearing her song on the radio.

"I've held you while you cried. You've held me while I cried. And... Tate?"

She blinks through unshed tears and looks at me.

"I want us to hold each other again." I drop my voice to a strained whisper. "*Please.*"

She blinks hard, her lower lip wobbling. "I..."

"Time to sing to the birthday girl!" the entertainer announces. "Where's Daddy? Can you come over here?"

I raise my hand and signal I'm coming.

When I turn back, Tate's already leaving.

The smiley face on her coffee leers at me in disgust.

You think she'll forgive you that easily? Think again, asshole.

47

TATE

I STARE AT THE STACK OF BLUE BOXES THAT I'VE placed on top of my drawers. I need to return them. There must be hundreds of thousands of dollars' worth of jewelry inside them. I know Sullivan wanted me to have them, but it feels wrong keeping them.

I open the one containing the daisy chain and stare at it, before carrying it over to my suitcase and placing it inside.

It's the only one I'll keep. That, and the coffee he made me at Molly's party yesterday are the things that have made me question whether I should listen to him and try to start over with him again. I laid awake half of the night considering whether I should go to his place in the middle of the night and tell him I wanted to try again.

Every cell in my body wants to be back with him and Molly.

But maybe it's too late, and I'm scared of getting hurt again.

I grab some T-shirts and place them inside my case, leaving out the old Linkin Park one that belonged to Brandon. That one's well overdue its journey into the trash can. The last

Ashley heard through some friends of Huck's—because the guy seems to know everyone—Brandon's back living in his parents guest room and hunting for a job. Whatever he ends up getting, I doubt he'll work in music again, something I think Sullivan will ensure, seeing as he also seems to know people everywhere. So at least I don't need to worry about bumping into him where I'm going.

An urgent thudding on our front door has me abandoning my packing and rushing out of my room, exchanging a puzzled look with my father.

"He's stealing it!" Larry yells through the door.

Dad opens it and Larry clutches onto the doorframe, his face red as he puffs out, "The guy's taking it!"

"What guy?" my father asks.

"A fancy suit. Probably a city inspector for noise or something. He's taking Tate's piano," Larry wheezes like he's run all the way from the basement.

"The piano?" I gasp.

"Yes. He and another guy are carrying it out like they own the thing. Parked their fancy car up, blocking the street."

I rush to the window, my heart in my throat as I scan the sidewalk below. I don't see anyone. But I see the car Larry's referring to.

My stomach twists into a knot and I push up the window and stick my head out.

"Oh my God, what the hell?" I gasp.

Cars honk angrily as they're held up, waiting for two men to wheel the old piano from the basement across the street to the other side. They stop directly in line with our window, and one turns his head, looking straight up at me.

My breath catches.

Sullivan.

"Stealing it!" Larry continues.

"Technically, it's his. He owns the building," I say, my voice sounding strange.

He's wearing a blue suit today. But he's taken the jacket off and has rolled his shirt sleeves up to his elbows to maneuver the piano. The muscles in his broad chest look puffed up, even from this distance, as he pushes a hand back through his dark hair.

He sits at the piano and lifts the cover from the keys.

For a moment, the street falls silent. No cars drive past, and the few pedestrians all slow their steps, looking at him in curiosity. Our neighborhood never usually sees cars like Sullivan's. And they certainly don't see designer suited men sitting at pianos first thing in the morning.

"This one's for you, Tate!" he calls up to our window.

I stare at him as he starts to play. Every note rings out perfectly, like they're imprinted on his soul.

I clasp a hand over my mouth as the notes of *Unstoppable* fill the street.

He turns and watches me, locking us in an intense gaze.

It's all too much, and I drag in a shuddery breath, a sob bubbling in my throat.

"Don't cry, Baby," he calls out, pressing on the keys harder. "I didn't want to make you cry."

A crowd gathers as residents of our building step outside to watch the spectacle and hang out of their windows to see.

"I'll keep playing all day until you understand," he shouts.

"Understand what?" I shout back.

"That I love you! You hear me? I fucking love you!"

He yells the words so I can hear, but he doesn't need to. They're in his eyes, pinned on mine, in the notes of the song, played to me.

He loves me.

"I'm coming down," I choke out.

I fly past my father and Larry and to the elevator. It arrives within seconds like it doesn't want me to wait any longer than necessary either.

Some of our neighbors are hanging out on the steps up to our building's door as I exit. Everyone's eyes are on Sullivan as he continues into his second performance of Unstoppable. This time the keys are pressed a little more gently. But the music still carries all the weight of his emotion with it as he meets my eyes across the street and holds them as I cross to him.

I come to a stop beside the piano, my eyes roaming over it. In the natural daylight, it looks even older and battered than in the basement. But out here it seems to play better. Sound different.

"I had it tuned yesterday while you were at Molly's party," Sullivan says, studying my face.

"You told me it wasn't you," I say.

The sheer passion in his eyes is spellbinding as he plays effortlessly, like he always does. Like the music is a part of him, the notes ingrained into his very essence.

Part of me fell in love with a man through his music that night in Grand Central Station. Something that had never happened before, despite all the other times I had heard The Masked Maestro play.

"And that's true. I'm not him, Tate."

I wait for him to play the closing notes of the song, and the air stills around us as the final one echoes out.

"But I was that night. I wasn't meant to be there. Something held the real Maestro up and I stepped in. He said some people *need* to hear his music, and he couldn't let them down. And I think I needed to play that night too. I was... I'd had a bad day, remembering."

"You had?" I whisper, hating the flash of grief that crosses his face.

"But I couldn't tell you it was me. It wasn't my secret to tell."

"You told me you didn't know how to play that song."

His eyes pinch. "I lied."

"You played all of the others from that night when I asked you to, but not that one."

Sullivan rolls his lips, whatever he's about to tell me obviously being hard for him to admit.

"Sinclair made a montage video for the funeral of my brother doing all the stuff he loved. All the risky stuff." He shakes his head, a sad smile on his face. "It's the song she put with it. For whatever reason, that night I wanted to play it. I don't even understand why. And when you asked about it I didn't know what to do. I was scared that if I started talking about Slade then I'd tell you about Molly. And as much as I wanted to trust you—"

"It's okay," I say gently.

He looks at me and gently places his hands onto my hips, guiding me to step between his legs and the piano. The heat of them against me has my breath hitching.

"Sinclair read out a quote at their funeral. It said some people make you feel happiness. Some teach you lessons. And others give you memories to carry with you for a lifetime. I didn't know it at the time, but Slade was also going to give me Molly. He gave me a reason to keep going, Tate. And as stupid as this might sound, I still feel him. Not just in here"—he takes my hand and places it over his chest where his heart is thudding in a deep, steady rhythm—"but in a way like he isn't really gone."

"He'll always be with you," I breathe.

His eyes mist. "I told myself I hated love because it could leave you. And even if it didn't, then it came with conditions. That no one would ever love Molly like I do. Like she's theirs."

"She *is* yours," I choke, my voice shaking as Sullivan lifts my hand to his lips and presses a featherlight kiss to the tips of my fingers. "And anyone who can't see what an amazing little girl she is doesn't deserve to be in her life."

"I know." His eyes soften. "You told me more than once. And you also told me you loved my daughter and no matter what I did, I couldn't change that. And... Tate? I never want to even think about trying. The way you love Molly is the one thing I couldn't ignore. I told myself I could cope without your smiles and your songs drifting around our home as you cooked. I told myself that I could live without ever waking up next to you again. Never being the one you looked at the way you did. I told myself a lot of things. But no matter what, all the time we've spent apart I've kept coming back to the same conclusion."

"Which is?" I sniff.

"Which is that I can't live without a woman who loves both of us, but who I'm pretty sure will side with Molly over everything as she grows into the incredible young woman that I know she will."

I laugh softly as he continues.

"But the day will come when Molly moves out and has her own life. And fuck, Tate, I don't want you not to be there beside me when she comes home to visit and brings boyfriends that I'm going to want to strangle."

"I could keep you in line." I smile as the first of my tears escapes down my cheek.

"Yeah, Baby, you could," he whispers.

My heart squeezes. *Baby*.

"I love you, Tate. I have loved you for longer than I've been able to admit to myself. But I'm not hiding anymore. I want you. Molly wants you. My family want you. All I've heard about is *you* since the party yesterday. They wanted to know where you'd gone."

"I'm sorry." I reach up and wipe my cheeks. "I needed some time."

"Do you still need it?" Blue eyes scan mine, back and forth with growing urgency.

I hesitate and his face falls.

"Tell me our song isn't over. Please, Tate."

"Sullivan..."

He stares at me as I take a deep breath, hoping I can get the words out. Because once I do, everything will change.

Again.

"I've been offered a job in California," I confess. "I met some people from another record label when I was on tour there, and they want to work with me. I'll be songwriting. It's my dream job."

"California?" he echoes.

I nod, my throat burning.

"What are you going to tell them?" he asks in a hoarse whisper.

Tears rush down my cheeks and I shake my head.

"I already gave them my answer."

"What was it?"

He stares at me and the devastation on his face is more than I can bear, so I turn away.

That's when I see it. A lone paper rose sitting on top of the piano. This one isn't white. It's blue. Just like his eyes. Just like Molly's.

I don't need to pick it up to know that the petals are made from the same musical score that he's just played for me. *Unstoppable.*

The final flower to complete my bouquet of all the songs he knows how to play by heart.

The most poignant one of them all, because it bares the deepest part of his soul to me.

His face blurs behind my tears as I turn to him.

"Yes," I say, my voice barely a whisper. "I told them yes."

48

THE WEDDING

SULLIVAN

"I'm turning around, Son."

"As best man, it's my duty to look out for the bride, so you turn at the correct time," I tell my father, making him chuckle.

"And as your father who hasn't seen his bride since we all had dinner together last night, I can tell you that's not happening. I want to see her the second she steps into view."

"Age has made you stubborn."

"Age has given me everything I've ever dreamed of. You, Sinclair, my family… and now Hallie and the baby."

I look up the aisle at Molly, standing in wait with Halliday's friend, and maid of honor, Sophie, her bottom lip poking out in seriousness as she grips onto her basket of petals.

"It'll be nice to have another little one for Molly to play with."

"You're a great father to her." My father's hand lands on my shoulder with firm, loving reassurance.

"Thanks, Dad. I learned from the best," I reply, clapping my hand on top of his.

My father stiffens next to me, and I follow his gaze to the tree line behind Sophie and Molly.

"Take a breath, Dad," I instruct in a low whisper.

His attention is fixed on Halliday, walking toward us in a silver wedding dress. My father composes himself with a slow inhale, a murmured curse of wonder leaving his lips. "I'm so damn blessed."

"We want you to be happy, Dad." I pat him on the back as Molly walks up the aisle, scattering her petals.

My throat seizes up and I blink hard.

One day she might be walking up here on my arm. And I'll be watching my little girl get married herself.

The thought is both overwhelming and bittersweet.

"I know, and I love you even more for it, Son," my father murmurs, completely transfixed by Halliday.

Vincent's playing the piano to one side, and the notes of the song drift sweetly on the warm breeze. I allow each one to sink into me as I allow myself another indulgent thought.

Maybe one day I'll be standing where my father is, watching Tate walk toward me.

Please, God.

I feel her absence today like a hole in my heart, surrounded by family and friends. All the people I love.

She should be here.

But the job she was offered was her dream. I couldn't let her go back on her word and turn it down. Not for me. Not even for Molly.

"She found the candy before I stopped her," Sinclair apologizes as she slides into the front row of seats.

My father chuckles as Molly flings petals about with delight from her purple candy-stained fingers. She reaches the top of the aisle after lots of 'awws' from the seated guests and holds her arms up to me with a proud grin.

It takes everything in me not to bawl like a baby.

"Good job," I whisper, scooping her up into my arms.

We watch as my father and Halliday recite their vows, and Molly points to the two pictures set up on a small table at the head of the aisle, positioned so they face the two of them.

"Who dat, Daddy?" she whispers in a sweet voice.

"That's Halliday's sister, Jenny," I whisper back. "She's in heaven too."

"Like Grandma?"

"Yes, like Grandma," I reply. I've told Molly about my mother, even though they never met.

My mother would have loved Molly.

"And Uncle Shade," Molly adds, pointing at the second photograph on the table and mispronouncing his name.

"Yeah. Like Slade," I answer, staring at the photo that's like looking into a mirror.

A lump forms in my throat, making it hoarse as I grip her tighter. Just me and her. The two of us. Like it's always been.

"Daddy sad," Molly whispers.

"Daddy's okay," I reply.

She gazes at me with wide eyes, then pulls me closer by tightening her arms around my neck.

The moment her soft little mouth presses a kiss to my cheek with a *mwah* sound, my heart cracks.

"Love you, Daddy," she tells me.

"Love you too, Sweetheart," I choke. "Daddy loves you too."

Jenson's holding Molly's hands and performing silly dance moves with her in the center of the dance floor. Her head is thrown back in delight as giggle after giggle spills from her.

"He's found someone to hang out with who's the same age of mental maturity as himself."

I snort as Vincent hands me a fresh glass of whiskey.

"I think Molly's more advanced, personally. And she wears a bear onesie better than him."

"True." Vincent chuckles.

We watch the two of them for longer before he asks, "So how are you doing?"

"Fine."

"Fine?" His tone implies he thinks I'm talking bullshit.

He knows me so well.

"I'm... wondering how she's getting on," I admit, begrudgingly.

"Tate's a smart girl. She'll be able to handle herself."

I drink some of my whiskey so I don't have to form an answer that's any more eloquent than a grumbled grunt of agreement. One that also hides the unnecessary flare of jealousy that strikes me as Vincent speaks about Tate with a small hint of familiarity.

She went on one date with him. *One*. And she told me she didn't want *comfortable*.

But the whole idea of her with any other man makes me damn *un*-comfortable.

Because she's *mine*.

At least, in my head she always will be.

And Vincent's right. She is smart. She's incredible. And I know she's got this new job in the palm of her hand. But I still struggle with the fact she didn't want me to help her iron out the finer details of her contract. It took a lot of persuading for her to relent and allow Jones to assist her, on the understanding that I stepped back and let her take the lead.

She wanted to do it herself.

She got this job off her own merit. And after all the ways

I've interfered, I get why she wanted to negotiate it on her terms.

I just wish I knew how the hell she was. We haven't spoken since I left for Cape Town a few days ago for the wedding.

The day I played to her in the street and told her I loved her.

The day she graciously declined my offer to help her set up things for her move to LA.

The day she also said she just needed time.

I'm trying so damn hard to give it to her, when all I want to do is call her and ask her how she is.

She's in LA today, signing the contract for her new job.

When Molly and I get back to New York it'll only be a couple of days until she leaves for good.

I'm praying to God the time she asked for results in her coming back and telling me she wants to make things work.

I can fly over there as much as possible. And fly her back to visit.

I'll do whatever I can not to lose her.

Even though the churning in my gut tells me I already did.

"How're things with you?" I ask Vincent, aware that I'm being a rude, self-pitying asshole.

"Good. Great, actually. Life in the shadows has it's advantages. You know there's a porn site where groups of guys are dressing up in balaclavas and banging people in organized orgies while playing live recordings of The Maestro's music?"

"Really?" I smirk.

"There are those who need to hear the music. And those who need to *feel* the music, I guess." Vincent chuckles. "Whatever man, I'm just happy it's spreading joy."

"And potentially STIs," I clip, earning myself a chuckle from him.

The band slide seamlessly into another song and Molly continues dancing with Jenson, surrounded by other guests, all dancing, including Uncle Mal and Aunt Trudy. Everyone around us is having a great time. My father's sitting beneath a fairy lit veranda talking softly to Halliday with one hand stroking her bump tenderly as she gazes at him with nothing but love in her eyes. Sinclair's melded to Denver's side, one hand on his chest, batting her eyelashes at him as he looks like he's grumbling to her about something. But his hand is still low down on her back, caressing her with tenderness.

Even Killian is sitting at the bar, flirting with one of the wait staff.

Everyone is together. And happy.

I clear my throat, then drain my whiskey.

"Another?" I invite Vincent, gesturing to the bar.

His attention moves from something behind me and settles on my face.

"Nah, Buddy. I think you're about to be needed." He slaps me on the back and wanders away.

My eyes snap to Molly, expecting her to be looking for me. But she's still happily dancing with Jenson without a care in the world.

"She makes a very cute flower girl."

I spin at her voice.

"Tate?"

My eyes probably look like they're in danger of falling out of my head.

She's not in LA. She's here.

She's here.

I stare at her for a few long seconds, drinking her in like a lone man in the desert who's just seen a mirage. A lush, tropical oasis that'll save his life.

She gives me a shy smile, her eyes glittering. "Hi, Sullivan."

"You're supposed to be in LA."

"I was. Now I'm here."

"Now you're here," I echo roughly, staring at her like this will all make sense.

None of it should matter to me. *She's here.* But it does matter. It matters more than anything.

I pushed her away once, thinking she was chasing her dream. But it was the wrong one. This time it's right. And as much as it pains me, I *need* to know she's not giving it up.

"Much quicker than I planned. My flight wasn't supposed to get in until tomorrow," she says.

"You had a flight booked? To Cape Town?"

Her eyes flick around at the wedding guests before coming back to meet mine and seeming unsure, like she's wondering if she made a mistake. I'm still unable to believe that she's here, right in front of me. Flesh and blood.

"I did. I wanted to see you. But then Jones ushered me onto a private jet."

Something inside me homes in on that information. "Private jet?"

"I told him I was planning on coming here to talk to you, and he said he could help. He must have made a call to Huck because it looked a lot like the jet Huck borrowed from a friend to bring me back from tour. All silver inside."

My narrowed gaze flicks to my father, catching him looking at us. He smiles knowingly, before turning his attention back to Halliday.

"Always useful to have friends willing to... *help out*," I comment. "How did the meeting go?"

Tate breaks into a smile. "Really well. They agreed to everything I asked for."

"They did?" My heart lifts. "Did you ask to work four days a week so you can come home for long weekends?"

I don't catch myself quick enough to stop the word 'home' from slipping out.

Her eyes pinch. "No... I didn't."

"You didn't?" A growing sense of dread starts winding its way around my windpipe, inching up slowly like a poisonous weed that's determined to destroy everything in its path.

This is it. The final goodbye. She's come to tell me it's over. She doesn't want to put us through the strain of long-distance, even though I'm more than willing to do whatever it takes to make it work.

I haven't allowed myself to consider it not working.

I can't.

"Tate—"

"I know we talked about it last time I saw you, but..." She sighs. "That's not what I want, Sullivan."

I struggle to hold it together as my breath comes in jagged pants.

I've lost her. She didn't even want to try. I messed things up that badly that she couldn't even bring herself to try in case I screwed up and hurt her again.

Now I'm going to have to explain to Molly that Tate's gone again.

And just like the first time, it's because of me.

She takes my hands and strokes them. I want to whip them away before the pain of knowing it's the last time she'll touch me takes over. But at the same time, I close my fingers around hers, pulling her closer until our bodies are flush, our chests grazing.

I don't want to let her go.

"I understand," I breathe, my throat burning as she looks into my eyes.

I can't look away. I want to sear the sight of her into my soul, so I have something to remember her by when I go to hell after what I've put her through.

I ruined us. I broke us.

I deserve this.

I should be grateful that she came to break it to me in person. That's Tate all over. Kind. Sweet. Thoughtful.

But all I feel is anger at myself.

"No. I don't think you do," she says, and it takes everything in me not to kiss her one last time. I haven't felt her lips against mine since the night she lifted me up off the floor and held me together when I thought I was going to shatter into a billion pieces.

The last time I kissed her it was tinged with the salt of tears.

"Sullivan," she urges, pulling me out of my head. "I didn't ask, because I want something else instead."

I fight the glimmer of hope away that's poking at my heart like an incessant itch. If I let it in and I'm wrong, then I don't know what I'll do, or how I'll survive.

"What *do* you want?"

Her eyes are glassy, her voice thick with emotion. "I told them if I couldn't work remotely from New York, then I wasn't taking the job."

I stare at her, speechless.

"I said I'd love to work with them. But that I loved two people in New York more. And without them, I wouldn't be able to write any songs, because their loss would be louder inside me than anything else. So, if they wanted songs, then I'd need to stay in New York in order to write them."

The itch cascades like a waterfall, transforming into a rushing blur of thundering noise.

"You love two people in New York more?"

She nods. "Molly and my dad."

She bites her lip, failing to hide her smile.

"I mean you, Sullivan," she whispers, reaching up to stroke my hair. "*I love you*. And I'm staying in New York. With you and Molly."

"You are?"

She nods.

I exhale shakily.

"Thank you."

I cup her neck between my hands and tilt her face up, searching her eyes.

"I love you, Tate. I love you so *fucking* much."

I don't care that my voice cracks as I speak. I don't care that I'm trembling. I don't care that my head's so light I'm in danger of passing out.

"I love you too," she whispers, drawing my eyes to her soft lips.

"Please, say I can kiss you," I choke. "Show me you mean it. That you're really in this with us."

"My heart's always been with you and Molly. *Always*."

She still hasn't moved closer, despite her reassuring words. Despite the way her pulse is thundering erratically beneath the pads of my thumbs like it's beating out my name in morse code.

"*Please, Baby*," I beg.

Her breath hitches, and for an agonizing second she's silent.

Then she nods.

One tiny, subtle movement.

But it's all I need.

My mouth descends on hers with fevered hunger.

I waste no time in making her mine again, tasting and exploring every inch that I've missed. Molding us back together, piece by piece.

I groan into her mouth, and she pulls back, biting her lip in a smile. "Sullivan?"

"What?" I groan, slanting my mouth over hers and kissing her again.

"People might be looking."

"People can mind their own fucking business," I rasp,

kissing her again. "You came back to us. You think I give a flying fuck who sees me kiss you? Besides, they're all family and friends. They'll see us kiss plenty at our wedding."

She pulls back again, and I chase her, letting out a desperate growl at being denied.

"What?"

"You said you're staying in New York," I explain in response to her shocked expression.

"I—"

"Tate. If you're coming back, then be assured, I will not fuck up again," I say with conviction.

Her eyes widen.

"I'm not making that mistake again. You'll be my wife... *One day*," I add, to ease her into the idea, even though my mind is already formulating a plan to make that day as soon as fucking possible.

She blinks before laughing. But stops abruptly as she studies me.

"You're serious?"

"Have you ever known me not to be?"

Her mouth drops open but before she can answer, a small tornado dressed in tulle runs over and crashes into us.

"Tate!"

I hoist Molly up into one arm. The beautiful smile on her face makes my chest fit to bursting.

"That's right, Sweetheart. Tate came. And aren't we happy to see her?" I wind my other arm around Tate's waist and pull her closer.

Molly nods eagerly and holds her arms out. Tate moves closer so she can wrap them around her neck.

My grip on them both tightens as they embrace, protected inside my arms.

My girls.

"Dance, Daddy?" Molly asks sweetly, her eyes bouncing between me and Tate.

"Absolutely." I smile at her.

"Go on. I'll..." Tate gestures to a table with some empty seats by it.

I arch a brow at her as I say to Molly, "You want to dance with both of us, don't you, Sweetheart?"

"Yay!" Molly claps her hands in delight.

Tate's eyes shine as I tip my head toward the dance floor. "Shall we?"

I take Tate's hand, keeping Molly held in my arm as I lead us in-between dancing couples. I turn and pull Tate into me, holding her close with my hand on her lower back.

She slides one hand up around my collar, placing the other around Molly.

The band moves into a cover of Ed Sheeran's "All of the Stars", and Molly rests her head against my shoulder, gazing at Tate with a magical smile, made all the sweeter by the innocence in it as Tate sings the words of the song softly to her.

I hold them both in my arms.

And we dance.

We dance until Molly grows heavy in my arms and her eyelids wilt. But still, my little girl fights sleep, not wanting to miss a moment. But as Tate smiles, first at her, then up at me, I realize.

Life will give me so many more moments like this now that I have them both.

"Molly gave me a reason to carry on after losing them both," I tell Tate softly. "And so many times I thought I was screwing it up."

"Sullivan," she breathes, her eyes pinching with emotion. "You weren't. Look how happy she is. You're an amazing dad."

I look down at Molly, settled happily against me, still fighting sleep.

My heart swells in my chest and I pull Tate closer.

"Then I met you. And I didn't look at it as a challenge that I was failing at anymore."

She blinks, tears building along her lashes. "How do you see it now?" She sniffs.

I smile softly. "As an adventure."

"*Sullivan*." She wipes at her eyes.

"Sorry to break up the happy reunion."

Tate's head snaps up as Sinclair holds out her arms, gesturing to Molly.

"But Denver and I want a dance with Molly." She throws Tate a wide grin. "Hi, Tate."

"Hi." She smiles back.

"Glad you could make it," Sinclair says as she takes Molly from my arms.

Denver's beside her, and he tips his chin at Tate. "Hi."

"Hi," Tate replies, before biting her lower lip and smiling up at me.

Sinclair's grinning, watching our exchange.

"Sullivan? Why don't you show Tate around? There are lots of really romantic spots around the property that I'm sure she'd like to see." She winks at me, then flicks her gaze toward Denver. "Aren't there, Brute?"

Denver's gaze burns into hers and he clears his throat and reluctantly agrees. "There are. Lots."

Sinclair giggles at the gruffness in his voice, before tipping her head at me, and motioning for us to go.

It's the first time my blood hasn't boiled at the insinuation of my sister's sex life before. In fact, right now I'm planning the ridiculously extravagant gift I'll get her for her next birthday.

"Let's go," I say to Tate, even though I'm already marching her off the dance floor, my rapidly hardening dick making it near impossible to move without urgency.

"Sullivan?" She laughs. "Won't people wonder where we've gone?"

"They won't be wondering, they'll know."

"Oh my God." She presses her hand over her eyes as I stalk to one of the entrances of the main house. The door's wide open to allow people to come in and out to use the ground floor bathrooms.

I turn back and sweep her up into my arms, making her gasp.

"Sorry. Was I not moving fast enough for you?" She giggles.

I stride inside the house and carry her straight up the sweeping staircase to the upper level. My footsteps are strong and purposeful as I take us down the hallway, past Molly's bedroom, and through the door opposite it that leads into my suite.

I place her onto her feet and lock the door behind us.

"Wow, this is beautiful," Tate exclaims, her head swiveling to look at the four-poster bed with sheer drapes secured back around it, and the balcony that overlooks the ocean.

"You can admire the view after."

She turns and her eyes drop to my chest as I waste no time yanking off my shirt.

"Oh, right." She bites her lip, lifting her heated gaze to mine. "It's like that, is it?"

"Sure is."

I step toward her, and our breath mingles in the hot, loaded air. For a few heartbeats, we just stare in longing, drinking one another in.

"Tate?" I whisper.

She licks her lips. "Sullivan?"

The trust in her eyes as she looks up through her lashes at me has my dick throbbing painfully against my zipper.

I stroke some strands of hair back from her eyes, groaning

softly as I allow the back of my fingers to trace down the side of her face, over her neck where her pulse is fluttering beneath her silky skin, and to her collar bones.

"Am I fucking you or making love to you first?"

"I get to choose?" She bites her lip playfully, matching my low, raspy tone. I'm barely holding back from throwing her beneath me on the bed, tearing her panties out of the way, and burying myself to the hilt.

"If it makes you feel better, call it choice. But I'll be doing both multiple times before the night is over. You can just decide how you want it first."

Her eyes drop to the tented bulge in my pants and her lips curl up.

"You think you can do slow right now?" She wraps her palm around my shaft and squeezes.

"Fuck," I hiss, gazing through hooded lids at her.

She strokes me through the material and pre-cum leaks so fast from my slit that a wet patch appears on the front of my pants.

"I can do slow," I force out through gritted teeth.

With skilled hands, she slides down my zipper and pulls my heavy cock out. I let out a tortured groan as my balls hike up to my body, desperate to unload inside her.

"Are you sure?" she teases.

"Tate," I warn. "I need you back on my cock, where you belong. So give me an answer I can work with."

She tilts her face up to mine, her tongue darting out and swiping delicately at her plump lower lip.

"Fucking," she whispers. "Fuck me first."

I grab her face and crush my lips to hers, making her gasp in surprise. Maybe she expected me to throw her down and sink inside her straight away. And as much as my cock is begging me to do just that, I want to kiss her first.

I *need* to kiss her, because my brain is still processing the fact that she's here.

And she's staying.

She's mine.

"You're beautiful. So fucking sexy," I pant roughly as I descend on her neck, assaulting it with kisses that I know might leave marks. She can wear them and show the world that she's goddamn mine until I get a ring on her finger and call her my *wife*.

The thought makes the throbbing end of my cock leak all over her pale blue dress.

"I ruined your dress," I grind out, baring my teeth to the swell of her cleavage as I bend to pull it into a biting kiss.

Tate shivers in my arms, her nipple tightening into a steeled peak beneath my exploring hand.

"It's fine. I can clean it. I have new dryers from my landlord at my place, remember?"

Even though I know she's teasing, the idea that it might still be her place when we return to New York, and that she might want to live apart sends a rush of white-hot rage-filled panic through me.

Her dress pays the price.

Her body is pulled toward mine, making her tits heave with a shocked gasp as I grab the neckline and tear the thin fabric right down the center.

"Now I really fucking ruined it."

"Oh my God." Her eyes are wide, but they quickly drop to a lust-filled haze. "I liked this one," she says, her cheeks all flushed and pretty.

"I'll buy you a thousand just like it."

I rake my eyes down her body ruthlessly.

"You're even more incredible than I remember," I say in awe.

I drop a hand to my dick and squeeze it, unable to help

myself as I lick my lower lip, eyes greedily ravaging her tits that are spilling out of her bra.

"Fuck yeah, Baby. You got even sexier."

I gather up a slick load of pre-cum and let go of my dick. Using the tips of my fingers I paint her heaving cleavage until it's shining with me.

"Do you like this bra too?" I bite my lip as I reach for it.

Before she can answer, I've forced my fingers through both thin lace cups and shredded them so her dusky pink nipples poke through.

"Sullivan," she gasps through a shocked laugh.

"You know the panties are next, Tate. Fuck me, I need to see that pussy of yours. I'll incinerate anything that's in my way of being with you."

She looks at me with a heady intensity.

We both know I'm not just talking about clothes and sex anymore.

Her eyes stay glued to mine as I lower my head and seal my mouth around one nipple. She sucks in a breath and sinks her hand into my hair, tugging it from the roots. I smile around her as I suck harder and lap at her with my tongue.

If I ever doubted that she's missed me as much as I've missed her, then her needy whimpers blow any doubts from my mind.

"I need to make you come," I groan, my attention on her breasts ramping up in intensity until I'm grazing them with my teeth and delivering little nips alongside open-mouthed, sucking kisses and licks. "Fuck, Tate. I need you coming on my face and my cock, Baby."

She moans with wanton need as I pick her up and place her onto my bed.

I hold her eyes as I remove my pants and underwear, until I'm standing at the foot of the bed, naked with my dick in my hand.

I give it a much-needed stroke.

"Look at you, Baby," I tsk. "Lying there with your pretty dress all ruined and your tits out like you're aching to be fucked."

"Oh God," she whimpers, arching up in the air and presenting her perfect nipples to me for sucking on again as I kneel on the bed between her thighs.

"That what you want? To be fucked?"

"Yes."

"Yes, what?"

"*Please*, Sullivan," she pants. "Take away the emptiness I've felt without you."

Her words make my throat thicken instantly, and our eyes lock.

"I'll never let you go again, Baby. *I swear*." My voice comes out hoarse and tortured.

But it's what she needs to hear.

It's what we both need.

Her eyes soften, love and lust glazing them as any last hints of doubt that could have been lingering there drift away.

She wriggles on the bed beneath me as I drink her in. Content to just look at her and bask in the glory of being able to call her mine again.

"Show me," she whispers.

I snap out of my haze as the soaked fabric of her panties rubs against the crown of my dick.

Looking down between our bodies I tut like I'm disappointed.

"What's this?"

"What?" She wriggles more as I sit back on my heels and watch the way she's desperately trying to rub herself against my rock-hard dick.

"This?" I repeat, dragging one knuckle down the center of the blue lace that's darkened into a wet strip. "All this"—I lick my lips slowly—"wetness. It's leaking out of your greedy little cunt."

She shudders as I drag my knuckle back up, circling over her clit.

"Now I know why you asked for fucking first," I say as I cinch the soaked fabric of her panties between my thumb and forefinger and pull it up toward her clit so that the swollen lips of her pussy spill out either side of it.

The resulting look is filthy and fucking fabulous.

She gasps as I lean down and suck one side past my lips.

"It's because..." I move to suck the other side, loving the gasp that comes from her pretty little mouth. "You know you'll not be able to take my cock slowly. Your wet little cunt's too greedy. It wants to be stuffed full of it, coming on it as I fuck you hard and fast, doesn't it?"

Tate whimpers.

"Doesn't it?" I nip her clit through the tightened fabric.

"Yes!" she cries, her thighs trembling around my ears. "Yes."

"You need to come for me, Baby?" I choke out, emotion building in my chest as I circle her clit with the tip of my nose, breathing her in, but purposefully making myself wait before I allow myself a full taste of her.

I need to savor it. Burn it into my memory.

I almost lost her.

"Yes," she whimpers. "Make me come, Sullivan."

I screw my eyes up, a guttural sound like that of an animal in pain rushing past my lips as I yank her panties to the side and press my open mouth to her.

Her taste explodes on my tongue, filling my senses, overtaking my head, becoming the only thing I can focus on as I sink into her, devouring her with rough, desperate sucks, licks, and kisses.

"Baby," I utter, diving even deeper into her until her

wetness is coating my tongue and gliding down my throat. "Don't ever leave me," I beg. "Don't ever fucking leave me."

Her hands work their way into my hair, holding on for dear life as I bring her to the edge.

"Sullivan..."

She's trembling and writhing beneath me, her voice filled with a dizzying lust and wanton heat.

"You taste so good."

She whimpers, her thighs shaking either side of my head as I eat her out with increased determination.

"Oh God," she whimpers.

I sink even deeper, lapping up every quiver of her pussy and swallowing down all the slick arousal that's dripping out of her.

"Come on my face, Baby. There's a good girl now."

She tenses, and her grip tightens on my hair making my dick surge with a wave of pre-cum, that drips onto the sheets.

The incredible sound she makes the moment she lets go is one I'll replay over and over in my head for the rest of my life.

"Sullivan! Oh my... Sullivan!"

She screams. My girl fucking screams my name as she squirts a jet of warm cum into my mouth.

I drink it down with a smack of my lips before sinking back into her, hungry for more.

"Jesus Christ, yes, Baby. That's what I'm talking about."

She whimpers and pants and wriggles, not knowing what to do with herself. I clamp my forearm over her hips, pushing her into the mattress as I work her back up with my tongue again.

"Sullivan!"

Her orgasm rolls into another delicious wet scream of my name.

If the band wasn't playing so loud then there's no doubt the whole wedding party would hear her.

I'm going for a third when she pulls my hair so hard I wince.

"Need you," she pants, "inside me."

I kiss her trembling skin, loving the way she sucks in a breath as my lips graze her puffy, silky little clit.

Tugging her panties down, I bring them to my nose. Her pupils blow wide as I jerk myself off at the same time as I take a deep inhale.

"I'm going to need to keep these."

"Are you?" she breathes, her eyes sparkling.

"Fuck yeah."

I drop my hand and scrunch it around the base of my cock, the other cupping my balls. I grunt as I jerk myself off again, this time with her panties wrapped around my shaft.

She watches me with flushed cheeks as I put on an obscene show, allowing my pre-cum to run down the sides of my length and sink into the fabric alongside her own arousal.

"It's been a long time, Baby. Maybe I should come first before I fuck you. Paint those juicy tits of yours instead. Otherwise you'll have me leaking out of you for days."

"I want that."

Tate holds my eyes, a dirty glint in hers.

I press my lips together in a tortured grunt.

"Fuck, Baby, you're killing me."

She smiles and I almost blow on the spot. "Come here."

I discard the panties aside and do as my girl wants.

Settling between her legs, she widens her thighs on instinct, inviting the pulsing head of my dick to slide through her wetness.

"You sure?" I rasp, hovering on my arms above her, our faces only a few inches apart.

I don't know why I'm asking. I've just devoured her like a starving man.

But this?

This feels like the final part of the puzzle. Like once we do this, that's it. She really is back. She really is mine.

Forever.

"I'm more than sure," she breathes, stroking my cheek.

"So am I."

I hold her eyes as I push forward and finally thrust inside her after months of being apart.

"Tate," I choke, my voice betraying me as I bottom out inside her tight wet heat.

Her breath puffs against my lips and she takes my face between her hands.

"I love you, Sullivan Beaufort," she says, her body rippling around me, relishing every inch of me being back inside her, where I belong.

"I love you too, Tate Miller," I say thickly. "I love you so, so much."

I press a kiss to her lips, and she smiles against my mouth.

"What is it, Baby?" I rasp as I pull almost all the way out before sinking back inside her with a shudder.

Every muscle in my body is taut, dangling on a pinnacle of losing all control.

"I thought the making love came after?" she says, kissing me again.

This time I smile against her mouth and bring our foreheads together.

"My girl wants to be fucked, does she?"

Her responding gasp as I pull back and thrust inside her with a little more force tells me all I need to know.

"Don't say I didn't warn you," I say, pressing a final light kiss to her lips before straightening up on my arms and widening my knees so she's spread out beneath me.

She's stretched, pink, and glistening, my cock stuffed inside her and making her so full that her swollen little clit has pushed free of its hood.

"Now there's a sight," I admire with pursed lips as I begin pumping my hips, watching the way her pussy stretches around me like it's only just managing to take me all.

"So good," Tate whines.

I keep a punishing rhythm as I drink her in, sliding my eyes up her body to where her tits are bouncing up and down her chest.

Fuck, she's right back where she belongs.

I'm going to love this woman for the rest of my life.

The realization hits me in the chest like an arrow to my heart and I let out a groan as my cock swells inside her.

"Tate. Fuck, Baby."

She widens her legs, gazing up at me.

"Harder. I need you to fuck me harder. Make me forget what it was like during those months where I didn't feel you inside me."

I pound her into the mattress, loving the way she throws her head back with ecstasy. Loving the way she cries out my name and her body clamps down on me like it never wants to let go.

She wants me to make her forget.

But I want to remember.

I need to remember what it was like without her. How I almost lost her. So I know I'll never be so fucking stupid ever again as long as I live.

"Sullivan," she moans my name, and a familiar tightness hugs my slicked-up cock.

"You going to come, Baby?"

"Uh-huh," she manages to utter through a panted whine.

"Good girl. Let it out," I coo, jerking my chin forward and pushing a little deeper so my pubic bone rubs her exposed clit.

She comes with a cry, her lashes fluttering as she struggles to hold my gaze.

"Good girl," I choke. "Your cunt's milking me, Baby. Jesus Christ."

I can't hold it any longer, as she spasms around me, I let go.

I come so hard my eyes water, and my hearing muffles.

"Tate," I grunt. "Oh fuuuuckkkk...."

The only thing I can focus on as I unload months' worth of pent-up sexual longing is her eyes.

Beautiful, trusting blue eyes that sparkle up at me like I'm her goddamn man.

I *am* her goddamn man.

"I love you." I kiss her roughly, sliding one hand to her neck and holding her in place as I thrust, making our mixed cum spill out over our thighs. "I love you."

"I love you too."

We're a sweaty, slick mess of hammering hearts and heaving chests as I slowly fuck the last pulses of my orgasm out inside her. Her body flutters around me with the aftershocks of hers.

I drop my forehead to hers and a serene smile paints itself over her face as we finally catch our breath.

"I didn't even congratulate your father and Halliday yet. Or say hello to any of the other guests. I'm so rude."

"Don't worry, he knows you got here safely on a private jet." I smirk.

"What? How?"

She waits for clarification, but I kiss her instead. She'll figure out my father's the one who owns a private jet with a *sterling* silver interior soon. He bought it for Halliday as a present so her parents could visit from England.

I'd usually hate anyone interfering with my personal life.

My father knows that.

Yet, he did it anyway.

And I need to thank him until my voice gives out.

Tate returned to me. Us. After the tour. And now.

She came back to me and Molly where I desperately wanted her to be, and where my father could see she belonged.

"Besides, you're not a guest," I inform her.

"Oh God. I wasn't even invited. I'm a wedding crasher!" She squeaks and it's adorable.

I chuckle and her eyes narrow playfully.

"It's not funny. There are members of your family here that I haven't met before, and now they'll have a bad impression of me."

I kiss her neck, savoring the scent of her that surrounds me.

"You're not a wedding crasher, Tate. You're one of us."

"What?"

"Family," I state. "You're family now. You don't just get me and Molly; you have to take us all. But there's no going back." I flex my dick inside her making her body clench around me. "We've consummated your return. You're mine now."

She chews her lip, her eyes sparkling.

"Hmm, I like the sound of that. I always wanted a bigger family. And lots of babies."

I groan and kiss her.

She winks at me and I'm a fucking goner for her all over again.

"Beauforts stick together," she muses.

"We do, Baby."

I'm already growing hard inside her again at her mention of babies. The idea of Tate with a baby bump, growing a little brother or sister for Molly is like a shot of adrenaline to my dick.

"But if any of my family think they're getting even a second of your time tonight, then they're mistaken."

I kiss her again.

"Because now..." I start pumping my hips, sliding in and out of her, nice and slow and deep. "Now I'm about to make love to the woman I'm crazy about."

Her eyes mist.

"I love you, Tate," I breathe.

"I love you too, she whispers, pulling me into a tender kiss that has my heart swelling.

Our hands entwine, fingers wrapped together as we move in harmony.

Like a perfect song.

One I'll be playing on repeat.

Always.

EPILOGUE

TATE

The morning after...

"Come again, Baby. That's it. Good girl. Just like that."

Sullivan's voice is like velvet being dragged over stone as he murmurs against my lips, emotion passing between us with every scorching and tender kiss we've shared throughout the night.

I shudder inside his arms, coming in deep, pulsing waves as I slide up and down his cock.

He grips my hips as I use my arms around his shoulders to support myself.

"Tate," he grunts, pulling me down roughly and coming inside me.

I kiss him through it, then break into a smile against his mouth.

"Hottest night ever," I muse, my voice hoarse from the number of times he's made me cry out his name.

I lost count of how many times we fucked. Made love. Kissed. Came.

They all melded into one another.

I just know I haven't slept. The rare moments when Sullivan wasn't inside my body, he was inside my heart, and head. Talking to me. Telling me all the things he wants to do together when we get home. All the places he wants us to go together with Molly.

As a family.

The happiness in his voice is unlike anything I've ever heard before. I'm loving it.

There was no way I was ever going to leave New York after that day he came and played on the sidewalk to me.

I knew from the moment I heard the first notes of that song, "Unstoppable", that nothing would keep me from them again.

Sullivan didn't want me to give up my dream job. He asked me to consider flying back from LA each weekend. To make it work long-distance. And maybe we could have. But despite him pretending that would be enough for him. It wasn't enough for me.

I want to be with him and Molly every day.

I knew the moment I walked into that meeting about my contract that I was going to be working from New York. So, I took a page out of Sullivan's book and negotiated like a shark, doing everything I could think of to get them to agree.

My song, "Blue Eyes", was the deciding factor.

I was prepared to let that song go. People already heard it when I was touring. I figured the new company would want fresh songs. And they do. But they want "Blue Eyes". They said it's the song that made them notice me in the first place and make me the offer of a job.

So I agreed.

It's as if Sullivan and Molly were in that meeting with me. And they're the reason it went the way that it did.

"Molly will be awake soon," Sullivan says, kissing me with a groan as he guides me off his lap and back against the soft pillows. I sink into them as he sits up.

"Take your time. We'll meet you downstairs in the kitchen."

I nod, happy to steal a few moments in his luxurious bed before I get up.

And happy to watch his muscular round ass saunter away across the room.

I didn't get to take in the décor last night. The bathroom is inside the bedroom, partitioned with a giant glass wall. There's a round tub with a floor to ceiling window beside it, showcasing an incredible view of the ocean. And a huge rainfall shower that Sullivan's turned on.

There's a door to one side which I assume is the toilet, but my attention glues back to the magnificent man inside the shower, head tipped back beneath the spray, eyes closed.

His biceps bulge as he slicks his dark hair back, then grabs a bottle of something.

It's like hot billionaire shower porn as he soaps up his toned, broad body.

Bubbles catch in the smattering of dark hair on his chest, and he drops his hand to his dick, soaping up the semi-hard length with skilled ease.

"How did I get so lucky?" I murmur.

I look up. His eyes are glittering, and his lips are tilted into a self-assured smirk. He totally busted me staring. But I don't care.

"You okay, Baby?" he calls in a rich, satisfied voice that seems to give away the fact he's been screwing all night.

"Yeah. Just watching," I muse. "I figure if I'm yours like

you say, then you're mine too. And I can perve on you and your billionaire dick should I wish."

He chuckles. "Look all you want, Baby. It's all yours."

He closes his eyes and tips his head back, rinsing away the suds.

My mouth waters as he shuts off the shower and smirks as he wraps a towel around his waist and walks over to the bed.

He leans down and kisses me, water droplets running down his tanned chest.

"I know that look. And believe me, I'd love to sit that pretty little pussy back on my face and make you come again before breakfast. But I have something to do with Molly."

"You don't need to worry. I'll be fine here in this ridiculously comfortable bed." I press a kiss to his lips. "But I am getting up in five minutes because I miss Molly and need to see her. We didn't get long together last night."

Sullivan's eyes soften at the corners, and he lifts my hand, kissing my fingers.

"She'll be so excited you're here, Tate. See you downstairs."

I take my time showering after he leaves, admiring the sunrise over the ocean from the balcony as I dress in a white sundress from my luggage that Sullivan brought up from downstairs for me last night. I smile to myself about him ripping off my blue one last night as I leave the room and pad quietly down the hallway toward the staircase.

It feels weird to be tiptoeing around one of his father's vacation homes when I haven't even spoken to Sterling since arriving. Sullivan said the immediate family are staying here, with the rest of the guests in a nearby hotel.

I'm hoping it's too early for anyone else to be up, because doing the walk of no-shame from Sullivan's suite isn't how I'd like to run into them again.

I need coffee before that.

Heading down the stairs, I follow the faint sound of a familiar sweet little voice that pulls at my heartstrings.

Molly's sitting eating at a long, gleaming marble table when I walk into the expansive kitchen. Sullivan looks up from where he's making coffee and catches my eye. The warmth in his gaze as he looks at me makes bubbles fizz in my stomach.

The glass wall behind him that shows the ocean stretching off to the horizon barely registers. Instead, with pure happiness guiding me, I make my way over to Molly.

"Good morning. Can I join you?"

She looks up and grins as she notices me, before nodding eagerly.

I slide into the seat beside her, feeling Sullivan's eyes on us.

"What you eating?" I ask, resting my chin on one hand.

"Pancakes," she replies, her bottom lip poking out in concentration as she collects a piece of pre-cut pancake onto her fork and puts it in her mouth.

"You ready for another, Sweetheart?" Sullivan asks, walking over with a large plate in one hand.

"Aww, you made bear pancakes? Are these ones yours?" I ask Molly, pointing to the messier attempts at bears on the plate.

She shakes her head. "Those Daddy's."

I look up at Sullivan, biting back my grin.

"It's the oven," he grumbles. "The ones I make at home come out better."

"You've been making bear pancakes at home?"

He nods and places the plate on the table. "Molly missed yours."

He walks back over to the counter and picks up two mugs. I know he doesn't mean anything by that. But knowing Molly missed me when we were apart makes my heart heavy.

Sullivan comes back, placing a coffee on the table for me.

"Thanks." I smile up at him gratefully and he leans down to kiss me.

I motion with my eyes to Molly who's too busy eating her pancake to notice. Sullivan's eyes twinkle and he pulls out the chair beside me and sits down.

"Sweetheart?" he says to Molly, keeping his eyes on mine. "Shall we show Tate that thing we talked about?"

"Yeah!" Molly bounces down from her chair and runs over to the counter, coming back, holding a book.

Sullivan's eyes are on my face as Molly thrusts it into my lap proudly.

"What's this?"

"Open," she instructs.

I look at the plain blue cover, then open it.

"What are these?" I frown as I turn the first three pages, staring at the small pieces of card stuck to each one.

"I think you know what they are," Sullivan says softly.

I glance up at him, my breath hitching. "You were there?"

"At every one."

My throat clogs as I trace a fingertip over one of the many ticket stubs. "Oh... wow."

They're all here. Every concert I ever played as a support act. All the different cities. All the venues in each one. Glued inside the book in chronological order, marking every moment we spent apart.

"I never saw you."

"You weren't supposed to. But I heard you. All of your songs. And I heard every lyric of *that* one."

I swallow. I know exactly which song he's referring to.

"Blue Eyes?" I whisper.

"Blue Eyes," he repeats, taking my hands inside his.

"I wrote that song before I left New York. It was about falling in love for the first time."

"I know," he rasps.

I look up at him, searching his eyes, a confession dangling from the tip of my tongue. "It wasn't—"

"About me?" He arches a brow. "I know." His eyes move to Molly, and they soften with adoration. "It was about Molly."

"It was," I whisper, the emotion in my voice turning into a giggle as Molly beams brightly at me.

"You were singing about her. And every time I heard that song I prayed that things could be different."

"Sullivan…" I give him a soft smile. "We don't need to go over this anymore. What's done is done. It's all in the past now."

"Let me finish, Tate." He strokes my hands inside his. "You love her the way she deserves to be loved. You love her like I do. You love her unconditionally, like a mother should."

I blink away tears at the tenderness in his voice.

"She deserves a mother like you."

He holds my eyes, his signature intensity burning brighter than I've ever seen it before.

"What are you doing?" I falter as he pushes back his chair and drops to one knee.

"Molly?" he instructs in a soft voice, his eyes staying on me. "You know the next part we spoke about?"

"Yes, Daddy," she says seriously as she comes to stand beside him.

He holds his hand out and she places a signature blue, Beaufort Diamonds box into his palm.

"Good job, Sweetheart." He kisses her on the head.

"Tate?" he says, his voice catching with emotion as he flicks open the box to reveal a ring inside. "Will you marry me?"

My heart stops. The platinum band has two giant stones set side by side so that they look like one giant gemstone.

Both are blue.

"A diamond from each of us, hoping you'll say yes to our proposal. Because we come as a package deal." He searches my eyes, an uncharacteristic vulnerability in his as he waits for me to say something.

I stare at him, then at Molly, who's looking up at me, all innocent eyes and round, rosy cheeks.

My coffee cup is beside her. I reach for it in a daze and dip my finger into the cocoa-dusted foam.

I draw a semi-circle and finish it off with two dots.

Sullivan's brow is pulled taut as he watches.

I rotate the mug so they can both see.

A face smiles up at them from the foam.

"Is that a yes?" Sullivan asks, the uncertainty in his voice making me want to grab him and kiss him.

"It's a yes." I smile at Molly, before turning to him. "Yes. To both of you, my answer is yes."

"Yes?" His brows shoot up and he lets out a shaky breath. "Yes?"

I nod. "An absolutely-one hundred percent-yes!"

My throat burns, and I can't stop the fat tears from bursting out as Sullivan pulls Molly into a hug with us and brings his mouth to mine in a crushing kiss.

Molly giggles as she's squashed in our embrace, and it makes me laugh too, breaking the kiss.

"You knew all about this?" I ask.

The proud smile on her face makes my heart melt.

I'm looking at her, soaking in the sound of her giggle as something is slid onto my left finger.

Sullivan's eyes heat as I turn to him.

I look down at the giant glittering ring on my finger and suck in a sharp breath. Seeing it there makes it so real.

"Me go now?" Molly asks, seriously.

"You can go now," Sullivan replies.

"We were only interesting for a moment," I joke, ripping

my eyes away from the ring to watch her leave the kitchen quickly, probably off to get her baby dolls.

"Are you sure about this?" I turn back to Sullivan. He's still on one knee in front of me, his gaze locked on my face.

"Are you?" he asks.

"Yes. If you really mean it."

"We mean it," he says with conviction. "You have no idea just how much we both love you, do you?"

I shake my head, smiling, as more tears threaten to soak my cheeks.

He cups my face in his hands.

"Your voice is the melody to my heart, Tate. I told you once, and I'll say it again and again until you understand it. You are more perfect than any song. Molly's always seen that too. But she knew how to love you properly from that very first day. I didn't. And I'll spend the rest of my life regretting the terrible job I did of showing you in the beginning."

I sniff, overcome with emotion that makes my chest tight. "It's okay. I understand why. You were protecting Molly. And besides, that was in the beginning. You didn't love me then."

He sighs and his lips lift into a soft smile.

"I've loved you a long time, Tate. Before I ever knew how to show it, I loved you."

He lifts my hand like he's admiring how the ring looks on me.

"Why do you have an engagement ring here? You didn't know I was coming."

"I had it in my pocket the day Cliff and I dragged that old piano into the street."

"You did?"

"I'd have married you right there on the sidewalk if you'd let me."

He looks up at me.

"I was going to ask you then, if you'd forgiven me. But

things went differently, and I've kept it with me ever since so I can look at it and manifest you coming back to me. Or something like that. Halliday told me it would help. But mostly, I looked at it and told myself what an idiot I was for losing you in the first place."

A small, shocked laugh pushes past my lips. "You're unfairly hard on yourself."

"I love you and knew that I'd lost someone really special."

I reach up and cup his cheek.

"You haven't. I'm right here."

He leans in to kiss me, but a loud bark makes me jump back from him.

Two dogs race into the kitchen, barking wildly, their tails flying about in wild circles. They're followed by a squealing Sinclair.

"Molly said you did it!"

"Did what?" Sullivan asks, moving back on to his feet.

"Oh my God, just move, please." She laughs and breezes past him, making a beeline for the empty seat beside mine.

Denver enters the room, carrying a grinning Molly. "It wasn't me," he rumbles.

Molly giggles in his arms as Sinclair reaches for my hand and takes it, studying the engagement ring.

"Don't blame Molly," she says. "Like I don't know you well enough, Sull. I knew you were up to something days ago. And you were all uptight about anyone touching your luggage on the flight over. And I can see why!" She squeals with delight. "You did well. It's gorgeous. I approve."

She meets my eyes and the pure, unbridled joy in them that she has for us threatens to set off my tears again.

"You know I helped Halliday plan this wedding. I still have loads of ideas. Just in case you were bored one day and—"

"Let my fiancée breathe, huh, Sis?"

I giggle at the face Sinclair pulls in response, but then beam at her as Sullivan's words sink in.

Fiancée.

Oh my God, this is real.

"I should call my dad, he—"

"He's due to land in a few hours."

"What?" I stare at Sullivan.

"I asked for his permission the day after I saw you back in the city. He's the only one who was supposed to know about any of this," Sullivan says.

Sinclair rolls her eyes, waving a hand in the air. "Yeah, whatever. I've known since those cat cookies that this day would come. I'm going to have a sister-in-law!"

Her excitement is infectious, and she pulls me into a hug and squeezes. Denver's shaking hands with Sullivan, congratulating him. And Sinclair's two dogs have calmed down and are sitting side by side at Denver's feet.

"They're so cute," I exclaim, spotting the small bowtie on the larger one, and white ribbon around the smaller one's neck.

"Don't let looks deceive you. They're high maintenance," Denver says. But the fondness in his eyes tells me he'd protect Sinclair's two dogs with his giant body as savagely as he would her.

"High maintenance must be your weakness," Sullivan quips, his eyes darting to Sinclair, who scoffs in mock outrage.

I soak it all in. I've never seen Sullivan joke with his family before. He's like a new man, growing happier by the day.

As hard as it was being apart, I can see now. We needed it. *He* needed it. He finally looks like a man who's healing.

His eyes soften as he catches me studying him, and he walks over and pulls me to my feet, wrapping me in his arms.

Sinclair rushes from the room and I widen my eyes at

Sullivan as she yells so loud I swear they can probably hear her out at sea.

"Everyone, get down here! Sullivan has news!"

He chuckles, his chest rumbling against mine as he embraces me.

It's not long before the kitchen is full. His father and Halliday, Mal and Trudy, and Killian and Jenson from their security team, are all looking at us.

It's his father who speaks first.

"Molly? What's going on?" he asks gently, like he doesn't already know. I can see in his sparkling blue eyes that are so like Sullivan's that he knows exactly why Sinclair gathered us all down here.

He's standing beside Halliday, one arm wrapped around her, stroking the underside of her baby bump protectively.

She smiles at me, glowing like a woman who just married the love of her life, and I smile back, beaming, like a woman who just agreed to marry hers.

"Daddy and Tate get married," Molly says seriously.

Sterling nods. "Ah. In that case, congratulations, Son. Tate."

He comes to me first, pulling me into a hug, before doing the same to Sullivan, saying something to him in a low voice that has Sullivan nodding and gripping him tighter.

The room fills with upbeat chatter, and I drink it all in.

Molly's giggling. Sullivan's smiling. And I'm floating.

It can't get any better.

"Will you let me help my fiancée?"

I narrow my eyes at Sullivan before laughing. "You can't use that word to get your own way, you know?"

"What? Help?"

"Fiancée." I snort, poking him in the stomach as we walk along the beach.

It's been the most perfect day. My father arrived, and the rest of the guests from last night came to the house for a huge lunch. I met Sterling's brothers and their kids and grandkids. They're all so alike. Warm. Welcoming.

"Think of it as a wedding present to my wife," Sullivan continues.

"I'm not your wife yet," I tease.

"But you will be. We can have whatever kind of ceremony and reception you want. Just as long as it happens soon."

I love how eager he is, like he's on a mission now that we're back together. But I still can't resist toying with him.

"I don't know. Sinclair has so many ideas. It might take us months to come up with a plan for how to do it all."

A muscle in Sullivan's cheek clenches and I kiss it, drawing a small smile out of him.

"Can we serve cocoa-dusted drinks after we eat?"

"We can serve nectar collected by diamond encrusted bees as long as you marry me as soon as possible."

I snort out a giggle. I'm loving this lighter, happier Sullivan. Even if he does say such things with the same dry sarcasm he's always had.

He's adamant he wants to buy an office space in Midtown that he can then lease to the record label who've offered me a job as a songwriter. He said their company reports indicate they want to expand their offices to the East Coast, and that it makes good business sense for them to begin with New York. He said it's another investment opportunity like my apartment block was.

I rolled my eyes when he pulled that explanation out. We

both know my shrunken uniform is responsible for that purchase.

"Fine," I concede. "Buy the building. Be their landlord. But that's it. I can't have you coming into work all the time. You're too hot, you'll be a distraction."

His lips stretch into a satisfied smile. "I'll tell Jones to draw up contracts."

"You do that." I giggle. "Now, can we enjoy the view without talking about work? It's so beautiful here."

Sullivan stops, pulling me closer beneath his arm as we gaze out at the sparkling ocean.

"Being back here has been..." He blows out a breath. "There are so many memories here, Tate. I haven't been back in years. But now I'm here, it feels like their loss is right in my face again. I see my brother everywhere I look. I don't get that feeling with Mom, only Slade. Maybe because we were twins, I don't know."

"It must be so hard. What can I do?" I ask, my chest aching for him.

He kisses the top of my head.

"Nothing. Just being here with you and Molly makes it easier. You know, I spent so long not able to accept what happened that day. Things didn't add up about the fire. About how fast it spread. And there was a big payment made to the Port manager's sister, like someone was buying his silence and paying it to her so it wouldn't be traced as easily. Just..." He sighs. "But we've searched for answers for almost three years. And got nothing. I need to move forward, Tate. I can't allow my past to dictate my life anymore. Not when I almost lost you."

I hold him tight. I love that he can finally open up to me. But it doesn't stop me from wishing that what he had to open up about wasn't so heartbreaking. I'd do anything to take his pain away.

"Halliday told me she saw him earlier. If she wasn't pregnant, I'd have questioned her sobriety." Sullivan chuckles softly, but there's no humor in it.

"Slade?" I look up at him in surprise.

"Yeah. When she was walking toward the aisle. She says she thought it was me."

"Do you think it could have been? I mean, does she see people who've passed on?"

"No. She's not psychic. She didn't see a ghost, Tate. I think it was the emotions of the day. She knew it was hard for my father coming here, but that he wanted their wedding here anyway. She saw what she hoped to see. Because if by some miracle Slade was alive, then it would make my father happy. It would make the whole family happy. But he isn't. I saw them both taken in front of me that day. They're gone. Dead people don't come back."

The finality in his voice makes my throat burn.

We stand in silence, soaking in the sounds of the waves lapping the shore. There's a couple in the distance, further along the beach. They're walking together with a little boy, who looks a similar age to Molly. He scouts the sand, stopping every few steps to inspect something. The man is tall with dark hair, and I narrow my eyes, trying to imagine what it would have been like for Halliday to see someone she thought looked so much like Sullivan that it made her question who it could be.

They move further away until they're out of focus.

"You okay?" I ask Sullivan, tilting my face up to him.

"I'm okay." He kisses my forehead. "Just thinking about how my family changed that day. And now it's changing again. Growing this time."

I give him a soft smile. "I'm honored to be joining it. Beauforts stick together. And that's what I want. To be here for you and Molly."

"They do. And we'll do the same for you, Tate. You'll always have us. I love you so much... The most beautiful song ever played," he murmurs.

"The most romantic thing anyone's ever said to me."

"That makes me both angry and happy at the same time."

I laugh at the deep crease that's appeared between his brows. "Now isn't the time to dream about murdering my exes."

"No, it's not." His face softens. "It's the time to tell my fiancée that not only is she the most beautiful song, but that she's mine to sing."

"I'm fine with that." I grin.

He studies me for a moment.

"There's one more thing I want to ask you. It's something for me... and for Molly."

"Whatever it is, my answer's yes. Anything you need from me that'll make you and Molly happy I'll do it. If you're both happy, I'll be happy."

I smile up at him. His eyes are on mine and it's a little scary just how intense they've suddenly turned.

"So it's a yes?"

"Y-yes," I say, sounding unsure as his gaze penetrates me until my bones heat.

He blinks, knocking his laser-focus down a notch, and brushes a strand of hair back from my forehead with painstaking gentleness.

"I want you to adopt Molly."

"You do?"

"I meant it when I said she deserves a mother like you. You love her. More than you love me. And all it does is make me love you even more. I want my girls together, Tate."

I blink back happy tears.

"I love you just as much as Molly."

"You don't have to tell me that to make me happy."

"Don't I?" I bite my lip, my eyes misting.

Sullivan cups my face tenderly. "No, Baby. But you need to answer my question."

My breath catches in my throat as I choke out a muffled sound of happiness and nod.

"Say it, Tate. *Please.*"

His voice has an edge to it. Like he has to hear the exact word. Like it has to be said in the correct way. Played at the perfect pitch and tone, like the opening note of the world's most beautiful song.

I smile at him as tears race down my cheeks and onto his hands.

He doesn't brush them away. He just holds my eyes with his own.

Blue Eyes.

Just like the song I wrote about his daughter, that's changed my life. My next word is going to change it again.

And I couldn't be happier about it.

"Yes!"

"Yes?" He arches a brow like he's still not sure I mean it.

I pull his mouth down to mine.

"It's a yes, Sullivan. A billion times. YES."

The End.

BONUS EPILOGUE

SULLIVAN

"That's so good, Sweetheart," Tate praises.

Molly's face splits in two with a grin that reaches straight into my chest and squeezes my heart.

"Shall we try one more time?"

Molly turns back to the piano, perched on Tate's lap, poking her lower lip out in concentration as she mimics Tate's fingers on the keys. They're playing the beginning of Chopsticks with mostly correct notes.

"Oh my goodness, you're the next Mozart!" Tate gushes, kissing Molly on the cheek.

My daughter giggles before sliding down and running over to me.

"You watch, Daddy?"

"I did. And you were incredible. Both of you." I look at Tate, admiring the diamond necklace I gave her. Her cheeks flush and she presses her fingers to it, reading my mind.

"Come on, Sweetheart. Bedtime. Auntie Sin and Denver will be here by the time we've read your story. They're going to stay with you while Daddy takes Tate somewhere, okay?"

Molly's getting too sleepy to protest, and I kiss her dark curls, looking at Tate.

"Let's go read," I say.

She smiles at me; the same beautiful way she does every evening when I ask her to come and read with Molly and me. It's like she considers each time as something precious. And she's right. Reading with my girls at the end of each day is the thing I most look forward to.

It's precious.

It's fucking magical.

We read Molly's favorite book, taking turns to do a page each, then I wrangle Tate out of the door before Sinclair can pull her into wedding talk. We've been back in the city less than a week, and usually I'd welcome anything that might mean our wedding will happen sooner.

But not tonight.

Tonight I have plans for us.

"Where are we going?" Tate asks.

Her eyes flick to Cliff as he drives, but he just smiles, keeping my secret.

She pouts adorably.

"You'll see," I rasp. "Patience, Baby."

BONUS EPILOGUE
TATE

"Can I look yet?"

"You can," Sullivan says with a deep rumble as he lifts the silk blindfold from my eyes.

"What the...?"

"Surprised?" he rasps.

I stare at the old beaten piano from the basement placed against the wall.

"Um... you could say that! What's it doing here?"

I whip my head side to side checking out the room. It's like something out of an interior magazine. All creams and whites with accents of baby blue. Two huge comfortable-looking sofas sit either side of a bleached wood coffee table. Behind them are bookshelves with a mix of music books on display. And there's a desk on the opposite side of the room to the piano, with a brand-new Mac on it.

"What is this place?" I walk over the plush carpet and gaze out of the windows at the billion-dollar view of Central Park.

Sullivan looks around like he's assessing it to make sure it's up to standard.

"Your new office."

"What?"

I spin to face him. His lips twitch.

"You're serious?"

"When am I not?" He arches a brow, and I shake my head, a surprised laugh huffing past my lips.

"I only agreed to let you help before we left Cape Town. How did you find somewhere for the label so fast?"

"I already owned this building. I was wondering what to do with the upper floors of it. Nothing seemed right... until now." He shrugs like it's no big deal. Like he keeps billion-dollar Manhattan real estate hanging out in his back pocket just in case he decides he wants it.

Who am I kidding. This is Sullivan. Of course that's what he does.

I swallow. Sometimes I forget how wealthy he is. He's just Sullivan to me. The man I fell in love with. Who likes piano music as much as I do and kisses me like he can't get enough. And most of all, he's Molly's dad. An amazing, doting dad who makes really bad bear pancakes, because despite what he said about the oven in Cape Town, I've seen his attempts since we returned, and they're no better.

"I don't know what to say."

I wander over to him, my head on a swivel as I keep spotting more and more beautiful things in my new office. Like the watercolor painting on the wall depicting a woman sat playing a piano just like the one that now sits proudly inside my new office.

"You don't need to say anything. But I hope you like it?"

He clears his throat and pins me under an intense gaze.

He's nervous.

"I love it. And I love you! Thank you so much." I wrap my arms around his neck and reach up to press a lingering kiss to his mouth.

His gaze heats immediately.

"I'm glad, Baby."

Baby.

No matter how many times he calls me that, every time I hear it rolling off his tongue, whether it be soft and smooth, like now, or rough and commanding when we're having fast sex, it makes butterflies swarm inside my core.

I run my thumb over his lower lip, dusting the tip over the edge of his perfect, straight teeth, following its track with a small sigh.

"Tate," he growls.

"What?" I pout innocently. "Are you telling me you didn't think I'd want to thank my generous, handsome fiancé with a kiss in my new office he so expertly had styled for me?

His pupils dilate as I slide my hand down and squeeze his dick through his pants.

He's already rock hard.

"You know I don't buy you things so you'll thank me. I buy them for you because the light in your eyes when you see them is so damn worth it."

"That light in my eyes is because of you. Nothing else."

I rub him through his pants, loving the way his jaw hardens and he lets out a deep groan.

"I love you." I tilt my face up to his.

He seals his mouth over mine, grabbing a handful of my hair and holding me still so he can ravage me with a deep kiss that has my thighs clenching and my toes dancing against the floor.

He pulls back, leaving me panting.

"Take your dress off. I want you naked. The diamonds stay."

I touch the necklace that he *enjoyed* a lot the last time I wore it, and a shiver of anticipation runs through me, making my panties damp.

His eyes are like two blue flames on me, heating my body as I uncover it inch by inch, rolling my stretchy wrap dress down over my powder blue lace bra and panties, until it drops into a heap around my feet.

"Good girl," Sullivan rasps, still standing fully suited, his eyes on me like a predator's. "Now show me those perfect tits I love to suck."

I unhook my bra and toss it to him. He arches a brow as he catches it with one hand. He strokes the soft lace with his thumb, letting out a quiet moan as his eyes zero in on my puckered nipples.

"So perfect," he murmurs.

"You want to touch them yourself?" I reach up and touch both of my breasts, giving my nipples a little pinch. I know he'll love that.

"Fuck, Baby," he barks out, almost sounding annoyed that his reserve has snapped so quickly.

He marches over, wraps one arm around me, and yanks me against his solid body. His hand goes straight to my breast, cupping it possessively.

"Mine," he growls.

"Yours," I breathe.

I arch my back and let out a delighted moan as he kneads my breast, circling his thumb around my nipple until it's painfully hard and aching for his mouth.

"Sullivan," I whine.

He knows he's got me just where he wants me. One touch from him and I'm putty.

"What do you need, Baby?" he rasps.

"You."

"Which part of me?"

I throw my head back as he rolls my nipple deftly between his thumb and finger, before giving it a light flick.

"Your mouth," I pant, needing it on me so badly.

"Your fingers," I gasp as he lowers his head and seals his mouth around my nipple and sucks.

"And your..." I whimper as he slides his hand into my panties and slips them past my clit, gathering up my wetness, before bringing his fingers back up to circle around it.

"My...?" He presses slow, hot kisses over my skin, all the way up to my neck, making me shudder.

"Your cock," I breathe. "Please. I need you inside me, Sullivan."

"Come on."

He takes my hand and leads me across the room. I trot after him in just my heels and panties as he takes long strides in his suit. The fact he's not even taken his tie off, and I'm almost naked, is so deliciously filthy that it makes my clit pulse hard against the soaked lace strip between my legs.

We stop in front of the piano and Sullivan hooks my chin with his thumb and finger.

"You're so fucking sexy, Tate," he drawls, slanting his lips over mine in a panty-melting kiss.

He pulls back and holds my eyes as he unbuckles his belt and pushes his pants down.

Then he sits on the piano stool with his back to the keys and looks at me expectantly.

"I fucked you on mine. It's only fair you fuck me on yours, Baby."

He leans back and his hard cock juts up arrogantly from his hips, heavy and glistening at the tip.

"Now take off those soaked little panties and sit."

My breath hitches, every cell in my body tingling with need as I hook my thumbs in the sides of my panties and drag them down my thighs.

Sullivan's gaze heats as he watches me, and he lets out a low curse.

"Fuck. Look at you."

He jerks his cock slowly, making the wet, sparkling beads on the tip glitter in the evening light.

I lick my lips, and he juts his chin at me.

"You can suck it, Baby. But then you're giving me that hot little cunt to enjoy."

It should be embarrassing how fast I drop to my knees and reach for his cock. But I'm so horny that I don't care. Besides, I know Sullivan likes it when I'm eager.

"Good girl," he hums, stroking my cheek as I wrap my lips around the head of his dick and suck up all his pre-cum with a little moan. "You love sucking my cock, don't you?"

"Mm-hm," I murmur, taking more of him into my mouth.

"Jesus Christ, I could fuck your throat right now, Baby. You're just so fucking tempting, you know that?"

I smile around a mouthful of dick and bat my lashes innocently.

"Come here," he instructs.

I let his dick pop free of my mouth and it bounces against my diamond necklace.

"Are you sure you don't want to come on it again while I'm wearing it for you?"

"I do. And I will. But not this time."

I pout and his lips curl into a sexy smile as he rubs his thumb over the tip of my tongue that's just tasted him.

"Why do you think I sent you so many diamonds? I want to fuck you in all of them and finish over every part of your gorgeous body."

"Sounds like heaven," I murmur.

His eyes darken.

"Now get on my cock where you belong."

I rise to my feet and lift a leg to straddle him.

"Nope," he tuts. "I want you to see your new office, Baby.

I want you to look out at the place you're going to create magic."

He takes my hips and spins me so my back is facing him.

"Such a nice view," he rumbles, using his thumbs to pull the cheeks of my ass apart.

My body makes a wet sound as my pussy opens up, and Sullivan sinks into it with a rough, heady groan, tasting me with determined laps of his tongue.

"So damn sweet." He slaps my ass and pulls back just as I'm about to grind against his face and let him eat me from behind until I come.

He widens his thighs, guiding me back with a strong grip on my hips.

"Good girl. That's it. Slide onto it, Baby. It's all yours. Take my cock like you own it."

I cry out in a hot, heavy moan as I sink down onto him inch by inch. He's so big and I feel so full like this.

I squeeze my thighs together, my breath catching in a whimper as my skin meets his and his balls press against me.

"So fucking good," he groans, his hands flexing on my hips with bruising strength. "Now work my cock, Baby. Make it give you that orgasm I know your cunt's so greedy for."

I place my hands on his knees and keep my feet flat on the floor so I can move. But it's still hard at this angle, and my thighs start to burn from hovering back over him.

He grunts with amusement, like watching me struggle to take his cock is entertaining. I let out a frustrated whine, and that's when he helps me. He lifts me up and down like I weigh nothing, taking all of the weight out of my legs for me, until I'm just able to enjoy the sensation of his cock thrusting in and out of me with the perfect power and depth.

"Sullivan," I mewl, my body making an obscene wet sound as he uses it like his personal lap-held fuck toy.

"Fuck, Baby. Is that clit out?"

I look down at the way I'm stretched wide around him. His balls are glistening with my wetness, the skin on them rippling each time they thrust up against my body.

"Yes," I cry, watching the way my clit's so swollen and visible as each of his thrusts parts my pussy lips wider until I look like I'm being split open by him.

"Good. Rub it for me."

I lick my fingers and let out a deep moan as I reach down and stroke circles around it. I'm so sensitive I could come any second without warning.

"Sullivan," I whimper.

"Come for me, Baby. Rub that little clit until your cunt's wringing my cock out."

I keep circling, faster and faster, more and more of our combined slickness making my fingers slide all over my skin.

"Sullivan..."

"That's it. Good girl. I can feel you strangling me."

I look down at his balls. They're tighter and fuller, pounding against my skin with each thrust.

"Do it, Baby," Sullivan grits like he's barely holding on.

His grip on my hips tightens, making my pussy clench around him.

"Fuck," he hisses. "Just like that."

My office might be beautiful, and I love it. But I can't peel my eyes away from the obscenely hot way our bodies look together as I teeter on the edge of an earth-shattering orgasm.

"Sullivan," I cry, everything inside me pulling tight.

"Go on," he urges.

I rub my clit faster and dig the nails from my other hand into his leg.

All it does is spur him on.

"Fuck, go on. Come on my cock. Your future husband's

cock is the only one your greedy little cunt wants. So let me have it."

His words are my undoing.

"Fuck!"

I come so hard my legs give way completely and Sullivan has to hook them over his thighs, so I don't collapse. But the position stretches me wider, leaving me at his mercy as my orgasm races through my body, making my vision blur.

"It's okay, Baby," he soothes.

His hand slides in front of mine, taking over as he continues thrusting his hips beneath me, and driving his cock up inside me.

"I can't..." I whimper, my clit throbbing with sensitivity.

"You can," he coos. "I'll take care of it."

I sink back against him, an incoherent, panting mess as he expertly strokes my clit, bringing me back to another orgasm with record swiftness.

"Sullivan," I cry out, struggling to get my breath as it hits me.

"Ssh, Baby. I just wanted you to come when I did."

I whimper in his arms as he presses his face into my neck and groans long and loud.

"Fuuuccck, Baby. Fuuuuckkk."

His cock swells inside me making me impossibly full as my body erupts into tight clenches around him.

"Oh God," I squeal as my orgasm is drawn out, my body squeezing his cock with a desperate intensity.

He fucks me through it, pulling every tiny little flinch and flutter out of me before I sag back against his body with an exhausted sob.

"You're okay, Baby. I've got you."

His deep voice is warm and smooth, ready to catch me and help lower me back to earth gently.

"You're a tyrant. You're going to make me come so hard that I'll pass out one day."

"I'd never let anything happen to you," he promises, all delicious and serious.

"I know."

I turn my face so he can lower his lips to mine.

"I love you."

"I love you too," he murmurs, smiling softly against my lips. "Now when you write your first song for the label you can think of fucking me in your office."

I laugh, kissing him again. "I told you you'd be a distraction."

He reaches up and strokes my cheek. "I'm proud of you."

My heart flutters. "I'm proud of you too."

He presses another kiss to my lips.

"I got you a new office present."

"The office isn't enough?"

His eyes soften. "Nothing will ever be enough for the woman I love."

I narrow my eyes. "You're going to keep buying me things, aren't you?"

He smirks. "Try and stop me."

I sigh as he kisses me again and slides out of me, helping me to my feet.

"You have your own bathroom through there." He points to a door I didn't notice before.

"I'm entry-level, and I have my own office with a *bathroom*? You know my new colleagues will know it's because I'm fucking the landlord, right?"

He does a stellar job of not reacting as I roll my eyes, before pressing a kiss to his mouth.

"I do love it, though. It's beautiful. Thank you."

"You're welcome."

His gaze is on me as I walk into the gorgeous marble bathroom to clean myself up. When I come back out Sullivan holds my clothes out for me and waits until I'm dressed before he fixes a wayward strand of hair for me.

"Last present of tonight, I promise," he says, his eyes glittering as I arch an unbelieving brow at him.

I take the large Beaufort Diamonds box and run my hand over the silk ribbon before undoing it. Their brand's boxes are so beautiful, they're a gift in themselves, before you even get to what's inside.

I lift the lid off.

"Sullivan?"

My voice catches in my throat, and he moves behind me, wrapping an arm around my waist and pressing a kiss to my hair.

"It's the one your dad took," I say, lifting the framed photograph from the box.

"When we came back and explained to Molly you were going to adopt her. I know," he murmurs.

I glance at him over my shoulder, then back at the photograph.

Molly's held in Sullivan's arm and his other is around my waist. Molly and I are holding hands, with them resting against Sullivan's chest. My ring's glinting in the sun. And we're all smiling.

Even Sullivan.

"It's perfect," I whisper.

He takes it from me gently, looking at it with a soft smile that makes him look so devastatingly handsome I want to pull him to me for another kiss and never come up for air.

He places it on top of the piano, then wraps his arm around me.

"There. Now, your new office is ready for you."

The End.

Are you ready for the final instalment of The Beaufort Billionaire's?
Get your copy of Book 4,
where everything will be revealed:
https://books2read.com/BBbook4

ALSO BY ELLE NICOLL

<u>**The Men Series**</u>

Meeting Mr. Anderson – Holly and Jay

Discovering Mr. X – Rachel and Tanner

Drawn to Mr. King – Megan and Jaxon

Captured by Mr. Wild – Daisy and Blake

Pleasing Mr. Parker – Maria and Griffin

Trapped with Mr. Walker – Harley and Reed

Time with Mr. Silver – Rose and Dax

Resisting Mr. Rich – Maddy and Logan

Handling Mr. Harper – Sophie and Drew

Playing with Mr. Grant – Ava and Jet

(**Forget-me-nots and Fireworks**, Shona and Trent — a prequel
novella to The Men Series)

<u>**Beaufort Billionaires Series**</u>

The Matchmaker - Halliday and Sterling

The Rule Breaker - Sinclair and Denver

The Love Hater - Sullivan and Tate

Book 4 - Coming Soon

ABOUT THE AUTHOR

Elle Nicoll is an ex long-haul flight attendant and mum of two
from the UK.
After fourteen years of having her head in the clouds whilst
working at 38,000ft, she is now usually found with her head
between the pages of a book reading or furiously typing and
making notes on another new idea for a book boyfriend who
is sweet-talking her.
Elle finds it funny that she's frequently told she looks too
sweet and innocent to write a steamy book, but she never
wants to stop. Writing stories about people, passion, and love,
what better thing is there?
Because,
Love Always Wins

xxx

Website – https://www.ellenicollauthor.com

www.ingramcontent.com/pod-product-compliance
Lightning Source LLC
Chambersburg PA
CBHW031733180726
48283CB00005B/1496